Praise for *The Art of Disappearing*

"Wonder filled and wonderful."

"A terrific page-turner about a sta_, textile designer who meet in Vegas and marry two days later, and all the mystery and mayhem that ensues."   —*Elle*

"There's a nice wistfulness in Pochoda's writing that makes you root for her characters."   —*The New York Post*

"A lyrical novel that will enchant you with a love story and with poetic, evocative prose."   —*Shelf Awareness*

"*The Art of Disappearing* has been compared to *The Time Traveler's Wife*, but Ivy Pochoda's prose is lusher, her characters more melancholy, her style more mysterious."   —*The Rumpus*

"Pochoda's debut is a magical tale of romance and loss, sweet and heartfelt."   —*Bookbitch*

"Pochoda's seductive debut novel is a phantasmagoric exploration of the ever-shifting line between destiny and coincidence."   —*Booklist*

"An uncommonly good first novel about the unlikely love between a lonely woman and a most unusual magician. It's a magical story, full of passion, heart-break, and wonder."
—Peter Hedges, author of *What's Eating Gilbert Grape*

The Art of Disappearing

IVY POCHODA

ST. MARTIN'S GRIFFIN

NEW YORK

ART OF DISAPPEARING. Copyright © 2009 by Ivy Pochoda. All rights
reserved. Printed in the United States of America. For information, address
St. Martin's Press, 175 Fifth Avenue, New York, N.Y. 10010.

www.stmartins.com

Book design by Maggie Goodman

The Library of Congress has cataloged the hardcover edition as follows:

Pochoda, Ivy.
    The art of disappearing / Ivy Pochoda.—1st ed.
       p. cm.
    ISBN 978-0-312-38585-9
    1. Magicians—Fiction. I. Title.
PS3616.O285A89 2009
813'.6—dc22

2009016207

ISBN 978-0-312-65099-5 (trade paperback)

First St. Martin's Griffin Edition: October 2010

10 9 8 7 6 5 4 3 2 1

To my parents, of course

One

I married Tobias Warring in the Silver Bells All-Nite Wedding Chapel in Las Vegas. It was a conventional start to our unconventional story. And it was an attempt to conjure something solid from the wind-scattered sands. Our faces were bathed in the pink and purple lights of the Stardust Casino flashing through a two-by-two-foot window behind the priest's head. Our witnesses were a couple of underage punks from the QuikTrip who demanded a six-pack for their services. "Have a nice life," lisped the boy with three rings through his lip, ripping the ring top from his beer. His girlfriend, anxious to reclaim her spot outside the convenience store, gnawed her chipped nails. The priest, an elderly Mexican in tinted sunglasses, complained about working the graveyard shift and told us he'd once led a pilgrimage of fifty blind children to the Corcavado, but had since fallen on hard times. He closed his Bible, switched off the crackly tape recorder playing "Love Me Tender," and it was over.

We toasted our wedding at the Treasure Island casino with pink cocktails garnished with canned pineapple impaled on miniature sabers. We spent our wedding night at the Laughing Jackalope Motel. Our first kiss had been suggested by the priest: "Joos may kiss if joos want."

I'd met Toby two days earlier in the Old Stand Saloon, which logged overtime as a casino, hotel, nightclub, restaurant, and employment center in Tonopah, Nevada—a five-minute town whose limits were marked by the Shady Lady brothel on the west and the Cherry Tree on the east. The black waiter, younger than the rest of the employees by at least thirty years, had a mouthful of shining teeth, sunken and scattered like forgotten headstones. When he told me that a man sitting in the back of the restaurant wanted to buy me a drink, his words whistled through the impressive gaps in his mouth. He said that the man had suggested white wine to go with my shrimp parfait. "Sounds good," I replied, trying to peek at the stranger through the dingy reflection in the restaurant's window. But all I saw was the waiter threading his way back to the bar, carefully avoiding an old man with an oxygen tank who was struggling to play the slots.

"I think the man in the back booth on the left," the waiter said when he returned with my wine, "would like to join you." He set down my glass with a wink that was misinterpreted by a retired madam at the next table eating the landlocked surf-and-turf special. She returned the wink, letting a shrimp tail drop from her lips. The waiter ignored her. "It's good to bring a little magic into your life," he added, showing me his disorderly teeth once again. "Not much blowing through this town nowadays," he continued, applying a graying cloth to a corner of my table. And then he lowered his voice. "He's a magician."

His quiet words reverberated through the restaurant. The eaters, the toothless chewers, stopped scratching their silverware on their plates and stared at the waiter, whose voice had shattered their slot machine soundtrack. The no-nonsense town of Tonopah seemed uncomfortable with magic and the magician. With a censorious lip smack, the retired madam tucked the tip she was going to leave the waiter back into her purse.

So I allowed Toby Warring to enter my life. "Send him over," I said, smiling at the waiter while twirling my wineglass on the uneven table. As I waited for the stranger to approach, I stared out the window, imagining a brief respite from my hours in empty buses and unfamiliar airport terminals—a momentary release from the hush of motel rooms and the solitary clink of my fork against my plate. I allowed my mind to wander, wondering whether the magician might, for a moment, make this particular set of surroundings feel like home.

As Toby approached, the jangle of the slot machines in the next room became a distant bassline clank, and their flashing lights spun into a steady orange glow. The silent eaters were content, for an instant, to savor their food, forks to their mouths. The clatter and crack of bused dishes vanished; even the waiter froze, his gray cloth dangling off the corner of a table. So it seemed that the magician and I were alone, moving toward each other at an accelerated speed—me leaning over the table, Toby striding silently among the immobile diners.

A glance would judge Toby surprisingly good-looking and surprisingly young for a guy who sends drinks to strange women. Although I had never seen him before, there was something familiar as he approached. His dark hair, dark clothes, and pale skin gave him a shadowy appearance, and somehow I felt that he, or someone like him, had often been watching me—from the back of classrooms or on the school bus, across the aisle in a train or from a corner in a museum gallery.

An uneven mop of black hair dangled in Toby's eyes and dusted his ears. His features were elegant and angular. His eyebrows arched sharply, while his high cheekbones sloped away gracefully. And from behind the ragged fringe of hair shone eyes the same gray blue as the summertime river behind my childhood home. As the magician drew nearer, I noticed a slight stoop to his shoulders and deep lines—rivers of frustration and worry—that flowed over his temples and streamed down from his eyes. His hands were prematurely knotted with years of forcing air, an untamable medium, to produce rabbits, doves, and sometimes to support full-grown humans. He splayed these hands, as elegant as tree roots, on the table, and began to speak, dispelling a little of the dusty silence of my desert days.

"I'm not a big fan of shrimp in cream. Maybe the wine will wash it down," he said, leaning over the splintering table. "Mind if I join you?" He had a voice that produced its own static, a voice that, while announcing itself grandly, was interrupted by blips of self-doubt, as if both the voice and the magician had grown used to mistrusting the physical world. A sandy voice filtered through the worn megaphone of the big top.

I gestured across the table. "Please." And we exchanged names: his—Toby Warring, mine—Mel Snow.

"So, you're a magician," I stated rather than asked. "Can I see something?" Then I blushed, embarrassed to have asked the obvious. My eyes lingered on his hands spread wide on the wooden table.

Toby's gaze followed mine. "At eight, I could stretch an octave. My adoptive mother said she'd never seen anything like it." He looked out the window. "She was a concert pianist. She looked like the innermost member in a set of Russian nesting dolls."

"I'm hopeless with music," I offered.

"Living with a pianist is no guarantee of talent."

I nodded.

"When I was old enough, my mother put away my toys and brought me to the music studio. We had a converted porch stuffed with four baby grands. I was terrible. When I played, it sounded as if I were grasping onto tree branches to survive a fall from a great height. My mother said my hands engorged the keyboard and spat out music." He laughed. "They never should have adopted me."

"And you, your father . . . ," I began, then clamped a hand over my mouth. "I'm sorry. I'm behind on conversational etiquette."

Toby smiled. "And I am happy to have someone to talk to. My father was an anatomist. He looked like an owl. And he was more interested in the dead than in the living. He had no idea what to do with me. After my brief music career ended, I returned to what remained of my toys. Basically a children's edition of *Gray's Anatomy* and my blocks."

"That doesn't sound like much," I said, trying to catch the magician's mercurial stare.

Toby narrowed his eyes. "Blocks are perfect for mastering the art of illusion."

"Good for substitution?" I asked.

"My blocks taught me that I could do magic."

I raised my eyebrows, waiting for him to explain.

He shook his head. "That would be revealing too much. And you have told me nothing."

"My parents aren't as remotely interesting as an anatomist and a concert pianist," I said.

Toby folded his hands.

I shrugged. "My mother doesn't work, and my father is a minor league baseball scout." Then I mentioned the name of the suburban town on the banks of the Delaware River where I grew up, which turned out to be only a few miles upstream from Toby's childhood home.

"Perhaps we passed each other at a game or a dance?" I suggested, even then trying to join Toby's story to mine without letting him know that I had barely attended school functions myself.

"Magicians don't go to football games or dances. I didn't even finish high school."

"You ran away to join the circus?"

"Something like that. I did a little magic show to earn money. Birthday parties and weddings. I guess my teenage anxiety came through in my tricks. My shadow projections wept blood. Rabbits I pulled out of hats were covered in fake gore. The flowers I found up my sleeves were dead."

"I guess you didn't get too many repeat bookings?"

"Even though I could make balloon sculptures of all the famous castles in Europe." Toby laughed. "So I left home. I went to a magic-and-circus school in California. I didn't last very long. My classmates started to suspect that I perform magic without illusion." He turned his hands over, showing me two square depressions.

"Your blocks?"

Toby nodded. "They showed up in places I never intended. Places I never sent them."

I smiled. "Now you are revealing too much again."

The magician bit his lip. "I didn't mean to. Like my magic, this confession is catching me a little off guard."

"How is magic performed without illusion?"

"Naturally."

I didn't reply.

"You don't believe me."

"I don't know." I took a sip of my wine. "What else do you have up your sleeve?"

"Would you believe me if I told you I have no idea?" Toby shook out his cuffs, producing nothing.

"I might. Can you change water into wine?"

"That's a miracle, not magic." He passed his hand over my glass, turning the last sip of wine from white to red. Now it was Toby's turn to smile, arching his thin lips upward with his eyebrows. "Any better?"

I took a sip. "Not really." I took another sip, trying not to wince. "Miracles," I said, letting the word melt on my tongue. "That's something I haven't seen in a while. But I've been waiting."

Toby held me in his gaze. "Have you?" He laughed and adjusted the cuffs of his shirt.

"Sure," I replied. "For a civil man to send me a drink in a small-town saloon. That's some sort of miracle."

The magician blushed under his ivory skin. "I don't know what your definition of miraculous is," he said, suddenly shy. Then he passed his hand over my glass once more, refilling it from his palm. "Will this do for now?"

"It's nearly water into wine," I said.

Now Toby looked out the window and took a deep breath. "I've been waiting, too."

"For?"

"In this restaurant now for three days. In this desert for several years, to see someone I felt comfortable buying a drink."

I felt myself redden and quickly smoothed my hands across my face. In an instant, Toby's surprisingly cool fingers covered mine. My cheeks burned. He withdrew his hand and looked away. A shrimp had appeared in my palm.

"I'm not going to ask how that got there," I said.

"I was hoping for something more romantic. Things get a little disorganized."

"Maybe it's better that way."

"Why?"

"A little disorder makes the order pleasant. It makes it bearable."

The lines in Toby's face smoothed out. "Everyone's always told me the opposite." He paused, hiding his eyes in the fading light outside the window. Toby pressed his fingers into the table. "Can I ask you something?" He didn't wait for my response. "Does a little company make the loneliness more bearable?"

What loneliness? I almost asked. Even though it had stopped being true long ago, I wanted to tell the magician, *I'm not lonely, I'm alone. There's a difference.* He, on the other hand, appeared always to have been lonely. But I didn't explain. So we sat in silence for a moment, our eyes darting from the wooden wagon-wheel chandeliers to the window. In the streaky pane, I caught our reflection—the shaggy hair and stooped shoulders of the magician towering over my desert-dried blond ponytail. And for an instant, it seemed that all the other diners had faded away again, leaving us glowing a little too brightly against the Nevada night. I saw my green eyes flash in the glass while Toby's gray irises slipped across the window like mercury. Before we could speak, we were disrupted by a clatter of falling coins.

I looked directly at the magician. He was shaking his cuffs. "Well, now," he said. "Not a miracle, maybe, but a minor windfall." He gathered up the coins and tied them into a polyester-blend gingham napkin. "Here." He handed the bundle to me.

I shook my head.

"Keep them. You might get lucky on the one-armed bandits."

"We'd have to split the money if that happened."

"Magicians don't gamble. Luck and magic don't mix."

I tucked the money into my bag. "For a rainy day, I guess."

Toby pressed his lips together. I saw them tremble. And then he laughed a laugh so cool, it made me forget—if only for a second—the dinginess of the Old Stand Saloon. "Not much chance of that out here. Rain."

"It wasn't that funny," I said.

Toby didn't reply. But his mouth and eyebrows arched into a silent smile.

I replaced my glass on the table. "For the wine, thanks." Sometimes I like to put the preposition first. I find it reassuring. Because I travel a lot, I like to give what I say a place and a purpose. While I'm on the road, I need an anchor, however temporary, before I'm swept along to my next small-town appointment. And now, in the company of this surprising stranger, I needed some ballast before the magician's words swept me too far into the desert night.

"My pleasure. Tonopah's not the sort of town you often find two strangers in. It's worth some sort of celebration," he said.

"To shrimp in a glass and wine from a box," I said, holding up my glass. "Are you here often?"

"I did a few shows at one stage. I pretty much keep to high school auditoriums and state fairs. I'm not what you would call one of the more desirable magicians."

"You seem like a pretty good magician to me."

"I am a very good magician, but there are magicians who don't think I should be allowed to perform in towns like this. Some people," he continued, "some whole towns, and especially some magicians can't handle the inexplicable, even if it's just a simple trick."

"Why don't you go somewhere else?"

"I've been here so long." Toby looked over my shoulder and

out the window. Then he waved his fingers, dispensing his words into the vapors of overcooked roast beef. "Anyway, I'm still waiting for my big break. One day I'm going to play Vegas." Now he fixed me with his glittering stare. "So, what draws you to a place like this?" he asked, leaning forward, making me worry about the cracks in my lips, the unripe olive tone of my skin—which was badly matched to my hair my mother always said—and the look in my eyes that may have betrayed my uncertainty about magic but not about the magician.

"I do a one-woman Penelope-and-Odysseus routine," I said. "I'm a textile consultant for the hotel and restaurant industries. So I do both the weaving and the voyaging. Without the Sirens and the suitors," I added. "Or the sorcery." I caught his eye.

"Suitors and sorcery," Toby echoed. I felt the silk slip of something between my fingers. I opened my hand and released a cascade of rose petals. "Perhaps that is about to change." Toby looked down at the petals. "I was aiming for whole flowers," he said, scattering the petals. "I'm distracted."

I laughed, crushing some of the petals into my palms, hoping to absorb their scent. "A bit closer this time." I rubbed a petal between my fingers. "You certainly come prepared. What else have you got up your sleeve?"

Toby laughed.

He ordered a whiskey for himself and another wine for me. The sweetness of the wine and the bitter aftertaste of its synthetic container made the flashing slot machines swirl in and out of focus.

In the beginning, Toby's arrhythmic speech caught me off guard. His pauses sneaked up unexpectedly, and he swerved from subject to subject like a racecar driver. With no indication to mark the end of our talk, he announced, "I'm off. It's not that I'm not enjoying myself. It's just that I'm getting a little tired." He cleared his throat. "Tired mind. Thoughtless hands. I wouldn't want to give you the wrong impression."

"It's been an interesting impression." I smiled, trying to draw him back but willing to let him go. "Maybe I'll get to see your show sometime," I added, even though I was planning to leave Nevada the next day.

"That might be sooner than you think," Toby said. "Circe held Odysseus for a whole year just with magic and wine."

By the time I'd thought up a response, Toby had vanished into the tangle of slot machines.

People always say how minutely they remember the details of the moment that changed their lives—let's say the waltz of light and shadow, the Greek key design on their coffee cup, the bitterness or sweetness of food, the dryness of skin, the specific pathway forged by adrenaline, the black and ocher hexagons on the carpet. What I remember most about that night, besides the stop-action motion of the Old Stand Saloon as Toby crossed the room to join me, is the restaurant's synthetic gingham napkins.

When I reached my room, I withdrew the napkin filled with quarters from my bag. I tucked the quarters away in a small pouch, then spread the napkin on the floor. From my sewing bag, I pulled out a needle and thread and a patchwork quilt—my traveling companion. When you move around as much as I do, you need your own map or trail—a time line to remind you of where you've been, how you got there, and if necessary, how to find your way back. Working quickly, I sewed some of the napkin into my quilt, hoping it would lead me back to the magician.

As I've said, my name is Mel Snow. I was born in the lull between a blizzard and a flood. My parents told me that it was the falling temperature that forced me into the world. I'm not sure I believe this. I do think the blizzard—its rampant disruption of our suburb—has contributed to the way I design my textiles. I love the patterns, the seamless repetitions, which are both effortless and expected, as clear and orderly as a marching band. But as much as I desire an unbroken chain of diamonds, leaves, or snowflakes, I cannot let them sit perfected and undisturbed. I want to turn up the volume, introduce a synthesizer or a zither, something out of place in the arrangement of the orderly orchestra. So I shorten a trapezoid into a rhombus, skip a diamond in a string of fifty, darken a white snowflake to an ashy gray. And in my designs, with their minute corruptions, I try to create a pattern of patternlessness.

When not disrupting my own textiles, I made a living comforting and reassuring the cheapskate owners of small hotel-casinos in forgotten Wild West towns. I had recently been working for Sew Low Fabrics, and I was struggling to get a handle on their clients who wanted to evoke a bogus respect for Native Americans. "How about something a little more Indian? One of those geometric prints in too many colors. The tourists love that stuff," they'd say. "No one wants to forget how the West was won," they'd add with a chuckle. The manager of the Old Stand Saloon was no exception.

I had hoped to catch a glimpse of the magician before taking the bus out of Tonopah that afternoon. But the manager had kept me overtime with a string of gripes about his order for curtains, bedspreads, and napkins, all patterned with an interlocking horseshoe motif—a bit of which I had sewn into my quilt. He had spent so much time telling me about how proud he was to "buy American," even though I'd noticed that he'd ordered his plates and flatware from Mexico, that I had only a few minutes to catch the bus. I dashed to the lobby, the clatter of the synthetic stain-resistant horseshoes drumming in my ears like a high-speed forge, and took a harried look around for Toby.

The waiter with the jagged teeth peeked around the door of

the restaurant, where he was arranging cutlery on the buffet. "He's gone," he said. I grabbed my bag and went to wait for the bus. The magician didn't appear.

Eighty miles outside of Tonopah, in a small town called Beatty, I had to transfer to another bus that would take me to Las Vegas in time for my midnight flight. As I got off, I asked the driver, "Am I going to make this connection?"

"If he comes, he comes," he replied, not looking my way. He closed the door, and with a hydraulic hitch, the bus was off.

I waited. The yellow sun began to melt and spread, dyeing the sky rust, then crimson, and finally cornflower blue. I dragged my foot through the loose stones and watched as the traffic began to pick up—the late-night convertibles and caravans heading for a night out in Vegas.

After two hours, I stood up, shouldering my bag, and prepared to walk to the gas station in the distance. I had gone only a few steps when a brown minivan came to a halt next to me. I picked up my pace, but my bag was heavy. I didn't turn around until someone lifted it from my shoulder.

"The desert is no place for someone named Mel Snow."

I faced the magician. "I missed the bus, I think." I tried to hide a smile. The sun reflected off the jet buttons on Toby's black cowboy shirt—the only visible manifestation of his time in the West. A tumbleweed rolled down the two-lane blacktop toward us. I stared beyond it, at the rusted desert disappearing toward distant mesas.

"You shouldn't mind missing things. Things go missing for me every day. Books, bags, even shoes, both of them. It's an art." Toby trapped the tumbleweed with the toe of his shoe.

"What are you doing here?" I asked.

"Looking for you." He bit his lip and looked away. I looked down at his angular shadow stretching across the highway.

"Really?"

"I'm not good with people, normally," the magician said, the static of his voice almost swallowing his words.

"I thought you said that I was the lonely one."

"Are you getting in?"

I already had my hand on the door. I peered into the back of the van. "No assistant?"

Toby bit his lip and shook his head. The bravado of the previous night was absent. He reached for the shift, brushing my thigh. My fingers extended toward his but coiled instead around my seat belt as he put the car in gear.

"My last assistant vanished," he said.

"In a puff of smoke?"

"Something like that."

I watched the desert stretch itself out alongside the road in swirls of sand and rough plants. When I shifted my gaze across the windshield, I often found that I was looking at the spot Toby's eyes had just left.

"You never told me where you're going," the magician said.

"You never said where you're taking me."

"To see my show."

I smiled as I watched the mesas pop up alongside us—tea tables for Titans.

The town of Intersection, Nevada, lies one hundred miles east of the Old Stand Saloon, just off the Tonopah highway—a slow road that's hardly traveled, on account of its two-lane nonsense and lack of exit signs. Intersection was built around a gas station that expanded into a convenience store, which expanded into a diner when the old highway was first built. Tract houses sprouted around the diner, and then a visionary from Reno thought he smelled gold and tried his luck with a casino. Then came a whorehouse and then more tract houses. And soon the town was crawling with a first generation of Intersection natives.

Greta Civalier, called Sunshine, who wove her story into mine and Toby's, was half Quebecois and half Navajo, and Intersection born-and-bred. At sixteen, she was attractive, but not so romantically attractive as the role she had written for herself. Although she had the benefits of her mother's sun-baked coloring and her father's elegant profile, she hid both of these under the tattered black trimmings of teen-goth style. Her thick brown hair was interwoven with patchy black dye. Chipped black nail polish covered her chewed nails. Stripes of dark eyeliner masked her eyes, while white makeup did its best to obscure the glowing skin beneath.

Along with her friends, Greta had experienced a period of eighth-grade rebellion, during which she haunted parking lots in ripped clothes and planned small acts of vandalism she never carried out. But when her friends moved on to the next fad—boys and glitter and faded denim—Greta's personal style grew darker. Her multicolored punk fashion gave way to a mall-goth look of platform boots and oversized black T-shirts advertising bands like Obituary and Cradle of Filth. Soon Greta, no longer wanting to be a billboard for music she really didn't enjoy, began to take an interest in the occult, finally fixating on death, dying, and the dead. At least death, unlike the rotating fads embraced by her friends, would never go out of style. Death was real. Immortality was even better.

The nickname Sunshine, taken from her mother's favorite clairvoyant on the Psychic Friends Network, was an attempt by the Civalier family to rescue their daughter. Greta's mother, who had abandoned her native religion, scorning its sweat lodges and canyon lore, tried everything to weed out what she called "that child's morbid fixination." She sent Greta to a summer camp run by a splinter group of fundamentalist Christians and enrolled her in several after-school Bible studies. But the Bible summer had served only to reinforce Greta's fixination, and she came home with stories about how her counselors were looking forward to the day of Revelation, the day when, according to Greta, "Everyone would be, like, totally happy to die."

We met Greta in the Route 66 Diamond Diner, which lies nowhere near the classic highway. After school, for $3.75 an hour, she tied back her half-dyed hair and traded her black uniform for a white apron and a sea green dress while she sloshed coffee, blended milk shakes, and cried "Order up!" Toby and I were seated at the far end of the counter, hoping to grab a quick burger before his show.

"Take your order?" Greta issued her questions without interrogatory words. It was just easier that way. She tapped her black nails on the counter and fiddled with the strands of ball-chain necklaces looped around her neck. Noticing that Toby was removing a creamer from underneath my chin, she said, "Cool." And then she looked at me with the teenage horror of having ascribed coolness to something that might not be so. "That all you can do?" she asked.

"All?"

"Like, can you do real stuff?"

"Depends on what you mean by real. But I can do more than this," he said, producing a saltshaker from the air with a *pop*.

"I was kinda into that when I was younger. But now it's pretty dumb, you know." She gave him a strange smile, one that seemed to mock the magician.

"I don't know. Tell me."

"Oh, not that you are dumb. Personally. It's just that I think card tricks are sorta boring."

"I don't do card tricks. I promise," Toby assured her.

Greta wandered off to the far end of the counter without taking our order. A moment later, she was back carrying a flyer. "You're not that magician? The one performing tonight?"

"I might be," Toby replied.

Greta tapped her nails on the counter. "Well, are you or not?"

Toby nodded.

"I saw your show."

Toby didn't reply.

"A couple of years ago. State fair."

The magician's jaw tightened.

"You made that woman disappear. Your assistant."

"Not quite," Toby muttered.

"So, then what?"

"Is our little punk girl bothering you?" a sandy-haired kid sitting farther down the counter asked.

"Shut up, Jimmy. I'm not a punk." Greta narrowed her heavily lined eyes. "That's my boyfriend," she said under her breath.

"Yeah?" Jimmy said with a laugh, "So, what are you?"

"I'm a nihilist."

"And what's that?"

"It means I think there's no point to anything, especially if you're stuck in a dumb town like this."

"Whatever, Sunshine," Jimmy said.

"Don't call me that." Greta turned back to Toby. "I was wondering when you'd pass through."

"Here I am."

"And with a new assistant," Greta said, looking at me.

I shook my head.

"No? So, you looking for one?"

"One what?" Toby asked.

"An assistant."

"No. I stopped doing magic with people."

"You think I'm going to work in this diner my whole life."

"I don't know what you are going to do," Toby said. "But I'm hoping that, at least for now, you are going to take our order."

"Yeah?" Greta fumbled for her pad. "I know what kind of magic you can do."

"I'm sure you don't," the magician replied, then consulted the menu.

"You ever do Vegas?"

"Soon."

"Like you're ever going to Vegas," Jimmy called.

"What do you know?" Greta snapped. Then she turned to Toby. "If you do Vegas, you'll need an assistant."

Toby shook his head.

"I'll come."

"Why don't you start by coming tonight?" Toby asked.

"You gonna do anything dangerous?"

"I might."

"Maybe. So maybe."

When I joined the thin line of spectators trickling into the Intersection High auditorium, I wasn't surprised to see Jimmy, Greta, and her two best friends already sitting in the second row, right down from the seat Toby had reserved for me. They looked around nervously, doing a poor job of smothering their excitement with teenage skepticism. There was an uncertain electricity running through the auditorium as people prepared to abandon their common sense.

Toby's show smelled of sideshow and vaudeville. Crushed velvet capes shiny with wear, three-note music box crackle, and black top hats green with age formed the backdrop that allowed him to be distrusted and believed. He had all the lines from magicians past. "Ladies and gentlemen, tonight you are going to see things behave in a way you never thought possible," he began, using the worn pomp and circumstance opener of any magic show. It was as if he was trying to conjure the image of a traditional magic show to distract the audience from his brand of magic—the kind that didn't involve tricks.

His hands—which seemed so much smoother onstage than they had on the Tonopah table—cut through the air with disarming grace as he opened with a series of shadow projections that showed the road from Beatty to Tonopah with its parade of passing mesas. As he bent and curled his fingers, the mesas ran together until they exploded on the screen as a rushing river.

Once Toby had folded away the screen, he took off his top-coat and turned it inside out. As he reversed the sleeves, the coat vanished and was replaced by a canopy of black silk on which local Native American cave paintings appeared. Then he wrapped the black fabric around his shoulders, and it transformed into a red robe embroidered with Chinese dragons.

Toby reached into the pockets of the robe, pulling out handfuls of sand that I'd seen him collect outside the auditorium. He flung these into the air, transforming the sand into snow. Then he reached up, capturing some of the swirling snowflakes in his fingers. He cupped his hand and put his lips to his palm, blowing the snow in a perfect helix that spun from the stage into my lap. As the snow descended over me, Greta looked in my direction and rolled her eyes. "Lame," I heard her whisper to her friends.

I don't think the Intersectioners noticed or appreciated how Toby conjured with objects he'd collected from their town that day—street signs, coffee cups from the Route 66 diner, a wreath from the war memorial. They had been expecting rabbits and hats and enchanted bottles. They didn't know what to think when Toby caused a seasonal shift onstage or when he made a bed of verdant flowers grow from the dry desert earth. They looked confused as he transformed one of the school's banners into a cactus shaped like a famous Vegas casino. I'm certain the audience didn't appreciate the greasy gingham napkin that produced a windfall of quarters. They simply slid to the edges of their seats, hoping that the traveling magician could offer them a low-impact release from the binding laws of crop cycles, ten-cent slot machines, droughts, and the rest of the everyday. They were hoping not for magic but for a church revival on the grandest scale—salvation instead of levitation.

I'd already had a foretaste of Toby's singular mastery of magic, his impressive tricks. Now, with all the awkwardness I'd seen in the car banished, his hands carved the air, finding pockets of space visible to him alone. He pulled statues and busts and paintings from nowhere onto his stage. He made them change shape. He made the figures in the paintings move, the eyes on the busts wink. And while he conjured, when he looked at me, his lips curved into a subtle smile.

While the rest of the Intersectioners furrowed their brows at the unfamiliar and all-too-real magic, I glanced over at Greta. What was she seeing in all of this? Not bizarre transformations that confused her friends. Not the red, oily tinsel that made the more religious members of the audience believe they were witnessing the devil's work. What Greta saw was frustration in Toby's magic. "Who cares," she whispered to Jimmy, "if a banner becomes a cactus?"

"I dunno," Jimmy replied. "It's just a show."

"Yeah, well, I thought it was going to be real," Greta snapped. "You know, dangerous."

Next Toby wheeled a bank of lockers onto the stage. He fiddled with the combination locks until they all opened at once. Inside each locker was a pet belonging to one of the audience members. Now the audience was engaged, certain that none of their family members would have lent a dog or cat to the traveling magician. Toby closed the lockers, and when he reopened them once more, the animals had vanished. Then a bark sounded from the back of the auditorium, and Billy Redtail McCallister's dog—a rusty animal that traced its roots back to the coyote—appeared from behind a dusty curtain, followed by the other animals.

Greta snorted. Best Friend Number One rolled her eyes and asked Best Friend Number Two "what Greta's deal is."

Her deal was this: "I thought he was going to do it for real."

"There is no real, stupid. It's a magic show," Best Friend Number Two advised.

But Greta wasn't listening. "Imagine if you could vanish for good. Now, that would be something," she said to Jimmy. "Hey!" Greta called loudly from the audience. "Why don't you make it disappear for real?"

Toby shook his head and smiled. Greta's friends squirmed as she opened her mouth again.

"I thought you were going to do something good. Like cut someone in half."

Toby didn't lose his cool. He just slid into his next illusion.

"You should cut someone in half," Greta managed before Jimmy silenced her.

"You'd love that," Best Friend Number One said.

"Only if it were real," Greta said.

The show finished. The audience filed out of the theater more baffled than entertained. I hovered in the wings, still warmed by the inexplicable thrill of the performance. Finally Toby emerged.

I rushed over to him and clasped my hands around his wrists. "That was incredible. The mesas. The coins and the napkin. It's like you made it up on the spot."

Toby winked. He leaned toward me, but I shied away. The

magician cleared his throat. "Sometimes the audience gets it, sometimes they don't. I'd say tonight was fifty-fifty." I let go of his arms. "But you know what, it doesn't matter. By next year, they'll have forgotten what they didn't like. And I'll be up there again with a completely different show." Toby looped his arm around my shoulder.

I allowed my head to rest against his arm as I watched the crowd disperse, wondering if the magician had forgotten his last assistant as easily as this audience would forget him.

Outside, Greta and her friends were loitering around their cars, smoking, flirting, cursing.

"Hey," Greta called, "I thought you said you were gonna do something cool."

"I thought it was cool," one of her friends said.

"Yeah, like with everyone's pet. That was cool," Jimmy offered.

"It wasn't," Greta said. "Nothing happened. Everything's the same as it was before."

"I don't know, Greta," Best Friend Number Two said. "Most of the show was, like, kinda too real."

Greta shrugged and turned her back. "Good luck in Vegas," she muttered.

We got in the car and drove out of Intersection. A few miles down the highway, we stopped for gas. I fiddled with the glove box, searching for a piece of fabric from Toby's show that I could join to my quilt. Finding none, I wandered into the small convenience store and waited for him to pay. Just inside the door was a solitary slot machine. I reached into my bag and found the pouch filled with quarters. I wriggled one out and fed it to the slot. I pulled the handle. The wheels whirred. Music clattered out of the machine. I looked over at Toby as he tucked his receipt into his pocket. Then money began to fall. It slipped out of the machine, tumbling down onto my shoes: $325.

"Well," the attendant said. "Well, well, well. She ain't paid out in a while."

I shook my head in astonishment.

"Three hundred and twenty-five's the max," he continued. "That outta do you just fine."

"For what?" Toby asked.

"For a Vegas wedding. That's where you're heading, ain't it? Same machine paid for me and my wife."

I married Tobias Warring in the Silver Bells All-Nite Wedding Chapel on the south end of the Las Vegas Strip. But you already know that. It was our way to end the procession of lonely roads and empty hotel rooms. For Toby, it was a way to conjure something permanent into his too-malleable world and perhaps, I wondered, to replace someone he'd made vanish. For me, maybe it was a way to fill the hole torn by my brother's defection—but that was a story I had yet to tell my husband. That night we shared a bed in the Laughing Jackalope Motel at the bottom of the Strip. The room had a vibrating bed, a quarter for fifteen minutes. I used three dollars of change to rock us to sleep. And we slept wound around each other, shaking like giant rubber teardrops.

Two

When I go to sleep after too many drinks, the evening's events replay themselves throughout my dreams in a narrowing spiral of convoluted and hyperbolic detail. And in the morning, when I enter an uncertain wakefulness, I am unable to distinguish between the mutations of the dream and real-time happenings. When the Las Vegas sun pushed through the fading and fraying trim of our curtains, I woke midgasp, head quivering three inches above the pillow, and realized that in the hysteria of yesterday, I had forgotten to panic.

My eyes focused on the brown-and-ocher decor of a motel past its expiration date. The furniture was scattered across the room, none of it flush to the walls, as if it were ready to pack up and leave at a moment's notice. And for an instant, I felt like I might follow. I let my gaze descend from the ceiling to the bed next to me, until it came to rest on the figure of the sleeping magician, his black hair spread out over his pillow like an ink stain.

Toby slept with his fingers curled tightly around the edge of the sheet. I inched away from him, unsure of what we would say to one another if he woke up. He sighed, and his lips smoothed into a smile. His sleep-breath deepened as he fell further away from me into his dreams. Then my heart crawled into my throat—inspired by Toby's too-calm sleep—forecasting the moment of panic that was just around the corner. I had married the magician. So I slipped out of bed and went to buy our wedding presents.

By ten, the temperature was already pushing ninety. The steam heat rippling off the road reached eye level and made crossing the street like going through a viscous-looking glass. Las Vegas isn't a town well suited to ambling. It isn't a town well suited to a pre-noon existence. At night, people are lured from the streets by a kaleidoscope of hypnotizing neon—and in the morning, the shops sleep as late as their customers. As I watched the ragtag remains of a bachelor party move toward me—a handful of men in disheveled sports jackets and ties struggling to walk in a straight line and negotiate the services of several hookers on the breakfast run—I came across what promised to be THE WORLD'S LARGEST GIFT SHOP: OVER 10,000 SOUVENIRS."

Just outside the front door was a battered pay phone. I checked my watch. My parents would probably be home. I traced my fingers over the scratched receiver, remembering the river behind my childhood home. I used to count the days until it was cold enough for the water to freeze, allowing me to play on the river without having to swim. I remembered the sharp smell of the winter air, the sting of gusting snow, and the burn when my skin touched the ice. I remembered my parents supervising my uncoordinated skating sessions. I closed my eyes, recalling the uneven surface of the ice that tossed me from my skates and the low moans from deep within the frozen river as it expanded and moved.

This was the season, the slow march of early fall into winter, when I longed for time to accelerate, for the temperature to drop, and the water to freeze. I suddenly yearned for the unmanicured lawn of my parents' backyard. I wanted my parents to tell me how wild they'd let the grass grow this year and how often the river had flooded the past spring. I wanted to know if they ever used the sinking picnic table. And I wanted to tell them about Toby. I wanted to be told that if this didn't work out, I could come home.

I pressed my finger onto the phone's chrome surface and watched my fingerprint cloud the greasy metal. It would be early afternoon. Midautumn. The phone rang. I wondered about how quiet the house had become with me and my brother gone. The fall river would be the only sound. I wondered if my parents avoided our rooms, or if they'd changed them into studies, guest rooms, or let them be as they'd always promised. The phone kept ringing. I imagined it echoing through the house, out the screen door that led to the porch. I imagined it being absorbed by the water-damaged curtains in our living room.

I didn't think about what I would say if someone answered. I wasn't sure how I'd explain my last three weeks. I was certain only that I'd tell them I'd be home as soon as it got cold. I would promise to stay through the winter. I would sleep in my old bedroom and be startled when the snow slid off the eaves. And I would bring Toby with me.

The phone rang several more times. I could no longer picture the late-summer tempo of my home—the slow creak of the porch swing, the tired rattle of the struggling refrigerator. The lazy trickle of the August river. My parents weren't there. I hung up and entered the store.

What do you buy for the man who could, with the slightest movement of his hand, have almost anything? I wandered through multilevel displays of shot glasses, snow domes, and ashtrays. The souvenirs pledged a solidity they couldn't provide. I discovered that the decorative ceramic bells airbrushed with pictures of the famous casinos had no clappers, the frosted champagne glasses lost their misty finish under the moisture of my fingers, and the ashtrays were made of tin that a cigar would melt. The shimmer and pageantry of the shop—its reduction of the Vegas experience into playing card coasters and poker chip chocolates—reminded me of the wedding chapel where I had pledged my future to a magician the evening before. Then the panic hit—a blow to the solar plexus that sent me tumbling into a rack of acrylic T-shirts. As I fell, I panicked hard about the small things bouncing around in the big picture. Was I going to live in a tract house on the outskirts of Vegas and turn orangey brown? Could I find a decent sunscreen in this sun-worshipping town? Was our marriage going to crumble like a miniature plaster casino or be stashed away and forgotten like the clapperless bells? Or would it hang on for years like the famous Las Vegas sign? Did the magician conjure me to his side? If so, how long would the trick work?

Usually textiles sing to me. Poly blends sound like synthesizers, while cottons are more like a big band orchestra. In the cluttered souvenir shop, all the materials—the plastics, rubber, plaster, and metals—were chanting and shouting, flooding my head with a frenzied orchestra. I gasped for air. To my surprise, I discovered that I was at the counter paying for a pair of frosted champagne glasses painted with the logo of the MGM Grand.

"Rough night?" the elderly cashier asked. She was wearing a straw sun hat and sunglasses, as if, even in the store's artificially cooled interior, she was under threat from UV rays. "You looked a little unsteady back there."

I turned my head and saw the scattered T-shirt rack.

"Don't worry about it. I've seen worse," she assured me. "This town takes its toll. You've got to be prepared." She touched her hat and began to wrap the glasses in tissue paper. "You'll want to be careful before you do something serious. There's a whole lot of trouble out there, just waiting to be had."

Trying to avoid eye contact, trying to hide the panicked light that I knew was flashing in my eyes, I counted out my money. "There you go," I said to the display of posters behind the cashier's head.

"Well, I see you've already found yourself a little problem. Doesn't take long."

"I'm okay," I replied, reaching for the bag.

The cashier wouldn't relinquish her grip. "Now, listen to me. I know the way things work around here. You look like a smart girl, but I can tell this heat's doing you no good. Once you cool off, you'll find a way out of whatever it is that you've gotten into." She let go of the bag so quickly, I almost let it drop onto the counter.

"Thanks," I said, hiding my dislike of advice from strangers. "But I'll never get used to the heat."

"Don't like the heat?" The cashier chuckled as I turned to leave. "Of all things."

Outside the store, I unwrapped the glasses and held them up to the bright sky. Their smoked glass diffused and distorted the harsh sun. I put them away before my hands began to sweat and destroy their finish. Then I walked back to the motel over the steaming asphalt. The last tremors of my panic were still making my arms shake and stinging my fingers. I looked at my watch. I had been gone for nearly an hour. That would have given the magician enough time to pack his things and slip out into the surrounding sand. I closed my eyes and listened to the lazy traffic inching up the Strip and the slow tick of the climbing heat. What did my magician's voice sound like? I remembered something of its static, but nothing of its lilt. I remembered his gnarled hands with their square depressions, but could not picture the arms that connected them to his elbows or shoulders.

And the face I remembered was that of the performer—the one coated with a sheen of stage light and fairy dust. It was a completely incomplete picture, one from which the subject could easily disentangle himself and vanish before I snared him in my net of details. Perhaps what had attracted me to Toby the day before had been an illusion. Or perhaps my first impression would last forever. I paused at the door of the room and realized I did not know what to listen for, what rhythm of breathing or dreaming should be coming from behind the wall. And just before I turned the handle, I wondered if the magician was waiting, hoping for the girl he'd banished from his stage years ago to step through that door.

Inside the poorly air-conditioned room, Toby was sitting up in bed. As I closed the door, I thought I saw a glimmer of panic wash off his face. His shoulders relaxed. "You're back," he said.

I leaned against the door, twisting my fingers through the plastic bag, and watched as the magician continued to smile. His genuine pleasure seemed at odds with the artifice of his craft. With sleep creased on his face and his hair wild, the magician looked handsomer than I'd remembered. It caught me off guard how striking Toby was, how naturally his face lit up without stage lights or magic.

To my surprise, his thin body was muscular and smooth. I closed my eyes, trying to recall what it had felt like to hold him the night before. My mind went back to all my empty mornings in remote motel rooms, and I wished that I had stayed in bed. I looked again at the magician, and despite what he had told me, and despite the loneliness I'd seen hugging his shoulders, I wondered if I wasn't part of his game.

"I thought you'd left. I didn't even hear you get up."

"I tried not to wake you."

"I told you, I'm uneasy with people. And when I wake up, you're gone."

"I'm sorry."

"I thought I'd sent you away."

"But my stuff is still here," I said, looking toward my suitcase.

"I guess that's right." Toby didn't seem convinced.

"You don't know me very well if you think I'd go anywhere and leave that behind."

"I hardly know you at all." With one elegant hand, he patted the bed next to him.

I wondered if it was an invitation to join him, and I hesitated. Before I stepped forward, Toby withdrew his hand from the pillow and gathered the sheet around him.

I turned my back and busied myself with my suitcase, glancing in the mirror as he got out of bed. It seemed strange that we had slept curled around each other, and now it was difficult to make eye contact and to form full sentences. The magician slipped into the bathroom. Soon I heard the clatter of water hitting the plastic shower cabin.

I began to dig through my suitcase for something better to wear. I had on yesterday's clothes. They smelled of smoke from the Treasure Island, where we'd had our first drink as a couple. When I'd decided on a yellow sundress with bright red flowers, Toby emerged from the bathroom wrapped in a towel.

"Shower?" he asked.

I nodded. On my way to the bathroom, our bodies touched. "Sorry," I said, trying to slip past him.

"Oh, sorry," Toby echoed, moving to the bed.

I stood under the shower, letting the water run cold, then hot, then cold, as I prepared again for the heat of the day. I examined the ends of my hair, wondering how much lighter it would become under the Vegas sun. I couldn't remember the last time I'd spent the night in a hotel room—or in any room—with a man. I couldn't even clearly recall my last date. It was probably some bungled affair toward the end of art school. As I began to shave my legs, I wondered whether Toby and I had actually dispensed with the awkwardness of the dating process—negotiating each other's likes and dislikes, the fear of revealing our true opinions.

I turned off the water and let myself drip dry. Then I stepped out of the shower and listened for sounds from the next room. I wrapped a towel around my head and leaned into the mirror. I parted my lips, hoping to think of something to say to the magician that would make him stand by our decision of the night before.

I put on my dress, pulled back my hair, and opened the bathroom door. Toby was sitting in one of the chairs with his legs crossed and one hand on the telephone. He was wearing all black again, a T-shirt instead of his Western shirt. He'd flung open the curtains, and the sun brought out the strange blue highlights in his skin.

His eyes lingered on my dress. Suddenly embarrassed, I said, "I should have worn it last night. It's the closest thing I have to a wedding dress."

"I like it."

I opened my mouth, but Toby got there first, his words tripping over mine. His eyes were sparkling. "It's finally happened."

I waited for him to continue.

"I just got off the phone with the shark who calls himself my agent. With my strange reputation, he's the best I can get. Anyway, he got me a gig. Here in Las Vegas." He stopped speaking, as if startled by his own words. "I can't believe it." Then Toby's eyes narrowed. His lips twitched. "You did this."

I shook my head.

"Yes. I'm sure of it."

"I don't know how."

"When I was a kid, I thought I couldn't have it both ways. I couldn't have love and magic. And after what happened with my last assistant . . ." Toby broke off and stared out the window. "It's strange. A magician can conjure anything but success. It took meeting you."

"I'm flattered," I said.

"It's not the classiest casino, but it's Las Vegas. And Las Vegas is what I've always dreamed of."

I looked at Toby, trying hard to imagine him entranced by all the neon outside.

He caught my eye and smiled. "I know what you're thinking. It's a strange dream. For anyone but a showgirl or a magician, that is."

I laughed.

"The gig starts the day after tomorrow."

"That great," I said, wondering where I fit into Toby's tomorrows. "And I have the perfect way to celebrate." I retrieved the plastic bag and handed it to the magician.

Toby removed the champagne glasses and held them up to the window. "The MGM. I'll get there one day," he said. "Well, I—" Toby stuttered. "—I have something for you, too."

He opened his palm. In the center of his hand was a silver band set with a single turquoise stone. He placed it on my finger.

"When did you have time—?" I began.

Toby shook his head, silencing my question. "I was worried that you thought it was a mistake." He stared out the grimy window. "That you weren't coming back."

I shook my head. "It didn't cross my mind," I said, speaking more honestly than I'd meant to.

Now Toby's lips trembled, and his words were filled with static. "So, what do you think?" He stopped. "About this. The motel. Las Vegas." He looked at my hand. "Your ring . . . The wedding."

"I'd always imagined something a little more formal."

Toby laughed. "But seriously."

"Seriously," I said, "I wonder what comes next."

Toby pursed his lips. "I don't know."

"But you're the magician. I expect you to know."

He shook his head. "I never got into fortune-telling or spirit cabinets. I can't look forward or back."

We held up our empty glasses.

"To us," Toby said.

"And to your name in lights," I added.

We stared at each other, and the distance between us shrank, just as it had in the Old Stand Saloon, until Toby's lips were pressed against mine and we fell backwards onto the bed. That's when the details of the magician's face imprinted themselves in my mind—the swirling blue eyes surrounded by their premature creases, the purple tint in his waterfall of black hair, the small twist in his aquiline nose, his symmetrical lips, the vertical divot in his chin. "I've been thinking about this all morning," he said as his kiss dissolved the heat and cooled the insistent desert sun.

Despite the weak air-conditioning and the pressure of Toby's body, I felt cool. I looked down and saw that the bright poppies on my dress had changed into snowflakes that sent delightful icy tingles across my legs and chest. Then with whatever magic he possessed, Toby lifted me out of the dingy motel room and high above the swirling sands. When we returned to the worn reality of the Laughing Jackalope, the magician said, "Now it's time for a honeymoon, Las Vegas style. But first, let's get some champagne to fill— and I guess, destroy—these glasses."

We spent‚ the rest of our wedding day on an around-the-world tour. We rode the taxicab roller coaster in New York, New York, climbed the Eiffel Tower outside the Paris, examined the mock sarcophagi at the Luxor, and relaxed in a gondola in the Venetian. We wound up at the ALL YOU CAN EAT SEAFOOD buffet at the Rio, where—having told one of the servers that we were newlyweds—we received a complimentary bottle of sparkling wine and a miniature wedding cake draped with carnival beads.

While fortune—good or bad—and intrigue follow a magician, paving the way for his next trick or move, the rest of us must stick to the laws of nature and necessity. So I spent the rest of the morning on the phone to hotels and textile companies, looking for work that might keep me busy in Vegas. I got lucky with an outfit called Fabrication, with contracts out to the larger hotels in the West. I held the receiver away from my ear as a loud grunt followed the sound of exhaled cigar smoke. "We've got a big job on the Strip. Not going to be an easy one," the director of Fabrication bellowed. He ran his business with no appreciation for the textiles. Quality and pattern were a distant second to volume and cost. "For this job, I need you to demand they go for the expensive stuff, and lots of it. They invented gaudy and glitz out there, and you're going to sell it back to them."

That's how I found myself in the office of the assistant manager of the Winter Palace, a "golden age of Russia" casino scheduled to open the next month. The backers figured that the cold war had faded enough for people to celebrate caviar, vodka, and a Russian version of *Riverdance*. The casino had taken more than five years to build, and the drawn-out construction and reconstruction of the Winter Palace had ruined its textiles. The plush red, gold, and black fabrics were scuffed by construction boots and stained from the overflowing fountains. In addition, the Winter Palace's managers had offered a three-day preview to Vegas bigwigs for whom every hotel room is a canvas for destruction.

"We are a classy casino. The new classy," Sandra, the assistant manager, explained, underlining her point by flicking one of the brass buttons on her white linen blazer. Sandra, who was about forty, had been born and raised under the Las Vegas sun. Her cleavage, tanned to a burnt umber and amply displayed even for a female interviewee, had the worn-in look of old suede. She piled her dark brown hair high on her head with a handful of gold hairpins and probably a substantial investment in mousse. Her makeup—coral lips and turquoise eyeshadow—was old school. "Our restaurants, shops, lounges, and suites provide a sanctuary from the ding-ding of the slots and the hustle-bustle of the tables. Remember, we are Russia. Not the *now* Russia, but the high-style Russia of Catherine the Great. Designer suits and hair-styles. Vodka and cigars. Russian *Vogue*. Think boudoir classy." She tweaked another brass button and sifted through the promo-tional literature.

The Winter Palace was shaping up as classy in a "new-money Mafia" way—quilted chintz, miles of brocade, plastic moldings, sconces, gold and glass furniture, and dozens of columns in the shape of matryoshka dolls. The exterior of the casino, with its onion domes and garish paint, looked more like Disney World than St. Petersburg. The ceiling had been painted with an artis-tic approximation of what a Russian sky might look like. The ef-fect was dismal, thanks to the painter's overly zealous inclusion of clouds.

"I know what you mean," I assured Sandra. I had tuned out most of her speech, entranced by the way the rich red-and-gold hyacinth motif on the carpet seemed to reduplicate within itself. I wasn't sure that the hyacinth was native to Russia, but the rich-ness of the flower did convey the old-fashioned luxury that the designers of the Winter Palace were after.

"Mel Snow," she said, reading from my résumé, "that's an interesting name. Of course, we don't get snow around here. Couldn't imagine being named after something cold. But you all do things differently in the East."

I nodded.

"Coldest I've ever been is when they accidentally turned off the heat in my condo's pool in December."

I twisted in my chair, bouncing on the fresh springs and tight upholstery. "I'm still trying to get used to the ins and outs of the desert."

"The ins and outs," Sandra repeated with a laugh. "Honey, the only way to get out is to get air-conditioning. Otherwise, it's just you and the sun, which is, of course, how we like it. But be careful of the sand. I know it looks pretty tame, but sometimes the wind kicks it up so badly, you can't go out. And then you can forget sitting by the pool." Sandra cleared her throat and resumed looking through the papers on her desk. "Well, you'll see about all of that soon enough. But as I was saying, classy. We're not looking for a makeover, a make-under, or anything like that. It took us five years to come up with the appropriate patterns for this place. And we're not going to change them much, that's for sure. But what we need right now is a consultant. This place is a fabric maze—"

"Textile."

"Excuse me?"

"I'll be working with textiles, not just fabrics. Vinyls and linoleums."

"I don't know from linen," she said, straightening her blazer. "That's your business. All I know is that I can see construction boot marks leading through the Grande Salle and some sort of black residue that keeps appearing on the petals of the silk flowers. But if you say textiles, then I'll say textiles. A textile maze. We need someone to manage that side of things until we open and also during our first weeks. Judge how the wear and tear are going to affect our fabr—I mean textiles. Let's walk," Sandra said, standing up and clicking her long fingernails together.

I've done this sort of work before in restaurants and small

hotels. The owners want to you be a fortune-teller, to predict when and where things will be spilled, how many people can sit on a velour couch before it starts to retain their imprint. They want to know when the shine will start to fade from their stain-resistant napkins. You've got to keep them happy, show them how to use the napkins in better rotation, soak them before throwing them in the wash, avoid the harsher industrial detergents. Tell them to brush the carpets every night, especially those in the entrance, rotating the fibers so that they won't get worn and matted. But I'd never tackled an enterprise the size of the Winter Palace. Sandra was right: It was a textile maze, a textile labyrinth. Instead of the fresco style favored by many of the other casinos, the Winter Palace's designers had covered the walls with a silk-screened mural of St. Petersburg. Plush ottomans and divans opened their arms to weary gamblers. Even the stools in front of the slots and the tables were upholstered with a polyamide nylon that would need consistent monitoring.

"Fabrication knows the size of the project?" I asked Sandra, waving my arm at the textile jungle outside her office. We passed out of the restricted area and entered the casino's main floor.

"They said you were good. They said you have a special understanding of fabric," she said. "I don't know what that means exactly, but if you can tell us how to get these scuffs from the horses' hooves off carpets, I'll know we're in business."

"Horses?"

"We planned to have horse-drawn sledges bring people up and down the mall, but the horses—well, they just created a mess." She bent down and showed me a depression in the carpet where horseshoes had ripped up the pile. "Now we're going to use them only at the opening. And we're going to cover their hooves with little velvet booties. Other than that, the sledges will be motorized." Sandra pointed to a track laid on the floor. "Unfortunately, they'll be more of a ride than a form of transportation, but they'll still be way more exciting than those gondolas at the Venetian. We've had someone do an exact copy of Catherine the Great's sledges, and we've piled them with all sorts of fake fur. I'm sure you'll love them, since snow's your thing and all."

"Sure," I said, wondering how the fake-fur throws would look at the end of a week.

"Speaking of snow, have you heard about the Hermitage Salon?" Sandra asked, grabbing my arm.

"No."

"You will love this. We can't go in now. They're doing some last-minute tweaking on the temperature controls. But let me tell you, there's an enormous frozen lake where professional skaters will perform and at mealtimes there'll be a band. And here's the kicker," Sandra said, extending her arms for emphasis, "once every half hour, we've arranged for it to snow."

"So whenever I'm homesick . . . ," I started to say.

"My thoughts exactly," Sandra said as her eyes lit up. "And vodka, do you like vodka?"

"Sure." I looked at my watch. "But not before noon."

"Me neither. But sometimes—well, sometimes. We've got well over two hundred varieties." She threaded me past the bustle of last-minute construction, through the completed shopping mall with stores waiting to unload gold jewelry and leather handbags, and into a vodka-themed bar called, oddly, Red Square. Except for a painter doing some touch-ups, the place was empty. Sandra dipped below the bar and retrieved a bottle of apricot vodka. "Occupational delight," she tittered, filling our glasses. "When we're up and running, this entire bar is going to be made of ice." She ran her nails along the recessed metal countertop. "So." She opened a folder that she'd brought with her and slipped back into her brusque business voice. "Let's discuss the terms of your employment. We are in a bind. We got our gaming license quicker than expected. A miracle, a real gift from God in this town. We need to get this place in order fast. Spotless. Showcase perfect." She resettled her blazer over her chest. "Fabrication has told us that you will do the job. I hope they're right."

"Of course," I replied, pleased to be employed by the only wintry oasis in the city. The overwhelming variety and opulence of the textiles were irresistible—a full-bodied orchestra waiting to unleash its music on my ears.

"From what I can see on your résumé, you're a traveling consultant. And what we need is for you to stay in one place."

"I'm planning on staying in Las Vegas for a while," I assured her.

Sandra frowned. "But what I'm thinking is that a traveling consultant doesn't have a place to live. Am I right?"

I told her that I was staying at a motel and that Fabrication would foot the bill during my contract.

"Well, that doesn't sound satisfactory at all. I imagine their air-conditioning isn't up to standard. And that will do you no good. Especially you, Mel Snow." She took a long sip of vodka. "A motel," Sandra repeated under her breath as she flicked through the papers in her folder with a click of her tongue. Satisfied with her search, she shuffled the papers into order, tapped the folder on its short end to make sure everything slid into place, and took another drink. "Until we open, you are welcome to stay here. We have several rooms set aside for consultants and important visitors, and I'm sure that I can arrange the Cherry Orchard Suite for you. Since you know how to manage fabrics, I don't have to worry about damages."

"Of course not," I said, surveying the shopping mall that was going to be part of my new home.

"You're alone?"

"Excuse me?"

"Are you traveling alone?"

It felt odd telling a stranger something that I hadn't had the courage to tell my parents. "Just married." For a moment, my words sounded so unbelievable that I worried I was lying.

"A Vegas wedding," Sandra said with a knowing nod. "I bet your husband's either a bottle rocket of passion—the can't-wait-let's-do-it-now type—or one of those never-going-to-commit guys you need to nail down in any way possible."

I was on the verge of telling her that I had no idea. "He's a magician."

Sandra took a last gulp of her drink and kept her opinion to herself.

My brother spent his childhood trying to convince me that I'm a lapsed water child—that if I were willing, I could have listened to the stories of oceans and rivers as their water slipped through my fingers. Well, it's not water speaking to me, but fabrics. It's been that way since I was a kid. Vinyls sound like an off-key oboe, chintzes like woodwinds in full flight, velvet like the comforting rhythm of a bass drum in an orchestra pit. Cotton, which many people find pedestrian, announces itself like a Main Street marching band—crisp and clean. Satin sounds like the blues, and organza like jazz. After Toby and I moved into our first home, the Cherry Orchard Suite, the textiles in the Winter Palace trumpeted their songs proudly and unceasingly in my ears. Even the stiff synthetics and polyvinyls, which usually sound like tuneless whistling, adopted the toe-tapping rhythms of European pop music. I enjoyed being alone among the textiles of the casino more than I expected. At night, I was comforted by the soprano sax sound of our sateen sheets and the swaying anchor of Toby's mid-dream conjurings.

The constant movement of his hands traced the pathways of my sleep cycles, and each morning a new object was sitting on our bedside table. Sometimes I recognized the things Toby produced with his nocturnal magic—a coffee cup from the greasy spoon where we ate breakfast, the elevator-capacity sign from the lobby of the casino, a handful of poker chips. Sometimes there were objects only I had come into contact with, such as fabric from Sandra's office or textile order forms. And finally he produced things that were a mystery to the magician himself—a wallet-sized snapshot of an unfamiliar family and an engraved money clip, unfortunately empty.

I tried to watch Toby's hands, looking for pathways along which I could follow his magic. But they flew from in front of my face to a pocket, tabletop, vase, or a stranger's coat. They moved so quickly that I lost them, literally in the blink of an eye.

"I used to be embarrassed by my hands," Toby said. "I'd keep them in my pockets, pushed them right down."

I took one of his hands in mine and massaged the deep crevices between his fingers. "They're beautiful."

"I didn't want my classmates to see what I could do." Toby laughed. "Then there was a year I barely used them at all. Right after I made my assistant disappear."

I wrapped one of my hands over Toby's to still its movement. I squeezed tight, bracing myself for his confession.

"It was an accident. A couple of years out of school, I shared a small circuit in the Four Corners area with a woeful magician, Jim Swenson. He called himself Swenson the Spectacular, but there was nothing remotely special about him. He could barely palm a dime." Toby's palm went cold inside my grip. "We had an assistant, Eva. Swenson wasn't too happy when she and I got together. He was always jealous of my abilities, and his jealousy soon turned into mistrust." Toby paused and exhaled. "I have never entirely understood how my magic works." He looked at me, to see whether I was willing to follow him down a path paved with implausibility. He saw no resistance and continued. "When I was at school in California, I tried to mimic the style and methods of my classmates. But everything came too easily to me. I saw paths for conjuring where my peers saw blockades. When they needed to palm an object and substitute another, I could simply lose something into thin air and discover the necessary replacement in my hand."

"How?" I asked.

"I'm not sure." Toby closed his eyes. "The best explanation I can give is that, for me, the air contains hidden dimensions. It has pockets and caves. It's like a maze waiting to be carved out of foam or sponge. I know this doesn't make much sense. All I can say is that empty space is as big or as small as what you choose to fill it with. And many spaces prefer to exist out of plain sight."

I nodded, although I didn't quite understand.

"You see," Toby said, returning to the middle of our suite, "there are endless patterns in the world that most people overlook. There are rhythms and pathways that are perfect for my magic. These unknown dimensions are what I find beautiful. They are untouched and unpolluted. They are mine. I consider them safe. By finding them, by paving and cultivating them, this is how I perform what you consider my tricks." He took a deep breath. "Imagine the joy I felt the first time I carved my fingers through the air and discovered a place where I could transform one of my childhood blocks into a plant or an alcove where I could produce birds and rabbits to keep me company." Now the magician smiled a smile that seemed to stretch back through time. Then he flopped back into the armchair. "Of course, I did my best to hide these methods from my classmates and later from Swenson. A year or so into our tour, Swenson started to suspect the extent of my abilities. He began whispering to Eva that I was dangerous. She ignored him."

I let go of Toby's hand and stood up and went to the minibar. I found a half bottle of white wine and poured two glasses. Toby took a sip and stared over the rim of the glass.

"It was supposed to be a simple trick: Here one minute, gone the next. I'd done it thousands of times before with statues, vases, flowers, even pets. I guess I never really thought about what would happen if I sent a person deep into the unseen labyrinth." Toby spun his glass, transforming the wine from white to red. "Eva was a great assistant. She had this wild beauty that brought an element of danger and mystery even to Swenson's magic."

I sipped my wine, trying not to picture Toby's beautiful girl-friend.

"I knew that Swenson and I were about to part ways. And I wanted to go out with a bang. That night was the first time that I didn't hide my talent from him. The delight had been going out of my tricks. I hated masking the thrill I felt each time I uncovered a pathway or pocket of air along which I could move something. I was suffocating my art with artifice. You understand."

"Yes," I said. I sensed that hiding the true nature of his craft was like my plugging my ears to the textiles' songs.

"I called the trick 'Lady in the Lake.' It was short illusion. It had to be. I constructed a large tank onstage filled with water. The tank was transparent on all sides. Eva was supposed to step off a platform and dive into it. Then she would disappear for a few moments. After a covering of lily pads appeared on the surface of the tank, she would burst through the water, carrying a flaming torch." Toby took a sip of wine. "She never emerged." He bit his lip. I watched as his teeth pressed deeper into his pale lips. Finally he continued. "I remember pushing my hands through the air. Then I knelt at the edge of the tank and combed the water. But I knew that it contained none of the compartments or pathways where I could search for her. I put my face into the water, but there was no point. The air, the water, the entire labyrinth had closed to me."

Toby stopped speaking and leaned back against the chair. "There was no explanation—no evidence, even—of what I'd done. At that moment, I couldn't say whether I'd killed her or misplaced her." The magician shook his head. "*Helpless* and *terrified* do not touch the surface of what I felt." He took a deep breath. "I gave up magic for a year. But for me, there's never been anything else. Slowly I started up again. But never using people. Since then, I've been hiding on whatever small stage I can find." Suddenly Toby stood up. "Maybe I shouldn't have told you this."

"Why not?"

"You think I'm dangerous or careless."

I shook my head. "Did you look for her?"

"I tried every body of water I came across and every stretch of desert. I checked every restaurant and theater. Then one day I stopped." Toby stared straight into my eyes. "Do you think that's terrible?"

"I stopped looking for my brother long ago," I said. "I moved to the one place he'd never appear."

That night I accompanied Toby to his Vegas debut at the Castaway, a small pirate-themed casino on Vegas's other strip, the unglamorous Fremont Street. The Castaway was once the most successful casino in town. Founded by a Texas rancher with a two-man body count, it was the epitome of hard-nosed, no-frills gambling and offered the highest limits of any casino in town—provided you staked it all on your first bet. By refusing to provide entertainment or amenities beyond the all-night grill in the basement, the Castaway had not budged from its diet of cards, smoke, and liquor for nearly fifty years. But a new manager, a cardsharp from Atlantic City, had come up with the idea that if the gamblers were shown a few card tricks—if they were teased with the impossible—they might get ideas about their own abilities and bet large. So the manager cleared the wobbly roulette tables and armless bandits from the small theater that, since the casino's construction, had been used only as a roughing-up spot, and he placed an ad for a magician.

Toby chattered nervously as we walked, explaining how he would stick to working with conventional objects like balls and glasses. He knew that his audience was looking for tricks not magic, and he didn't want to draw attention to his unconventional talents.

Toby performed his first show for an audience of twelve who had mistimed the start of the Fremont Street Experience—a laser show that played out hourly over the domed roof of the Fremont Street esplanade. On a shoddy stage in the Castaway's neglected theater, Toby began his display of close-up magic. He opened by producing coins from the air and transforming ties into yards of silk handkerchiefs. His patter was mechanical, as he matched his magic to the tricks the audience was expecting, switching balls underneath cups and slipping cards into his sleeves.

Toby worked slowly, giving the audience his best attempt at a straight-up magic show. He wanted to tease them, pretending to show the strings that supposedly held his tricks together. He stepped off the stage and took a seat in the third row, allowing the audience to examine the slow movements of his hands. With his feet up on the seat in front of him, he produced a languid sequence of small-scale conjurings that made the audience gasp with delight each time they almost saw his method. Like the light falling off a July Fourth sparkler before the waver has completed his midair circles, Toby left a nearly discernible trail behind his tricks. But no matter how slowly he worked and how closely they looked, the audience could not decipher his methods. Unlike other magicians they'd seen, there was no explanation for the mundane magic that flowed from Toby's hands.

That night after the show, we drove out to the point where the fringe casinos of neighboring towns recede into the desert. Toby was silent, his hands as still as the sand around us. We bought coffee from a roadside stand called Jim's Big West Donut and drank in silence by the side of the road. The darkened sky had done nothing to cool off the day. I sat on the ground and tried to bury my fingers in the sand, looking for an oasis that had escaped the burn of the sun. And when I failed and allowed the hot grains to crawl beneath my fingers, I began to assign a pattern to the nocturnal sands. I traced one ripple as far as I could before I realized that I must have lost the original strand miles back. I didn't notice that Toby was gone until I saw his footprints disappearing around the back of the doughnut shop into the outstretched blackness. Fitting my small feet into the prints of Toby's larger ones, I followed the path until I caught sight of his angular figure in the distance.

The magician stood a hundred yards out in the desert, a black stencil against the inky sky. He was back in his training ground, in the empty expanses where he'd tried to tame and understand a magic that was not based on illusion or trickery—the conjurings with their surprise endings. Toby lifted his head as I approached. "Those cups and balls might be good enough for a small theater, but you deserve better."

His arms fluttered through the sky, rippling the solid darkness like a flip book. Then Toby grabbed the sand from around his feet, cast it into the air, and watched it rain down again. As they fell, the grains took the shape of wings extending from the magician's body. The wings fluttered once before dissolving into the desert floor. Toby fanned his fingers wide against the sky and then snapped them shut. The sand rose up to meet him.

I was trembling. I knew he had a knack for producing saltshakers and seafood, but this was different. The whole desert seemed to be at my magician's command. I wanted to draw closer, but did not want to disturb the dancing sand. Castles rose to my husband's fingers. Then the sand took the form of enormous flowers. He made rivers flow and snowflakes fall. When his hands dropped to his sides and remained motionless, I ran toward Toby and wrapped my arms around him.

"That was astonishing," I whispered, not wanting to disturb the magic in the desert air.

Toby's hand slipped over my fingers, lingering for a second on my wedding band. When we returned to our suite, the turquoise stone had been replaced by one that captured the colors of the desert's setting sun.

Three

I was born at home during a dramatic rise in temperature that transformed a blinding snowstorm into a flood. It was a freak occurrence, resulting in three days of heavy rain that ravaged our state. I know now that my brother, Max, was more pleased with the rapidly rising river than with his new sister. But it took me years to accept that he loved water more than he loved me.

Max was a water baby. Soon after he was born, my father decided that the best way to protect him from the river behind our house was to teach him to swim. On his first half birthday, my father took Max to the local pool. Holding him by the ankles, Achilles-like, my father eased my brother into the water. Max kicked free, dipped his face, and casually came up for air. My father applauded and promptly enrolled him in infant swim classes.

By the time he was three, Max was spending his evenings submerged in his bathwater, training himself to hold his breath for over a minute. By the time he was four, it was clear that Max preferred water to land. When no one was looking, he jumped into pools, fountains, even the ocean. At first my parents encouraged his swimming—driving him to pint-sized swim meets, timing while he held his breath underwater in the tub, taking him to the university to watch the Olympic trials. But when I was born, everything changed.

There had been no time to get to the hospital as the temperature began to rise, the barometer to fall, and the snow that had been predicted to last until the morning of my birthday gave way to torrential rain. So, with her Jiffy Pop belly about to burst, my mother rolled from the couch to the floor, and the water and I picked our moment to arrive. When I entered the world thirty hours ahead of schedule on our imitation oriental rug, my father swung me into the air, rescuing me from the floor that was already sagging under the weight of the creeping water.

My parents hadn't considered that a house by a river might not be watertight. Ours was always ready to leak. Squirrels, termites, and carpenter ants had spent years snacking on the roof and the sills. Over time, the foundation had sunk into the river-dampened soil. If my parents had ventured into our shallow basement, they would have discovered an *Alice in Wonderland*–style Caucus-race among the chipmunks, squirrels, raccoons, and mice who circled a permanent puddle on the floor.

While we were growing up, my brother would often whisper to me about the way the water had worked its way in from the corners of the house, surged around the moldings, and sneaked in behind the carpet runners on the day I was born. He told me how it had slipped over doorjambs and seeped into the cracks of our imperfectly sealed floors. It had advanced slowly, he said, carefully lapping the cream-colored tassels on the edge of the rug. Then, like an orderly phalanx, it had begun its attack on the orange-and-blue carpet. Wave after wave of water had marched forward, sinking deep into the synthetic fibers, and finding no resistance, it had stayed for the night. And despite the fact that even now, if I close my eyes and roll myself into a ball, I can remember the damp welcome that greeted me before I was whisked from the rug and held above the rising water, I was never seduced by Max's stories.

Max watched my arrival from between the peeling rungs of the banister on the second-floor landing, waiting for a moment when he might be left alone. He got his chance when the doctor arrived and transferred me and my mother to a bedroom upstairs. Max dashed out to the garden, tilted his head toward the sky, and let the icy rain slip across his face. He skipped across the cold, swampy lawn down to the river that had overflowed its banks. But as he dipped a toe into the rushing water, my father arrived, grabbed him by the collar, and swept him back to the house.

My mother spent the next three days in bed, listening to the rain that hadn't taken a break since I was born. The light drizzle that tickled the roof and windows in the early evening became a full-strength assault, drumming the house on all sides with a heavy metal beat. My parents didn't hear the slate tiles stripped from the roof by the wind shatter on the driveway, leaving our house defenseless. It was Max who discovered the new leak—a playful drip that came in through the roof, descended into a crack in the attic floor, and charmed its way through the plaster of the third-floor ceiling, until it was able to fall, one droplet at a time, onto the hall carpeting. He stuck his head out into the hallway just in time to catch the slow descent of the first drop.

That was where my father found him. At first he watched Max in silence, unwilling to break the spell on the openmouthed boy. But then a drop of water that had trembled for several minutes in the cracked ceiling made its swift descent. Max shut his eyes as the drop hit the back of his tongue. He closed his mouth and swallowed, savoring the taste of rain and wood and plaster.

My father moved forward to speak to him, but the water had taken advantage of his delay to launch its invasion. It started pouring through the ceiling. Five leaks sprouted in the hallway, three more in Max's room, four in my parents' bedroom, and one in the guest room where my mother was nursing me.

From that day on, my mother blamed Max for inviting the water into our house. She blamed him for leaky bathtubs, burst radiators, broken pipes, and most of all for the occasional surging of the river. Each winter, she would count down the days until it would be cold enough for the river to freeze and the rain to turn to snow. Snow was her elixir. And more important, snow made things match. It smoothed rough edges and harsh contours. It erased the garish paint jobs on new cars and undermined families who had trimmed their houses in a Caribbean palette. It masked badly pruned hedges and covered lawn ornaments. Snow, according to my mother, brought tranquillity and beauty to a mismatched world. As she saw it, a good snowstorm would be better than a baptism.

When I was seven and Max was eleven, the remnants of a tropical storm moving up the coast raged against the house for three days. My mother insisted Max stay indoors. He stomped his foot with the agitation the storm was whipping up inside him. Our mother shrugged her shoulders and turned back to the stove, where she was fixing steak and fries.

But that night, even the prospect of all-you-can-eat fries and cake for dessert couldn't calm the frustration that was consuming my brother. As my mother cooked, Max rattled his fist against the window, trying, it seemed to my mother, to add to the force of the furious storm. Thunder cracked in the distance. Max beat his fist against the window again, causing more droplets to slip onto the sill, and then he marched up the stairs.

He did not come down at dinnertime. His plate of food cooled. My mother wavered between distress at her son's unhappiness and a desire to show him the dangers of the storm. After dinner, I helped her load the plates into the dishwasher. She called to Max, "If you're going to wash your face before bed, do it quickly." Unsupervised, Max often plugged the bathroom sink, filled it with water, and practiced holding his breath.

"One day, he'll forget what he's doing and simply pass out under there," I heard my mother whisper in my father's ear. So my father volunteered to be a lifeguard during his son's bathroom aquatics. But Max complained that our father's presence prevented him from reaching the underwater peace he sought. And late at night, when my parents were asleep, he would return, fill the sink, and dunk his head.

That night, on my way to bed, I pressed my ear against the bathroom door, listening for gurgling. But there was only silence. I got into bed, and my mother wrapped the covers around me. When I closed my eyes, I imagined the gnashing teeth of the hungry river. That was the first night the water teased me in my dreams.

Until then, I'd always dreamed of dry land. That night I was dreaming of the botanical gardens, with their lanes of cherry trees winding away and doubling back, making room for busy traffic that shouldn't have been there. As I wandered, a distant note like a muffled trumpet began to slither among the trees. Then the mute was removed, and my ears filled with an orchestral roar. I heard the water before I saw it. It spoke a foreign language, filled with sibilant sounds. I tried to cover my ears. But my hands slid to my sides, as if they, too, wanted to listen to the unfamiliar music, to touch it, to let it slip between their fingers. And when my hands fell, I heard the water call my name as it licked the bark with its wide tongue—the soft M's rising and falling among the invisible ripples, the M's that I imagined looked like waves. I felt the water before I saw it—the smooth tickle of its lips on my ankles, a buttery touch that made me want to fall into its embrace. I started to shake when the water, now visible, began to rise, bringing with it a carpet of fallen cherry blossoms. It reached my ears and began to repeat my name, a velvet calling, an invitation. And ignorant of how to behave underwater, I opened my mouth to reply, and the water flowed in, cascading down my throat, bubbling in my lungs. I sputtered, coughed, and woke up.

I bolted up in bed, forcing the water that wasn't there out of my lungs. I could still hear my name, as sung by the water, hovering in the room. My window had blown open in the storm, and my cheeks were splattered with rain. I could hear the river howling in the distance. Hungry, just as Max said. So I ducked back under the blankets and covered my ears.

Perhaps my mother sensed the treachery of my dream. Or maybe she believed that the water had leaked into my head, intending to drown me as I slept, because only moments later, she was sitting on the edge of my bed. "Mel. Are you under there?"

"Mmmmm."

Then she ran her hand across my face and felt the cool traces of the raindrops. She sprang up and closed the window.

"Mama? Why does Max love the rain so much?" I asked.

"Max," she said, considering her oldest child's name. "Max," she repeated, springing up from the bed although she had just lain down. "I forgot to tuck your brother in."

Thunder pounded near the house, mimicking my mother's rising panic. "Max?" she screamed. The thunder cracked again. My mother reappeared in my doorway. "Do you know where your brother is?"

"No," I replied. I followed her into the bathroom. Max's towel was gone.

"Max!" she hollered, trying to outdo the thunder.

We stood on the steps of the back porch, which ended on the flagstone path that led down to the river. My mother was counting aloud, never quite getting to the number three that would send her out into the storm. Then she took a deep breath and held it, preparing to dive into the storm. She didn't move.

"Is Max by the river?" I asked.

That did it. She took me by the arm, her human lifesaver, and we plunged into the darkness. It was my first exposure to a thunderstorm, a hot swirling assault that cut maniacally through the August night. This was not the dangerous calm of the water in my dream, but an active aggressor that blinded my eyes and swam up my nose. The whip-crack thunder urged the storm forward, driving it around the final post. The rain and wind that shook the trees resounded in my ears like breaking glass. And in the distance, I could hear the angry stomach growl of the river.

We crossed the lawn, now a plush swamp of muddy grass, and arrived at the gate that divided our backyard from the dirt path to the river. When my parents first moved into the house, they had scrambled down this muddy path, picnic basket in hand, to eat by the water. But as the water became their enemy, their picnics retreated—first to a blanket spread just inside the gate, then to the middle of the lawn, and now to a modern picnic table a few feet from our back door. My mother had not been down to the river or even opened the gate since I was a year old. Only Max, during his forbidden solo explorations of the riverbed, had prevented a rusty arthritis from immobilizing the latch.

My mother's legs and hips banged against the gate. Over the pounding rain—which sounded more like the emptying of

buckets than like the simultaneous splatter of individual drops—
we could hear the deep snarl of the river as it rushed past us,
chewing up the bank and swallowing rocks and tree branches.
This was not the water of my dream, which had held its hunger at
bay. This water was insistent and unwilling to compromise. And
although I tried to listen for the song that Max heard in the rain
echoing in the swirling river, I disliked the water's angry voice. I
knew that if I fell in, it would chew me up and spit me out against
the shore. My mother sucked her breath in again and pulled me
down the muddy path.

We half walked, half slid as the warm, soft mud cushioned
our tumble. The river had already devoured most of the bank,
leaving less than two feet between the bottom of the path and
the edge of the water.

"Max!" my mother shouted, her voice melting into the wind
on its downstream course. "Max!"

"Max," I cried, my voice not even penetrating the storm's outermost shell.

"Flashlight, flashlight," my mother said, frantically patting
her pockets. "Oh, God," she cried, discovering that she was un-
armed.

We squinted over the riverbed, trying to separate the rain
from the dark. The thunder cracked hard and close. My mother
counted the seconds between each thunderclap. Ten seconds.
Nearly overhead. As the thunder approached, chariot driven, its
horses madly pawing the earth, it brought with it sheets of lightning that electrified the whole riverbed, illuminating it with a
phosphorus white.

Another sheet of lightning shocked the storm to life, showing
the spidery outlines of the tree branches, the tumult of the water
at our feet, and a small white rock bobbing in the middle of the

river. When the next white sheet descended, the rock was gone. My mother gripped my hand. Her other hand seemed to be groping in the dark, either reaching out into the river or looking for a light switch to keep the storm's electricity running. It was him—the next flash of lightning showed—floating in the river. Max seemed to be both fighting the storm and delighting in it. One moment, his arms would churn wildly, searching for some stability in the fluid madness—and the next, he appeared to be lying calmly, waiting for the river to sweep him along.

My mother let go of my hand and crept into the water until it reached her knees. I moved backwards onto the shrinking shore and held on to a tree branch that protruded from the small slope. "Max!" she shouted. "Max!"

The sky lit up, and we saw Max turn toward us, his face contorted with a look of surprise.

"Max!" my mother cried, taking two more steps into the river. "Stay there." Then the thunder cracked, and she whirled around, looking for me on the muddy bank. "Mel! Mel, are you holding on?"

Tears choked my reply as I watched my brother's head devoured and regurgitated by the black water. My mother retreated to the bank and extended a hand to me. I could feel Max's eyes penetrating the ferocious storm. Then my brother blinked and allowed his head to be swallowed once more by the blackened water. "He's gone," I wailed, flapping one hand in the direction of the river.

"What?" my mother screamed. She turned again to the river, but her water baby had disappeared. She extended her arms out into the water, hoping they would reach where her feet would not take her. Max's head resurfaced. He stretched out his body, relaxing on his tumultuous water bed, and began to make his way downstream, gently carried by the manic water.

Our mother fell back, buffeted by her own fear. She sat in the river as it gnawed her legs and back. She sat, quietly counting between the thunderclaps as the eye of the storm passed overhead, and she allowed the rain to cry for her.

Four

As Toby had promised when we first met, he trapped me with magic, wine, and—now that I remember my Homer properly—sex. Las Vegas had everything necessary to make me forget the world beyond. Our hours were punctuated by the scheduled eruptions of the Mirage's volcano and the performances of the *Pirates of the Caribbean* spectacular at the Treasure Island. At night we were mesmerized by the pillar of light shooting out of the Luxor's pyramid. Las Vegas seduced us. It was equal parts Circe's island and Land of the Lotus-Eaters.

When my workday was over, I loved accompanying Toby down the Strip to Fremont Street, marveling at the exploding multicolored fountains and improbable buildings as if he had created them just for me. We lost ourselves among the gaping tourists, watching them as they mistook Toby's magic—a handful of new flowers, for instance, that burst from one of the Bellagio's impressive bouquets—for Vegas's own. The town seemed to summon

Toby's craft, and tricks tumbled from his fingers. The deep lines in his face, the ones I thought were forged by frustration and worry about the limits to his art, had vanished, and for the first time, Toby seemed not to care who took notice of his art.

One Sunday, we decided to leave the lights and glitz of Vegas and drive into the desert, an expanse that I no longer associated with loneliness, but with color and possibility. We headed east until we came to the westernmost edge of the Grand Canyon. Just off the road where a Navajo woman was selling blankets and jewelry, we parked and watched a distant thunderstorm develop across the canyon. By the time the crack of thunder reached us, it was muffled and distorted. Lightning danced along a distant rim, descending from isolated black clouds. When the storm ended, vanishing to an invisible region of the canyon, Toby and I headed back to the car, passing a display of native crafts.

I'm not often enticed by these stands that pop up along all the well-traveled roads in the West. Mass-produced knickknacks like coasters and picture frames decorated with Southwestern motifs have replaced traditional artisan work. But here the blankets caught my eye. They were not the usual Mexican serapes, but authentically Navajo. I picked one up, drawn to the colors that mirrored the rusty canyon and the blue-black storm in the distance.

Toby nodded his approval. "I knew you'd pick that one," he said.

"Did you?"

He fluttered his fingers over the blanket, "You know sky and sand, or water and sand." He tapped the blanket's opposing colors. "How could you resist?"

I smiled. "Obviously I can't."

As I got out my wallet, the vendor tried to interest me in

several other blankets, but I shook my head. "Okay, okay," she said, placing my blanket in a bag and handing it to me. "This one is a good choice. Navajo marriage blanket. Very beautiful."

I reached over to take the bag from her, but the woman didn't let go. "If the marriage does not work out, the blanket must be cut," she said. "This is very important." Her dark eyes darted from me to Toby. We both laughed. "Very important."

"All right," I said.

"This blanket is too beautiful for cutting," she continued before letting go.

"I know," I replied.

Toby wrapped his arm around me as we walked back to the van.

We drove away from the canyon, back into the desert, where we found a convenience store on an empty stretch of road. While Toby went inside to buy beer, I watch a rusted FOR SALE sign sway in the wind. Several miles up the highway, we parked and walked into the sand. When the road had faded sufficiently into the distance, I spread the blanket on the ground, and we lay down.

Soon Toby propped himself up on his elbows and looked away from the highway and into the desert.

Before I could stop myself, I asked, "You're still looking for her?"

The magician shook his head.

"Then what?"

"Habit."

I nodded. "I know. Even when you suspect someone will never turn up, you keep looking."

Toby turned away from the desert, popped open the beers, and stared at me.

As we watched the lightning in the distance, I was reminded of the storm that stole my brother. "I know my parents didn't expect Max to return from the river the night he went swimming in the storm," I said.

I took a sip of beer and cleared my throat.

"That night on the riverbank, when I clung to a branch and watched the storm," I began.

Toby leaned back on his elbows.

I let my mind return to the moment when the storm had watched us with its unblinking eye like a liquid Cyclops. Satisfied, the eye closed, dried its tear ducts, and released us from its stare. "The wind continued whipping through the trees, hurling raindrops from their leaves. There was no lightning left to illuminate the blackened water or the disappearance of my brother." All there was, I remembered, was a contented, rhythmic grumble coming from the river, a sure sign that it was delighted with its digestion of an eleven-year-old boy.

"My father brought my mother and me back to the house and called the police," I said. "We remained inside while he joined the search party. Eventually I fell asleep. The last thing I remember seeing was a single tear trapped in the corner of my mother's eye. I still wonder why it didn't fall. Finally, when the last of the afternoon light had disappeared, a fireman arrived, carrying Max, drenching our floors with mud and water. Max's arms looked translucent as they swung free from the fireman's hold. His dark brown hair, matted with mud and small sticks, was caked in a helmet around his head. My mother moaned and slapped her hands against the sofa. Before she could speak, the fireman told us that Max was sleeping."

"Sleeping?" Toby asked.

I nodded and smiled. "My brother had some extraordinary talents. Sleeping in water is one of them. The fireman told us that he found Max in a little creek two miles downstream. He said it was a miracle that the water hadn't pulled him under.

There was absolutely nothing wrong with him. Not even a mosquito bite. I think the fireman wanted to tell us that that was a miracle, too, but my mother would not listen. She didn't want to encourage Max's water-lust." I spun my beer bottle in my hand and looked directly at the magician. "You know your pattern of watching and waiting here in the desert."

Toby nodded.

"That night, my own vigil began. I was so worried that Max would return to the river that after he fell asleep, I crept into his room and sat in the rocking chair next to his bed and watched him." I sipped my beer. "I woke him up and asked him why he'd gone down to the river. He told me, as if it was the most natural thing in the world, that he'd gone there to swim through the surface of the moon."

"That sounds reasonable."

I stared at Toby. "Maybe it does now. After that, I returned to Max's room nearly every evening, trying to prevent his escape. I tried to keep Max as close to me as possible. And when I couldn't, I guess you could say that I memorized him." I laughed at the memory. "After the night he spent in the river, Max's hair turned a light straw color. Within six months, the color deepened, acquiring a rich gold hue that sparkled in the sun and glowed in the dark. My mother thought the river had leaked inside his head."

"Maybe it did."

"I think so." I finished my beer. "Soon after his hair changed, Max experienced a strange growth spurt that not only made him taller, but also disproportionately elongated his limbs, fingers, feet, and toes. My parents are compact, and when he was young, Max had been a miniature version of my father. But then his arms and legs grew until he looked like a monkey puzzle tree. His hands and feet followed, until we had to compare them to flippers. Eventually his skin paled to a translucent opal. I learned so much from Max. The only thing he couldn't teach me was to love water. So I couldn't follow him when he finally left."

"And here you are in the desert."

I looked over the canyon and nodded.

"Did you try looking for him?"

I shook my head. "Despite all my watching and memorizing, it took me years to figure out that Max never really returned from the river that night." I dug the bottom of my beer bottle into the soft earth. "But that doesn't prevent me from expecting him to turn up around every corner."

Toby looked off across the empty canyon and said nothing.

In the month that I had been working for Sandra, I began to catalog her suits and became convinced she rarely wore the same thing twice. Today it was a coral pink number that gripped her waist, chest, and rear with magnetic force. The 2 percent spandex content of the fabric caused it to emit country music squawks each time she sat. Of course, she couldn't hear this. All she knew was that her new suit felt like a second skin and deepened the dark leather hue of her tan.

"You're the one who knows about fabric and all," she said, pulling the bottom of her jacket so the neckline plunged to a dangerous low, revealing the turquoise lace trim of her brassiere, "but these synthetic blends are a gift from God. Sometimes I feel like my old linen suits hang on me like garbage bags. They make me feel like a pioneer or a settler—dowdy and homespun." She gave her skirt a little twist. "This might be the desert," she continued with a flick of her wrist, "but it's not the prairie. No choice but to look good."

"Spandex and nylon add shape," I said, "but they don't breathe as well as natural fabrics."

"Breathe? Who needs them to breathe? Who goes outside? Everywhere has air-conditioning."

This was true. Moving sidewalks and towering skywalks transformed the Strip into a synthetic biodome. Like moles, we traveled through cooled tunnels from parking lots to hotels and from movie theaters to shopping malls. Monorails ushered us from one casino to another, while galleries and promenades sheltered us from the high midday heat. Everyone—locals and tourists alike—worshipped the heat from a safe distance. So, when Sandra wondered aloud for the second time that morning, "Who really goes outside, except to the pool?" I just nodded and examined the skin on my forearms.

We were reviewing the uniforms of the cocktail waitresses. The designer had taken a nineteenth-century Russian dress and crossed it with cancan outfits from the Moulin Rouge. With the hemline raised by nearly a foot, the overall effect was of a peasant costume run through a shredder.

"These crinolines look a little limp," I said, fingering the built-in petticoats underneath the dresses. "If you want that bunny tail look, you should starch them or attach some wires."

"Sure," Sandra replied distractedly.

"And as long as you've got good servers who aren't going to spill drinks on themselves, the fabric should hold up perfectly. It'll even absorb stains." I let the pop-music polyester slip through my thumb and forefinger. "But, I'd advise you to forbid smoking in these. A little ember, and they're gone."

"Right," Sandra replied. The crisp tone that she used when discussing Winter Palace matters was gone.

"But these stockings," I continued, "these you've got to change. You can't protect stockings from rough corners and cigarette ash." I stretched the fabric of the black lace nylons so that

Sandra could see their faults. "A snag in the wrong place, and these will disintegrate and curl away from each other." Through the synthetic spiderweb, I caught Sandra's gaze. She was peeking at me. She squinted slightly and then looked away. I continued pointing out the stockings' flaws.

"My advice would be to get solid hose with the lace pattern printed on them. Get something like they use in musicals. That stuff is really sturdy but also breathable." I folded the stockings and placed them in the clothing pile. When I looked up, Sandra was staring at me.

"Is something wrong?" I asked, strumming the stockings so they twanged like an out-of-tune banjo.

"Wrong? No, of course not," Sandra said, recovering herself. "I just had a question for you."

"A question?" Sandra was usually so businesslike that she moved through sessions with her employees without pausing for air.

She took a little breath, "You're married to the magician, right? The one who works at the Castaway?"

"Why?"

"Well," Sandra began, "people are starting to talk about him."

"They are?"

"He's making quite an impression up and down Fremont Street," Sandra explained. "His show is incredible."

"Really?" When I had seen Toby's show, his magic had not been anywhere near as incredible as it had been in Intersection.

"Haven't seen his show?"

"Once," I answered. "But it's probably changed a lot since then."

"Well, you don't know what you're missing. He works the tables and—I won't lie to you—the ladies like a pro. Slick as can be."

"He works the ladies?"

"I wouldn't exactly say that he's flirting. But it's something in his eyes. Something intense, like he's trying to look through us."

"Us?"

"Well, he doesn't look at the men that way. In fact, not many men come to his shows. It's pretty much an all-female audience."

"Really," I said, trying not to sound surprised.

"And those eyes of his—they can just drill into you, like he's trying to dig out your thoughts, you know?"

I knew. I knew the probing, questioning stare that tried to work its way into the corners of my mind. I was surprised that he unleashed it on others.

"What a catch," Sandra said with a wink. "Most magicians are—you know—unattractive," she added with a whisper. "But yours—"

"Toby."

"Yeah, Toby—he's not just good-looking, he's—" She stifled a laugh. "—enchanting."

"Oh, really," I said, smiling.

"I'd always imagined magicians were weird and kind of awkward. You know, like the kid who sat in the back of the class and played fantasy role games or whatever. But not yours. I mean, between shows, all the ladies want to buy him drinks."

I shook my head, remembering the lonely man I'd found sitting in a corner booth in Tonopah.

"I'll admit that even I offered him a cocktail." Sandra laughed. She waved her pearly manicure in my direction. "I've been in this town my whole life, and I've never seen a magic show like his."

"How many times have you gone?"

"Just twice," Sandra answered. But twice seemed to have been enough for her to fall under the new powers of my magician. "And it made me wonder what it's like."

"What what's like? Living with a magician?"

"No," Sandra whispered, leaning in close, "sleeping with one." She recoiled, as if she'd shocked herself with her curiosity. "Growing up in this town, I've had singers, race car drivers, boxers, even a member of *Riverdance*. But never a magician."

I'm not fond of discussing my personal life with close friends, let alone with acquaintances. My childhood taught me to take my heart off my sleeve and bury it. But now I needed to claim the magician as my own, trap him in my web of description and detail. "Well," I began, searching for a suitable metaphor, "it's a bit like sleeping with an octopus. You know, many hands and one mouth. He can be everywhere at once while being right there in front of you."

"An octopus?" Sandra gasped. "I'm not sure whether that excites me or disgusts me."

"Take your pick. Many women would kill for an extra pair of arms."

Sandra squinted, puckered her lips, and nodded in conspiratorial agreement.

I knew she wanted all the details, but I preferred to keep to myself how Toby's hands flew across my body in a maniacal sign language. When I could have sworn that he was massaging my shoulders, suddenly he was tickling my toes. And when I looked at my toes, I noticed that his hands had moved to my hair. And all the time it appeared that he hadn't taken his lips from mine. Sometimes he managed to make the bed vanish as if we were floating toward the ceiling in an erotic levitation. Sometimes the ceiling itself seemed to disappear and the room flooded with the sky. After it was over, after my magician's hands, which had doubled and redoubled as we reached the finale of our private magic show, had collapsed onto the sateen sheets, I woke up to find the remnants of his conjuring pressed into my body. I found coins on my inner thighs, poker chips on my lower back, the jack of diamonds stuck to my left buttock.

I wasn't sure that Sandra would appreciate the combination of magic and sex, so I told her what I thought she wanted to hear.

"Wow," Sandra breathed when I had elaborated on several of Toby's more impressive manipulations. "You are a lucky woman." She readjusted her jacket. "I think I'll go down for a vodka. Coming with?"

I looked at the tiny gold wristwatch dangling on Sandra's wrist. The scrolled hands told me that it was before eleven. "I'll pass."

"All right," Sandra answered, sounding a little deflated. "But maybe I'll see you this evening?"

"This evening?"

"At the Castaway."

"Sure," I said, "I'll check it out."

I left Sandra's office, navigated my way through the well-secured administration wing of the casino, and onto the gambling floor. The tech men were testing the sound system. The music was just loud and snappy enough to maintain the players' enthusiasm without agitating them. The soundtrack was a hybrid of Russian folk songs and Muzak. Unmuffled by the jangle of spinning slots, the clatter of roulette wheels, or the shouts of gamblers, the sound of synthesized zithers blared through the pits. I walked past the craps tables, examining the skirts I had commissioned to protect the carpet from the more aggressive dice throwers who took running starts and whose stiletto-heeled girlfriends jumped up and down, tearing the pile with their shoes. Examination complete, I headed to the exit, past the Revolution Bar, where hipsters were encouraged to drop money on aristocratically priced drinks while contemplating the ironies of the Winter Palace.

Out on the Strip, the heat reminded me that I hadn't been properly outside in more than thirty-six hours. I was starting to lose track of the day and of the time. Despite the temperature, I was hungry. In fact, I was craving a steak—a flat, greasy diner steak. There was a joint just off the Strip I hoped would offer low-key relief from the elaborate Vegas buffets. I was tired of big spreads where cold cuts cuddled up to sashimi, dim sum next to seared quail. But worst of all, buffets sapped my hunger before I even sat down. Overwhelmed by choice and fearful of making a poor selection, I became a grazer, sampling drumsticks and spring rolls to see whether either was worth adding to my tray. By the time I reached my seat with a plate of food, I was unpleasantly full.

The Red Rock Diner offered a steak dinner that got cheaper as the hours got later. At 11 A.M. the price of a well-flattened sixteen-ounce sirloin with "any sort potato" had risen to four dollars from its low of three dollars, 2 A.M. to 6 A.M. At noon, the trampled steak had hit $5.50. During the dinner rush, it would peak at $6.75, before plummeting at 10 P.M. to $4.50, and then back to its 2 A.M. low. Before I sat down, I spun one of the vinyl-covered stools at the lunch counter. It creaked and wobbled until I stopped it with the weight of my body. The Red Rock's chrome decor was tarnished by a layer of grease from the grill. Years of fry fat, cheese oil, and burger juices settled over the counter, napkin holders, seats, and silverware, giving the restaurant a speckled sheen.

"Steak dinner," I said to the waitress when she appeared in front of my stool. I was busy finding hidden patterns in the Formica counter and didn't look up.

"So you know, we don't do rare, medium rare, anything like that," the waitress said to my bowed head. "We just do steak."

"That's fine."

"And the potato? You want fries?"

"Anything else? Can I have baked?"

"Baked?" the waitress snorted. "It's only eleven. You got a while?"

I found it—a widespread pattern of larger and smaller rectangles, each unit of the pattern containing twenty-eight shapes. Task complete, I looked up.

"Yeah?" the waitress asked, casting around the nearly empty diner for someone more important. "Maybe you do have all day?" she said, tapping her nails on the counter. "So—fries, or what?"

She was younger than her voice and wore a mint green uniform that she probably expected to fill out one day. And even though she'd bleached away some of her dyed-black hair and scrubbed the goth eyeliner from her eyes, I recognized her.

"Greta?"

The impatient tapping of her nails ceased. "What?"

"Greta. The girl from Intersection. You were at the magic show."

"Greta?" the waitress repeated loudly enough for the other two diners, and probably the guy in the kitchen, to hear. "Greta," she said again. "Intersection?"

I stared at her. "Sure, Intersection."

"Never been there," she said with a click of the tongue. "So who is it you want me to be?" Her eyes narrowed fiercely.

"No one," I said, deciding to humor the teenager. "Fries will be fine."

"Fries?" she repeated, letting her mocking smile salt her words. "Yes."

She made a note on her pad. "By the way, my name is Paula," she added with a flick of her name tag and a familiar smirk that intimated, as it had before, that she just knew better.

"Okay, sure," I said as she went into the kitchen to relay my order.

The air conditioner hummed weakly as I counted the minutes

until my lunch arrived. Finally, the cook slammed his hand onto the small bell and slid my steak to the newly christened Paula, who thrust the plate in front of me with an arrogant thump.

"Can I have a cup of tea, as well?"

"Hot tea?" she snickered, lifting her eyebrows and betraying her age.

"You've never heard of drinking hot tea on a hot day?"

"Never."

Greta took her time getting my cup. She chatted with the cook and wiped down the far end of the counter. When she finally returned, I had grown tired of looking for a way to hide the fries. "When you've got a minute, I'll take the check. Thanks." I watched amber tentacles spiral out from the tea bag and into the cloudy water.

"When I've got a minute," Greta said with a look around the empty diner. Then she cast an eye over my plate. Devoured steak. Untouched fries. "Why'd you order them if you didn't want them?" she asked.

"It was simpler," I replied.

The other two diners dropped their money on their table and left. When the door shut behind them, Greta came over to me.

"So, is all you do hang out in diners?"

"I do a lot of things," I said.

"Like follow around that magician?"

"We're married."

"Oh," Greta snorted, not quite believing me. "He still doing the lame show?"

"It wasn't lame."

"Whatever."

"Well, he's got a permanent gig."

"Where?" Greta asked, looking away, trying to hide her interest.

"Here."

"In Vegas?" Her eyes lit up. "For real?"

I nodded.

"'Cause since I got here, I've been looking—"

"The Castaway."

"Never heard of it."

"It's on Fremont Street."

"That's not the good part of Vegas."

"He's pretty much the biggest thing on that side of town," I said, echoing Sandra.

"Sure."

Greta walked away, forgetting my check. At the far end of the counter, she picked up one of the greasy chrome napkin dispensers and used it as a mirror to reapply her lipstick.

"The check," I reminded her.

She clicked her tongue against her teeth and then dropped the check in front of me. "So, is he still looking for an assistant?"

"I don't think so."

"'Cause I'd be perfect."

"Toby doesn't use assistants."

"He will."

I shook my head and didn't answer.

"If he's gonna be big, he's gonna need an assistant. You'll see."

"Greta—"

"You said the Castaway?"

"Aren't you a little young to be hanging out in casinos?"

"Don't you get bored of hanging out in diners?"

"Not really," I said, overtipping her before walking out the door.

Day passed into night, but the interior of the Winter Palace registered no change. The lighting was planned so that the patrons would not notice the hour. Inside the casino, it was always mid-afternoon. After Toby's first week at the Castaway, his contract had been expanded to include a six and an eleven o'clock performance in addition to his nine o'clock spot. So, after consulting my watch to make sure I would avoid the crowds in front of the Treasure Island waiting to watch the naval showdown between the buccaneers and the British, I began the long walk to Fremont Street, where the glitz of the Strip gave way to pure gambling grime.

Once called the "Glitter Gulch," Fremont Street was the birthplace of Vegas, but unlike the popular casinos on the Strip, Fremont's were free of special attractions and prom-night themes. They stood, like over-the-hill athletes, content to remind the rest of the city how great they'd been without making any effort to regain their former glory. The only nod to the once-spectacular Glitter Gulch was a strip club by that name offering free entrance, free table dances, and eight-dollar bottles of Budweiser.

The magician was leaning casually against the door of the theater when I entered the casino. He was wearing a suit I had never seen before—a green silk blend with a gangster gleam.

"I was wondering when you'd make it past the door," he said.

"It seems like I'm the last woman in town to fall in love with your show."

Toby raised his eyebrows.

"Sandra," I said.

"Oh," the magician replied. "I've been drawing a different sort of crowd lately. Not a conscious decision."

"And I hoped I was the only woman inexplicably drawn to you."

Toby leaned forward so his thin lips brushed my ear. "You are. The rest come for the show."

I pulled back and scanned the room, looking for the women Sandra had described.

Suddenly, Toby smiled broadly, and the corners of his mouth jutted dangerously toward his cheekbones. "Pick a card," he said, fanning a deck in front of my face.

"No thanks."

"C'mon, pick a card."

"No," I said. "Try it on someone else. Anyway, I thought you didn't do card tricks."

"Okay, then," my magician replied, "I'll pick one for you." He inched a card out of the deck.

"I'll choose my own, thank you." I wiggled a card out from the far left of his fan. Nine of clubs. I replaced it in the deck.

A bell rang in the distance. "Oops, out of time," Toby said, putting away the deck. "Show's about to start."

"But my card," I said, grabbing Toby's sleeve as he slipped into the theater.

"I thought you weren't interested."

"Of course I'm interested."

"After the show," Toby promised. "You'll get your card after the show. And about the women—for that, you'll have to wait and see as well."

I ordered a vodka tonic from a passing waitress. When she returned, I took a generous sip, exhaled sharply, and entered the theater. Inside, I found Sandra and a friend of hers, a bar manager at Circus Circus, already seated in the back row. Sandra shushed her friend as I approached.

"What?" I asked when their giggling had subsided.

"Nothing," the friend squealed.

"Trina, remember Mel?" Sandra said, jabbing her companion under the collarbone. "She's Toby's wife."

"Toby? Who's Toby?" Trina said.

"The magician," Sandra whispered in a stagy voice, and the two of them burst into fresh laughter.

When they collected themselves again, I suggested that we move to the front of the theater.

"The front?" Sandra hollered. "All the action goes on back here."

I had just enough time to fall into a seat before the lights went out. A single grimy bulb lit the stage, illuminating the entrance of my magician. There was something sultry about his appearance. The stage lights erased the creases from his eyes and added a new depth to his hollow cheekbones. His movements were tauntingly languid, as if he were almost inviting his audience into the secret. But the angular shadows Toby cast on the tattered curtain and splintering stage made him seem mysteriously vacant—and they made the spectators want more of him.

As two smoky-voiced catcalls echoed through the theater, Toby paused center stage. Then he smiled an unfamiliar smile that mixed charm with subterfuge. Sandra pinched my arm. The magician began his show with a few unremarkable tricks—he made flowers grow from an empty vase and produced a goldfish in a bowl. After three more tricks, Toby pulled a highball from his jacket.

"Name your poison," he said, stepping off the stage and approaching a woman in the front row.

"Bourbon," the woman announced.

Toby filled the glass from an opaque bottle he had brought down from the stage with him.

The woman took a sip. "Four Roses?" she asked. She took another sip. "It is Four Roses."

Toby moved through the audience, taking drink orders and filling glasses from the same bottle. Out came whiskey, vodka, rum, and cognac. Out came tequila and gin.

Sandra squawked with delight when Toby poured her a glass of Absolut Peppar. Trina asked for gin and received a glass of

Bombay Sapphire. I noticed that she stroked my magician's fingers as he passed her the glass.

I asked for whiskey, but got a glass with the nine of clubs.

"Is that your card?" Toby asked.

"How does he do it?" Sandra demanded as I fished the card from my drink.

Toby put down the enchanted bottle and walked out of the theater. The audience stood up to follow. The girls in the back row now had front-row seats for the rest of the show. I hesitated for a minute until Sandra tugged my arm. "This is the good part," she said, dragging me along.

Toby walked through the slots. Cigarettes appeared at his fingertips. They appeared in the mouths of the slot players. Rows of flaming 7's appeared across the pay bars of the slot machines. As he passed, a woman discovered that her nearly empty coin bucket had filled with nickels. A cocktail waitress with an empty tray found herself carrying six old-fashioneds. The audience, following several paces behind the magician, gasped and laughed. At the tables, a gambler put down his drink, and a full one appeared in its place. The man on his left found two cigarettes tucked behind his ears. Toby made dice hover in the air before they fell. He made the ball on the roulette wheel disappear. He conjured a pentagram on the bingo board.

But with the women, with the hardened Vegas broads, the gamblers' wives, and the newcomers, he was especially slick. He pulled fistfuls of chips from a woman's plunging neckline. He lit another woman's cigarette from ten feet away. He transformed the cards of an elderly woman who was losing at poker into aces. Bouquets of flowers materialized in empty arms. Swing music flowed from cigarette lighters. Lipstick shades turned from pink to red.

Toby moved about the casino with the silence of an Indian tracker. The audience was unable to keep up with him. First he was causing an olive to appear in the martini of a woman playing blackjack; then he was making pink smoke rise from the drink of a lady by the bar.

For his finale, Toby chose a blackjack table, pulled out a chair, and placed a bet. The cards began to gallop across the felt. Chips followed suit. A cigarette appeared in the magician's lips. He dropped it in an ashtray. When he looked up, a fresh one was hanging jauntily from his mouth. He deposited the new cigarette in the ashtray and discovered that another had found its way between his lips. Soon a delighted cry rippled across the table. All the players revealed their cards—six identical hands of twenty-one—all made up of the king of hearts and the ace of hearts. The dealer placed his cards on the table. They were identical to those of the other players. "Tie goes to the house," he cried. Toby stood up, took a small bow, and the surrounding tables and spectators burst into applause.

"That was different," I said, maneuvering around a woman in a sequined suit who had cornered my magician. Toby was having difficulty extracting himself from her grasp.

"Did you like it?" Toby asked.

"Absolutely," I replied, although I did miss the natural elements—the sand, water, and flowers—that I had come to expect from Toby's magic.

"Lemme buy you a drink," the sequined woman pleaded.

"No thank you," Toby said, unwrapping her hand from his wrist.

"Why don't you buy me one, then?" she wheedled. "My husband's over on the craps. Blind as a bat."

"Sorry. I don't socialize when I'm on duty," Toby lied.

"So when do you get off work?" another woman wanted to know.

Toby grabbed my wrist, and we wove our way to the bar.

Women popped up on all sides. They wanted their cigarettes lit. They wanted their drinks refilled. They wanted to slip twenty-dollar tips into the pockets of Toby's green suit.

"Wow," I said when we found space in the bar off the casino's main floor. "What's that all about?"

"I don't know," Toby replied. "Started two weeks ago. I was meant to lure the husbands into emptying their pockets, but it seems I've won over the wives. The manager was angry after the first week. Said that I was hired to charm the gamblers, trick them into loosening their purse strings. He said I should give my show a more masculine angle. For a few days, nothing worked. Gamblers, especially in this place, are tough guys. They don't want flowers or silk handkerchiefs. They want top-of-the-line card tricks or they want to see girls being cut in half. Blood or money. But then the women started coming. All sorts of women."

"What made them come?"

"I don't know. There was a poker tournament in town. Maybe that was the reason—something to distract them while their husbands sweated it out at the tables. Maybe they were bored with the testosterone of Fremont Street. Or maybe it was just a coincidence."

"You are very charming," I said.

"Sometimes," Toby replied with a wink. Then all the playfulness left his face. "This is the first time in ages that I've had the chance to be charming." He laced his long fingers through mine. "You started all this. You were the first."

I shook my head. "Meeting you was just luck."

"A good magician doesn't believe in luck."

"What about the one-armed bandit at the gas station?"

Toby shook his head.

"Then what?"

"Some things are meant to be, and some are brought about by circumstances we don't understand."

I stared out over the rippling lights on the casino's floor, over the coiffed heads of Toby's new fans and wondered how he was luring these women to him. Then my thoughts rewound to the Red Rock Diner, to another girl Toby seemed to have pulled to his side. And finally my mind landed in Tonopah, where we met and where this chain of women seemed to start.

The noise on the casino floor was growing louder, a cacophony of smoky cackles and hoarse titters. The bar was starting to smell like a mixture of damp perfume and hairspray. I looked around. Women were standing in an imperfect semicircle around my magician. They were watching Toby over the rims of their glasses and over their shoulders. "There are so many," I whispered.

"Yes. Tonight we have Jacqui Masterson, who likes gold-tipped cigarettes, Manhattans, two-piece suits, but can't wear heels because of a herniated disk. Her husband is at the Golden Nugget, but she spends most of the day over here because when he drinks, she can't stand the smell of his sweat. Then there's Selena Baxter, whose husband was banned from the casino after pulling a knife on a dealer. She likes cognac, doesn't smoke, and wishes she were still a showgirl," Toby said.

"How do you know all of this?"

Toby looked over the crowded casino floor. "See that woman over by the nickel slots?"

I peered through the fronds of a plastic fern and saw a tall woman with a hive of dyed-black hair smile at Toby through her empty highball.

"She's trouble. Evelyn Langhorn. Never been married. Grew up in a casino. Thinks she's seen all there is to see, so she's looking to create something never seen before."

"Did they tell you all this?" I asked.

"No."

"Then how—?"

"In the dark, no one knows how much you can see."

The bartender placed a whiskey sour in front of Toby. "I'm not sure who this one's from, Mr. Toby," he said, gesturing at a gaggle of middle-aged women hovering by the dollar slots.

"Thanks," Toby said, casting aside the cherry garnish.

The women were approaching. Before they were within earshot, Toby whispered in my ear. "C'mon," Toby said, taking me by the hand, "let's get out of here."

Several doors down from the Castaway, we found a slots hall with a Caribbean theme. We sat in front of a pair of complicated-looking electronic poker games while women in canary yellow Carmen Miranda outfits with headdresses of fruit and fake feathers brought us foot-long glasses of beer. Our seats faced the enclosed promenade of Fremont Street. As we sat, the Fremont Street Experience laser show played across the domed roof of the esplanade. We sat in silence, listening to the tinkle and whir of the slots and the electronic music from the laser show.

Suddenly Toby grabbed my hand, nearly upsetting my beer. "Isn't that . . . ," he began.

I followed his gaze and saw a familiar figure with badly bleached hair saunter down the street. Greta had changed out of her waitress uniform and into her usual goth garb.

"It is," I said. "I saw her earlier today. She's working in a diner off the Strip."

"Another diner," Toby wondered.

"Well, she'd gladly trade it in to become your assistant."

"I thought she said my show was lame."

"She did."

"So?"

"So, she's a teenager. Anything to get attention."

"I guess I wasn't a typical teenager," Toby said. "I've got to get ready for my next show. Coming?"

"I'll leave you to your ladies," I said, kissing him.

I took a sip of beer and watched Toby vanish into the crowd outside. Then I slid into a seat in front of one of the slot machines, fed it five dollars, and began to play. The machine was one of the old-style games with a cup holder, an ashtray, and a low payout. After I lost five dollars, I decided to give it five more. I had just spun the wheel when someone reached over and tapped a cigarette into my machine's ashtray.

"Excuse me," a man's voice said.

I looked up, irritated that the speaker hadn't used any of the ashtrays on a dozen other machines.

"It's a fool's game," he continued. He was older than Toby, with greased black hair and skin that was either too tan or caked with makeup. He wore a black leather car coat and a tight white T-shirt tucked into black jeans. Years ago, he might have been muscular, but his physique was melting into paunch. When he put his cigarette to his lips, a large gold signet ring glinted in the flashing lights of the slots.

"Doesn't bother me," I said, swiveling my chair away from him.

"I don't believe in luck," the man said.

"Then you're in the wrong place."

"Actually I'm not." He stuck his hand out in front of my face. "Name's Swenson. Swenson the Spectacular."

"Mel," I said, pulling away from Toby's old partner.

"Do you believe in luck, Mel?" Swenson asked. He plucked a cocktail in a plastic cup from the top of a nearby machine and took a sip.

"I don't know," I muttered, wanting to be rid of Swenson.

"Well, maybe you believe in coincidence."

I spun the wheels and won a dollar.

Swenson cracked an ice cube in his teeth. "Would you say it's a coincidence if I told you I'm a magician?"

"Why would that be a coincidence?" I asked, keeping my back turned. "Anyway, I already know you're a magician."

"So, I'm not the only magician in your life."

"I'd hardly say that you're in my life."

"Not yet."

I spun the chair round and faced Swenson. "What is it that you want?"

"I've known Toby Warring a long time. We go back."

I didn't reply.

"Did a show together at one point."

"I've heard."

"Now, what have you heard?" Swenson lowered himself into the chair next to me.

"That you're not the best magician." I spun the wheel again.

"Hmm." Swenson cracked another ice cube. "That pretty much sounds like Toby." Now he wrapped a large hand around my wrist. "At least I'm not a dangerous magician."

I pulled free. "I don't know what you mean."

Swenson smiled. "I think you do."

I spun the wheel and lost all my money. Out of the corner of my eye, I could sense Swenson staring into the gritty esplanade of Fremont Street.

"I wonder," he said, jostling the remaining ice in his drink. "I wonder."

When I didn't respond, he drained his glass and replaced it roughly in the cup holder in front of him. I was about to feed the machine another dollar, but Swenson stopped me. "I wonder," he said again, "how you make someone disappear."

I shrugged, and slid the dollar into the machine.

"I'm not talking for a split second behind a screen. But really disappear." He waited for a moment, then rapped his signet ring on the plastic front of the gambling machine. "What I'm talking about is making someone vanish for months. Or years."

"I don't know," I said finally.

Swenson laughed and winked. "Exactly. Neither do I. And I've been a magician half my life. A trustworthy magician." He drained his drink and winked once more.

"I loved her. Obviously more than he did."

"Who?"

"Eva, our assistant. And Toby ruined everything."

"I'm not sure what you want from me."

"There's absolutely nothing I want from you, sweetheart." He smiled and nodded slightly. "I'm just worried about you. That's all."

"I can take care of myself."

"That's what she thought." He reached over, spun the wheel on my game, and lost. "Such a disaster."

"Some people prefer to be absent," I said, thinking of my brother.

"Most don't." Swenson trapped me with his red-rimmed eyes. "And most magicians don't like renegades like your husband. Not even in dives like the Castaway."

I looked away.

"We have a code."

"I'm sure you do."

Swenson's face wore an indulgent smile. "Drink?"

I shook my head.

He withdrew a handkerchief from his pocket, draped it over the top of the machine in front of him. When he whisked it away, two fresh cocktails had appeared. "I'm afraid you don't have a choice."

"No thanks," I said.

"You see, *that* is magic." Swenson smiled. "Now, if you want to see a real show, you should check out my North American Wonder Show."

"No thanks," I repeated.

"I've got the biggest tour going in the Canadian provinces."

"And?"

"It's a lot better than what your husband will have when people discover that he's not to be trusted. You think this side of town is bad. I can't imagine where you two will go next."

"Why would we have to go anywhere?"

"Ah," Swenson said with another patronizing smile, "by now you should have learned that a magician never reveals what is up his sleeve."

"Toby never has anything up his sleeve," I said.

"That, sweetheart, is precisely the point."

Five

If Toby had been perturbed by my meeting with Swenson, he didn't let it show. He simply told me that things were going too well for Swenson to interfere with him now. In fact, attendance at Toby's show at the Castaway was so good that the management had offered him a yearlong contract, which Toby had yet to sign. He had a feeling a better offer was waiting in the wings. Getting stuck on Fremont Street when the Strip was calling would be a disaster.

Like a fish in a tank, I had grown used to living without natural light since arriving in Vegas and mistook the city's shrunken castles and palaces for the real thing. I was drugged with the lazy promise of simple days, of conveyor belts that moved me, slots that might make me rich, and around-the-world trips that were just across the street. Most of all, I was drugged by the calm that descended every morning when I opened my eyes and saw the sleeping magician. We always slept tightly wound around each other. When we woke, we would open our remote-controlled curtains, revealing the empty desert flowing away from the Strip. Then we would sit up, conjuring our future from the sun-baked sands.

To my surprise, I was beginning to look forward to settling in the desert. On Toby's day off, we'd drive out of Vegas, heading deeper into the desert, navigating the dirt roads with Toby's creaky van. We sometimes drove in the direction of the spot where Toby had made the sand dance for me. It was near there that we discovered a solitary blue ranch house, its unusual cornflower color fastened brightly to the rusty hues of the surrounding desert.

An abandoned model home from the early seventies, it stood, framed by two distant mesas, waiting for a suburban sprawl that never arrived. Shag carpet, brightly colored living room and bedroom sets in shades of blue and green, all pretty much intact. Toby sprung the lock, and we stepped inside. Despite the lack of air-conditioning, the interior was cool and soothing. We linked hands and toured our desert home.

When Toby was working, I often joined him between shows at the Castaway's bar, stealing the magician from his women, at least for a couple of moments.

"Toby, Mrs. Toby," the bartender said, setting our drinks in front of us.

"Thank you," I replied, removing the maraschino cherry from my whiskey sour. Except for an older man, dressed too warmly for the Las Vegas weather, we were alone at the bar.

"Hey," Toby said, removing his silk coat and tapping me on the shoulder. "I've got a surprise for you."

"Should I pick a card?"

The elderly man moved a few seats closer.

"It's nothing like that." Toby laughed and showed me his empty hands. I thought I saw our new neighbor smile.

"What, then?"

"Sandra was at the last show. She says it's her tenth time."

"That's surprising." Sandra's fascination with Toby was beginning to irritate me. "I'd have thought she'd seen you more than ten times by now. She thinks you're the best thing since Wayne Newton."

"Anyway," Toby said, dispelling my comment with a wave of his hand, "Sandra asked me if I'd do a version of my act at the opening of the Winter Palace. A small show on the tables."

I was too happy to wonder why she hadn't mentioned this to me. I leaned over and kissed Toby's thin lips.

Toby ordered another drink and began to describe several of the ideas he had for the Winter Palace. The usual crowd of women was hovering behind us. Toby looked over his shoulder at the older man next to him, then bowed his head closer to mine and described two potential opening illusions.

Suddenly a hand came between us. I looked down at chipped black fingernails as Greta drew up to the bar. "So, the Winter Palace," she said.

For a moment, Toby was too startled to speak.

"How could you know that?" I asked.

Greta shrugged. "Must be a big deal."

Toby recovered himself. "I don't think you're old enough to be here."

"Hasn't stopped me before."

"I've noticed," Toby said. "But I could say something."

The teenager rolled her eyes. "Like anyone cares." She turned her back, showing me the uneven roots of her hair.

"Greta, he's right. I'm sure there are better places for you to spend your time."

"Like?" she asked, tapping her nails.

Suddenly all my answers—the mall, the movies, a high school

dance, or the library—seemed too juvenile for the girl with her back to me.

When I didn't reply, she continued, "You've gotta do a way bigger show than in this place."

Toby stared into his glass. "That's my business."

"What'cha gonna do?"

"Don't you know a magician never gives anything away?" I said.

"I'm sure no one wants to see card tricks and that kind of stuff at a casino opening," Greta said.

"They don't," Toby said.

"So?"

Toby didn't reply.

"So, now you're gonna need an assistant." Greta kept drumming her nails on the bar. The ball-chain necklaces around her wrist rattled on the wood. "Well?"

Toby shook his head.

"You think I like listening to people slurp their coffee in a diner? No way. I came here for you." She pressed in closer to Toby.

"This isn't going to work," I said gently.

"What do you know?"

Toby wrapped his fingers around her wrist. "That's enough. Go back to your diner or to Intersection." His voice was firm.

"No way." Her words were sharp and insistent.

"Listen to me, Greta. You will not be part of my show."

Greta shook her head.

"I've told you, I don't work with an assistant."

"Only because you lose them."

Toby opened his mouth. But Greta got there first. "Remember, I was there. You made that woman vanish."

The magician shook his head.

Greta smiled. "Well, I think your old partner, Jim Swenson, agrees with me. I met him the other day outside your show."

"Why don't you be his assistant?" Toby asked.

"Swenson says you're a dangerous magician."

Toby shook his head.

"So, why would I want to assist him when I could assist you?"

"Swenson is an idiot."

"Whatever. But you're gonna need someone like me. Someone who's not afraid of your tricks."

"I don't work with assistants."

"This is Las Vegas. Every show needs a girl onstage."

"We'll see," the magician replied.

"No, you'll see," she said, waltzing off through the crowd of older women.

I put my hand over Toby's and was about to speak, when the man sitting next to him spun his glass on the bar in a spiral, drawing our attention. "Teenagers," he said. "They never know what's good for them."

I nodded.

"I'm sorry to interrupt," the man continued, "but I was impressed by your show." His voice and his manner were too elegant for Las Vegas, especially the Fremont side of town. He spoke with an accent, savoring each word as it slipped over his tongue. He had a head of sleek sliver hair and an ivory face that looked as if it belonged on top of a Victorian walking stick. "I'd say it's a little bit like Kellar and a lot like Cardini." The man lit a gold-tipped cigarette, and I noticed that his hands looked as if they were covered in melted wax.

"All the good tricks seem to be taken," Toby said.

"Your tricks are better than good." He trapped Toby with his strange hypnotic stare. "But they're not really tricks, are they? My name is Theo van Eyck," the older man said, offering a long gnarled hand. He flipped Toby's hand over and examined his fingers. I realized a glove of burns covered the older man's fingers. Then Theo van Eyck smiled a thin smile that reminded me of Toby's. "Long ago, my hands were very much like yours." He released Toby from his grip. "You see, once I also could do magic." He fell silent, waiting for his words to vanish with his cloud of exhaled smoke.

"What kind of magic?" I asked.

"I'm fairly sure I do not need to explain that to either of you." Theo looked behind him at the women. "Shall we?" he asked, indicating a far corner of the bar.

Theo ordered another small gin. "Do not be alarmed when I tell you that I have been hearing about you for some time."

Toby sipped his drink.

"It isn't often we find another true magician."

"We?" I asked.

"In Amsterdam, where I live, I have gathered a small circle of men who are dedicated to preserving the art of real magic. Men who still wish to push the limits of our craft beyond the second-rate showmanship you see everywhere." Theo glanced over his shoulder. "Especially here." Now he swirled his drink and considered Toby. "You have quite a reputation."

"For what?" Toby asked.

"We have been following your career ever since you left school. Details of your performances in obscure places have made their way back to us. I think that you have been persecuted long enough."

Toby smiled faintly.

"In my day, it was the other way around: I wasn't chased from town to town when people began to suspect the reality behind my tricks. I was in demand." He sipped his drink. "But conjurers have been replaced by tricksters."

"Tricksters," Toby repeated.

"Tricksters and showmen. A trickster certainly wouldn't be able to make a woman disappear for real."

Toby pushed his drink away. Theo wrapped a hand around his wrist. "Magicians often make mistakes. It is not the end of everything."

"It almost was."

"Have you ever wondered how you managed it?"

Toby shook his head. "I was more concerned with finding her."

"Finding her means undoing the trick. Undoing the trick means knowing what went wrong."

"I've given up on that sort of magic."

Theo smiled and shook his head sadly. "We would like you to join us in our circle before the glitz of Vegas obscures the beauty of your tricks."

"I'm happy here."

"Are you? In this theater, hiding your true talents from people who think you have perfected the card trick?"

"It might seem strange, but I like this town. I guess that's what happens after all those third-rate venues. Las Vegas becomes the goal. It's a city of illusion."

Theo shook his head. "It is a city of weak tricks and weaker magicians."

"Vegas," Toby said, "is the perfect place for magic. Where else do people flock in groups to be tricked out of their everyday existence? Look, they know the miniature Eiffel Tower outside the Paris is a poor copy, but they have their pictures taken in front of it all the same."

"Again, you are talking about trickery, not magic."

"Maybe the magic you've seen here isn't up to your standards."

"It isn't even magic." Theo finished his drink.

"But the potential exists. Here everyone wants bigger and

better. I am the one magician who can give it to them. When I get to the big stage, no one will wonder if there is artifice behind my tricks. They will be stunned by spectacle, which is precisely what they want."

"Spectacle? Is that what magic is to you?" A look of displeasure crossed Theo's face.

"Not entirely. Or rather, not personally," Toby replied. "But spectacle is what the audience wants, and spectacle is what sells." He suppressed a smile. "I've booked a casino opening. It's all coming together."

"I have heard," Theo said. "But it will be the same there. Ultimately, your magic will leave you unsatisfied." The elegant magician flexed his fingers. "My talent is drying up. It would be pleasant to have a young magician around. At the very least, we can give you a place to hide from the eyes of your rivals."

"I have Las Vegas. I don't need to hide."

"Once the inexplicable catches up with you, what will you do?"

Toby shrugged. "I'm not counting on that happening."

"I know that you cannot explain to me, or even to yourself, exactly what went wrong that night. How will you explain it to someone else?"

"I hope I won't have to."

"You hope," Theo said, his voice suddenly cold. "A good magician never hopes." He examined the tips of his fingers, as if looking for his fading magic. "It is remarkable how often inferior men get in our way. I have come so far to see you. I wish you would show me more than this small stage show."

"What did you expect to see?" Toby asked.

Theo sighed. "I know what you are capable of."

Toby shook his head.

"I had heard about a magician who could command the sand and manipulate the sky."

Toby bit his lip. "No."

I tried to catch his eye, but Theo had trapped it once more with his swirling stare.

"Really?" he asked in a cool voice.

"Yes," Toby lied.

"A shame. Then perhaps all these rumors aren't true."

Toby drained his glass. "That is the nature of rumors."

Theo ran his fingers along the bar. "In Amsterdam, we have an illusion I imagine would interest you. I am too old to make it work. But you . . . Well, perhaps it would help you discover what went wrong with your assistant."

"It's a little late for that."

Theo smiled. "The beauty of a trick like the Dissolving World is that it is never too late for anything. Toby Warring, you are blinded by the lights of Las Vegas." With some difficultly, he snapped his fingers, summoning a handsomely engraved business card. "For when you change your mind."

We celebrated our one-month anniversary with a candlelight cruise on the *Desert Princess,* a paddlewheel boat that circled Lake Mead. Although the sand no longer suffocated me with loneliness, Toby and I both needed to wash off the desert—even if it meant dining next to tables of tourists. But we soon forgot the family next to us as the boat glided between canyon walls that were spackled with the last light from the sun.

The smell of the lake was refreshing. We slipped out before dessert to walk on the deck and lean over the railing. The magician cupped his hands and released a cascade of sand that spiraled into a helix of colors before it reached the water. I linked my fingers with his, indicating that for the moment his magic was unnecessary. With my eyes closed, I put my head on his shoulder, listening to the soothing rush of the paddlewheel. We worked our way around the deck, pausing to let the spray from the wheel bathe our shoulders and arms. Music picked up belowdeck, followed by the muffled sounds of chairs scraping along the floor as couples stood up to dance.

The sun had disappeared beyond the western canyon edge, leaving the deck in darkness. I looked into the blackening water at the swaying reflection of the boat's lights. The band below had launched into a swing medley. Far in the distance, the hydraulic roar of the Hoover Dam continued. The boat gathered speed. The paddle rotated faster, sending up more spray. The white wall of the dam soon grew invisible as we turned into a small offshoot of the lake. Here the canyon walls drew close, the frantic swing music below echoing madly from one side to the other. Toby had his hands cupped again, collecting water from the accelerated spray of the paddlewheel. I looked into his hands. The droplets of water had become iridescent. As Toby started to bring his palms together, we heard steps on the deck.

"You should have stuck to the small towns, Tobias Warring."

Toby brushed the water from his hands onto his pants.

"No one cared about you there."

"Swenson," Toby said as the other magician appeared from the shadows, his leather coat creaking as he approached.

"And you are still Toby Warring. A magician without a stage. Until recently." He smiled. "I didn't know the Castaway had a theater."

"I would have thought the Castaway was too seedy even for you, Swenson."

"Yes, but not clearly not for you. Although, I'm surprised you even dare perform."

Toby grasped the railing.

"Yes," Swenson continued, "it all comes back to that."

"That is something you can never understand," Toby said. "An accident." His voice was tight.

Swenson looked at me. "I see this one's managed to stick around." He winked. "Not everyone's been so lucky."

"I thought you didn't believe in luck," I said.

Swenson winked again. "I don't." Now he turned to Toby. "You ruined two lives that night. Hers and mine. I couldn't work for months after what you did. All my bookings were canceled."

"That's because I was the main attraction." Toby's words sliced through the dark.

"Times have changed, Toby. I've got my own tour now, and you've barely got the Castaway."

"He's booked the Winter Palace opening," I said.

Swenson looked from me to Toby. "Do you think that's such a good idea?"

"Why not?" Toby asked.

"Your secret isn't going to remain yours for long. People are starting to talk."

"Only because you are gossiping," Toby said.

Swenson smiled. "If you really were a perfect magician, the things you made disappear would stay that way."

Toby clenched his fists. I heard the crackle of glass, and a waterfall of crystal splinters fell from his cuffs.

"Kinda dangerous, don't you think?" Swenson asked me.

The *Desert Princess* moved deeper into the little canyon. The echo of the music and the churning paddlewheel grew louder. Toby turned around. Swenson drew his face close to Toby's. For an instant, the canyon was illuminated by a blue light, and their shadows appeared on its wall.

"An interesting choice, restyling yourself as a ladies' magician. You think that by drawing all these women to you, you can make up for the one you sent away."

Toby's hands were still. "I'm not trying to compensate for anything."

I looked past his shoulder, watching the walls of the canyon widen behind us.

"Good, good," Swenson said, sucking his cheeks with a clicking sound. "It would never work anyway. Neither of us would forgive you." He rubbed his hands together.

"Us?" Toby asked.

"You think when she came back, she'd return to you?" Swenson smiled broadly and nodded. "Yes, yes. When she came back."

The two magicians looked at one another. Toby's eyes narrowed. Footsteps echoed from the other side of the deck. He glanced over Swenson's shoulder as a long, thin shadow stretched toward us from the open door.

Eva was silhouetted in the stairwell. The first things I noticed about her were her perilous heels and her immaculate hairstyle—a crisp bob that framed her jaw.

Toby blinked, then squinted in the dark. He shook his head. "No," he whispered.

"Wouldn't that be simpler?" Swenson muttered.

I tried to catch Toby's eye.

"Why do you look so surprised?" Swenson asked. "Every good magic trick needs a resolution. Even if it's years too late."

"Eva." The name barely escaped Toby's mouth.

Eva looked nothing like a magician's assistant. With her dark suit and red lipstick, she looked as if she belonged at the head of a conference table instead of under stage lights. Her small features were accentuated by dramatic makeup—a streetwalker palette, my mother would have called it, of bright red and smoky black.

Eva said nothing as she came to stand in front of Toby. She cupped the bottom of her hair in one hand, then let go and waited.

"Eva," he repeated.

"Toby Warring," she said in a precise, quiet voice, like that of a long-distance operator. I stepped away.

"I have always wondered . . . ," Toby began.

"What you would say when I turned up." Eva linked her hands together and let them hang below her waist.

"Where you went," Toby said.

"Where you sent me, you mean."

"Yes, where I sent you."

"I have never felt anything like the sensation of plunging into that tank of water. It was as if everything fell away from me. I never hit the bottom. You said I wouldn't."

Toby nodded.

"But you didn't tell me what would happen."

"I didn't know," Toby admitted. "Everything always turned up where I expected it."

"People are not things," Eva said. Her voice was calm. "It was as if I was skydiving. I was spinning and rotating. A hundred black-and-white movies seemed to be rewinding through my head. I felt as if I were in a plummeting airplane." She pulled down the cuffs of her suit jacket. "I arrived on a mesa. Yes, a mesa. So perhaps, Toby, your instinct was right, to look for me here in the desert. But I always wonder why it took you so long to start searching."

"I didn't know how."

Eva shook her head. "If you try to lose someone into thin air, you better learn how to look for her."

"It's not something I'd ever try again," Toby said softly.

"You would have found me on a mesa, the bleakest place I can imagine. I felt suffocated by the absence of people."

"I'm sorry," Toby said.

"How did you do it?"

"An accident," he repeated.

"As if that explains anything." Eva smoothed her immaculate hair. "I was absent for eleven months. It was both an eternity and a millisecond." She wrapped one hand around her forearm. "Sometimes, I wonder if I'm even back. Maybe this is just somewhere else, another place from where we began together. Anyway, Toby, you've moved on," Eva said, turning in my direction.

"Mel, yes." Toby stumbled over my name.

I nodded.

"Don't worry, Toby. I've no illusions. I'm just hoping you play safe from now on." She looked at me with cool eyes. "Especially with her."

"I would never," the magician began.

"You see, I always knew you preferred magic to me." She smiled. "That trick was just more important to you. Imagine, what it takes to make someone disappear for good. It's easier than loving her forever, right?"

"Eva, you make it sound like I did this on purpose."

She shook her head. "No. I'm just saying you didn't understand your own intentions. And if you're not careful, you'll do it again."

"No." Toby's voice was firm. "Never."

"Careful, Toby. Don't get carried away by your tricks."

Toby turned away from Eva and stared at the looming canyon wall. After a moment, he said, "So how did it end? How did you make it back?"

"I'm not sure. Slowly people began to appear. And one day, I felt the same nauseating whirl and the desert where I'd found myself literally came to life. There was wind and tumbleweed. A car drove past. I flagged it down. The driver told me the date. Eleven months had passed. I hadn't even noticed."

Toby shook his head.

"Do you know what the worst part is?" Eva asked. "No one believes me. How could they? I plummeted into a tank in the middle of a magic trick and reappeared in a world created from your loneliness. Toby, you were always a lonely magician. No friends. Nothing but your incomprehensible tricks." Now Eva laughed a laugh that sounded like cascading gravel. "That's why I am so surprised you didn't look for me. I wound up in the perfect place for you and your magic." She blinked again, her smoky lids eclipsing the whites of her small eyes. "That's why I'm so surprised you didn't come."

Toby cleared his throat. "I didn't know how to find you. All I could do was wait."

"For some reason, I don't believe you." She folded her arms across her chest and looked at Swenson.

"I'm getting seasick," he muttered.

"There's more," Eva said. "I still don't know where I am most of the time. I don't trust my surroundings."

"That's your work, Toby," Swenson said. Then he turned to Eva. "You should see him with the ladies following him around the casino. Wonder where they're gonna wind up."

Toby turned to Eva. "You're going, already?"

"I don't stay in one place for very long. That is what has happened to me."

Swenson tapped his ring again. The boat was approaching the dock. He linked his large arm through Eva's and began to lead her belowdeck.

"Careful with your tricks," Eva said, her words light and fading. I watched her walk away, jealous of her carriage and her clothes. Then she and Swenson were gone.

We stayed on the top deck as the other passengers disembarked.

"I'm sorry," he said.

"At least you found something you were looking for."

"No," Toby said, "she found me. It's different."

"Why?"

The magician didn't reply, but kept his eyes on the spot Eva had left.

Six

In the days following our anniversary cruise, Toby clung to me but never mentioned our meeting with Eva. He threw himself into the preparations for the Winter Palace opening, crafting a show he hoped would be unlike anything Las Vegas had seen before.

I never told Toby that when he was busy I often ate my meals at the Red Rock Diner simply to see if Greta was all right. When it was crowded, I tried to avoid her section, choosing to watch her from a distance. Greta made no secret about which customers she preferred, but I could never decipher her preference. I simply felt sorry for the people whose cups came half-empty and whose orders were never quite right. Of course, whenever it fell to her to be my waitress, Greta gave me special treatment—sometimes waiting ten or twenty minutes before taking my order. And yet, on certain occasions when the diner was empty, she would linger, doodling on her pad as I considered the menu. I knew she wanted to ask me about Toby.

In recent weeks, she had begun to scrub off her goth façade. First the chipped nail polish went, replaced by a well-maintained beige. Then she'd trimmed her hair and recolored it an unremarkable shade of honey brown. Her lipstick went from dark purple to red, then to pink, and finally to a coral gloss that would have pleased Sandra. Greta swept neutral eye shadow over her lids and coated her lashes with brown mascara. Between shifts, she had made time for sunbathing, darkening her already coppery complexion. She might have passed now for a run-of-the-mill teen working at a diner to save for her prom dress.

I was not particularly hungry when I opened the door to the Red Rock. The grease and steam from the industrial dishwasher hit me full on. I saw Greta at the far end of the counter near the kitchen, examining her freshly painted nails as she flirted with one of the cooks. The diner was nearly empty, so I sat at the counter. I didn't bother to signal to Greta. She'd come or she wouldn't.

As I waited, I pulled out a textiles catalog and began to note bulk prices for some replacement fabrics I thought the Winter Palace should keep in stock. Without warning, a cup of hot tea slid down the counter, landing in front of me and splashing onto the open page.

"Greta, thanks," I said. I didn't bother looking up. I figured that by the time I did, she'd be gone. But as I lifted my cup, she was there.

"So. How's it going?"

I looked up. "I'm fine."

"I'm not asking about you."

I sipped my tea.

"How's the show coming? Toby's show."

"I'm sure that's fine, too."

"So, he keeps secrets from you, too."

"He's a magician. That's his business."

Greta patted the top of her neatly combed hair. "Must bother you."

"It doesn't."

She considered her nails once more. "But when he gets an assistant, he'll share everything with her. It'll bother you then."

"I keep telling you that Toby doesn't work with an assistant."

"He will."

"Greta, it's getting old."

She waited a moment before giving me her mocking smile. "Who are you to talk about what's getting old?"

I opened the menu and pretended to be interested in it. Greta reached over and drummed her nails on the lacquered page.

"What do you think of the color?"

"Your nails?"

She nodded.

"Pretty basic."

"So you think I should go longer. Brighter, maybe? You think hot pink would be more suitable?"

"For what?" I asked.

"For the stage."

"And what stage might that be?"

Greta removed her hand and took away my menu. "You know."

I shook my head. "Give it a rest."

"Even Jim Swenson said Toby's going to use an assistant eventually."

"Please stay away from Jim Swenson."

"Whatever," Greta said, walking away without letting me order. In a moment, she was back with a new cup of tea. "I'm just saying, two people ordering hot tea on a hot day is kind of weird."

"I didn't order," I reminded her.

"Well, you know."

I hadn't wanted either cup of tea. I'm a coffee drinker. But since our first encounter in the Red Rock, tea was all Greta ever served me.

"I don't know what's up with people like you."

"People like who?" I asked.

"You and that other lady. The one with the tea. Sitting in that booth." Greta rolled her eyes across the diner. "The one in black. Don't know how you can walk in shoes like that." She tapped her nails. "Well, unless you work the Strip."

I tried not to laugh.

"Hey, ma'am," Greta called, inching down the counter. "More tea?" It was a condemnation, not a question.

The woman turned. Her coiffed hair was unmistakable. In an instant, Eva was on her feet, heading toward the kitchen.

"Greta," I called.

"Paula," she reminded me, flicking her name tag.

"Is that an exit?" I pointed in the direction of the kitchen's swinging door.

"Not really," she replied.

I stood up to follow Eva.

"I mean, not for you," Greta said.

But I had already pushed through the swinging door and was standing in the steamy kitchen. Eva wasn't there. At the far end, near a walk-in refrigerator, was another door, which probably led outside. The teenaged cook tried to stop me as I passed him.

After the steam of the Red Rock's kitchen, the Vegas heat was strangely refreshing. The grimy parking lot was littered with Dumpsters for various businesses. At the far end, I saw Eva, her slim black figure opening the door of a car.

"Eva," I called. "Wait."

To my surprise, she stopped.

I hurried toward her. "Please," I said.

"I'm waiting."

For a moment, we looked at each other.

"You're expecting the circus girl Toby probably described?"

I shrugged.

"People change. Can you tell me what you want?"

I was staring at the fleur-de-lis motif on her stockings and shoes. "Not really. I thought you were leaving Las Vegas."

"So did I." Eva laughed. "But it's difficult for me to go when and where I please." She looked at me, searching for some sign of comprehension.

"I'm sorry, I don't know why I came out here." I looked back at the door of the Red Rock.

"Not jealousy, I hope."

"No," I replied, "not at all." I ran my fingers through my hair, which next to Eva's seemed brittle and unkempt. "I guess I thought talking to you might help me understand Toby a little better."

"You've married someone you don't understand?"

"Maybe."

Eva smiled, and suddenly I got a glimpse of the person who got lost inside one of Toby's tricks—a captivating woman who commanded the audience's attention while the magician put the finishing touch on his latest illusion. She walked around to the driver's side of her car, opened the door, and got behind the wheel. The window on the passenger's side rolled down. "Get in."

Eva drove fast, zigzagging through the traffic on the Strip. We shot out of Vegas in the direction of California. Using the rearview mirror, she applied her murky red lipstick. Then she lit a cigarette. "You haven't known him long, then," Eva said.

I shook my head. "A couple of months. We met in a small town a few hours from here."

"I don't think I ever really knew Toby at all. I was a different girl back then. I wanted a boyfriend. That's what you want when you're young, isn't it?"

"I guess," I said. I fiddled with the clasp on my seat belt. "Where are we going?" I asked.

"Somewhere important." She tossed her cigarette out the window and exhaled a last burst of smoke. "Maybe you and Toby will have a life—" She paused. "—a normal life. I don't know. But he told me when we first got together that love and magic don't mix. After a few months, we both forgot about this. When it was too late, I realized that the kind of magic Toby aspires to leaves no room for others." She looked at my wedding ring. "But he hasn't quite figured that out yet."

"You're wrong."

Eva shook her head. "How can you be sure? You didn't know him before."

"I know him now."

"It won't last."

"How do you know?"

The car sped along a two-lane highway.

"Toby has the ability to pull the perfect person to his side at the perfect time."

"I don't see it that way."

"So you think it's a coincidence that you two met in some middle of nowhere?"

"Yes, I do."

"I wouldn't be so sure." Eva's words were bitter. "Keep in mind, if he is able to pull you to his side, he can send you away again."

I decided not to respond.

"He might not mean to. In fact, he absolutely wouldn't mean to. But he will."

I glanced at the speedometer and wished Eva would slow down. Or stop. "You sound jealous," I said. I unrolled my window to breathe the air outside. "In fact, maybe you are. I'm having no trouble staying at Toby's side."

Eva put her foot on the brake. The car fishtailed to a stop in the middle of the highway. "Mel," she began. I was surprised that she remembered my name. "I live inside a magic trick. I have no jealousy." Eva stared at me. "I'm not trying to frighten you." Then she pressed on the gas. "I'm just trying to help you. When Toby sent me into that trick, he destroyed a part of my will. I don't want that to happen to you." She glanced in the rearview mirror. "Or to anyone else." Eva lit a new cigarette.

"Why would that happen?"

She exhaled. "Toby doesn't understand the sacrifices he is willing to make for his craft."

I looked out the window and wondered about the truth of this.

The sunset began to spread at the far edge of the desert, sending long shadows across the sand. If I squinted, the land looked tiger-striped.

"I was a city girl," Eva said. "I never thought I'd spend so much time out here." She laughed. "I was popular, too. Now it's simpler to know no one."

"Me, too," I replied.

"You, too, which?"

"The part about the desert." The other part was true as well, but I didn't want to admit it. Eva looked at me out of the corner of her eye. Her glance told me she knew better.

I wanted to ask how much farther we were going, but I knew she wouldn't answer. What I asked instead was, "What was he like?"

"You assume that the magician is different now."

"I think Toby was probably always a little different."

Eva looked at me again with her cool gaze. And for a moment, I wondered if there was a possibility that we could be friends.

"Toby is indifferent. He never understood what effect his magic might have on other people."

"That's why he no longer does magic involving people," I said. My defense of Toby sounded tired, even to me.

"Toby's ambition is to be the greatest magician who ever lived. And he could be. But at some point, his audience will insist on tricks using people."

I shook my head. "He's resisted before."

"It's easy to resist in a forgettable desert town."

Before I could reply, she pulled off the highway and onto a dusty service road. We passed rotting fences that enclosed vast patches of dust and sand. When I looked over my shoulder, the lights of the highway had vanished.

"Mel," Eva said. My name dropped from her mouth like a pebble into a lake. "What is the loneliest you've ever been?"

I knew. The nearly deserted motel where I'd spent my first night in Nevada. Being lost in a cornfield when I was a kid. Listening to the empty echo of the house after my brother left. Staring at my half-eaten dinner in a restaurant full of happy couples. "Watching my brother slip away downstream," I said.

"But you weren't alone," Eva replied.

I hadn't mentioned my mother. "It felt like it."

"You had the river for company. Even a little sound can be comforting."

Eva finally stopped the car. Leaving the headlights on, she opened her door. I followed. The light illuminated a small mesa. Eva walked around the side of it, until the car was out of view. Then she began to climb.

Despite the dark and her high heels, she walked confidently, but my shoes tangled in the bristly grass, and I often had to grab the brambles for support. It took us almost half an hour to reach the top. When we reached the plateau, I was out of breath, but Eva was as cool as ever.

Neither Las Vegas nor the highway nor anything else was

visible. No lights danced in the sand. No sound rose from the desert. I bent over, trying to recover from the climb. Before I could right myself, Eva disappeared around a jutting rock that divided the plateau. I found her standing at the base of an old radio tower that stretched fifty feet into the air. At the top of the tower, a red light was flashing, soundlessly interrupting the solid night.

I wanted to say that I hadn't noticed the tower as we'd climbed the mesa, but Eva spoke first.

"This is it."

I placed a hand on the iron base of the tower and felt the rust flake off.

"This is where I wound up."

I looked over the mesa and across the desert. The silence and the dark were overwhelming.

"Of course, it's not exactly the same," Eva continued. "When I arrived, this mesa was a figment of one of Toby's tricks. I imagine it's a place he'd noticed once on his way to school in California. I bet he never really thought about it. It just stuck in a corner of his mind. Then he sent me here."

"The signal, what is it?" I asked.

Eva shook her head. "At first I thought it was a dream, that I had been knocked unconscious at the bottom of the tank. But you can't bang your head against a dream, and if you scream in a dream, you wake up." She took a breath. "I was awake. I was underneath the signal tower. I sat there for so long that my pulse fell into sync with the flashing light. The night stretched on forever. Literally. The sun didn't rise. There was no wind, not even any sound from the desert below."

"And you didn't go down?"

"In the dark?" Eva laughed. "I had just been in front of a large audience. I had just felt my boyfriend's hand on my back, urging me into a tank where lily pads were supposed to bloom. And now . . ." She stretched out her arms. "As I told you on the boat, over time, the mesa started to change. It was as if it were waking up, leaving Toby's imagination and rejoining the world. One day, I noticed a car in the distance. Even though the trick—whatever it was—was dissolving, there was one thing I already knew." Eva paused and looked at the beacon. It flashed three times before she continued. "I could never really go back." She dragged her foot across the dusty plateau. "It was his doing."

"But an accident."

"An accident is still somebody's fault."

I started to back away from the radio tower, ready to leave the mesa.

"Toby didn't think. And he still hasn't learned that his magic is harmful. It's painful, and he will hurt someone. You need to convince him. He will listen to you."

"Convince him of what?"

"That his magic is dangerous."

I opened my mouth.

"Not always, but sometimes. And that is enough. It is the dangerous tricks that will appeal to him the most. Keep him away from these."

"Even if that were true, I'm not sure I could."

"But you will try."

"I've never seen Toby try anything dangerous." I headed for the large stone that divided the plateau.

"That is because you didn't know what to look for. The very fact that he doesn't understand how his magic works is danger-ous enough. You could at least tell him that."

"He's heard." I took a few steps before I realized that Eva was no longer following. I whirled around. "Eva."

No answer.

"Eva," I called again. But my voice was swept away. "Eva," I cried, stretching my voice as far as I could. No sound came back to me. There was only the persistent heartbeat of the radio signal above my head.

I sank to the ground beneath the tower. I felt as if the whole desert—the whole world, in fact—were being pulled toward this signal and then transformed into nothing but a repeating red blip. I struggled to control my breath. Surely, Eva would return. If she didn't, would Toby come? Would he think to look for me in the desert?

Eva had asked me a question about loneliness. It prompted another. What is the darkest place I'd ever been? Until then I'd thought it was the river that had taken my brother during a storm. I'd been wrong. Now I knew: the top of that mesa.

Oddly, I was relieved that Eva had gone. The Toby she knew and the one I married were different men, different magicians. I felt the night draw closer, enveloping me in Toby's lonely magic. But unlike Eva, I wasn't its captive. I stood up and started to walk. I felt my way down the mesa. My shoes filled with pebbles and dust as I walked along the dirt road back toward the small highway to hitch a ride back to Vegas. I could not tell Toby where I'd been.

Seven

Sandra was getting under my skin during the days leading up to the Winter Palace's grand opening. I had agreed to help her find the right dress for the VIP party. She dragged me through the malls at Caesars Palace, the Venetian, and the Aladdin until we found something suitably unsuitable. When she was not pinching me and pulling me from one boutique to another, she was back at the Winter Palace, hovering around my magician as he paced the main floor of the casino. She and her coworkers tittered, whispered in Toby's ear, and bought him drinks, but Toby said nothing about his plans.

I knew that Toby's silence concealed excitement. We sat up late, working on his show. While I sewed his costume—an elegant black suit lined with silk that captured the colors of the setting sun, he dreamed up illusions, made lists of materials, and considered how much of his remarkable skill he could display to the patrons of the Winter Palace and how he would trick them into believing that what they were seeing was not real.

Three hours before show time, the Winter Palace was crowded with middle-aged women who twirled their VIP passes, snatched blintzes and caviar canapés from passing trays, and flirted with the bartenders. Their heels were already doing a number on the red carpet. The explosion of fireworks from the Winter Palace's minarets echoed through the building. A traveling branch of the St. Petersburg Orchestra was tuning up in the theater while the Flying Karamazov Brothers tested their juggling equipment in the wings. Cocktail waitresses in skimpy peasant outfits circulated with trays of champagne and White Russians. Sandra was tipsy. She was wearing heels that she described as "absolutely Ivana Trump," and she looked, as she had wished, like something out of the pages of Russian *Vogue* circa 1985.

"Fantastic!" she trilled, popping a hand-cut potato chip loaded with caviar into her mouth. "Mel!" she yelled in my direction. "Mel! The curtains, fantastic. Everyone, just look at those curtains. Look how rich. You just want to roll around naked in all those folds. It's too bad we can't keep Mel around forever. Genius. She's a genius."

We were standing near an ice sculpture that Sandra had commissioned. It showed a family of caribou frolicking alongside an ornate sled filled with Russian royalty. The attention to detail was impressive, from the animals' chin hairs to the patterns on the rugs warming the passengers. "You like?" Sandra said, accidentally showering one of the caribou with champagne. "I knew you'd like it. All that snow and ice."

I thought how nice it would be to cool my cheek against the flank of a caribou. "It's fantastic," I replied.

"We're keeping the sculptor on the premises for the first month, in case we have a meltdown. After that, we'll call him in every other month or so for a touch-up." Sandra paused and adjusted the neckline of her dress. "You know, I must have taken twenty calls in the last two days about this show. All of my girlfriends were dying to be in it."

"I can imagine."

"But I made the best choice." Sandra swilled her champagne.

"Choice?"

"I wanted only the finest showgirl."

"For what?"

"For Toby's assistant." Sandra gave me one of her conde-scending looks.

"Assistant?" I asked.

"Your husband is sex on legs, but you've got to appeal to the men, honey. They're the big spenders."

"What assistant?" My mind was racing back to Eva and the mesa—to the warning I thought Toby didn't need to hear.

"Every good show needs a showgirl. And I got him the best. She's the lead dancer at the Rio. Guys come, literally, from every-where to watch her shake it."

"But Toby doesn't use an assistant."

"Yeah, yeah, yeah," Sandra said, polishing off her drink. "But we told him—no assistant, no show. And he's pretty excited, let me tell you. She's a real showstopper."

I grabbed a drink from a passing tray and took a generous sip. "Sandra, this is a bad idea."

"It's not like he's going to cut her in half or anything."

I clutched her wrist. "He's not supposed to use an assistant."

"Is this jealously talking?" She tried to pull out of my grasp.

"You don't understand—he *can't*."

"Honey," Sandra began in her mock whisper, "there is no *can't*.

It's already done." She stepped away from me. "You're never going to make it in this town if you're afraid of a showgirl."

"Sandra—"

"Done," she called over her shoulder.

My heart pounded as I watched Sandra slip into her crowd of girlfriends and vanish in a swarm of high hair and sequins. I edged over to the gambling pits and set my drink on one of the craps tables, wishing I could find the magician and ask him why he hadn't told me about the new addition to his show. I scanned the crowd for his familiar crown of shaggy black hair, but I knew that Toby was hiding. I exhaled, trying to expel the panic and numb my ears to Eva's warning.

"Not on the felt, please," a voice barked, making me jump. Even though my glass hadn't been on the felt, it was returned to my hand. "Can't put anything on the tables. Against the rules."

I looked around and saw Greta in one of the cocktail costumes. The bodice drooped. She'd frosted her hair and pulled it back in a tight bun. Her nails were long and bright pink. If it weren't for her voice, I might have mistaken her for one of the Winter Palace's trainees I'd used as a model for the outfit she was wearing. "I didn't put my drink on the felt," I replied. "And can you bring me another?"

"Close enough," Greta replied, ruffling the skirt for my benefit. "The edge is close to the felt. And on the felt is against the rules."

"I know," I said. "I make the rules."

"Then you should know how to follow them. I'm circulating over there next," she said, gesturing toward the ice sculpture. "So I wouldn't wait around for that drink."

"How did you get a job here?" I asked.

"You think I'm gonna work in that dumpy diner my whole life?"

"I don't know."

Greta took a step back and reconsidered me from top to toe. "You said you work here?"

"Yes."

She lowered her voice. "I'm only hired for the night. If I do good, I get to stay on. Not that I'm gonna be a waitress forever."

"I'm sure," I said, trying to get away.

"It's a shame that magician didn't give me a chance."

"It's too late. He found his own assistant," I muttered, finishing my drink.

"Who?" Greta's voice rose above the polite cocktail party murmur.

"The Winter Palace found her for him," I said quietly.

"So, he does keep secrets from you."

"I guess so."

"Should have been me."

"Shh," I said, lowering my voice and hoping that Greta would do the same. "It wasn't supposed to be anyone. Toby is not supposed to use people in his tricks."

"You keep telling yourself that. But it looks like you're wrong."

"It must be a mistake," I repeated, talking more to myself than to Greta.

"The only mistake your magician made is not choosing me." Greta's voice carried over the crowd.

Several partygoers looked our way. One of the floor managers started to head in our direction.

"He's made a mistake," Greta repeated. She was nearly yelling now. "Your magician has made a real mistake. I was meant to be in that show."

The manager approached our table.

Greta turned and faced her. "I was just telling this lady to keep her drink off the felt," she said, gracing me with her mocking smile.

"But I guess she didn't listen." Then she raised her tray to shoulder height and left.

I was about to follow her when the ladies' magician entered from the Empress Buffet. He walked swiftly, so that his jacket blew open, showing its multicolored lining.

The women pushed forward. They ran their hands along Toby's sleeves, slipped money into his pockets, and tried to whisper in his ear.

The husbands bowed their heads and muttered. "Don't much like magic myself," a man standing next to me said. "In fact, I used to think that it was a dangerous waste of time. But this guy's done wonders for my wife. Turned her back into the little dynamo I married fifteen years back."

I looked at the impromptu stage of backgammon tables. The question of whether the felt would survive the magic was eclipsed by my fear for the assistant Toby had invited onto his stage.

When Toby's assistant appeared, the crowd of women dispersed. As Sandra promised, she was captivating. She wore a black velvet burlesque costume with red satin ribbons that trailed behind her as she walked. Her black hair was sculpted into an impossibly high tower on the top of her head. Her lips sparkled with vibrant, iridescent red gloss. Her heels looked poised to kill. She towered over the magician, and it seemed to me that she could certainly do him more harm than the other way around.

Toby walked to the gambling floor and hopped onto one of the tables. His assistant stood below him. Standing on the tabletop, he produced a bottle in each hand and began to fill the glasses she held. He poured pink champagne, regular champagne, and even a sparkling Italian red. The assistant passed the drinks while Toby made the table's chips rise from the felt into his hands.

Toby had refined his Castaway routine. No more wicked

winks and naughty smiles—he was all turn-of-the-century elegance. He did not speak, and his silence doubled the distance
between him and his assistant. Once the drinks were distributed, the assistant held up a cue card that read MANUAL MAGIC:
THE DEXTEROUS DANCE.

Toby shook his cuffs to show that there was nothing concealed
in his shirt. Then he fanned his fingers and shot a stream of small
sparks from his right thumb. When he touched his right thumb to
his index finger, that, too, lit up with a stream of sparklers. He continued using his thumb to ignite one finger after another until the
tip of each finger was alight with a small fountain of fireworks.
Then, starting with his right thumb again, he touched his index finger and extinguished the sparks until all the fires died down. Fanning his fingers one more time, he shot a single, strong stream of
sparks from his index finger, held it aloft, and traced it through the
air, describing the word WELCOME.

The audience applauded politely, shifted their weight from one
foot to another, and sipped their drinks. The assistant held up a
card that read FROZEN FOUNTAIN, then handed Toby a red-and-
gold brocade cloth that I had selected. He displayed both sides of
the cloth. Waving it with the challenging grace of a bullfighter, he
lowered the fabric until the bottom edge touched the blackjack
table. He whisked it away, revealing a porcelain fountain filled
with porcelain lily pads and birds. Toby lowered the cloth over the
fountain. The gold fabric seemed to bulge. He withdrew it, and
water poured over the fountain's sides. With one more whisk of
the cloth, the lily pads began to bob and the birds came to life and
flew into the casino. Toby lowered the cloth once more, restored
the fountain to its original state. Then the showgirl wheeled it
away. He took a bow.

After these two tricks, I relaxed. It was clear to me that the
magician was going out of his way to avoid contact with his as-

sistant. His fingers never grazed hers as she passed him things. She was decoration.

In a number called ADRIFT, Toby updated a classic illusion by levitating two statues of Catherine the Great and sending them over the crowd and into the far reaches of the gambling floor. In MIND YOUR VALUABLES, he produced dozens of items, which he had lifted from the audience, dropped them into a giant glass vase, filled it with water from the palm of his hands, covered the vase with a black drape, took a hammer and smashed the vase to bits, and then lit the drape on fire. After the drape disintegrated into ash, he directed the audience to look at another table, where they saw a gold box filled with their possessions. Toby hopped off the table and, without asking anyone to come forward, handed each item back to its owner.

Now the assistant held up a cue card for Toby's final illusion. It read CATCH ME IF I FALL. Like any good magician, Toby knew he had to include one dangerous element. Although he had been fairly secretive about his preparations, he had assured me that he would make himself the subject of any dangerous trick he did. He did not mention that he was considering the BULLET CATCH.

Toby took his mark on one of the blackjack tables while the showgirl held a gun up to the audience. She distributed bullets to people, asking them to mark the shells. She then loaded the gun and tested it, firing at one of the statues of Catherine the Great and shattering the tsarina's left shoulder.

Coyly, the assistant asked for a hand climbing up to a table facing Toby's. Several men jumped forward to assist her. She posed for the crowd, then pointed the gun at the magician. My heart rose. Toby held up a finger. The assistant smiled. She put the gun down and held up a new cue card: VOLUNTEER PLEASE — CATCH HIM IF HE FALLS. The ladies of the Winter Palace moved forward, hands waving. I saw Sandra's pastel nails fluttering furiously. And from the corner of my eye, I saw a pale figure in a neat, black sheath dress. Eva's red lips were pressed together as she stared at the magician. He looked away, searching the audience for someone else to stand behind him and catch him if the bullets struck.

Hands waved and heads turned, searching for the person Toby would choose. Then I caught sight of one supplicant. She might have been any cocktail waitress. But I knew she wasn't. Her pink nails caught the light.

"Me," she cried.

I felt Eva's cool glance on my back. I wanted to stop the magician. I raised my hand. "Me!"

The magician paused and glanced my way with a questioning look. "Me," I demanded. Toby gave me a nearly imperceptible shake of his head. I tried to insist, but he turned away.

"No." The teenager's voice was cool and confident. "Me."

Maybe Toby couldn't see past the shredded peasant costume. Maybe he was eager to finish the trick and escape Eva's gaze. He nodded in the direction of the voice.

That settled it. Greta approached the stage.

Toby did not seem to recognize her. Keeping his distance, he allowed the assistant to show Greta where to stand and how to spread her arms. Toby took his place several paces in front of her. He pulled a blindfold from his pocket and tied it over his eyes. Greta looked the audience over, a superior smile on her lips. The assistant climbed onto the facing table. The audience took a collective step back as she raised the gun and pointed it at the magician.

The sound in the pits wound down, and Toby's updated vaudeville music seemed to be squeezed out of the speakers one note at a time. The assistant cocked the gun. The click echoed through the room. The moment before she fired, I heard the sound of crunching ice and turned to see Swenson behind me, draining his drink. Eva was next to him. With his mouth full of ice, Swenson smiled, showing me his nicotine-stained teeth. He raised his eyebrows and nodded toward Toby. Eva didn't take her eyes off the stage.

I wanted to cry out. The showgirl pulled the trigger. Everyone leaned back as the bullet cut through the air. Toby stood still, his feet firmly planted on the table, his arms clasped behind his back, his mouth slightly open. Suddenly, a cascade of gold coins burst from the bullet's wake and fell to the table. As the coins appeared, Toby lurched back slightly, then recovered himself. Greta rolled her eyes, but remained where she was. Toby removed the bullet from between his teeth. He tossed it to the audience so they could check for the mark.

When the coins had settled onto the table, Toby nodded to the assistant, and she raised the gun again. Swenson muttered something. Eva closed her eyes. "You should have said something," she whispered. Before the assistant fired, Greta looked out over the audience, searching for someone who might take notice. All eyes were on the magician and his assistant.

Another explosion ripped through the blackjack tables as the showgirl fired for the second time. The audience recoiled again. Now a waterfall of petals emerged in the bullet's wake, spinning lazily toward the table. Again, Toby staggered backwards before righting himself. Again Greta rolled her eyes. The audience exhaled. Swenson crunched another ice cube.

The assistant took aim again. The audience was barely ready. "I don't know if I can take this," one well-coiffed woman squealed. "I don't know how he does it."

Toby adjusted his feet on the table and clasped his hands.

Greta stole another glance at the audience.

"Daring," the well-coiffed woman's companion replied.

Greta was glaring at them. Then she caught my eye. She shook her head, summoning a composure I'd never seen before. She gave me her mocking smile before returning her attention to the trick.

The assistant cocked the gun. Greta held her head up high, her arms out. The assistant extended her arm. Toby steadied himself. And Greta, with quickness I'd never have expected, leapt in front of the magician.

This time, there was no transformation of lead to rain or snow or gambling chips. There was no miraculous waterfall of conjured objects to mask what was happening on the table. Greta extended her arms, as if reaching for the bullet, hoping to catch it like a football. It sailed into the space between her open arms, tearing through her dress and cracking her breastbone. An explosion of blood, the shape of a narcissus blossom, shot from her chest.

Toby whipped off his blindfold in time to see Greta tumble at his feet. As she fell, she turned in my direction. Smoke and the acrid stench of singed polyester filled the air. My scream kept rising from my throat as I watched the teenager's blood pool around Toby's shoes. The assistant dropped the gun. Someone stepped forward to catch her, trampling her fallen headdress as he approached.

I remained still while the audience rushed by. A few people tried to help the girl on the table while others slipped to the sidelines to watch the spectacle unfold.

My mouth was still open when Eva appeared in front of me.

"You didn't try to stop him?" she asked.

I shook my head. "I didn't know."

"You did. You just didn't believe me."

And suddenly, I had the answer to Eva's question about my loneliest moment. It was here, in this chaotic gambling pit, surrounded by hundreds of guests in cocktail clothes. I saw a string of dingy motel rooms, leading me back across the country. I saw myself at the counter of nondescript diners. The faces of the stampeding audience were cold. Then I felt Toby's eyes.

He reached down to Greta. Blood covered the front of his suit. A small fire seemed to be burning in his pale cheeks. His jaw was trembling. Our eyes didn't leave one another until he turned away and gathered Greta in his arms. Pressing her limp body into his, he stepped off the table and carried her out of the casino. No one followed him.

I don't know how far Toby went before he was intercepted by the police. At some point, I remember Sandra tapping me on the arm, telling me that he'd been taken to a precinct near Fremont. Somehow, she had managed to steer the remaining guests into the Hermitage Salon.

I spent the night on a bench outside the Las Vegas Police Department. I had my sewing basket and my quilt. As I watched the parade of witnesses—the showgirl assistant, the casino doctor, and Greta's mother, who had been summoned from Intersection—I attached a scrap from the cocktail waitress outfit to the edge of my quilt. In the sharp, fluorescent glow from the police station, my quilt looked lifeless.

Folding it, I left the bench and crossed the dusty road to a phone booth. The dial tone surprised me as it cut through the Nevada night. I punched in my parents' number, wanting to hear that I wasn't alone. I imagined the phone ringing in their dark house, shaking them from their sleep. But no one picked up. Soon the answering machine clicked on. I opened my mouth, but my words dissolved in tears.

At 7 A.M. Toby emerged. "Death by misadventure," was all he said as I took his hot, dry hand and wove my small fingers inside his. Greta's mother confirmed Toby's innocence when she explained that she had been expecting something like this ever since her daughter had run away. When she emerged from the station, she had Greta's ball-chain necklaces twisted in her fingers like a rosary.

Toby and I sat in the minivan in front of the blue ranch house. It was two days after his accident, two days of ballistics tests and investigations into the legality of the bullet-catching illusion. I wanted to see the house and brush my fingers over a future that was slipping from reach. Toby waited in the car while I slipped inside the house and took a green-and-yellow-flowered dish towel for my quilt.

Back in the car, I turned on the ignition. A mile from the airport, I asked Toby, "Why didn't you pick me?"

It was a moment before he replied. "There's a place for you in my magic. But it's not onstage."

I unrolled the window. "You thought something might go wrong."

"No." Toby looked away from me, out the window. "The moment I met you, things fell into place. I'd been wandering in circles, one small town to the next, one uninterested audience after another. Not to mention the hours alone. And then, there you were in the Old Stand Saloon. I can't tell you how many times I'd been in there." He fiddled with the door locks, making them dance up and down. "Never saw a friendly face. I was almost ready to head home, or try out my luck in sideshows in Mexico. And then . . ." His voice trailed off. "And now—"

"And now, I can't help."

"When I was a teenager, I always got teased for being a magician. You can imagine I wasn't the coolest kid in school. But no matter how bad it got, magic always made things better. Nothing seemed out of reach, and I could shape my world to suit myself. Who cared what anyone said?" Toby clenched his hands into fists. "There've been a few ups and downs in my career. But magic got me through. This is beyond my powers to fix. And it wasn't even my fault. I will never be a Las Vegas magician." He shook his head as his eyes ran over the desert. "I wonder if I'll ever be a magician at all."

I placed my hand on his leg. "I could have prevented this," I said.

Toby turned from the window.

"Eva told me something would go wrong. She said you'd be tempted to use an assistant. I didn't know how soon it would happen."

"It wasn't the decision to use an assistant or a volunteer that was the problem. It was Greta."

I looked out the window, wondering if Toby wasn't really at fault.

We sat in silence for a moment.

"What should we do with the car?" I asked.

Toby didn't reply.

"Your van?"

He shrugged.

"Toby."

"Leave it," he muttered.

"We can't do that."

"It's just a car."

"It's more than that."

I let the car idle. The engine rattled. The magician said nothing. He simply crossed his arms over his chest.

"All right," I said. "Let's go." I took the keys out of the ignition.

Then I put them back. "I hope someone comes along and enjoys it," I said.

"What?" Toby asked.

"All I'm saying is I hope it makes someone else happy."

Toby didn't reply. He just shouldered his bag and walked toward the airport.

Eight

Amsterdam seemed to me to be tinted with the last paint coaxed from the corners of a once-vivid watercolor palette. The sky that peeked between the gabled buildings was not the blue promised by the famous Delft tiles, but a blue that had been stretched thin, made gray with too much water. With its muted colors— always more gray than blue and rust than red—reflected in the placid canals, the city had an illusory quality. Its narrowness, the hair's-breadth houses and one-way streets, was exaggerated, thrown back by the dark canal water. The reflected city appeared as deep in its own canals as it was narrow on land.

Amsterdam was the perfect place for illusion. The long and interwoven streets, Palmgracht, Palmkade, Palmstraat, Palmd-waarstraat, beguiled with their similarity. And the shop, the restaurant, the small café where you wasted the afternoon, disap-peared with a turn of the calendar page. Over time, I learned that Amsterdam was capable of this sort of trickery—the place that took you a half hour to find often turned out to have been only a few blocks from where you started.

For me, the city was an unlikely choice—a head-on collision with my water demon. But Amsterdam was a city that promised to shake off the desert, and just maybe, its canals would give me a glimpse of my brother's watery shadow.

The train from the airport rattled into Amsterdam Central Station. The commuting crowds cleared to reveal a withered man in a heavy wool overcoat waiting for us near the first car. With light but slow steps, he approached.

"Piet Boerman," he said, offering a dry hand, which Toby shook reluctantly. "Theo told you that I'd be waiting." Piet blinked his watery blue eyes, then smiled so half moons rippled on his cheeks.

"Thank you," I replied.

In those last days in Las Vegas, I had retrieved Theo van Eyck's business card from Toby's wallet and phoned the old magician. And although he'd sounded surprised, something told me that Theo had been expecting my call.

"I don't live very far away," Piet said as we headed away from the platform. "If you don't mind, we can walk."

Toby nodded and synchronized his long strides with Piet's stiff gait.

Piet turned to me as we crossed the canal closest to the station. "Like Theo, I, too, was a magician of sorts." Then he looked at Toby. "Tomorrow after you've rested, we will see Theo, a far more impressive magician than I. More impressive than nearly anyone, except you, I've heard." Piet smiled, but Toby managed only a small nod.

Piet Boerman lived in a canal house that had been in his family for generations. Over the years, it had been turned into a museum of magic—smaller illusions stored on the top floors, and the devices for large-scale conjuring below. Now in his mid-eighties, he could no longer mount the steep stairs to the upper two floors. So he offered us the studio in his attic. Its only window looked out on the mismatched gables of the houses across the canal. Our room was too high up to see the street or the canal, so our view reduced Amsterdam to a uneven row of house tops, a disarray of step gables, bell gables, neck gables, and spout gables that looked like the peaks of Victorian circus tents. From our window, the city was cut off from its streets, canals, and human traffic. Our view showed everything and nothing—the endless run of amputated rooftops and the open sky with its magic lantern of weather.

In this attic, with its delightful combination of crisp air, rough sheets, and homespun blankets, I fell into a deep sleep, finally forgetting the face of the teenager who had sent us across the ocean. Soon, from somewhere inside my dreams, I heard Toby's voice calling to me. I tossed and turned, trying to locate the magician. Then I woke. He was sleeping soundly next to me, his hands balled into fists and tucked under his pillow. His lips were pressed together. But I could still hear his voice whispering indistinctly in the cold air.

"Toby?"

The magician didn't move.

"Toby?" I looked around the attic. The house creaked and re-settled. I shook my head, trying to dislodge the magician's voice. I plugged my ears. "Toby, stop."

"What?" the magician muttered, and rolled over.

I got up, pulled on a sweater, and tiptoed to the landing. The hallway of the floor beneath the attic was strewn with boxes bursting with playbills and leaflets. Out of the shadows, I could just make out the face of a Chinese conjurer printed on a cracked poster. I felt his eyes on me as I continued down the stairs. Now my magician's voice was joined by dozens of other whispers calling to me from the boxes and muttering from the posters and play-bills.

I began to hurry, taking the steep steps two at a time. The canal house shrank around me. Big devices with blades and saw teeth waited behind half-open doors. A gust of wind blew into the stair-way. A handbill with the image of a magician dressed as a swami fluttered down from the floor above. He wore the same expression of dangerous superiority as the Chinese conjurer in the upstairs hallway. As I let the paper fall from my hand, the swami winked.

On the second-floor landing, a dark hallway stretched in front of me. The house heaved and breathed. At the end of the hall, a door blew open. The magicians' whispers stopped. I squinted at the column of light that leaked into the hall, and saw a bit of fab-ric fluttering through the open door. As it rose and fell, Asian mu-sic filled my ears.

Even in the low light, I knew how this silk would feel as it slipped across my skin—like cold-melt mercury. I pulled the door open and, with a creak of hinges and floorboards, entered a chilly bathroom with a claw-foot tub. On the back of the door was an ex-quisite silk robe. I stared, hesitating to lift it from its hanger. Its music filled my ears. I grabbed the robe and swung it around my shoulders. The music swelled, drowning out the night noises of the old house.

The robe was the color of air—the silver of the clouds and the almost imperceptible blue of thinnest sky. The front of the coat was embroidered with two golden dragons, and on the back, an enormous phoenix burst from multicolored flames. I ran my hand along the wall, looking for a light switch. With a click, a weak bulb flickered to life, illuminating the robe's rich colors. I approached a mirror and lifted my arms above my head. The dragons shifted.

Then I spun around and watched as the phoenix flew high above the fire. The music escalated as the robe prepared to carry me away.

"You've found the phoenix." Piet stood in the doorway behind me. Even in old age, he possessed a talent for surprise.

"I'm sorry."

"You're finding it hard to sleep," he said, placing a hand on my arm. "It's not the jet lag." He raised his white eyebrows. "It's the secrets. It's hard to sleep around secrets."

"I thought I heard the robe calling me. From the hallway."

"Did you?" Piet replied. Then he nodded. "Perhaps you did."

I began to take the robe off. "I design fabric and textiles—and this silk, the music, its music, is unlike anything I've ever heard."

"You hear music?" Piet asked.

I nodded and returned the robe to the hanger. Then the old magician placed his dry hand over mine. "No. It's yours." He tightened his grip. "I insist. This was from our end. From the moment when our magic stopped. If you hear music where I only see pain, you should keep it."

"I couldn't."

"Please, a little souvenir to inspire you and Toby."

I looked at the robe, suddenly unsure. "Thank you." I draped the robe over my arm, exposing a label sewn inside the collar. "'Made by Special Order by the People of the South,'" I read aloud. "For you?"

"Not for me. For Theo." His words escaped from his lips, carried on uneven currents of breath. "His magic was the beginning and the end for us all."

"But he no longer wants it?" I asked, running my hand across one of the phoenix's wings.

"Theo?" Piet shook his head. "For him, the phoenix was a false friend. But that's his story."

The shadows in the hallway had shifted, smoothing themselves into benign shapes. "I sleep irregularly," Piet said. "I can offer you some tea, provided we drink it the Dutch way—no milk and a little sugar."

Still carrying the robe, I followed him to the kitchen.

I slept late the next day. When we finally left Piet's house, the sun had vanished, leaving Amsterdam under the blanket of coal gray evening. At the end of his cobbled street, Piet stopped and leaned on his silver-headed walking stick. "Theo lives in our famous redlight district. He has been looking forward to your arrival." He pulled up the collar of his overcoat. "We all are. It has been so long since someone joined us. Fifteen years is too long to spend in the company of the same faces. I think we fail to realize how old we've become."

"No one new has come in fifteen years?" Toby asked.

"Some have left," Piet replied. "Theo's name shone brighter than any of ours. He brought us together to rekindle magic's golden age. It almost happened. And then, it didn't. Now, we are falling apart."

Red lightbulbs framed the canal bridges, dyeing the water with suggestiveness. The women in the windows gyrated impassively, beckoned halfheartedly. Their bodies did the work—moving to music that was out of sync with the rhythm of the street. They perched on the edges of red leather stools, bursting the seams of their lingerie. Some yawned, some filed their nails, others chatted listlessly. The red lights appealed to me. I liked the uneven chain of the glowing windows that ran up and down the canals. I liked the red-bulbed arches under the canal bridges that disappeared into the distance like a row of open mouths. A modern-day Roman feast stretched along the district's canals—slot machines, fast food counters, and bars filled the gaps between the famous windows. There was a guttural symphony of indulgence that accompanied the area—a bass clef composition of moaning, chewing, slurping, and the *clink-clink* of coins.

Toby's face registered nothing as barkers called to us. He didn't flinch as the scantily clad women tapped on their windows, inviting him in.

At the end of a covered, cobbled alley stood a white farmhouse unlike the narrow step-gabled buildings along Amsterdam's canals. As we stood before the door, the noise of the district faded into an improbable silence. The house was set in a small courtyard filled with unruly vines. Opposite it stood a pair of matching carriage houses with splintering wood doors.

Piet reached up and pulled a cord. A bell responded from deep inside the house. As we waited, Toby shuffled his feet on the cobblestones, flattening the raindrops, while I tried to trace the path of a single vine as it climbed up one of the courtyard's walls.

After several minutes, the top of the door opened with a creak and Theo van Eyck's ivory face emerged. In the faded light, I recognized the Chinese conjurer from Piet's poster. He looked past me and Piet to Toby. "Ah," he said, "Finally."

He unlatched the bottom part of the door, then released the iron gate, slowly coiling his scarred fingers around the latch.

Toby opened his mouth, but said nothing.

"No, no," Theo said. "There's no need to explain."

Toby nodded. "Mel brought me here."

"I know," Theo replied, placing a hand on my back and leading us into his home. "Welcome." He closed the doors behind us and sealed us in his world.

We were standing in an enormous room that filled the entire ground floor of the house. At its center was a wide staircase. The room's narrow windows were located near the ceiling so the light shone in dusty shafts, creating a pattern of squares on the floor. A helix of blue smoke curled down the staircase along with the sounds of men's voices. Somewhere someone was running through scales on an accordion.

In the checkerboard light, I could make out the stately decay of the room's furniture—Queen Anne chairs with split velvet cushions, splintering steamer trunks, fraying tapestries, candelabras hidden beneath stalactites of wax. A collection of scales, crucibles, and test tubes was scattered across a long table with cabriole legs. A large map with curling, yellowed corners hung over the fireplace. An air of lax suspicion filled the room, and I felt as if we were being watched. I don't want to say that it seemed as if time had stopped inside Theo's house. Time had been ignored.

At the far end of the living room a roaring fire with flames more blue than orange was burning in a vast fireplace.

"Upstairs, there is drink. Down here, only the fire," Theo said, heading for the staircase. As we started up after Theo, a chair near the fireplace scraped along the stone floor. Theo stopped and peered at a seated figure. We followed his gaze and saw a short man with salt-and-pepper hair dressed in a worn smoking jacket. He was sitting with legs crossed, holding a birdcage on his lap. Inside, a dead dove lay on its side.

"Lucio," Theo said quietly. "Once a great spiritualist. He'll never bring that bird back or hear it singing in the afterworld."

Lucio removed the cage from his lap, placed it on the floor next to him, and stood up. "This is?"

"Toby Warring," Piet said.

Theo placed a long, crooked finger to his thin lips, "Ssh." Then he continued up the stairs.

On the second floor, a labyrinthine library with floor-to-ceiling bookcases created corridors and alleyways so that there was no clear sight line from one end of the large room to the other. Here and there in the stacks were massive armchairs, some occupied by men reading by candlelight or oil lamp. One read with no light at all, simply turning the pages in the dark. As we passed, Theo let out a small laugh. "I am not as old-fashioned as it seems. My house has electricity. It is their choice to be this way."

In a corner of the library, we came to a set of steep stairs that ended in a heavy velvet curtain. The older magician slid in front of me and lifted the drape. I heard a few bars of a cabaret song and the whine from the accordion. I turned and smiled at Toby. His fingers were wrapped around the railing. His breath emerged unevenly as he craned his neck to see the magicians in the room beyond. "A new home for your magic," Theo said, pulling back the curtain. And before Toby could object, Theo brought us inside.

It took me a moment to adjust to the strange light. The room was lit with a combination of kerosene lamps and stage lights, some covered with cracked, colored gels. This apartment resembled at once a gypsy caravan and a Victorian fun house. Like the city, it seemed to duplicate and double back on itself—fading away in places and presenting many odd corners in others. This illusion was the result of beveled mirrors hung haphazardly along the walls. Broken wooden pillars with peeling gold paint, remnants from some superannuated stage set, were stacked in one corner, and a pile of worn velvet curtains covered in a plush layer of dust lay in a heap opposite.

"Our sanctum," Theo said. "You are standing in the remains of one of the last Spiegel tents. These tents have as many secrets as we do. Their name comes from the Dutch word for *mirror*. I journeyed with this one across Eastern Europe on my last grand tour. She was wrecked during a storm in Poland. This is all I saved." He waved an arm around the room. "She might be a little worn, but more elegant than any Las Vegas theater."

A circular table surrounded by chairs upholstered in old

brocade occupied most of the room. An enormous electrified art nouveau chandelier hung overhead. Several of its bulbs were missing, and the others flickered weakly. A mixture of cigar, cigarette, and pipe smoke curled upward and swayed slowly in the dim lights.

A dozen magicians were seated around the table. They, too, looked as if they'd been left behind at the close of magic's golden age. Their suits smelled of theaters and sideshows. The smoke that hung in the room seemed to have worn itself into their faces, tanning them like stage makeup. Two of the magicians were playing checkers. One used coins for his pieces, the other animal teeth. It was a game neither seemed to be winning.

Another group was immersed in a card game. Some of these men conjured as they played. Their magic was rusty, and I could see how they used their bodies in their art. A stocky magician, no more that five foot five, practiced a coarse, physical magic. He pressed the objects he wished to conceal—cards and chips—against his torso and inflated his bulky chest to mask his deception. When the time came, he produced what he had hidden with a swift, resounding thump, like a woodchopper splitting a log. His magic was strong, simple, and rough. The paper-thin magician who sat to the stocky man's right used the hollows between his jutting bones as hiding places, easily concealing the end of a rope or the head of a cane in his skeletal frame. Lucio, who had somehow arrived in the sanctum before we had, rubbed his enormous hands together forcefully, conjuring more blood to his cheeks, as he squinted at the faces of the other players, trying unsuccessfully to read their minds.

Theo considered this group, then turned to Toby. "They may not look like much now, but they were once the best in the business." He took Toby's elbow and drew him closer. "Like you, we were capable of the tricks others can only pretend to do. Unlike

you, our art has escaped us." A thin smile broke across Theo's lips.
"You would never guess that the company you see here made their
living performing for royalty in exile. From the Middle East to
Russia, we were sought by hidden kings and queens and their de-
scendants. And we amazed them."

Theo cleared his throat, and the men around shifted in their
seats. Their expressions mixed frustration with anger at a physical world that no longer seemed at their command.

"Gentlemen," Theo said.

The magicians looked up.

"May I present Toby Warring."

The checker game stopped. The cards disappeared along
with the inhospitable looks. The room glowed with expectation.

"Good evening," Toby replied, almost as if he were about to
begin a show.

"And his wife, Mel Snow."

But all eyes were on Toby. I moved to the back of the room
and found a comfortable chair.

"You have come from Nevada?" the skinny magician asked.

"Yes," Toby said as they made room for him, Theo, and Piet at
the table.

Wine bottles appeared. Glasses were filled. The stocky man
brought one to me. After a toast, a strange silence filled the room
as the magicians stared at Toby, waiting, I imagined, to see his
magic.

"You are a natural magician, like Theo," Lucio said. "That is
what we have heard."

Toby said nothing. He tapped the stem of his wineglass un-
easily.

"We have not seen real magic in years," the skinny magician
said. "Perhaps I can show you something?"

"Gideon was a formidable quick-change artist," Theo said.

Toby nodded, and as he did, Gideon switched from his tattered suit to an old gypsy costume. Toby and I clapped.

Then the plump magician produced another bottle of wine. The bottle shook as it appeared, and I worried that when it hit the table, it would break. The men continued to introduce themselves, each one displaying some element of his magic. When it was Piet's turn, he shook his head. The purple shadows played across his white hair. "I never did magic. I only built illusions."

Next came Lucio. The spiritualist took a deep breath and squinted at Toby. His cheeks burned with the force of his concentration. No one spoke. The smoke began to settle over the table, as if it, too, were waiting. Finally, Lucio took a deep breath. "The desert," he said. "I see you in the desert. Again."

"Not likely," Toby said. "The desert and I no longer get along."

Theo looked at Lucio and laughed. "These days, Lucio's prophecies mostly pertain to things that have already happened."

The spiritualist glowered and polished off his glass of wine.

Theo glanced around, half-disappointed, half-amused by what he saw. "I'm sorry that our magic no longer lives up to our reputations. Although, our reputations are faded as well. There was a time when we could baffle even one another with our talent. Now, we leave that up to you, Toby."

"No."

"No?" Theo asked, his voice still cool.

"No," Toby repeated. "So, I believe it is your turn."

The magicians shifted uncomfortably.

Theo gave Toby his showman's smile and leaned toward him as if he were about to share a secret. He wrapped his waxen fingers around Toby's. "I told you when we first met that my hands were not so different from yours." He laughed. "Maybe now you find this hard to believe."

Toby withdrew his hand.

"I would almost say our hands were identical," Theo continued. Then he looked at Piet. "Wouldn't you agree?"

The oldest magician nodded.

Toby clasped his hands together and placed them in his lap.

Theo pressed his palms onto the table. "But there is nothing left in them." He clapped, and a sound like thunder shook the sanctum. I stared at the skylight, worried its glass would crack. "When I was still a real magician, there was nothing I couldn't do." The room stopped shaking. "But now—" Theo pressed his fingertips together. "—this is it." A weak flame flickered from his hand, trembled, then died. "Such a shame when the hands cannot keep up with the mind."

"What happened?" Toby asked.

"An accident."

The magicians looked away from Theo.

"What kind of accident?" Toby asked.

Theo exhaled and looked at Piet. "I let someone die on my stage."

"You let someone die?" Toby's voice was calm.

Theo trapped Toby in a hypnotic stare. "I killed my assistant, if you prefer. This is the mistake that brought an end to our golden age. No more bookings, and I could no longer conjure."

Toby pressed his hands together and looked away. "Why didn't you tell me?" He sounded tired.

Theo laughed. "You wouldn't have come."

"No, I wouldn't have."

"But you're here now," Theo said.

"I'm sorry. I will disappoint you. At the moment, I'm not up for magic."

"Then magic will abandon you. As it has us." Theo rubbed his hands together, trying to massage his twisted knuckles. "We had our own theater. We traveled through Asia, India, and Russia.

Then we lost everything. We want our world back, and we think you can help us."

"I'm not here to do magic," Toby said. "And I can't help you."

Piet leaned over the table and lowered his voice. "Then why have you come?"

"To hide." Toby looked at his hands, still cupped in his lap.

Theo curled his hands into fists. "No, you've come to be the best magician you can be. That is why you've come."

"That used to be my ambition," Toby replied. "It's no longer possible. No one will hire the magician who killed a volunteer."

"No one in Las Vegas," Theo said coldly.

"Despite appearances, I am a Vegas magician. Or I almost was. I'm through wasting my magic in dusty and forgettable places."

"A different world is within your reach," Piet said quietly. "When you see what you can do, you will love magic more than ever. You will allow us to show you what is left of our world?"

"Of course." Toby flexed his fingers and placed them on the table. "We can take you to a place where your magic can thrive," Theo said, wrapping one of his scarred hands around Toby's.

"The one place I'd set my heart on is out of reach."

"If you come with us, none of that will matter," Piet said.

"You'll forget about Las Vegas soon enough," Theo added.

For a moment, silence filled the sanctum. I imagined it pouring down from the skylight and flooding the old Spiegel tent.

Toby waited as Lucio refilled his glass. "When I was younger, my greatest fear was of not being able to put back together the things I was discovering I could take apart. Now it's happened. Twice." He paused. "The craft I love has betrayed me."

Theo's face sharpened. "It is the other way around." Then he looked up at the skylight. "Our sanctum is crumbling. But our memories will teach you how glorious our magic was and how much greater it could have been." He snapped his fingers, and the plump magician produced more wine. The candles seemed to burn brighter, and the talk turned to shows and illusions.

I closed my eyes, carried off by a combination of wine and jet-lag and the low light of the sanctum. I listened as the magicians began to recount their adventures. They told Toby about performing in a Mongolian court and about traveling on the trans-Siberian railroad. They told him about being persecuted in a Catholic village in Sicily when the spectators suspected they were in league with the devil. I opened my eyes from time to time, trying to imagine the withered speakers in the fantastic tales they told.

Finally, Toby stood up and tapped me on the shoulder. Except for the two of us and Theo, the sanctum was empty.

"Did you hear anything you like?" Theo asked as we headed down the stairs.

"Of course," Toby said.

"This is only the beginning of our stories. We will bring this world to life for you as much as we can. Then, perhaps, you will like magic once more."

"I like the stories," Toby said, and shoved his hands deep into the pockets of his coat.

It was a relief to escape from Theo's musty house and immerse ourselves in the humming red-light district. Night had fallen, and the ladies in the windows picked up their pace. Their music was louder and their gyrations quicker.

"What did you make of them?" I asked after we'd left Theo's.

Toby shook his head. "I've always known that magic is an old-fashioned art, but I didn't know it was petrified."

"Some of them seem nice enough."

"Sure. It's no secret that I'm not the most up-to-date person." Toby pinched me on the shoulder. "And neither are you. Who quilts these days?"

I laughed.

"Is this what my magic will come to? Tops and tails?"

"They don't seem too keen on women."

Toby glanced at the windows as we passed. "They could use a dose of this."

I laughed.

"Theo's magic is appealing. So are his stories. But does the setting have to be so dour? You'd think they were a secret society rather than showmen. The best tricks magicians perform are for each other. But those guys are extreme, hiding away in that mausoleum." He stopped and looked at the canal and the black-lit windows running alongside it. Dance music poured out of the windows of a nearby bar. "I like it out here." Toby looked up and down the canal.

I nodded. "It's like Las Vegas."

"Without the fairy-tale architecture."

"Which is better."

"Maybe," I said, pointing toward a large fountain in the shape of a phallus lit up with pink and purple lights. "I think they're into a different kind of illusion around here. But it could be a good place for magic. Maybe we could find you a small theater. Though I don't think you'd be as successful as the ladies' magician."

"Probably not. But you never know. Fremont Street was a real men's club."

"Until you."

"Until me."

We left the red-light district and walked toward the Royal Palace and the Dam Square, where the carnival was running. "Magic is like growing up," he said. "As you get older, you start playing with more significant objects, but you miss what you conjured with as a child. It's silly to think of doing magic with blocks for the rest of my life. But sometimes I think it might have been better."

"Except you wouldn't have grown up."

Toby was silent for a moment as we listened to the various amusements competing for our attention. "I was naïve when I first discovered that I could do magic. I thought my talent could win me friends." He smiled. "I tried to use my skill to impress my classmates. I knew better than to head for the popular kids. Instead I latched on to those just on the outskirts of popularity."

"Like me."

"Probably like you. There was one girl, Madeline. I had a thing for her. She was pretty but awkward. The kind of girl who's going to be popular eventually but doesn't know it. Just looking at her, I knew that all the boys would be turning her way in a couple of years, when they got bored with the clones who are the focus of early teenage affection." Toby draped an arm over my shoulder and looked at the sky as he talked. "Oddly, Madeline was interested in magic. I showed her only the little things—flowers and vases, silk scarves and card tricks. And she liked them. Every day she'd ask what surprise I had in store for her. Of course, most of my surprises were small gifts in disguise—candy, bracelets, stuff like that. So her interest was partly material." Toby shook his head. "I never learned when to stop. I still haven't. The kids in school were really getting on my case. They laughed at me and lumped me in with the math geeks and role-playing game misfits. I had a feeling that Madeline might soon see things their way. Instead of playing it cool, I upped the ante. We were lab partners in biology class, the only class I really enjoyed. At the back of the room, they had all these reptiles in formaldehyde. They must have been twenty or thirty years old. I found them intriguing, but they terrified Madeline. She was the kind of girl who got an excuse note from her parents on the days we were due to dissect something."

"That sounds familiar."

"Growing up with a father who was an anatomist, I was the opposite. I couldn't wait to get inside a piglet or a frog to see how everything worked."

"I can imagine that."

"So Madeline and I were in the back of the lab, cataloging fossils. She couldn't take her eyes off the formaldehyde animals. She said she felt them watching her. She said they were making her sick. So I—"

"You didn't."

Toby nodded. "Before I knew what I was doing, I'd transformed one of the small preserved turtles into a live animal. Madeline screamed. Everyone was staring at me with these expressions that were both condescending and terrified. She would not stop screaming. I tried to explain that it was only a trick. No one listened. The whole school rose to her defense, to protect her from a freak like me. As if I had done this to scare her. Within a month, she was on the arm of some baseball player, and I had lost my last friend."

"But gained a turtle."

"True. If I'd stuck to my blocks, things would be easier."

I shook my head. "You'd be dating homecoming queens, and where would I be?"

"That day in the lab, I realized that all I'd ever have is magic. When I got home, I lay in bed, unable to stop my tricks. I conjured until I blocked out the jeering voices. I conjured a whole world to replace the one I was cut off from." The flashing lights from the carnival danced across Toby's face. "But then I began to see my magic differently. I mean, I transformed a nasty, preserved turtle into a live creature. What could my classmates do?"

"Nothing like that."

"Nope. So even if it meant being the ultimate outsider—"

"A dangerous freak."

Toby laughed. "Yes, almost that. Even if that's what it took, I was going to keep exploring this world."

"It's a great place."

"Better now," Toby said, pulling me tighter.

"You never tell me stories," I said, hoping for another.

"My stories are all the same."

We had arrived at the foot of an enormous, gaudy Ferris wheel in the middle of the fair. We looked up at the wheel circling through the nighttime sky.

"Shall we?" Toby's face brightened as he led me toward the ticket taker. A brusque man with fingerless gloves ushered us into one of the compartments and dropped the safety bar. The flashing lights encircling our carriage began to dance as we left the ground. I looked down to see the carnival recede.

"This is better," Toby said.

"What is better?"

"It feels safer up here."

We rose toward the pinnacle of the ride. The wheel moved slowly, stopping to let on more passengers. When we reached the top, it shuddered and stood still.

As we fell, Toby began to talk. The words tumbled from his mouth. "It was so quick," he said, raising his voice over the swirling carnival noise. "I heard the bullet. Then I have only a split second to transform it. It's not difficult, but the timing must be perfect. My mind must be still."

My thoughts flashed back to Eva standing in the audience, her presence perhaps clouding Toby's concentration.

We passed the lowest point of the ride and began to ascend.

"I felt her behind me. How could I have been fooled by that costume? You designed it well, I guess. Conceals people. Isn't that what is required to work in Vegas? Pretending to be someone else. A different someone to everyone. Well, it worked, and I chose her. And that was my mistake."

"You should have chosen me," I said.

Toby looked up as we began to rise. "No. I never mix love with magic."

We reached the top of the ride. I braced myself for the stomach-lifting fall. "I could feel her behind me. I didn't want to acknowledge her. A second mistake. I should have presented her to the audience, made a big deal. I guess I was arrogant. And angry. Her tension was distracting. I could feel her eyes boring into me."

We passed the bottom of the ride once more and heard an exhilarated whoop from another passenger.

"She jumped in front of me." He paused. "The reverberation was the worst part. It shocked my whole body. A wall had been thrown up in front of my magic. There were no pathways or tunnels through which I could undo what just happened." Toby closed his eyes. "I could feel her life pouring out onto the table. Everything was spinning, but I couldn't move. I couldn't even be sick or shout." He paused again. "It was a sick combination of mortality and failure. And then she was gone."

We were at the top once more, looking over a maze of gables to where lighted bridges were reflected in the Amstel River. Far above the neon advertisements, the clattering trams, and the tacky department stores, Amsterdam still looked like a fairy-tale city.

Then the wheel pitched forward and began to accelerate. Toby stopped talking and grabbed my hand, allowing me to consider the scenery. The sky fell away as we plummeted downward. The windows of the department store and the wax museum directly in front of the wheel went out of focus. The palace on the west side of the square dissolved into an abstraction of brown and gray. The erratic lights and wind-up music of the carnival below swam past in quick flashes that reminded me of the fluorescent flares of deep-sea fish that Max had once shown me.

As the wheel spun, I could feel Toby relax and let his body slump against mine for the first time in days. I lost sight of the river. I leaned over the safety bar, trying to glimpse the water, but all I saw was a whirl of lights. And then we were back at the top of the ride. I looked down along Amsterdam's main street and let my gaze turn east, searching for the river. But the primary north-south street had changed. The tram tracks had vanished, and so had the shop windows. Instead of reaching the river, the street—now more like a road—disappeared into a horizon that was no longer bounded by the city. I thought I saw a brothel at one end and a saloon in the middle.

"Tonopah," I whispered. I looked at Toby. Then I squinted, trying to bring the horizon closer and see what lay at the road's end. And for a moment, I thought I glimpsed the blue ranch house. The wheel rose over the crest, the road seemed to lengthen, its horizon pulled back into the distance, and the house vanished. Then Amsterdam appeared as it should. "But I thought you weren't going to do magic."

"It only lasts for a moment."

Nine

For some people, the best way to get to know a city is through its restaurants. Others prefer nightclubs, parks, or a day of shopping and sitting in cafés. For me, it has always been through exploring used-clothing stores. In the same way that Toby was able to learn so much about Jacqui Masterson and Evelyn Langhorn by watching them from his stage, I can learn about people and places by rifling through racks of old clothes. Their wearers' stories—but not their names—rub off on my fingers. Sometimes I'm able to discover something about a neighborhood's history and its residents. I find clothes that have been separated by death and divorce. I listen to stories of first loves and forgotten cocktail parties.

Amsterdam was full of secondhand clothing vendors, from high-end consignment shops and hipster hangouts to local stores crammed with housecoats and junky jewelry. Old clothes speak to me. I could not wait to hear Amsterdam's stories.

Toby and I wandered through the cobbled streets of Amsterdam's Jordaan neighborhood, a district of family homes, art studios, and stores selling everything from antiques to junk. We paused in front of a shop window that contained a wild array of games. Hand-carved pieces, trapped in irresolvable challenges, faced off on strange boards. Toby squinted and leaned in close to the window. I saw two pieces from one of the games change position. The magician blinked, and a fresh card flipped over on a mysterious deck.

"I thought you didn't do card tricks," I said.

The magician smiled and squeezed my hand. Behind the window, two cruciform pieces danced in place.

I was about to urge Toby on, when a store across the street caught my eye. It was filled with clothes from the 1950s and early 1960s. The window display featured cat-eye glasses arranged on top of elegant hatboxes and suitcases. Airplane and train tickets were strung into streamers and hung like beaded curtains from the top of the window.

I left Toby staring at the games and stepped across the street. The store was split into two levels. The main floor was filled with garments in perfect condition—immaculate bouclé suits, fur-collared coats, and pink-sequined sheath dresses. I wandered around the top floor, trailing my hand across the racks. I paused, letting suits tell me of cruises on the Holland America Line, or whisper about the city's post-war climate. There were photo-print dresses that mumbled something about jazz clubs and artist squats.

The downstairs was crammed with jumbled racks of funkier items. Here a poufy coral party dress gushed about a New Year's party at the Hotel Europa, and a black velvet number worried that it had been mistaken for something that belonged in Amsterdam's red-light district. I started browsing at the far end of the racks, fingering fraying crocheted dresses and pink swing coats with missing buttons. Soon my fingers latched on to a black velvet trapeze dress with a wide lace collar and long floppy lace cuffs. I pulled it out of the rack. I put my ear to the fabric and heard a familiar sixties pop tune. I closed my eyes and began to whistle along.

When I opened my eyes, a woman was standing in front of me. She was short, and her cropped hair was tipped with purple. Her features were small, almost elfin, and she wore a long deconstructed wool cardigan sweater and an enormous knit scarf. Beneath the scarf, a tattoo snaked up her neck. She stood with crossed arms, listening to me. I stopped whistling and felt myself blush. She laughed and extended a hand. She wore fingerless gloves, and her nails were painted green.

"Olivia," she said.

I shook her hand. "Mel."

Olivia took the dress from me. "I get it. It kind of makes you want to dance." She spoke clear English, hardened with stiff Dutch consonants.

"I guess it does," I said. "But not to my kind of music."

"It's got its own music?" Olivia held the dress away from her. The music grew faint in my ears.

"Well, sort of," I said. "Or maybe not."

"No," she said, taking one of my hands in hers, "tell me."

"It's silly."

"I'm sure it isn't." Olivia fixed me with her blue eyes. They were the color of the cornflowers that grew behind my parents' house. Her gaze was earnest.

"Well," I began, "sometimes fabrics sing to me, sometimes they speak. Not for long. Just for a couple of moments."

"You're kidding." Olivia dropped my hand and turned around, taking in the jumbled racks and, I thought, trying to imagine their hundreds of songs and stories. "I work for a designer. He makes wild clothes, but none of them sing." She grabbed a party dress with a velvet bodice and a long plaid skirt. "What's this say?"

I leaned in close. "Instrumental Christmas music. Live." Olivia held out a psychedelic bubble dress. "Sounds like surf guitar."

"How do you do it?" She gathered a pile of dresses into her arms.

"I'm not sure. I design textiles, so it comes in handy sometimes. Sometimes, it's distracting."

Olivia held up each of the dresses to my ear. Jazz, bluegrass, Dutch folk music, some kind of Bavarian beer hall chant, I told her. Then she pressed her ear into the fabric, straining to hear what I heard.

"I can't," she said, hanging up the dresses one by one. "They all sound like the seashore." Olivia began sifting through the racks until she found the black velvet dress I'd been whistling along with. "You need this."

"I do?"

"I'm having a party. Well, not me. My boss, Leo, is. His parties are the best. This one has a burlesque carnival theme." Olivia led me to a clearing between two racks and spread the dress on the floor. "I'm thinking you could cut out the bodice and lace it with red ribbon," she explained. "Then you could fashion the bottom into pantaloons." She pinched the bottom of the dress together. "Very cool."

"What about the collar?" I asked.

"You've got to leave it. It will look Victorian. A good contrast." I nodded.

"And shoes. We need to find you some shoes." She jumped up and handed me the dress. "Try it on. I'll be right back."

I ducked behind a curtain at the back of the store and slipped into the dress.

While I was changing, Olivia thrust a pair of red boots with silk laces under the curtain. "I'm sure they're your size."

I stepped out into the room. Olivia knelt down and began to pin the dress into pantaloons. "It's not perfect, but you'll get the idea."

Suddenly, I heard a low whistle coming from the stairs.

Toby had stopped mid-descent and was staring down at me. He wore a top hat he must have taken from one of the shelves on the upper floor. "Two days in Amsterdam, and you're turning into . . . Well, I don't know what you're turning into. I like it." The magician continued down the stairs.

"Olivia, this is my husband, Toby."

Olivia sprang from the floor to shake Toby's hand. "It looks like he's already started on his costume."

"Costume?"

"We're going to a party."

"Tonight."

"Tonight?" Toby and I asked in unison.

"So, you better get started on your alterations," Olivia said. Then she dug into a pocket, pulled out a small laminated invitation, and handed it to Toby.

"'A Burlesque Carnival,'" he read.

"The top hat is perfect. You see?"

"Not much of a costume, in my case."

Olivia looked at me.

"He's a magician."

Olivia grabbed Toby's wrists. "You have to come. A magician at a carnival. It's perfect."

It had been dark for hours when Toby and I headed out, wearing overcoats over our costumes. I'd taken the top hat Toby had found in the clothing store, and he wore the phoenix robe and a faded turban from Piet's collection.

"You're definitely on the carnival side rather than the burlesque," I told Toby as I pinned the turban into place. He didn't mind.

The invitation directed us to the side door of a church in the north of the city. A flight of stone stairs led down to the catacombs. As we approached, I could feel the steamy pulse of the party. We slipped into a crowd of revelers in floating velvet garments, fishnet stockings worn as sleeves, oversized tailcoats draped over peasant skirts.

This was the kind of slow-burn party where no one shouted introductions or stopped to wonder what you did or where you came from. The crowd swayed to low-key trance music. A series of stone corridors lit with torches were filled with twirling dancers without partners who raised their arms to the arched ceiling. I'd driven past parties like this before in the Nevada desert—tribes of millennial hippies circling a bonfire as they worshipped the desert or the sky. But I'd always kept on going.

Toby and I were swept into a throng of dancers who led us deeper into the catacombs until we found a square room ringed with a colonnade of arches. This was the official dance floor. Olivia appeared in front of me. She was wearing cropped tuxedo pants held up by suspenders over a white tank top. I looked down and admired her red fishnet stockings and impressive black patent leather heels laced with straps that came halfway up her calves. She'd powdered her face white, applied electric-blue eye shadow, and painted her lips ruby red. Without a word, she took my hand and pulled me deeper into the dance floor.

At the center of the crowd were two acrobats wearing tailcoats over Lycra leggings. They had slicked-back hair, and their makeup matched Olivia's.

"Those are the Christophs," she said over the music. "One is Dutch, the other Belgian. They also work for Leo."

The dancers made room for the Christophs as they launched into a series of impressive acrobatic moves. They did handstands on one another's shoulders. They linked their arms and feet and formed a human wheel that rolled across the floor. They flipped and twirled and landed in each other's arms. And when they were done, they slipped into the crowd, and the dancers closed over the open space they'd left behind.

The air was filled with incense and alcohol. The music crept inside me. I lost Toby. I looked across the room and saw his silk robe vanish into one of the corridors. A man dressed as a snake charmer took my hands and twirled me into the air. He set me down and disappeared. I turned in circles until I stumbled out of the room. Soon Olivia and I were moving deeper into the catacombs, stepping over partiers who'd sunk to the floor, staring at tarot cards in the torchlight or drinking hot cups of twiggy tea.

The party spun away from me on all sides. I saw someone swallow a sword. A contortionist squeezed herself through a tiny hoop. The music grew darker, its beat deeper. The light from the torches licked the archways with tendrils of orange flame. I ducked into a corridor and saw bodies slumped on velveteen cushions while a silent movie of a vaudeville act played on the wall.

Toby stood at the deepest point of the catacombs on a stone platform beneath an arch that framed his head. His features were crossed by shadows—his face almost opaque. But even in the dim room, the phoenix robe glowed. The dragons on the front slithered to the music, and I imagined the phoenix on the back rejoicing in the flaming torches.

A crowd had gathered. A ball of fire burst from Toby's clenched fist, then shot upward and hovered in the air while the magician conjured another. When he had five balls at his command, he began to juggle. He tossed the balls in the air, sometimes shooting them over the crowd so they formed an ellipse that circled into his hands. Then he threw them over his head, and they swirled around him like a halo.

Olivia and I drew closer. Toby gathered the fireballs into one flaming mass, which he stretched into a semicircle. I felt someone move into the space between me and Olivia. A large man dressed in a maroon velvet tuxedo stared at the stage.

"Leo!"

But Leo didn't answer Olivia.

Finally, Toby clapped his hands. The fire shot out over the crowd in two thick streams, then spread across the ceiling and vanished. Toby stepped off the stage. The audience swayed and twirled to the music.

Olivia and I rushed to Toby, but Leo got there first.

"This robe," he said, lifting one of Toby's arms and stroking the silk. "Where did you get it?"

"Mel, my wife," Toby stuttered, looking my way, "someone gave it to her. To us." He was not ready for conversation.

"I made this robe," Leo said. "I made it with my partner, Erik." He let go of Toby's arm and offered him a oversized hand. "I am Leo, and this is my party."

"Toby Warring."

"A magician," Leo said.

"And this is Mel," Toby continued.

"A fabric designer," Olivia added. "Fabrics sing to her."

Leo clasped my small palm in both his hands. "Do they?"

I nodded.

"Then we have much to talk about," Leo said, leading our little group to a stone alcove piled high with velvet cushions.

A lantern swung from the top of the alcove, casting a glow on Leo's mane of sleek gray hair. His face was long, with plump lips and a hooked nose, rounded at the tip. Despite his ungainly size and his age, his carriage was graceful. Even as he sat, he seemed to radiate a strange vitality. My eyes lingered on his suit.

"You are American," Leo said, taking four glasses of wine from a passing tray.

Toby and I nodded. "We've been here only a few days," Toby said.

"You are, I imagine, staying with one of Theo's magicians. Or perhaps with Theo himself."

"With Piet," I explained.

"Piet." Leo let the name hang for a moment. "Piet, I always liked best. He's the one who didn't do magic."

"You don't like magic?" Toby asked.

"Magic was Erik's domain. We lived together for more than thirty years. He disappeared during a hiking trip in the Dolomites." Leo looked out over the room at the dancers watching the snake charmer who'd taken Toby's place on the platform. "We met Theo and his company in Japan. They had just performed at the Royal Palace. We saw them in Kyoto. There was something odd about Theo's shows. I found them unsettling. But Erik was transfixed."

"What did he do?" Toby asked, waving his palm over Leo's glass, changing the wine from red to white and back again.

Leo laughed and sipped his wine. "The first show we saw was astounding. He made oranges turn into doves in the middle of the air. The doves flew through the audience and turned into smoke. That very night, Erik decided to make this robe. He wanted to make something that captured the flow of Theo's magic. His idea was that the robe's design would be choreographed to the illusions. He never imagined that it would take four years to complete."

"Four years?" I asked.

"Erik's relationship with fabric is not easy to explain."

Olivia winked at me.

"And I," Leo continued, "had to embroider the thing myself."

"You embroidered this?" I held Toby's sleeve.

Leo nodded. "Erik designed it. He researched the phoenix and the dragons for a long time. Then he designed it, and I followed his instructions." He finished his wine and sighed. "I thought seeing it again would bring Erik closer." He shook his head. "It doesn't. It reminds me more of Theo." The snake charmer left the platform, replaced by a burlesque dancer.

"Leo and Erik made many costumes for the magicians," Olivia added.

"Yes. We did swamis, Sikhs, Chinese mystics. Very old-fashioned costumes. I'm sure Piet has them tucked away somewhere."

"Oh, he does," Toby said. "I can't imagine him throwing anything out. Not even a single set list."

Leo smiled. "So, you are here to carry on the strange tradition of Theo van Eyck."

"No," Toby replied. "I always wanted to be a Las Vegas magician. Although my tricks might seem old-fashioned, Theo's style is antique. There's something about the modern grit of Las Vegas that speaks to me."

"Then why bury yourself in a house full of crumbling men?"

"Because, Las Vegas spat me out. My magic is no longer welcome there or maybe anywhere."

Leo nodded. "There is a gritty side to this city, too. Maybe it will inspire you. But be careful: Amsterdam is a magicians' graveyard. Secrets come here to die." He shook Toby's shoulder. "But you are too young for that."

Olivia popped a cigarette into her mouth. Toby cupped his palms. In an instant, the space between his hands began to glow. Olivia leaned forward. Toby clapped, and the light in his hands went out.

Olivia sat back and exhaled. "Some trick," she said.

A woman in a long pink wig, a rhinestone bodice over denim shorts, and stockings held up by black garters peered into our alcove. "Found him," she called over her shoulder.

Toby looked up.

"You're the man who can play with fire," she said.

The magician smiled. "Sometimes."

She leaned in close. "Come," she said, pulling Toby to his feet. "Unfair of you to hide in the corner." Then she noticed Leo. "Sorry to steal him from the host."

"Be my guest," Leo said.

Toby hesitated. I put my hand on his back, urging him up.

"They all want to see," the woman in the wig whispered.

Toby turned to Leo, who extended his hand. "You'll come visit us sometime."

"Of course," the magician replied.

Toby stepped into the corridor, and the flames on all the torches turned from orange to blue.

Leo watched him go, the phoenix dancing at his back, then turned to me. "I haven't forgotten that fabric sings to you."

"Not at the moment," I said. "The wine and the music are taking care of that."

"We have many things to discuss. But now you two should be dancing."

Olivia extinguished her cigarette.

"Olivia, make sure Mel comes to the villa."

Olivia nodded.

Leo fingered the red ribbons that dangled from the bodice of my costume, holding their ends up to the lantern. "Since Erik disappeared, his fabrics seem lifeless. Perhaps you can bring them to life. If only for a moment."

"I can try."

"Now, dance. It's the reason I throw these things."

It was my turn to lead, drawing Olivia from the alcove and onto the dance floor. On our way, she grabbed two mugs of tea. It tasted of twigs and earth. Olivia finished hers in one gulp and followed me.

The pace of the music picked up. I lost Olivia and found myself between the two Christophs. Soon the dance floor began to glow. The Christophs stopped dancing. The crowd parted, and the fiery silhouettes of two dragons and a phoenix began to sway in time to the music. In the center of the three was Toby. He was dancing.

We slept until lunchtime the next day. When I got out of bed, leaving the magician to his dreamtime conjuring, my head felt swollen and my legs were uncertain. I crept down Piet's perilous stairs, hoping for coffee and solitude, but found Theo sitting alone at the table.

"Good afternoon," he said.

"Hi," I replied.

"Piet's gone out," Theo said.

"Would you like coffee?"

Theo nodded. "It is the jet lag?" the elegant magician wondered as I filled the pot with water.

"Something like that."

"And Toby?"

"He'll be down soon."

"Good. This will give us time to talk."

I brought the coffee to the table and poured it into cups.

"Tell me, how often do you think about your hands?" Theo asked.

"Excuse me?"

"Your hands."

I looked down at my short fingers and my square palms. Square palms—the sign of an artist, someone told me once. "Sometimes," I answered. "From time to time."

"From time to time," Theo mused, spooning sugar into his cup. "Your husband has the most extraordinary hands."

I nodded.

"I hope he does not plan to suffocate their potential. There is so much he can do."

I sipped my coffee.

"We can help him."

"How?" I asked.

"There are tricks that will restore his faith in magic. When the time comes, I hope you will convince him to do them."

I shook my head. "When it comes to magic, I can hardly convince Toby of anything."

"That is because you haven't tried."

I refilled my cup.

"You volunteered for Toby's trick in Las Vegas."

I nodded.

"Why?"

I looked into Theo's eyes. His irises swirled, holding my gaze until I answered. "I was worried something would go wrong."

"And why was that?" The elder magician wouldn't look away.

"The woman Toby made disappear warned me that it would."

"But you didn't tell him."

I shook my head. "Toby's magic wasn't what went wrong at the Winter Palace."

"Anytime a magician invites someone onto his stage, that person becomes part of the magic. Your husband should know that." Theo blinked and released me from his stare. "Perhaps you should have said something."

"Maybe."

"Let us hope that the next time you have the opportunity to advise Toby, you will take it."

"I can't see when that will happen."

"Soon. We have a trick that will make magic meaningful for Toby once more. He is a magician, like I was, and knows nothing else. When the time comes, convince him. Magic is his happiness. It is his calling. I'm sure there's nothing you wouldn't do for him." Theo reached across the table and tapped the back of my hand with his hardened fingertips. "This is why you came to me."

Something in Theo's tone wouldn't let me admit he was right, so I pushed my chair back and collided with Toby as he walked in.

"And why have we come?" Toby asked. He sounded cheerful, as if last night's party had set something free in him.

Theo smiled. "So that I can show you what remains of our little golden age." He winked. "And so that you can explore some of Amsterdam's best secrets."

"Secrets?" Toby said. "I cannot have secrets before coffee."

The stately theaters that line the east side of the Amstel are hospitable to musicals, opera, and ballet—really, anything that comes their way. Theo led us down a small street between two of these theaters, where props and posters were stacked against stage doors and I could hear a show tune being rehearsed in one of the buildings. At the back of the alley was a limestone building nearly obscured by vines. A small flight of steps led to the entrance. As he approached the door, Theo kicked aside a carpet of leaves and crumpled paper and withdrew an impressive iron key for the large rusted lock. The door opened with a groan, admitting us to dust and shadow.

"When my company was in its prime, we had our own

theater." We heard the click of a switch, and a weak yellow bulb flickered to life. "This is it."

We were standing at the edge of what once must have been an elaborate cabaret. A sign that read LA GAITE in art nouveau letters hung over the stage. A small flight of stairs led down to a seating area lined with banquettes upholstered in cracked crimson fabric. Dozens of round tables, blanketed in dust, each with a silk tasseled lamp, were scattered through the room. Theo fussed with switches until yellow bulbs hidden inside unevenly spaced glass sconces shone weakly.

"When I was on tour, I always made sure that one of the other magicians was performing here." He brushed dust from his fingertips. "I have never considered selling the place. Please look around."

Toby and I climbed the steps to the stage. Lights with cracked gels pointed at the dark ceiling. Toby walked in a circle, his long shoes leaving a trail in the thick dust. I slipped into the wings and was caught in a tangle of backdrops and props.

The theater smelled of mothballs and mold. Indistinct secrets whispered from the walls. There was an uncertain majesty to the place, a tense combination of mystery and elegance—as if it were holding its breath, waiting for what might come next.

I wandered until I came to a small dressing room. A decaying tailcoat was draped over a chair, and pots of dried grease paint lay along a table in front of a cracked mirror framed with bulbs. A disintegrating set list, written in an elegant old-fashioned hand, was tucked between the glass and the frame. Several top hats lay on their sides on a shelf above a mirror.

The magicians' voices carried from the stage into the wings.

"It might not look like much to you now," Theo said. "Once this was our sanctuary. A home for our magic. It was packed every night. Not with children and tourists, but with people who understood what it meant to be amazed."

I imagined Toby's shoes tracing circles through the dust as Theo spoke.

"Magicians from all over the world came to watch us. In a few years, we would have become as famous as Kellar or Carter. We were on the verge of greatness unparalleled in the world of magic, because there was no artifice to our shows. It's a difficult task, winning people over to illusions that cannot be explained."

"I know." I thought I heard Toby tucking his hands into his coat.

"The average magician possesses a finite number of tricks that he combines and recombines to baffle the audience. And the audience knows they are being tricked. They simply cannot decide which of these tricks is in play at a given moment." Theo lowered his voice. I could imagine his face growing stern and his irises beginning to swirl as they had in the kitchen that morning. "It is our job to trick the audience into believing they are being tricked, when they aren't." The elder magician paused. "It is our job to convince the audience that the danger they are witnessing isn't real."

At the back of the dressing room, a door led to another dressing room, where a white silk robe with gold trim lay on a slipper chair. I took off my coat and slipped the robe over my sweater.

"It is easy to win an audience on tour," I heard Theo say. "Convincing audiences night after night to come back to the same cabaret is more difficult. My greatest feat was accomplishing just that." Theo stopped speaking. I could hear Toby sanding circles in the dust with the soles of his shoes. "My accident ended everything. I know that if my hands hadn't been burned, I would have brought people back. Audiences would have forgiven me for letting my assistant die. But the fire claimed her and my skill. Without magic, I was helpless." The elder magician cleared his throat. "I want to go back to that moment when my magic was at its prime. When it mattered."

"Then you and I want the same thing."

"No," Theo said slowly. "I want to go back to a moment when all magic mattered. The magic you perform hasn't begun to have meaning. It's merely trifles for tourists. You live in the wrong time for magic."

"It doesn't matter anymore."

"We can change that."

In the patchy light, I could see a couple of framed pictures on the dressing table. I held them toward the mirror. A couple in wedding clothes stood on the deck of a boat. The woman's face was shaded by a large white hat. The man, with his polished, austere features, was clearly Theo van Eyck. The second photo was a publicity still from a magic show. Here, Theo, dressed as a Sikh, held a sword above his head, with his assistant seemingly impaled on the blade.

"Your skills, remarkable as they are, are limited to the world of magic," I heard Theo say. "You cannot use them to pull an airplane out of the sky. You cannot use them for mundane things like cleaning your house or cooking dinner. You cannot save a life."

I heard Toby mutter something.

"You can only do magic. And if you choose, I will make this your home."

Still wearing the white gown, I stood up and left the dressing room. I found myself in a small hallway lined with flats and withered scrims.

Toby cleared his throat. "All I've ever wanted," he began, his words full of their usual static, "is to be the best magician. If magic was going to separate me from everyone I knew, at least I wanted to be a success. It's what I required to make sense of the craft."

"And now?"

"Two disasters are enough."

I examined the flat before me—a depiction of the courtyard of an Italianate villa with fountains and colonnades. One of the colonnades ended in a double door.

I heard Toby flex his fingers with a crack. "The only way I could ever perform again is if I were unable to undo what I did in Las Vegas. But I can't. As you said, I have many skills at my command, but I cannot retrieve a life." Toby paused, letting his words drift to the charred ceiling.

I reached out and touched the door at the end of the colonnade. I felt myself falling forward. I stumbled and was standing on the stage behind the magicians. Toby turned around.

"Sorry," I said as I righted myself.

Theo smiled. "You are the victim of one of Piet's trick doors. We built them to keep other magicians out. I'm surprised they still work."

"It's an astonishing theater," I said.

"Your wife is right." Theo gave me a conspiratorial smile. "I have to leave you for a moment and inspect a few details in the back of the building."

When we heard the stage door shut, Toby looked at me. "Nice dress."

I tied the robe properly. "It's creepy here, but also kind of alluring. Like a ghost town."

"It is creepy."

I circled around him, letting the robe flutter behind me.

"Do you think Leo made that?" Toby asked.

"I have no idea. It's so much nicer than anything they wear in Vegas shows."

"I like Las Vegas. We understood each other. There was a kind of give and take between me, the city, and the audience. I didn't criticize the people for their attitudes, and they didn't look too closely at my art. We enjoyed each other despite our mutual short-comings. Or maybe because of them. I came so close."

Dust rose from my feet and swirled toward the lights. "But imagine if this was yours. It would be perfect for a close-up show like the one in the Castaway."

"Do you really think this is something I should do?" Toby stared into the vacant stage lights.

"Magic is how you connect to the world. It seems a little silly to save all your tricks for me. Here is as good as anywhere as long as you make it your own."

"And as long as I stick to the basics."

I nodded.

Toby flattened his palms and held them out over the stage. "So that's what it's come to, a close-up show. I'm to be a card-and-coin man."

"And the rest of it." I jumped off the stage and sat in one of the banquettes.

"I suppose you are already redecorating."

I pressed my hand into the stiff fabric, feeling the springs resist my touch. "Well, I hadn't thought about it, but I could." I lay my head against the top of my seat, listening for the fabric's song or story. But all I sensed was silence. Then I reached out and ran a finger through the faded fringe on one of the small lamps.

It was silent. "Strange," I said. "There's no music. Not even a murmur."

"Maybe they're keeping their secrets," Toby said. "This place was built by a magician."

"Maybe." But the fabrics in Piet's house never hesitated to

talk to me. "If you take Theo's offer, we'll have to do a serious exorcism on this place."

"If." Toby's single word trailed into the wings.

"We could do it together," I suggested.

"When I'm ready."

"Of course."

Toby sensed my disappointment. "So, tell me," he said, joining me and putting an arm around my shoulder, "what fabrics would bring this place to life?"

"Why worry about that now?"

"I want to know. I want you to tell me."

I hesitated.

"A saloon theme," Toby said, prompting me.

"Not bad."

"Ever since I arrived in Nevada, I'd always dreamed of a saloon-themed show."

"Corny but clever."

Toby nodded. "We'd have to make it a little classier than the Old Stand, of course."

I laughed. "I've already done their fabrics."

"And I already have the black Western shirt."

Ten

In the days following the miraculous return of my amphibious brother, I became his watcher, his secret guardian, locked in a nightly vigil that I believed could hold him close. At least I thought that was my purpose.

Over the next few weeks of summer, I dreaded the start of school, when Max would be out of my sight. And I knew that before this separation, I had to memorize him. My study was careful and methodical. By fall, I could predict the clothes he was likely to wear the following day. I could tell whether he was about to hook his hands into the waistbands of his pants and if he would have trouble falling asleep at night. I knew the arch of his eyebrows when he encountered an unfamiliar word and the swift pucker of his lips when he was preparing to make a joke. I knew the number of wrinkles around his knuckles and the exact length of each of his toes. I knew that he preferred to cross his right leg over his left and that he held his breath when he climbed up the stairs. And I knew best of all the feeling of radiated calm that blanketed my body a split second before Max spoke to me.

Before I became a master of my art, I shadowed my brother from room to room, clinging to every word he said. But then I learned to dissemble—I figured out that I would learn more if he didn't know that I was watching. I learned to peek around the corners of books and listen through walls.

I clung to every detail of my brother—the trefoil pattern of moles on his right forearm, the slight depression on his left earlobe, the way he ate cereal with water instead of milk, the number of minutes—eleven—that he spent in the shower. While I was oblivious of the latest developments in the coolest TV shows or what songs were on the charts, I was an expert in the minutiae of Max's life—the inseam of his rented tux, the minimum SAT score it would take for him to get into a college with a good swim team, which words he missed on his French vocab quiz.

I was a devoted but powerless watcher, a lifeguard who couldn't swim. Despite my careful vigil, Max started to sneak out of the house. After I watched him pass through the gates of sleep, I would return to my bedroom and pray for a sleep of my own. But the moment Max moved, I was jerked from a patchy slumber, attuned to the smallest disturbance in the air on the other side of our thin wall. I'd tense as I listened to him open his window, slide down the drainpipe, and alight on the soft grass below. And when I heard Max's footsteps crunching over the gravel in our driveway, away from the river, I would exhale and wait for the stop-start sleep that came until he returned.

My twelfth birthday was a disaster. A raging storm stranded my father on a scouting trip and confined my mother to her room.

Max and I spent the evening in front of the TV, devouring cake straight from the box. When I fell asleep, he carried me up to bed.

I was dreaming of a blue swimming pool covered with birthday cakes like lily pads when Max came to get me.

"It's time to go," my brother said, taking my arm. He put his hand over my mouth.

"Don't you want to see your birthday present?"

I nodded and followed him to the car.

I dressed in the dark, slipped out my bedroom window, and slid down to the wet ground in a rough imitation of my brother's method of escape. Max was already in the driveway. We crept into the car and gently shut the doors. Max lifted the emergency brake and shifted into neutral. The car rolled quietly down the wet gravel.

"Excited?" Max asked, rolling the car out of the driveway without turning on the ignition.

I nodded.

We were heading toward the city. My heart rate quickened with the acceleration of the engine. I watched Max's right hand move from the steering wheel to the shift, flicker around the radio, and then hover for one moment above my leg before he had to return it to the wheel.

"Your present is at work."

"At the aquarium?"

Max turned the corner into an empty lot behind the aquarium.

"Come on," he said, popping the door locks.

"You have the keys?" I was amazed that anyone would trust my brother with the keys to an aquarium.

"Of course," Max said, producing a jailer-sized key ring. He selected one of the twenty and fitted it into the lock on a side entrance. I held my breath.

He took my hand and led me down an empty hallway. The

daytime excitement of tourists and school groups was replaced by a dark undersea world muffled by the sleep of thousands of creatures. The glow from the emergency-exit light was not enough to guide us, but Max had developed a sonar of his own, and wove around dark corners and past unseen obstacles.

He led me back to the laboratory where he worked on the weekends, testing pH levels and the algae content of the tanks.

"First stop," he said, switching on a small desk lamp. From underneath a pile of papers he produced a gaily wrapped box from the aquarium's gift shop. Inside was a bathing suit—a strange present for someone who doesn't swim. I unfolded it and held it up to the light.

"So?"

I didn't know what to say.

"Why don't you try it on? There's a bathroom in the hall."

After the dark hallway, the buzzing fluorescent light that flooded the white-tiled bathroom burned my eyes. The Lycra was three gradations of blue—a light aqua at the top that melted into indigo around the stomach and finished a dark cobalt. It fit perfectly. I stood in front of the mirror and tried to imitate the diving poses I had seen Max and his team strike before they plunged into the water.

"How's it fit?" Max called through the keyhole. I dropped my arms to my sides.

"Come in." I tucked my hair behind my ears and snapped the straps on my shoulders.

"Perfect," said Max. "An official racing suit, you know."

"I know," I replied, self-consciously wrapping my arms around my waist. I felt exposed under the bare fluorescent bulb.

"Turn around," Max commanded.

I spun around in a graceless pirouette.

"You look like a professional."

"A professional who can't swim."

In an instant, Max folded his long body in half and retrieved my clothes from the floor. "I don't know about that."

"Where are we going?" I asked as I tried to keep up.

"It's better in the dark," Max said, gesturing to the hundreds of tanks. "It's the closest you'll get to the center of the ocean without getting wet. In the dark, you can feel the pressure of all the animals."

I paused and listened to the gurgle of the tanks.

"The ocean hums more than it bubbles," Max explained. "It's the buzz of everything inside it."

The repetitive gurgling was teasing me.

"Come on," Max whispered. We flew past the fish tanks. I tried to recall some of the things he'd told me about the fish, but the tanks melted into a silver swirl, a reverse floating current that allowed no time for reflection.

We headed out from the main exhibition hall and stopped at a door with orange tape and a sign that read EMPLOYEES ONLY.

"What are they building?" I asked.

"If I told you, it would spoil the fun," Max replied, slipping underneath the plastic curtain. He fumbled with his key in the lock. I began to count the seconds. When I reached thirty-seven, Max opened the door and we stepped into a pitch-black room. I could tell by the delayed echoes of our breath and footsteps that the room was enormous.

"Wait here," Max said, abandoning me in the darkness. Soon a low hum began to hover at the corners of the room, and a few soft lights rose from the floor, illuminating a huge tank. "I could put on the overheads, but its much nicer this way," he said, reappearing at my side. He was wearing his swim trunks.

I looked from my brother to the monstrous tank, "Max, that doesn't have a shallow end."

"I've thought of everything." He unfurled a small inflatable rubber raft that he'd been hiding somewhere.

"A raft?"

"I'll be right there. You can hold on to me."

"All right."

A ladder led to the top of the tank, and we began to climb. The twisted iron rungs were cold and dug into the soles of my feet. As I approached the end of the twenty-foot climb, my arms ached. Max, who took no time at all to reach the top, extended one arm and hauled me up.

"It's deep," I said, staring at the water.

"Over twenty feet. But I'm going to be there the whole time. You can even hold on to the side of the tank, if you want."

My eyes traveled over Max's skin. I could imagine settling into the 110-degree crook in my brother's elbow as he rescued me from a watery plunge. But as I looked from Max to the water, not even the promise of my brother's water-smooth grip could calm the panic that jumped at me from the tank. "I don't know. I'm not sure anymore," I said, retreating from the edge.

"Come on." He led me back to the water and pulled me down on the cold platform. Max began to inflate the raft. I gripped the edge of the tank until my hands went numb. I looked deep into the tank, to the place where the lights faded away. As the little raft took shape from Max's lips, the water appeared to heave and sigh with sleep, resettling in its tank like a house in the night.

Max set the raft in the tank. It looked as insignificant as a handkerchief floating in the ocean.

"Now?" I asked, my voice rising and falling like the swaying raft.

"Not yet," Max replied. "There's one more thing." He got down on his knees and fanned his fingers underneath the surface of the water. He fluttered his hands, scattering droplets over the platform and causing the raft to scratch against the side of the tank.

"Max?"

But my brother couldn't hear me. He had dipped his face into the tank and begun to blow bubbles. And now a strange clicking noise, an underwater static, rose from his head—the same noise that leaked through the keyhole of his bathroom door when he was supposed to be washing his face.

"Max?" I repeated.

After two minutes, he withdrew his head from the water. Without even the slightest gasp for air, he said, "Don't worry." He puckered his lips and began to chirp. The chirp became a series of squeaks. Max lowered his face to the tank and plunged his head back into the water. I leaned in to peer at the watery shadows dancing on his white face. As I watched, the white opal of Max's face was eclipsed, overshadowed by a darkness that rose from the center of the tank. I stood up and retreated from the edge of the platform. The tank trembled as if a volcano of water were preparing to rise from its interior. I covered my eyes, squeezing them tight until I could hear the blood rush through my ears.

Then the water sighed. It gasped for breath and heaved itself over the tank, splashing my toes. I peeked through a gap between my fingers.

"Mel," my brother whispered, "come here. She won't bite."

I pried my fingers from my face. Max came into focus—his face intact and above water. At his feet bobbed a gigantic creature, full-moon white.

"This is Sophie," Max said. "She's the first trained white whale in America." Max uttered another series of clicks. The whale bobbed her head and replied with a staticky whistle.

I stared at the whale. She was the same white as my brother, a white that glowed, a white that sang, a white that was marbled with silver crests and valleys.

"She won't bite."

I tiptoed closer. Max drew me to his side and twined his fingers with mine. Together we reached out over the water. I closed my eyes, relishing the slipperiness of his touch. Our hands collided with the warm water and dipped several inches below the surface. Max pressed down harder on my fingers, driving them into the pool. And just when I began to fear the unreachable bottom of the tank, my hand hit something solid but smooth. I opened my eyes. Max had released my fingers, and the titanium white skin of the whale pressed into my palm. Her body had the texture of washed silk, smooth and chalky. Against the whale's massive body, my palm's diameter seemed to shrink—a pebble thrown at the moon.

"She's so white," I whispered to Max. "How can something be this white?" I shook my head.

The whale drew closer, sending small waves onto the platform as she rose. When her head broke the surface, I could see depressions and scars carved into her alabaster skin, like inside-out scrimshaw. I put my hands on either side of her head, absorbing her texture, which was both hard and slippery, firm but melting. A strange song, like a flute being played over a crackly radio, rose from deep within the whale—a purer version of Max's call.

I tried to read Sophie's head with my fingers. I wanted to memorize her curves, contours, and scars, so I could conjure her in my empty hands later on and summon the sensation of her bumps and depressions. I was so consumed by my exploration that I didn't object when Max slid me onto the raft and brought me eye to eye with a creature bigger than our family car. I had plunged into a waking dream where scale and measure had become deformed. It was a dream in which my only choice was to accept the marriage of the real and the impossible.

"You're swimming," Max said.

"What?" I answered, fingering the ridges on Sophie's forked tail.

"Swimming or floating at least."

I looked at the deep pool of water surrounding me. Size and scale swelled and shrank; the sky turned back into water. The moon became a whale again. And then I felt the fish tank smallness, the eyedrop confinement of the massive animal. I closed my eyes and saw a wild expanse of ocean big enough to reduce the whale to a comprehensible proportion. I let go and imagined a body of water large enough to accommodate schools of ten thousand of the alabaster creatures. The water engulfed my mind, swamped my brain, crashed on the insides of my eyelids. The water in the tank took advantage of my moment of panic, flying up my nose, burning my eyes, and tearing into my throat. I grew faint and slipped off the raft.

"Mel," Max cried, grabbing the back of my hair. "Mel!"

The top of the water slipped away. The white whale became black. Max's words were drowned out by the curtain of water between me and the surface. My ears and throat opened, and the water crashed in. It broke through all the barriers of my body, rushing and roaring and pulling me down. I thrashed and kicked. And then I felt the silky tentacles, the graceful arms of my brother, around my waist.

Max drew me into the crook of his elbow, as I knew he would. I relaxed into his arms and let my head sink into his chest as we rose to the surface. Our heads broke through the water, and I snapped out of my reverie, choking and sputtering.

"How much of that stuff did you swallow?" Max asked, helping me up onto the platform.

"I don't know. I just closed my eyes, and the water seemed to expand." I scrambled away from the water's edge.

"You just plunged off the raft and headed down. I think you've had enough water for one day. Do you mind sitting here while I take Sophie for a swim?"

Max dived from the platform, more like a dolphin than like a whale, and headed for the middle of the tank. He popped out of the water and beckoned to Sophie with his arms. I tried to trace their progress under the water, but they were lost in the unlit circles. Two minutes later, Sophie's head crested the surface; then her whole body breached with Max sitting on her back. He waved at me before the pair plunged below the surface again.

After several trips around the tank, Max brought Sophie over to me. "It's time to say good-bye," he said as I reached for the whale. He hauled his dripping body out of the water.

"Bye, Sophie," I whispered. She turned around and dived back into the depths of the pool—the moon eclipsed by the night.

In silence, we headed down the ladder. In the hallway, I slipped my clothes on over my wet bathing suit. Outside, the night had turned cold, and the sharp January air pinched my wet skin. The rain had stopped, and a few lonely flurries started their languid descent from the sky.

Max started the car and turned on the heater.

"Thank you," I said, beaming at my brother. I was shaking all over—trembling with the memory of my plunge and the magnificence of the whale. And I was trembling with delight at discovering that the other girl in my brother's life was a giant sea beast.

Eleven

The week after our trip to La Gaite theater was a week of rain. In Holland, a rare blue sky can immediately darken and be disrupted by bullet-sized hail; five weather systems can pass through in a single day, throwing the city from relative warmth into freezing rain. A twenty-minute walk can take you through a year's worth of weather. Like my magician, the Dutch weather distracted with an honesty—a golden fan of sunlight leaking from behind a cloud—while it put the finishing touches on the storm waiting in the wings. Unlike the rain that flooded my childhood, drowning our house, the Dutch rainstorms passed by swiftly, eager to take their havoc elsewhere. The Dutch rain didn't threaten, but performed, showing off its dexterity, its scope of pressures and wetnesses. It wasn't dangerous and malicious like the rain that had made the river rise and the house fall down around my family. It was cheeky and wicked. It spoiled a blue sky without warning, fell on one side of the city but left the other dry, and it teased—hiding in an oppressive blanket of gray for an entire day without falling.

At night, Toby and I were carried off to sleep by the rain tapping on the roof—and in the mornings, we were summoned awake by fresh gusts of wind driving the rain against our small window. We had traded the permanent sunshine of Las Vegas for its opposite: an unceasing backdrop of gray. The rain washed away the thrill of Leo's party and obscured the faded glory of La Gaite. The weather made exploring the city forbidding. So I remained in Piet's house, letting one day slide into the next as I watched the old man dig through his boxes, holding up memorabilia from Theo's triumphs for Toby.

And then, one morning we both woke up agitated. I'd slept later than usual, the constant gray of the sky making it hard to distinguish the morning hours from the early afternoon.

When I opened my eyes, Toby was standing in the attic doorway, staring at the window. "Rain."

I pushed my head into my pillow, struggling to regain the warmth of sleep.

"Why does it always have to rain? I feel like I haven't seen daylight in weeks. And there's nothing I can do about it." He looked into his palms.

"So come back to bed."

"That doesn't help."

"Maybe in your dreams it will be sunny."

"You don't want to hear about my dreams." Toby moved to the window and watched the gray clouds blow across the gabled buildings opposite.

"Maybe our next stop is a snowy place. That would suit me perfectly."

Toby turned from the window. "Of course it would, Mel Snow. But I don't think there's much call for a magician in Finland or the Arctic."

"Magic doesn't have to drive the train."

Toby returned his gaze to the window. With a finger he traced the pathway of a droplet as it slid down the windowpane. "I guess not," he said after a moment. Then he hit his hand against the glass, scattering the drops. "Want to see something green?"

"What are you going to do?"

"It doesn't always have to be magic, does it?"

"Certainly not," I said, letting Toby lift me out of bed.

We dressed and headed outside. Out on the street, Toby offered me a new angora scarf and an umbrella.

"You come prepared," I said, wrapping up.

"Always."

"Where are we going?"

He didn't answer.

We walked to the end of Piet's street and began to wind our way through his tangled neighborhood. Soon the elegant houses gave way to modern flats whose façades pretended a historic authenticity. We crossed a large canal and waited in front of Amsterdam's largest parking garage for the tram. The wet air had condensed into a light rain—a noncommittal spray that brushed against our faces and settled on our hair. The inside of the tram was streaked with footprints, remnants of an early-morning rainstorm. The hinged carriages creaked and squealed over the wet rails as the rainy city smells came in through the doors. We headed east across the Amstel River, which was shrouded in a mist that rose up to meet the falling rain. At the next stop, Toby pulled me from the tram and into the rain, which had upped its tempo.

"Only a short walk," he assured me.

"How do you know where you're going?" I asked.

We crossed a sleepy canal that was being tickled and refreshed by the fat raindrops. We passed the hibernating zoo with its lingering scent of hay and wet fur. I kept my hand inside Toby's, enjoying the warmth of his fingers. We crossed the street and stood in front of a black gate that joined two white buildings.

"The Hortus Bontanicus," Toby announced.

"The botanical gardens?"

"Of course. Where else could we see something green?"

As soon as the turnstile clicked into place behind us, the sounds of the city evaporated—the rattle and squeal of the trams, the splash of car tires crashing through puddles, the whir of bicycles and the sharp ring of their bells. The gardens, which were no bigger than a playing field, had been designed to obscure the city that ran along their edges. Small paths wound through stooped trees that hummed with life. Our feet crunched over the gravel, disrupting the glassy silence of the small park.

"This way," Toby said, leading me to a row of three narrow greenhouses.

He parted a rubber curtain, and we stepped inside. The damp chill of the air gave way to a tropical warmth that hugged our faces and caught in our throats. The greens in the misty interior were as dark as the deepest forest, as pale as the oldest sea glass, as electrifying as the harshest chemical. I breathed deeply to fill my lungs. Then the trees began to shake and tremble as an explosion of butterflies burst from their leaves. We threaded our way along the narrow path at the edge of the small greenhouse, watching the butterflies as they sucked nectar, danced among the trees, slept on the undersides of branches. All the colors that had been drained from the Dutch city sprang to life. They vibrated and shook. By the time we emerged from the greenhouse, having let the butterflies deposit farewell kisses on our necks,

Toby's face had smoothed into a smile. I took his hand and led him into the next greenhouse.

On either side of a path, thousands of cacti were stacked so high that they blocked the light from the windows. Some of them were minuscule, no bigger than my fingers, while others had towering tentacles with threatening spikes. It was as if Toby and I had stepped back in time, to the remarkable climate that had somehow drawn us together. The heat was the same: static and dry. The silence was the same: undisturbed by the quiet gaze of thousands of prickly plants.

I opened my mouth, letting the artificial heat fill my lungs. We didn't speak as we examined the cacti's confident poses and listened to their stagey silences. The plants were old. They had guarded their secrets for decades, not yielding to the scalding warmth or the scratchy soil. They seemed to be watching us with their needle-eyes, quietly confirming the match they had made in the desert months ago.

"Incredible," Toby whispered as we stepped out into the chilly air. "So warm."

We continued along a sand-colored path, ducking underneath the drooping branches of a weeping tree, and arrived in a small courtyard with an enormous glass atrium.

"I think we're the only people here," I said.

"I hope so," Toby muttered.

I followed him up a set of stairs that led to a walkway forty feet above the greenhouse floor. We made our way through three climates—the familiar scorch of the desert, the wet burn of the tropics, and the searing humidity of the subtropics. Here the plants and trees came in shapes wilder than anything Toby's hands might have conjured. All the patterns missing from the disorderly city appeared in the tripartite greenhouse—the veins spidering out over the rich green leaves, the perfect coils of bark winding around the exotic trees, the petals immaculately dispersed on the tiniest flowers.

I followed Toby out of the greenhouse toward an enormous glass structure as elegant as the palm trees arching toward its domed glass ceiling. We went up a wrought-iron staircase to a vertiginous semicircular walk through the tops of the palms. The trees grew thick and dense, often obscuring the path. I clung to the railing.

"The palms are so silent," Toby whispered, parting two trees that had interlocked over the walkway. I gripped the railing and closed my eyes. He was right. Unlike the trees in American forests, which bustled with life—shedding their leaves, changing their colors, and giggling in the wind—the captured palms covered us in an umbrella of quiet. They seemed to absorb all sound into their flat leaves.

I pushed ahead and arrived at another helixlike staircase at the end of the walk. But before I began to descend, I felt the magician pull me back. I turned around. Toby was standing where I'd left him. I brushed the spot on my shoulder where I'd felt the cool touch of his hand. Then I rustled toward him through the curtain of fronds.

"Ssh."

"What is it?"

We were standing in front of a palm with dark green elliptical leaves. "Look," he said, pointing at the tree. He took one of the fronds between his fingers and began to rub it. A single note from a distant woodwind rose from the leaf. The magician took a deep breath. Then slowly, he began to rub the frond once more. The single woodwind note ran along the leaf to the trunk of the tree, then coiled up the bark toward the palm's crown. As we listened to the palm's music, to the hollow sound of a tropical jungle, the expression on his face was the same as when he had made the sand dance into his hands.

He hesitated before reaching back into the tree. I bent over the railing and stared into the maze of leaves and bark. I felt the tree sway as if a wind had leaked into the greenhouse. It swayed again. And then the fronds began to rub against each other like cricket wings. The music that rose from the tree sounded like the secret voice of the forest. It was the music of the soil. It was as complicated and as textured as the roots of ancient trees. The music flew to the top of the atrium, where it collided with the raindrops falling on the glass roof. Then it echoed along each panel of the glass before descending over the sloped edges of the dome like a waterfall.

Now Toby waved his arms again, calling down a crescendo from the trees. He fluttered his fingers along a small frond, summoning a harpsichord solo. He shook a massive palm, from which a drumroll and cymbal crash erupted. He reached out toward a distant tree, calling down a flight of oboes and bassoons. At his command, a palm tree with thin fronds exploded in a jubilant string arrangement, and a tree with narrow, tubular fronds sang with the strength of ten flutes. Toby kept his head thrown back, his arms stretched forward, and his fingers waving madly.

The music of the palms and their hidden orchestra was majestic, but Toby had promised me. I took his wrists in my hands and pulled them downward, ending his concert.

"It doesn't always have to be magic," I said.

He didn't reply.

"You said so this morning."

"I thought you loved the magic."

"I love you. It's different."

"But I'm a magician."

"I don't have to love you for being a magician," I said, heading down the wrought-iron staircase, wondering for the first time where the magician ended and my husband began. I knew he didn't know.

"I'm afraid there is little else to me."

I took a deep breath. "I'll be the judge of that."

Toby took a few steps down the staircase, then stopped. "If you grow tired of the magic, you'll grow tired of me."

"Never."

"I've pushed everything aside for my art. And why not? There's a malleable world at my fingertips. I never have to settle for things the way they are."

I turned and faced him. "But sometimes you should just accept them."

"Why?"

I didn't know.

"If I can make a dead plant bloom, why shouldn't I? If I can make these trees sing, why should I stop myself? If I am the one person on earth who can do these things, is there any reason I shouldn't? My art is like a trick box. I keep going deeper inside it, finding another box, leading to another dimension. The nature of my magic is its limitlessness. Why stop with one trick when there is another unfolding behind it? It's like a kaleidoscope— one spectacular combination sliding into another. How can I look away?"

"I don't know."

Since our arrival in Amsterdam, Toby's sleep had become erratic and almost reckless. In Las Vegas, the thrill of his next performance propelled him from bed with the rising sun, but sometimes he now slept from the moment he finished his dinner until past breakfast. On those nights, he would curl himself into a ball at the far edge of the bed with his hands tucked underneath the pillow. His sleep was impenetrable, resistant to any touch or caress, or even a lingering kiss in the shadowy hollow beneath his cheekbone. On other nights, however, Toby could not remain still. After we had gone to bed, something would jar him from his sleep. For the rest of the night, he would move about the house. Sometimes he would come to rest on a sofa or landing, and then set off again on his nighttime ramble. In the morning, I might find him slumped over the dining room table or nestled against a newel post.

I woke up just past four in the morning. Toby had left our bed hours earlier. I shivered in the cold attic air before finding a sweater. Downstairs, I could hear the rustling of paper. In the living room, I found Piet kneeling next to three large boxes of playbills. He rarely slept, and had taken to cataloging and rearranging his memorabilia.

Toby was standing by the fireplace, one arm outstretched, his hand curled around the edge of the mantelpiece. His head was bowed and his cheek pressed against his shoulder.

"He's sleeping?" I asked Piet.

He nodded.

Toby opened his eyes and looked from me to Piet. His expression was slightly angry, as if I had intruded upon something private.

"Where were we?" he asked Piet.

"Let me get you both some tea."

When the magician left, I led Toby to the couch, where he put his head on the arm and allowed me to curl up next to him.

"I miss you," I whispered.

"I'm sorry."

I stroked his arm and closed my eyes, listening to a creaky

bicycle pass outside. As we waited for Piet to bring the tea, I felt Toby's body relax.

Scrapbooks filled with black-and-white photos of magic shows, many of them at La Gaite, were open on the coffee table. "Maybe Theo is right, and I do live in the wrong time for magic." Toby put his head on my shoulder.

Piet shuffled into the room, carrying a tray of rattling cups and saucers and the pot of hot tea. "Let it sit for a moment. At this hour, I think it is best if the tea is strong." He switched on a lamp at the edge of the couch, bathing our faces in soft light. "We can sit here until nearly eight without it becoming much lighter," Piet said.

When the tea was ready, Piet filled our cups. "This house keeps me up at night as well," he said. "I have every illusion I built for Theo stored here. I was a traditional craftsman until I met Theo. Something about our work together brought my illusions to life in ways I couldn't imagine." He picked up one of the scrapbooks and flipped the page. "I built La Gaite for him. In a way, the entire theater is one illusion. No two visits there are the same."

"How did it work?" Toby asked, keeping his head on my shoulder.

"I'm not entirely able to explain it. I can tell you that I built secret doors and hidden hallways that Theo could shift with a flick of his imagination."

Now Toby sat up and took several of the scrapbooks onto his lap. He leaned in close as he flipped through the pages.

Piet shook his head. "You will not be able to find what you are looking for that way." He stood up. "I want to show you something. It's the last illusion I ever built. It's my best work," he added, "but also the most disappointing. Come." We followed Piet into his workroom.

The room was packed with all sorts of contraptions—ornate

birdcages, trompe l'oeil paintings, blades and saws, marble statues and fountains. Piet went to the window and pulled back the curtain, filling the room with the glow from the street lamp. A tall box, roughly the size of a sarcophagus, stood next to the window. It was shaped like a pagoda, with a peaked roof, and was painted with Japanese ornaments and characters.

"The Dissolving World," Piet said, laying a hand on the box.

"The Dissolving—," I began. And then I remembered the trick Theo had mentioned to us at the Castaway. The trick he'd wanted Toby to do. I looked at Toby. He was approaching the box, no trace of recognition in his eyes.

"Maybe this can wait until morning," I suggested, hoping to prevent Theo from having his way, at least for one more night.

But Piet and Toby were already standing in front of the illusion.

Unlike the rest of the illusions in the room, the Dissolving World looked new. The paint had not chipped. The wood had not splintered. I ran my hand over the decorations. "It's beautiful."

"She's painted to resemble the many pagodas found in Japan." Toby nodded.

"Remember those tricks where a magician seemed to conjure any image of his choosing onto a blank canvas?" Piet looked from me to Toby.

He nodded.

"For most, it was a trick of the light or a hidden dimension in the canvas. For others, like Theo, this was accomplished through those talents that I know you possess." He glanced at Toby. "I hope my old toy still obeys me, if only for a second."

Piet slid his hand down the side of the box until he reached a small gilded handle in the shaped of curved bamboo. He closed his eyes, then opened the door. "Follow me." Swirls of dust from inside the box were caught in the glow of the street lamp.

Toby and I exchanged looks. The box certainly wasn't big enough for all three of us. "After you," Toby said.

I stepped on the edge of the Dissolving World, nearly treading on Piet's heel. I could feel Toby pressed behind me. I fought back a sneeze. Piet took several steps forward into a space that hadn't been visible from the outside. Toby and I followed and stood at his side. Suddenly it felt as if all my pores had opened at once, then closed with a strange sucking sensation, as if I were being pulled into myself. My legs wobbled and my stomach lifted. I blinked, and in my mind's eye I saw a blur—the passing scenery from a high-speed train, the manic rewinding of a movie. I opened my eyes. The dust had vanished. The interior of the box was beginning to lighten. I felt dizzy and unsure of my footing.

Piet urged Toby to reach forward. Toby did so, and the darkness at the end of his finger began to take shape. His finger worked like a tuner on a old-fashioned TV, dialing the image into focus. I could smell cigarette smoke and whiskey. My legs found equilibrium.

And now we are standing in the back of a cabaret theater. It's La Gaite many years ago. The round tables with tasseled lamps are almost all occupied. The audience talks quietly as they sip their cocktails. Smoke is caught in the light of the lamps and swirls upward. I lace my fingers through Toby's and squeeze tight. I do not dare look at him. I worry that if I turn away, the stage might vanish.

"I think this is as far as we can go," Piet whispers.

He's right. When Toby and I try to step forward, we are blocked. The stage, the audience, and the show that is about to start are just out of reach.

The house lights dim. The stage lights come up, revealing a set that looks like a Victorian drawing room. The furnishings are familiar—murky landscapes in gilt frames, brocade furniture, and animals in bell jars. A long wooden table faces the audience at the front of the stage. Dead birds lie in ornate cages. Bronze candlesticks peek from behind curtains of melted wax. The lighting is designed so that the shadows stretch to the ceiling. A man strides onto the stage. He is wearing an exotic robe, the color of air. There are two dragons on the front, and when he turns, a phoenix on the back. Gloomy stage lights illuminate the man's face. It's Theo, many years ago. He walks to the right of the stage and raises his arms above his head, casting a shadow over the theater. He lifts the top of a bell jar that contains a stuffed weasel. The weasel comes to life. It's beady eyes glow red as it disappears into the wings.

Next Theo summons a hawk frozen on a withered branch. It flies toward the stage lights. A raven flutters out of a hanging cage. Animals thrash inside their domes and dioramas. They gather at the magician's feet. He ushers them into a giant fireplace at the center of the stage. From the dark interior of the hearth, their eyes glow. The only sound is the whisking of tails and the tapping of claws. From the tips of his fingers, Theo blows a fireball into the hearth. The flames highlight the audience with yellow and orange shadows. Then, with an explosion, the fire goes out. The entire theater is dark. We can feel Theo's presence as he steps into the center of the stage. A dark shadow on a dark stage, he opens the phoenix robe, revealing the yellow glow of his animals' eyes. Slowly and soundlessly, they slip down the magician's body and scurry into the wings. The lights come up. Theo is holding two rabbits.

There is a large glass canister sitting on a wooden table. Theo places the rabbits in the canister, then places the canister over a burner. He lights the burner. The flame grows until it obscures the rabbits entirely. Then smoke begins to rise from the canister. It takes the form of featureless smoke-silver rabbits. Soon the smoke-rabbits dissipate into the stage lights. The fire from the burner dies down. The glass canister is empty. Next to me, I feel Toby shiver.

The audience shifts in their seats, waiting for the return of the rabbits. There's a small commotion at the front of the theater. Two young men sitting near the stage begin whispering. One is slight with sandy hair. He begins pointing at the stage, indicating the place where the smoke-rabbits vanished. His companion, a larger man with a mane of bushy black hair, tries to calm his friend. The two spectators fall silent. The larger of the two turns to look at the back of the theater, and I recognize Leo.

The rabbits don't return. Theo moves on to his next illusion. He clears the wooden table of its bell jars and dioramas. Now an assistant steps from the wings. She's dressed in a white chiffon dress that trails behind her and obscures her hands. She lies down on the table.

Theo stands behind the table and raises his hands above his head. The tabletop begins to separate from its legs. It floats over the magician's head. He brings his hands together. The table spins. Then Theo claps, and I hear the thunder that shook the sanctum. A ball of fire shoots from his clasped hands and flies toward the floating table. It collides with the wood. The table ignites, flames spreading from the underside to the woman on top. Theo rubs his hands together, and the table spins. He continues to rub, and the flames orbit the spinning table like the rings of Saturn. The flames leaping from the table take the form of dragons that fly out over the audience. Then there is a crack, like the splitting of a log in a fire. And part of the wooden table crashes to the stage.

Theo whirls round. His back is to the audience. He extends his arms frantically toward the burning table. He's trying to bring it toward him. But it won't fall. Now a new scent fills the air: a smell, first of fabric, then hair, then flesh on fire. Before I can scream, Piet grabs my hand and steps forward. We do not step into the theater, but with the same sucking sensation, we are through the other side of the Dissolving World and in the workroom. The last thing I see as we go is the burning table fall into Theo's waiting hands.

The workroom was still cold, its air crisp and smoke-free. We heard the door of the Dissolving World shut behind us.

"How did you do that?" I asked, forgetting never to ask a magician about his tricks.

"How did I?" Piet smiled. "I didn't."

Toby and I waited.

"One of a magician's greatest tools is suggestion." He looked at Toby. "It was my memory mixed with your magic." He waited a moment.

Toby took a step back and sat on a rough workbench. "I—" He couldn't find the words.

"Yes." Piet nodded slowly. "You made it work. But not perfectly."

I opened the door of the box and looked inside. All I could see was the dusty space enclosed by four walls.

"My memory is also a dissolving world. I don't remember the details perfectly. And you have seen La Gaite only in ruin and in pictures." He joined Toby on the bench. "So, you cannot actually take us there."

"But it was right there," Toby said.

"I didn't build this box so you could look at another world. I built it so you could go there." Without further explanation, the oldest magician stood up and left us.

For a moment, Toby and I sat in silence.

"Now I understand why La Gaite felt so eerie when we were there," Toby said. "It really is a ghost town."

"I much prefer our version."

Toby said nothing. He was staring at the Dissolving World. "You know. A Wild West cabaret."

The magician nodded absently. His eyes lost focus, and I knew he was no longer thinking about the future.

Twelve

In the three days since Piet had taken us into the Dissolving World, Toby's skin had turned from its elegant alabaster to a pallid gray. From the moment he woke up and until dinner, he remained in the workroom, and often inside the box itself. Sometimes I sat at the worktable, listening to him rattling around in the finite space in the pagoda. Other times, a sudden silence told me he had slipped into a world of his imagining. At dinnertime, Toby would emerge, looking haggard. And when we went to bed, I knew that during the night I would lose him to the trick in Piet's workshop.

One morning when Toby was still asleep, I sneaked into the workroom first, planning to intercept him when he arrived. After a few hours, he appeared in the door, a cold cup of coffee in one hand. His hair stood on end, and his shirt was buttoned erratically. He took one step toward the Dissolving World.

"No," I said. "Not right now."

"Mel, please." Toby sat at the worktable. "You have no idea what it's like." He rubbed his hands together. "I see it over and over and can't do anything."

"What?" I knew the answer.

"I see you in the audience. I see myself looking at you. I see myself ignoring Greta until she's jumped in front of me." He paused. "I see her swift motion, the bullet flying, her collapsing at my feet. I can't stop it. I can't prevent it, but I can watch it."

"Stop looking. It's simple."

"I can't."

"You'll have to."

The magician shook his head.

"At some point, you will."

"Piet said that it could take us back. But I'm just watching the same reel rewind again and again. I can't get there."

"What happens if you get there?" I asked.

"I can save her."

We sat in silence for a moment. "It's only a trick, Toby. You'll only save her inside an illusion."

The magician stood up and approached the Dissolving World. "That will have to do."

I shook my head. "Let's get out of here. I'm going to visit Leo today, and you're coming."

Toby wrapped his hand around the gilded handle. "Just give me today."

"And then what?"

"I don't know. But give me one more day, and I'll make it work." He let go of the door and enveloped me in his arms. As he pressed his body to mine, I could feel a new angularity to his bones and an unnatural coolness to his skin. But when Toby kissed me, it was as if nothing had changed. His kiss sent me into the outside world, staying with me on my journey to Leo's.

Piet told me that Leo lived in a small town not far from Amsterdam. He suggested that I ride his bike there, and if the weather changed, I could take the train back. The cold air stung my nose and burned my lungs as I took off down the cobbled street. I rode until I came to the Amstel River, then followed the bike path out of the city. Soon the last of the glass office buildings disappeared and I entered a small park shaken from its winter sleep by the sharp sunlight. Just beyond the park, the Amstel widened, breathing a sigh of relief at having escaped its city confines. The water glittered icy-clear and lay as flat as glass. Along this section of the river, enormous gated mansions and small thatched cottages lined the bank. Behind these, a dense woods obscured the freeway and the modern apartment buildings that ringed the city. Old-fashioned houseboats were anchored at the water's edge. As I rode, I felt the river's current urge me forward past a grand hotel, a riding school, and a charming pancake house that was serving late afternoon lunch to a group of women on a bicycle tour. I rode faster, willing to follow the river to the open mouth of the sea.

The farther I went down the Amstel, the further back in time I seemed to go, until I believed that I would arrive at the Dutch golden age—that is how this hidden section of the city appeared, like a painting by Nicolaes Maes or Jan Steen. Eventually, the path brought me into a large clearing, where a windmill watched over the river—its latticed blades dividing and organizing the unblemished sky.

Later, I came to the town Piet mentioned. I followed the magician's directions until I came to an impressive wrought-iron gate onto which the words THE PEOPLE OF THE SOUTH were welded in ornate script. Through a stand of fir trees, I could make out the roof of a large villa. I pressed the bell and waited. Olivia had said that Leo's house was built by one of Holland's great spice traders during the country's golden age. It was foolish, but as I waited, I inhaled, hoping for a lingering note of cardamom or cinnamon. But all I smelled was the cold sting of damp November air and the pine-pitch of the trees.

In a few minutes, Olivia appeared. She was wearing overalls, clogs, and a long striped scarf that hung below her waist. "I'm so glad you made it," she said, kissing me three times. "We've all been wondering when you'd come. How are the magicians?"

"Old."

"Not your magician." She laughed.

"Not yet," I said. "I need a day off from their memories."

Olivia looped her arm through mine. "Well, you should have come sooner."

"You're probably right. I get stuck in the past in Piet's house, and it's hard to leave. Then I look up and the day is over."

Olivia turned and looked at the villa. "You've come to the perfect place. I'm cutting patterns now. For three-quarter-length shearling coats. Maybe later you can help me." She pinched my arm. "You know, tell me what the fabrics say."

"Of course," I replied, wondering why I hadn't indeed come sooner.

We followed a path through the pines and arrived in front of the villa. It was enormous—so wide, in fact, that standing in front of the main entrance, one found it impossible to take in the whole façade. The building was made of limestone, with bay windows stacked on top of one another and gabled windows protruding from the roof.

I started for the door.

"I'm going to take you around back," Olivia said. "To the garden."

I pulled my coat tighter against the chill.

"You'll be warm, don't worry."

At the end of the path through the pines, Olivia opened a small wooden gate, admitting us to a lawn that led from the back of the villa to the riverbank. In the middle of the lawn stood a bright yellow Bedouin tent. "The river runs along the property," Olivia explained, pointing past the tent. "In the summer, there are swans, but now I don't think you'll see any."

We had come to the tent.

"So, this is where I'm leaving you." Olivia lifted the flaps and pinned them back.

"Someone will bring tea. Make yourself at home. Leo will be down soon or sometime, I forget which."

I looked around, admiring the tent. It was made of hand-dyed and hand-painted canvas covered with exotic flowers. Although I couldn't identify their species, the botanical detail was astounding. I leaned in close. The heavy fabric smelled like sunlight. But the music that rose from the canvas was like nothing I'd heard before. The songs of most fabrics tend to be generic, a Muzak version of swing or a medley of arias, but the tent sang a specific, highly individual composition of Eastern and Western music. The longer I listened, the more carefully arranged its music appeared to be—a series of movements that rose and fell with the twisting flowers.

After a while, I turned to examine the interior of the tent. The floor was covered with brightly colored rugs, hand-dyed in wild approximation of Berber style. These rugs were also draped over two wooden chairs that stood below the tent's peak. Between the chairs was a low Moroccan table made of hammered metal. Two humming heat lamps emitted a pleasant orange glow and warmed the interior.

I sat in one of the chairs. It was surprisingly comfortable. Beneath it, I discovered a small footstool. With my feet on the stool and my head against the high back of the chair, my gaze slipped over the lawn and down to the river, where the water was perfectly framed by two tall pines. With half-closed eyes, I watched the winter-gray water for a while. Then I shut my eyes and let the warmth of the heaters, the colorful rugs, and the painted walls carry me off.

When I woke, Leo was sitting in the other chair. He was dressed in a long suede coat lined with fur. Beaded tassels dangled from the cuffs and collar. He wore a large onyx ring on one finger and a sweeping scarf with crystal beads.

"I'm sorry," I said.

"What have you done?" Now he laughed a full-bodied laugh that shook the tent. He spoke with a deep baritone voice that reminded me of storybooks and radio plays.

"I fell asleep."

Leo shrugged.

"This tent is so relaxing," I said, sitting up and taking my feet off the stool.

Leo waved a hand in my direction. "So, relax. I see you've escaped from those dingy magicians."

I nodded.

"They've sealed themselves in a world of magic."

"Which is sad, because they can hardly do magic anymore," I replied.

"But Toby can," Leo said with a wink.

"Toby is more like them than he realizes. His life is dominated by the past."

Leo shook his head. "For two years after Erik's disappearance, I tried to recapture our life together. It doesn't work."

"I saw you," I said. "I saw you and Erik."

Leo raised one of his bushy eyebrows and waited for me to continue..

"You were there the night Theo's assistant died."

"His wife."

I nodded. "In the front of the theater."

"Piet has photographs?"

I shook my head and stared over the lawn at the winter-dried grass running down to the blue-brown river. "It's an illusion," I said. "An illusion that lets you look into the past. That's where I saw you."

Leo clasped his large hands together and placed them on his stomach. He leaned back in his chair and closed his eyes. "As long as you are only looking at the past."

"For Toby, looking won't be enough."

Leo lowered his voice and bent toward me. He locked his eyes with mine. "You must pull Toby away from this trick."

I lifted the edge of one of the Berber rugs draped over my chair and examined the pattern. "Toby has had two accidents. He thinks this illusion of Theo's can reverse what he's done."

"What do you think?"

I shook my head. "Sometimes I think I'm as much to blame as he is."

"How is that possible?" Leo asked.

"Someone close to Toby once told me that there is something unstable in Toby's magic. She told me to warn him not to use people in his tricks until he understood this. I didn't bother passing her warning along. And then the night of his biggest show, he used both an assistant and a volunteer."

"And everything went wrong?"

I nodded.

"But that's not your fault."

"I'm not so sure."

"What makes you think he would have listened?" Leo stood up. "Don't dwell on the past. It is human to want to change things, but also foolish." The designer extended a hand to me. He wore several large rings with dark stones. "And remember, there are consequences to this kind of magic." I let Leo pull me to my feet. "There is something I want to show you before I lose you to Erik's studio."

We left the tent and headed into the gardens. "We've arranged these both by season and by smell," Leo said, pointing from one end of the garden to the other. Even in winter, the colors that burst from Leo's plants were more vibrant and exotic than those at the botanical garden. "There's a small citrus grove in that hothouse, and the grasses that grow around it are all lemon-scented." He showed me a sandy patch where he and Erik had planted Eastern spice plants and another area they'd dedicated to Mediterranean herbs. He told me that the plants that grew alongside the villa, underneath his bedroom window, were fragrant at night.

We left the manicured lawns and gardens and headed into the woods. Soon I could see a ramshackle building surrounded by chicken wire. From a distance it looked constructed of dozens of boxes piled on top of one another.

"What is that?" I asked.

"This is what I wanted to show you. It is something I cannot bear to part with."

He set off in the direction of the fenced enclosure. As we drew near, I realized that the boxes were actually dozens of stacked rabbit hutches. "Rabbits?" I asked, looking past the fence.

"Those are Erik's rabbit ghosts."

The hutches were empty.

"The rabbits were part of the reason Erik was drawn to Theo's magic. Each night, Theo made a rabbit disappear. Each night it was a different rabbit. Sometimes it was two rabbits. Other magicians would eventually have retrieved them from a sleeve or a top hat. Not Theo. His magic was a one-way street."

I nodded, remembering Theo's performance at La Gaite and the chill I felt when the rabbits vanished.

"Erik always wondered where the rabbits went. So he built homes for them if they came back."

I wound my fingers through the fence.

Leo removed my hand and held it. He looked me in the eye, "You know as well as I do that those rabbits are gone."

I nodded.

"After Erik disappeared, I started coming out here. I used to daydream that one day he'd reappear with his ghost rabbits." Leo shrugged. "But I cannot wait for him. There is no point." Leo continued up the path into the woods. "However, there is one thing of his that I do want brought back to life."

"His fabrics?"

Leo wrapped an arm around my shoulder, pulling me alongside him.

In a few moments, we came to a tiny saltbox house with shingle siding. "Erik's studio," Leo said, opening the door. Inside was a large drafting table and numerous art supplies, including a silk screen and several cameras. Fabric swatches were pinned to one wall.

Leo unlatched a large cabinet and pointed inside. "Silk, felt, wool, chamois—who knows," he said. I turned around, taking in the contents of the studio. "You can do whatever you like," Leo said.

"What do you want me to do?"

Leo looked at the contents of the cabinet. "Erik put so much into his textiles, it seems a shame that his absence should ruin them for the rest of us."

He took me by the shoulders. "Bring them to life. You said fabric sings to you."

"Yes."

"Well, take your time. I cannot bear the silence. Cut, sew, whatever you like." He paused and looked me in the eye. "Unless, of course, you don't want to."

I laughed. "I'd love to."

The designer stooped down and kissed my cheek. "I don't know what to expect. But I expect something great."

The moment the door closed, I pulled a stool from underneath the drafting table and looked out the window. A long thicket of ferns reached from the studio to the winter pond. Their fronds were thicker and rougher than their deciduous cousins. Beyond them, I could just make out the river. I closed my eyes and listened to the arboreal silence. Then I stood up and opened one of the large cabinets.

Bolts of hand-dyed, hand-printed, computer-printed, and embroidered textiles were immaculately folded and stacked from my feet to high above my head. I reached up and let my hand run down the bolts like a pianist testing a keyboard. After a moment, I sat down with my back against the bolts. Then I heard my brother's voice.

It was Max's land voice, dry and crystal clear, and it was rising from the bolts behind me. "Lapsed water baby," he said. "Mel melts the snow," he chanted. "But will she ever understand why?"

"Max?" I whispered.

"Mel who swam with a whale."

His voice was coming from the bottom of the pile. I reached my hand into the bolts, lifting and removing some of the fabric until the voice became clearer. "You should try it sometime. Sometime you should try to swim through the surface of the moon."

From the bottom of the pile, I pulled out a velvet. It was turquoise with dark blue and green paisleys. It had the colors of the open sea, from the crystal blue water that hovers at the surface to the murky green that lives in the lightless middle ocean. "Someday you'll join the boy who swam through the moon."

"You know," another voice above me chimed in, "you know, I never really believed in magic. It's totally for little kids. Like, who really thinks that a rabbit can get pulled from a hat, right?"

I leaned into the cabinet.

"But I'd do anything not to have to wear that stupid uniform anymore. Who wants to be remembered for working in a diner? That might be cool enough for my friends, but I went out with a bang. I was the girl who died center stage. That's how you live forever. Wasn't it amazing? Wasn't it magic?"

"Yes," I repeated despite myself. "Yes, Greta, it was amazing."

"You gotta have guts to do what I did. Sure, I'm gonna miss the prom and stuff like that. But I'll get more pages in the yearbook than anyone else in the history of the school."

Greta's voice was chirping from above my head. I stood on my toes and pulled out the bolts until I came to a yellow cotton printed with red polka dots. As I withdrew the fabric, I heard a distinctive gum-snap. "I wonder what sorta stuff my friends are up to."

Then Sandra spoke up. "Aren't you the lucky one to tame a magician. Never seen anyone hold on to her man as well as you did. Had all the Vegas ladies in knots. He's a keeper, all right. Just don't let him wander off. Might transform into I-don't-know-what and never come back." A deep sigh resounded from a coral pink cotton-spandex blend. "Now wouldn't that be a shame."

"Loving water," Max's voice whispered from my feet, where I

had placed the paisley velvet bolt, "doesn't mean you need to ignore everything else. Maybe I loved water a little too much," he sighed. "I didn't know what else to do. It claimed me first." I reached back into the cabinet and withdrew six more bolts in variegated blues.

"Snow," my mother's voice cried from a white sateen. "Don't forget where you come from. It's dangerous to forget where you come from. Look at the mess you got yourself into in the desert. You might as well spend your life on drugs as spend time in a desert. All that heat melted your brain." The white sateen clicked its tongue. "Might as well get hooked on drugs."

I gathered the bolts in my arms, listening to the voices from my past, and some I thought were calling to me from my future. But none of the fabrics spoke in Toby's sawdust circus voice. I placed the fabric around the drafting table and wondered what was going to happen next. The voices kept talking, their words overlapping, swirling together. And finally, when I feared their stories and explanations would deafen me or drive me mad, I picked up my scissors.

I've been here and there in my life with fabrics, but they had never spoken to me so clearly and never had they spoken with familiar voices. My fingers were thrumming. The velvet paisley fabric was in my hand. And then I heard my brother's voice once more as the paisleys took the shape of waves, crashing over one another, each one dissolving inside the next. They became the surf and the undertow. They were the currents and the tides. Max ducked and swam inside them. He dived and crested on the worktable. He submerged for minutes before coming up for air. The paisleys became rivers, then my family's river. They became creek beds and estuaries. They transformed into harbors. And in all of these, I saw Max swimming, riding over the rounded crests of the paisleys, diving down into their valleys, and then ascending to their pointed tips. Several times, I thought that I'd lost him in the whirls and whirlpools of the pattern. But he always resurfaced, bobbing up and down on another shape. And then in the middle of the clearest blue of the pattern, Max waved goodbye, pointed deep into the fabric, and disappeared.

While I had been watching my brother, I had been cutting the blue fabrics, reducing them to squares and rectangles of various sizes. I found a needle, threaded it, and without regard for pattern or style, began to sew. My hands went their own way. The needle struck its own rhythm as it wove in and out of the fabric.

I have no idea how long I sewed, but soon I had created an underwater patchwork world. I shook off my thimble and dropped the needle. I held the quilt to the light and stared at the motionless water created and trapped by my hands. The paisley print that spoke with Max's voice flowed in and out of a host of different blues and greens. Among these was a chintz printed with algaelike flowers and a brocade with twisting plants that could be mistaken for seaweed. In addition to the familiar waters of my youth—the Delaware River and all the pools I had never dared to swim in—I found dozens of bodies of water that I hadn't ever known or imagined.

I peered closely at this quilt and imagined joining Max's water to the fabrics from my last hotel job. I reached under the drafting table and withdrew several red bolts. Some of them whispered with Eva's faraway voice; others simply sounded like the windwhipped sand. Soon these were cut and ready to be joined to the oceanic blues. First, the desert of Tonopah and Intersection where I had met the magician and watched him work his imperfect magic. This was the desert where we had been blown together along with the sand and tumbleweed. These patches were the dirty red of distant mesas and sacred kivas. They were red with the burn of the relentless sun and the blood of the gum-snapping girl. The fabrics were scratchy and rough—coarse linens, poor felts, even frieze. While I had been watching the colors and the textures of the desert, she appeared—the yellow-and-red-polka-dotted Greta. I looked down at my hands. I could feel the familiar depressions from the scissors loops on my thumb and middle finger. My fingers didn't stop. A new desert began to emerge with all the colors of Las Vegas. Boisterous sequins, relentless polyvinyls, plush terry velours exploded from my scissors. My needle, threaded with fire-engine-red thread, began to join these newcomers to the scratchy fabrics of the first desert. I strip-pieced the pattern that the wind etched into the sand. The desert that I was piecing together hummed with the voices of the fabrics I was using. Finally, my hands shook off the thimble and dropped the needle. I looked up. Night had fallen. The river had been claimed by the dark. The only light was a distant glow from the villa.

I left the table and ran toward the house, passing the ghost rabbit enclosures. I found Olivia sprawled on a sea of shearling in the main hall in front of a roaring fire.

I grabbed her hand. "You have to come."

She staggered after me. I pulled her through the woods, her scarf catching on branches and brambles as we went. We arrived at the studio, breathless.

"What?" Olivia asked, her hands on her knees.

"Look." I pointed at the quilt I'd draped over the worktable.

Olivia straightened up. "What is it?"

"A quilt."

She bent over the mysterious patchwork. "Where did it come from?"

"I made it."

Olivia gave me a look. "When?"

"Today." I rubbed my sewing hand. "Or maybe it made itself."

"These are Erik's fabrics. How?"

I shook my head. "I don't know."

"It's wonderful. There's some rhythm to these patches that I don't get. I know it's there, like a song you can't quite remember. When the melody is just out of reach."

I took the quilt from Olivia and spread it on the floor. I motioned for her to sit next to me on the ground. I wrapped my hand through hers and led her fingers to the first square of the quilt. "It's my story, my time line," I said. "The only thing missing is Toby." I squinted at the quilt and wondered when Toby would appear. In none of the squares that described my desert life could I find a trace of the magician. His actions, his desert magic, were visible, but Toby himself was absent. "But the story is there anyway."

"Story?"

I opened my fingers. Olivia did the same. Keeping my hand on top of hers, I began to trace the patches of the quilt. "I married Tobias Warring at the Silver Bells All-Nite Wedding Chapel in Las Vegas," I began. Then the story flowed from my lips as seamlessly as the quilt had emerged from my fingers.

When I was finished, Olivia curled up on the patchwork. "What comes next?" she asked in a distant voice that seemed to be nearly lost in a dream.

"I don't know," I said as the quilt carried us off to sleep.

Thirteen

I returned to Piet's just after breakfast. The house was silent with an air of abandonment, like school corridors during the summer. I noticed that Piet's walking stick was missing. I was not surprised to see Toby's coat. Something told me that the magician was both home and away.

I was curled up in bed with the quilt that I had taken with me from Nevada, wondering how these patches would connect to those I'd left behind at Leo's, when Toby appeared.

"Still sleeping?" he asked.

I was dressed in yesterday's clothes with raindrops threaded in my untidy hair, but Toby seemed unaware that neither of us had slept in the attic yet. I nodded, not wanting to explain that he was not the only one who didn't make it into our attic last night.

"Come," Toby said, extending his hand.

I hesitated.

"You said I had one more day to make it work." Toby paused.

His face relaxed, and I saw relief rise to the surface, overtaking exhaustion. "I did."

We stood at the entrance to the Dissolving World. I looked at him uncertainly as he opened the door. Toby smiled and urged me forward. We took two steps into the box, which stretched out before us as before. Soon I felt that same inward suction, followed by a massive release, as if all my cells were being packed together and then redistributed. Inside my eyes, I saw the snow-blind blur of TV static, and my ears rang with dozens of weak radio frequencies all fighting for stability. I lurched to one side.

Toby caught me. "Open your eyes," he said.

I braced myself against his arm and did as I was told.

We are standing on the banks of the Delaware River. Not the part behind my parents' house. Somewhere farther upstream. It's cold out. A spiderweb of ice is starting to form over the river.

"Go on," Toby says, "You can touch the water."

I shake my head. I never go near the river until it's frozen over. Not even inside a magic trick.

The magician hands me a coat. "It's your favorite time of year."

"It is," I say with a shiver. But there's something strange about the river. As I watch the current slip underneath the thin ice, I realize that it makes no sound. In fact, there isn't any sound at all. I breathe deeply, exhale loudly, to shatter the quiet.

"I don't know where you live," Toby says as we begin to walk along the riverbank.

I squint downstream. "Ten miles from here, I guess. I'm not sure." "I can't believe it," I say. "How did you do this?"

"It was easy. I just needed a little practice."

As we walk, our steps are the only noise. No cars rumble across the rusted bridges. There's not even the shatter of fresh ice colliding on its way downstream.

"Where is everyone?" I ask.

"Who did you expect?"

"Where is everything?"

"It's all here. What I remember of it."

The silent river makes me shiver again. Toby thinks it's the weather that's making me cold. He wraps an arm around me.

"Where are we going?"

"Home."

Toby and I tuck our hands into his jacket pocket. Eventually we turn away from the river and walk across a small backyard to a one-story house. An enclosed porch, twice the size of the house, extends from the left of the building. As we draw near, I see that the porch is crowded with four baby grand pianos.

"Your home?" I ask Toby.

The magician nods.

He slides back one of the screen doors and the glass door behind it, and we are in Toby's childhood home.

Like the river outside, the house is not just silent, but emptied of sound. Toby leads me past the pianos, three black and one white. I want to stop and examine them, but it's clear that the magician wants to move on. We climb three steps covered in mustard shag and are in the main house.

"This is the day I left," Toby says, peering into the kitchen. Orange ceramic canisters in the shape of pumpkins line a shelf. "Ernest had already died. And Pia was making stew. It was cold for March."

On the stove is an orange pot. Next to it on the counter, a cutting board with vegetables and a knife. But there is no smell of cooking. I turn around, expecting Toby's stepmother to return to the stove.

"I think it took her a few days to notice I'd gone. She'd stopped whatever she was doing in here to bang out some Beethoven. At the crescendo, I ran away."

"To join the circus?"

"Pretty much."

I try to picture the house filled with music. I want to imagine Beethoven pouring from the music studio, disrupting the unnatural silence. Toby senses my discomfort. "It was always like this. Music or silence. The silence was unbreakable."

We leave the kitchen. The living room has a conversation pit in front of a small fireplace. Framed photographs on the mantel show a small woman with her arm around the shoulders of several different children—none of them Toby. The living room has a subtle musical theme—a lamp made out of a clarinet, cocktail napkins with bass clefs, brass paperweights in the shape of trumpets. There is nothing to suggest the presence of a teenage boy. There is only music and its absence.

Toby is still looking at the mantel. "Pia kept exactly one photo of her husband after he died. And one of me."

"Playing the piano?"

"I was terrible."

At the back of the living room, near the sliding glass doors that lead to the yard, there's a well-polished dining table. "Holidays only," Toby says, pointing at the table. "And recitals."

We pass the table and enter a small room at the far end of the house.

I clap my hands. The sudden noise startles me. "Your room."

"You're the first girl I've brought home."

"Ever?"

"Absolutely," Toby says with a wink. "And my parents are away."

As I knew it would be, Toby's room is unlike the rest of the house. There are several books on a table next to the bed. One is a *child's edition of* Gray's Anatomy. *The shelves that line the walls are cluttered with objects—from someone else's family photograph to a small antique hand mirror. I pick up the mirror.*

"The collection of a young magician?" I ask.

"All of it," Toby says, gesturing toward the shelves. He picks up a set of Russian matryoshka dolls. He opens the largest doll and finds the smaller one inside, then a smaller doll inside that, until he comes to a doll so small, it doesn't open. He replaces all the dolls in order, then reopens the outermost one, only to find that it is empty. "Pia loved these. There's a set in every room. I don't think she knew what she was getting into when she gave them to me." He places the nested dolls on the shelf and lifts the top half of the outermost one again. The smaller dolls hop out of the big one like an orderly army. "I spent hours with these. It made my stepmother nuts when she'd open one to find it filled with pennies or soap bubbles."

"I always wondered whether there's something hidden in the smallest one," I say.

"There might be."

Among the knickknacks are two identical blocks. Toby and I notice them at the same time—though, of course, he must have known they were there.

"My blocks." The magician gathers them into his hand. Then he flops back onto the single bed and beckons me to join him.

"And now I have a girl in my bed," he says. I can't see Toby's face, but I know he's smiling.

I close my eyes and feel Toby's hands start to move through the air. There's a comfortable rhythm to his movements, like a pianist playing a favorite piece in the dark. With his shoulder, Toby gently nudges my chin. I look up and see his blocks floating over the bed. With one arm wrapped around my shoulder, he reaches into the air. His fingers fan wide as he conducts the blocks. They orbit each other. They inscribe invisible spirals and loop into figures of eight.

Then he snaps his fingers. One of the blocks disappears. The other still floats. The hand around my shoulder wiggles, and I feel the pressure of smooth wood.

Toby tosses this block into the air, and together the small wooden cubes resume their dance. Sometimes the blocks become one. Sometimes they multiply. Sometimes they disappear and then reappear between my feet, beneath the small of my back. I want the trick to go on forever.

When it seems the blocks have gone for good, Toby lets his hand fall to his side then reaches over, pulling me on top of him. Next he covers my mouth with a kiss that fills the emptiness of the Dissolving World. The kiss breathes life into the silent objects staring at us from the shelves. And in this timeless world, this kiss lasts so long, I fall asleep, perhaps for hours. When I wake, the blocks are back on the shelf. It is quiet again.

Toby stands up and pulls me to him. "Let's go."

"Where?"

"To your house."

"Ten miles?"

"Distances can be as close or as far as you wish," Toby replies.

"How will you know which one is my house?" I ask as we step outside. The winter trees are swaying silently in the silent wind.

"You will tell me."

How can you describe a visit to a place that exists in someone else's imagination? Once we leave Toby's part of the river and head downstream, details become fuzzy or misaligned—the rapids are out of place, a bridge is too far north. But others are perfect, like the boathouses I'd always admired when I was young. We are walking out of the magician's memory and into his imagination.

"Tell me about your house," Toby reminds me.

I begin by describing the porch that overlooked the river. I tell

Toby about the leaky roof, the unsealed basement, and the sunken picnic table. I describe the rusted iron gate that led to the small path down to the riverbank. I tell him how my bedroom was next to Max's. There was a drainpipe between them. That was how Max escaped at night to swim with whales or whatever else he did. In the middle of my story, I turn to Toby. "How do we get out of here?" The silence is so heavy that I'm worried I cannot crawl out from under it.

Toby doesn't reply.

"I told you that I always liked it best when it was cold. From my bedroom window, I'd watch the river freeze." As I'm talking, the air gets colder.

The riverbank changes. And soon a white house with a porch and a drainpipe is visible uphill to my right. From a distance, it looks like my house. But some of the details are blurry. I understand that unless I'm clearer in my description, we can't approach it. I also know that like the rabbit hutches, my house is empty. It's not just empty; it's filled with emptiness. The house both comforts me and makes me homesick.

I turn away. While we've been talking, the river has frozen over. The ice is thick enough to drive on.

"Now?" Toby steps onto his Delaware.

I follow. I look upstream and downstream. We have the river to ourselves.

"So what do you think?" Toby asks, opening his arms wide, trying to encompass all that he has created in the Dissolving World.

"I don't know what to think. I don't know if it's real."

"At this moment, it's real."

Carefully we walk along the frozen river. I miss the low groan of shifting ice. But I don't mention this to Toby.

"The last time I walked on the Delaware was the afternoon before

Max left for the second time." I kick the ice, testing its solidity. "He hated winter. He always thought the river was trapped by the ice. Somehow that day I forced him to come with me."

It is hard to imagine that my walk with Max along the frozen river took place roughly where Toby and I are standing. Maybe because Max left the next day, every sound, every detail of the river during that walk is still clear to me. I remember the low moan from the ice that punctuated our conversation. I remember how long a car had idled on the iron bridge or where I was standing when an ice skater fell nearby.

"Ice makes the river blind, Max told me. I told him it made it safe." I explain to Toby that Max and I had this disagreement every winter. Then I look down at the ice and for the first time, I think that Max was right, the river is blind. But this is not the real river, I remind myself.

"We can leave whenever we want?" I ask Toby for the second time.

"You want to leave?"

I shake my head. "I just don't want to stay forever."

I imagine a hint of disappointment crossing Toby's face. I kiss him with cold lips. "I knew that I couldn't keep Max out on the ice for very long. He felt suffocated by the trapped water. He kept telling me how dangerous ice is. Then he reminded me that my birth had melted the snow. Melt Snow. He said it over and over. I put my hand over his mouth to silence him. He was so pale then. A pale boy against the pale ice. He had been slipping away from us for so long. He looked like an underwater sea creature. Then he stepped in front of the sun. And for an instant, the light eclipsed him and Max vanished." I spun in a circle on the ice. "Of course, he was still next to me. And he still wanted to go back to the house. I agreed, but only if we explored a jagged inlet where the frozen river wound through a collection of rocks and trees."

As I expected, as soon as Toby and I arrive at the riverbank, the rocks and trees are there and the frozen river is laced between them. The inlet is not exactly as it was in my memory. But it's close.

"This is my favorite place on the river," I tell Toby. "At least it was. When the river was frozen, I imagined that with all the rocks peeking out and the tree roots just beneath the surface, I was looking at the surface of the moon."

"Isn't that what your brother was looking for?"

I nod. "But not in winter. Max was done with the river. And he headed to the shore. I ran in the opposite direction, back into the center of the ice." Toby and I return to the middle of the river. "I kept calling his name. All I heard in response was 'Melt Snow. Melt Snow.'" I paused. "Max was walking up the path. He was in a red coat climbing up a small brownish hill." I closed my eyes for a minute, pretending that the house up the hill is really my house. "I held my arms up in the air. Max didn't turn around until . . ." I stop talking. But before I know it, I'm finishing the story. "He heard the crack. It was like a spinal snap as the ice opened and I fell in."

The river trembles. The ice beneath my feet starts to move.

"Toby, no."

With one hand, he's reaching out for something only he can see. The ice parts. I fall in as Toby grabs my hand and pulls me through the other side of the Dissolving World.

The cold water stung my feet and legs as I slid onto the floor of the workroom.

"I'm sorry," Toby muttered. "I didn't know. I just wanted to give you ice and sunlight."

I wrapped an arm around him. "It's all right." I took a deep breath. My mind was still on the frozen river.

"It's just a trick," Toby said, patting the box. "Not real."

But I had fallen. My head was numbed, my arms and legs

would not pull me back to the surface. In the darkness, a whole world had emerged—mysterious rock formations, intricate underwater plants swaying in the current, even, I imagined, schools of slippery fish gliding past. I'd rolled over and stared at the distant, ice-blurred world above. I don't know why I didn't panic. Then I'd opened my eyes to see a long shadow stretched on top of the ice. Max's face had peered into the crack. His long white arms had reached into the water and pulled me out.

Fourteen

As Max and I got older, his nighttime departures became more frequent. He would slip down the drainpipe three or four times a week. My parents, heavy sleepers, never noticed his nocturnal disappearances. But I could detect the slightest movement in my brother's bedroom. Driven by his swim team discipline, Max went to bed every weeknight at ten. Just after eleven, the rattle of the chain on his bedside lamp told me that he had gone to sleep. I'd wait a few minutes, until I could hear the first bass notes of his deepening breath, and creep into his room, slide into the empty chair at his bedside, adjust the chair's angle toward the window, and make sure that Max was safe inside his dreams. On the nights when the rain was riling the sleeping river, I shut the window next to his bed to protect him from the water's call. Just after midnight, my vigil ended. I'd readjust the chair and walk out of the room, keeping my eyes on my brother until the last possible moment, memorizing the shape of his sleep. But I was always an imperfect guardian, for I knew that after I left, he would wake up and vanish into the night.

When I learned about the whale and the purpose of Max's night outings, my own sleep started to come quicker and snatch me away faster. Soon my vigil grew shorter and less diligent. The beep of my brother's alarm at 1 A.M., the opening of his window, his descent along the vines and drainpipes, the soft thump of his feet on the grass, and his eventual return a couple of hours later were camouflaged by my dreams.

By the time Max entered his final year in high school, he had metamorphosed into a strange sea creature. His skin was not the healthy tanned hue of a beach bum, but pale and translucent, an odd bluish white that came from spending too much time underwater. He passed through our rooms carried on his own current. His appearances at the dinner table or at picnics in the backyard were fleeting. He often disappeared from family outings, lured by a nearby river or lake. Max slipped away gradually. Until the day after I fell under the ice—then he vanished altogether.

After that, the house seemed to shrink inside its foundations. We circled around his room, his chair, his pile of flippers and bathing suits. During the first days of his absence, I blamed myself for his escape. He had vanished on my watch. After many false starts, the moment that I had trained for had come and I had let my brother slip away. I waited for him to call or write, but grew bored with my vigil. It was hard, I learned, to create an engaging routine out of absence—out of the phone that didn't ring, the mail that didn't come, the empty bedroom that never creaked. And when the quiet of Max's room began to lull me to sleep rather than keep me awake, I stopped listening for my brother's return. I knew not to make the same mistake twice, not to sink into a myopic observation of Max, or of his absence. So I began to look elsewhere, at the interlacing branches on the trees, at the new tiles our mother ordered for the kitchen, at the school windows streak-stained with steam from hissing radiators. And one day I noticed that I wasn't waiting for Max at all. This might sound heartless, absorbing Max's disappearance into the everyday. But it became clear to me that, in the absence of a coherent or pleasant pattern to his disappearance, I had jumped the gun once again. Max's leaving was not the vanishing I had been dreading since the night he jumped into the river. He would wash ashore somewhere.

Two months after Max left, his correspondence started. At the beginning, his letters were stubborn and jerky. His first postcard came from Florida, where he was working with a group of marine biologists in the Everglades, studying plant life. Two weeks later, we got a letter saying that he would be sailing up the coast, creep-ing under piers and crawling along the bottoms of ships to exam-ine the effects of pollution on barnacles. As Max slipped further underwater, shrugging off dry land for the deep sea, his letters be-gan to arrive in waves. After barnacles he dived deeper to study the sleep patterns of flounder and halibut. Max began to live up-side down, his feet pointing toward the sky and his eyes combing the cool darkness of the lightless sea. He was a mountaineer whose thrill came from reaching the lowest point. Max described his undersea world with cartographer's clarity, painting maps of sea caves and the interlacing networks of tidal beds.

Max described the different sounds of the deep ocean—the heavy murmur a hundred feet down, the light buzz that hovers around large reefs, the delicate whistle that skims along the sur-face. He believed that he could hear a storm in the distance as it drummed back and forth between the waves. He told us how mollusks and seaweed tasted fresher when eaten in the sea and that eating an oyster underwater was like kissing a mermaid.

Every so often, Max promised to come home. But we knew

he wouldn't. Somehow he was always buffeted by the tides before he reached our shores. We grew accustomed to his excuses and deferrals. Then Max called to say he was in Costa Rica and would arrive in Bermuda for an open-sea swimming competition the following morning. The next day, a plane ticket was waiting for me in our mailbox.

Max's letters had described several of these extreme swims, these Tidal Roars, as they were called. Held two or three times a year, depending on conditions, the contests summoned competitors to battle the currents of the toughest water—Hawaii, South Africa, the Philippines. In his letters, Max had mentioned huge swells, waves that loomed like houses, tunnels that could hold a city block. He described the blackout pressure of the water crashing over his body and the vacuum suck of the waves pulling him backwards.

When I remember Bermuda, I prefer to think of its oddly tangible nighttime sky. When the sun falls away, the horizons pull in tight and seal the island beneath the dome of the approaching stars. Then the earth's curve swells, pushing the land higher, so that it seems you could reach up and pull down one of the passing clouds or comb your fingers through the gray velvet of the darkened sky. Nighttime in Bermuda is like being trapped inside a lightless snow dome, the lapping of the water from all sides confirming your confinement. But at the first leak of light, the seal breaks, the sky recoils, and everything bursts into blue—a long call and response between turquoise water and azure sky.

I took a taxi to the hotel and flopped on the bed, listening to the rhythmic whip of the fan blades as I willed my body to cool. Eventually, I crept into the hallway and tiptoed to Max's room. I crouched down, my ear to the keyhole, held my breath, and listened. At first, all I could hear was the rolling of the waves in the bay outside the window Max had flung open. Short-long, short-long the waves arrived at the dock, licking the cruise ship and jostling the small boats anchored opposite the hotel.

The door was open. Max knew I would come. Against the languid backdrop of the waves, his breath was deep and melodious. A hot wind was blowing the curtains, and there, almost floating on top of the sheets, was Max. He slept on his stomach, his face turned toward the door, his arms and legs spread like the outline of a crime scene. The wind lifted his hair. He had lost the solidity of his swim-team days. His limbs had strengthened and dried like driftwood. And like driftwood, all the unnecessary bumps and muscles were sanded away.

When I returned to my room, I could not sleep. The dry cool of the air conditioner parched my throat, and the machine's rattling cycle chased my sleep. Having used up all the cool spots on the pillows, I gave up and propped myself up in bed to wait for morning and for Max. I stared at the door, willing it to open, but my eyes let me down, and I slept.

A sliver of light was trickling underneath the curtains, streaking the floor with a single stripe of sun. I flattened the pillows underneath my head and tried to recapture sleep. As I did, gathered into a dream like a fish in a fisherman's net, my cheek met with a damp patch on the pillow. The last strains of an unfamiliar water song were echoing in my ears. Max had come and gone.

The boat for spectators who wanted to watch the Tidal Roar left from the pier opposite the hotel. I went aboard and rode four miles out to sea, where the race began. My fellow passengers were a ragtag bunch of extreme sportsmen, reddened by the sun and roughened by the sand, and they whooped and hollered each time a wave broke over the prow of the boat. I heard Max's name spoken several times as the likely winner.

It took us almost an hour to navigate our way to the start boat. The water was no longer the vibrant blue and green I had seen from the airplane. Dark patches began to bubble up from the bottom of the sea and spread out like a lazy inkstain. While I examined these puddles, I sensed something cool and still hovering above the choppy water, something as placid and motionless as a fish eye. It was Max. As I watched the reflection of the start boat bobbing upside down on the white-capped waves, I saw my brother arrive on the deck—a pale blue figure among a crowd of sun-dyed surfers. A jellyfish among the dolphins. I watched him, distorted by the waves, bend and curve into impossible contortions. And I realized that I was not watching a reflection but seeing the actual ebb and flow of the underwater Max. It was his aboveground self that was the reflection—the unreal distortion.

"Max!" I yelled, looking from the water to the boat itself. "Max!"

My brother lifted his head and stared in my direction.

"Max!" I cried, fighting the sound of the motors and the waves.

Then almost without moving, he dived into the water and disappeared—a wave resettling into the sea. For an instant, his head broke the surface and I imagined that he called my name. Then he vanished.

The swimmers entered the water after Max, and the race began. As we waited for them to return, the waves began to grow, slapping harder against the side of the boat and pulling the prow deeper into the darkening sea.

"Swimmer! Swimmer!" someone cried, nearly dropping his binoculars.

"Swimmer."

Everyone jumped up.

"Ten bucks that's Max," someone behind me called.

But as the exhausted swimmer pulled into view, cresting and crashing the waves, I could tell it wasn't Max. Max would arrive with ease, slipping through the water without trying to subdue it. The panting swimmer was dragged on board. The winner rolled onto his back, lay still for a moment, and then pumped his fists in the air. "Some water," he bellowed, coughing and sputtering. "You've got no idea where it's taking you. Fifteen-footers. Beautiful black on the inside." He wrapped himself in a towel. "You know," he said quietly as he leaned against the railing of the boat, "I've never seen it so beautiful out there. Like a sapphire city."

Two more splashes broke through the surface. Neither was Max. Nor was Max with the pair who had to be rescued by a Jet Ski. The penultimate swimmer arrived on the horizon. When he was pulled on board, he fell in a heap. His eyes were panicked. He panted and heaved, expelling water from his lungs. After five minutes, he was able to speak. "That was rough. Beautiful, though. I took a beating, but it was worth it." He let his head drop back against the deck. Five seconds later, he bolted upright and looked around him. "Hey, where's Max?"

"Not in yet. Probably taking one of his long routes," one of the rescued swimmers suggested.

The other swimmers laughed.

"I saw him out there," the final swimmer said. "We both got pulled way off course by this monster. Swallowed us whole right near the turn. It was sort of strange. Max stopped swimming and started treading water, looking out at another monster building in the distance."

His words flowed away, and I felt a spark of fear. If the other swimmers had seen an indescribable beauty at the water's surface, Max would have certainly known about caves and pockets of wonder deeper inside it. The water's call was so loud that day, even those who didn't speak its language had heard its voice. But such enticements were lost on me, and all I heard was the victorious laugh of the ocean.

This was the event I had been waiting for—an oceanic swallow, not a simple disappearance into a rainstorm. Max had been practicing for ages, seeking the combination of current and comfort that had borne him downriver, asleep and unharmed. And all the nights of water whispers, the drowned dreams, had prepared me for his final swim. He had painted a picture for me of his future—a home he knew I would never visit.

I should have told the captain to turn back, that it was pointless to try to reel my brother in. Instead I remained silent, staring into the storm. The CB crackled. Our driver informed the start boat that Max was missing. The coast guard was alerted. Two hours passed. A tour boat radioed to report that Max had passed it five miles farther out, a solitary swimmer cresting the waves. A search party was dispatched. But I knew that by now Max would be looking for his underwater dinner, his mermaid kiss of oysters, his salad of kelp and seaweed. Later, he would bed down on his massive water bed and be rocked to sleep. Night fell. A fisherman's voice crackled over the CB. Max had slipped past him in the dark water. He said the moon had broken through the clouds as my brother passed, a solitary swimmer centered in its reflection. I felt the ocean rise up over the edge of the boat, and I reached out to accept it—a good-bye kiss.

Fifteen

The chill from falling through the ice remained with me for days. I stayed in bed, shivering despite the tea and medicine Toby brought me. While he tended to me, a collection of objects from his past appeared, refuse from his explorations of the Dissolving World. I would wake to find his children's editon of *Gray's Anatomy* or the nesting dolls from his bedroom next to my pillow. His high school yearbook materialized between the sheet and duvet. Other objects that I did not recognize formed a trail from the bed to the door. The eerie overflow from Toby's other world amplified the cold that filled me from the inside out. When it became unbearable, I would slip downstairs, where Piet would build a roaring fire.

Toby often sat with me there. He'd hold me in his arms until I stopped shivering. As he did so, I noticed small changes in his appearance. Toby's edges seemed to have blurred, and the sharp contrasts between his hair and skin had faded. I looked down at the hands wrapped around my body. Moons had appeared in his thumbnails, and pale suns set across the screens of his fingernails. From the jagged tree roots that I loved, a smooth pair of alabaster hands had emerged. I took one of his hands in mine. "Do you miss the way your hands used to look, all dry and desert tough?"

"Miss?" Toby replied, holding me tighter.

"You lost them somewhere between Nevada and Amsterdam."

Toby fluttered his fingers. "I could find them, I guess."

I shook my head. "Leave it." I ran my fingers over his, reminded of how Max's new body had broken though his childhood shell.

Toby squeezed me tightly, and for a moment his strength subdued my shivering. "I summoned this cold. I should be able to banish it."

"Some of your tricks are one-way streets," I said. "You still won't accept that."

Toby shook his head. "It doesn't have to be that way now." He turned my head so we were eye to eye. "Let's go somewhere warm."

"It's winter."

"Not everywhere."

"No, Toby. I'm not going back in there."

Sometimes, I slept in the living room while Piet passed through during the night, keeping the fire alive for me. On one such night, Theo and Lucio arrived and settled in the kitchen to wait for Toby. I fell back asleep, waking later at the sound of my husband's voice.

"I didn't know you were coming."

"It's been a while," Lucio said. "We're wondering if you're ready to show some of your incomprehensible magic."

"That depends on what you want to see."

"There is one thing we are particularly anxious to see," Theo said. "Piet says the Dissolving World is keeping you busy."

Toby was silent.

"You make it work?" Lucio asked.

"That depends what you mean," Toby replied. "It takes me many places. But there are still some that are forbidden."

"Ah," the mentalist replied. "In time, it will all work out."

"I don't know," Toby said. "No matter what I accomplish there, when I emerge, it is as if I've done nothing."

"That is one of the rules of the Dissolving World," Theo said. I heard him uncork a bottle and fill three glasses. "Piet built the trick as a sideshow piece, something we could bring on tour with us. We planned to set it up outside the theater to lure people into our shows by giving them a glimpse of another world." He paused for a moment. "Of course, this is the most pedestrian use of the contraption. What the Dissolving World can really do is make that other world a reality." I heard him sip his drink. "There are limitations. Once the magician who has conjured this other world, whether from imagination or from memory, leaves it, that world is shattered and everything returns to the way it was before he stepped into the box."

"All magic has its limitations," Toby murmured.

"Or it wouldn't be magic. It would be sorcery," Theo replied. "You can save that girl over and over inside the box. But once you return, it's as if you never went back."

"Of course," Lucio said, "there are other small consequences of going back and meddling with the past. None of them is important at first. But the more you go and return, the greater these will be."

I thought of the detritus from Toby's explorations of the Dissolving World that was filling our attic room.

"The thing is," Toby began, "I can't even get close enough to save the girl. That memory is shut off to me. I can go almost everywhere else but there."

"But why save the girl?" Theo asked. "Saving the girl will mean remaining in Las Vegas. And that is no place for your magic."

"There are so many better places for you to go," Lucio added.

Toby cleared his throat. His words emerged, devoid of their usual static. "I need to see whether I can save the girl before I can decide whether or not I want to go back there or anywhere else. I will keep trying until I save her."

His visitors said nothing.

"I will keep trying," Toby repeated.

I shivered and wondered if Toby would ever consider the charm of the present. "If that is what it takes for you to move on, then perhaps I can help you," Lucio said.

"How?" Toby replied.

"Did you ever wonder where you sent your assistant?" Theo asked.

"Of course." Toby sounded tired.

"I would think it's a world not unlike the one you find inside that box. A world sprung from your imagination," the elegant magician continued.

"Maybe you will not believe me," Lucio began, "but you have always been able to conjure a world of your imagining. You are probably not aware of it."

"Clearly not," my magician said.

"Now," the Italian said, lowering his voice, "have you ever conjured the perfect person to your side at the perfect moment?"

"I'm better at sending them away."

"No, no," Lucio said, his voice slipping into a smooth stage patter. "Think."

"I can't think of anything."

"How did you and your wife meet?" Theo asked.

"Mel?"

"Yes."

"We met in a small town in the middle of nowhere. A couple of hours outside Las Vegas."

"And you got married that night?" Theo asked.

"Yes."

"You must have been lonely," Lucio wondered.

"Life on the road is lonely, and then—poof—there she is," Theo said with a laugh.

I didn't stay for the rest of the conversation. I forgot the cold and rushed to the attic, where I lay under several blankets feigning sleep until Toby arrived.

In the morning, Olivia picked up the phone on the first ring. Despite the hour, she was cheerful. I closed my eyes, imagining her standing in Leo's world.

"He conjured me," I said.

"What?"

"Toby conjured me."

"When, just now?"

I took a breath, trying to suppress my panic. "No, from the beginning. It's all an illusion."

"Mel," Olivia's voice was sweet and soothing, "That can't be true. First of all, you're giving him too much credit. If he conjured you, which I'm fairly sure he didn't, it was your choice to stay with him, right?"

I nodded in invisible assent.

"And there's no way he keeps conjuring you morning after morning."

"I guess not."

"Anyway, Toby clearly loves you. Maybe it's hard to tell

sometimes behind all that magic. I mean he is a little strange, so he probably has strange ways of expressing himself."

Despite myself, I wanted to laugh.

"It probably makes Toby feel better to think he's conjured you. If you left, then he'd have a way to get you back. His greatest worry right now is that he's going to lose you on top of everything else."

"I wonder. But if he's worried I'm going to leave, why doesn't he ask me?"

"And why don't you simply ask him if he conjured you?" Olivia didn't wait for my response. "It would be too easy, right?"

"I guess. But sometimes I can't shake this feeling that something in our relationship is just a game to him."

"Magic is a game, isn't it?"

"Sort of."

"Look, these magicians are overgrown boys who are used to getting what they want. But there are many things their magic can't do. One of them is making you stay somewhere you don't want to be."

"What if you're wrong?"

"Well," Olivia said brightly, "if you really think he conjured you, let's conjure him."

"What do you mean?"

"Your quilt," Olivia said. "It's magic, isn't it?"

"I don't know. Probably not."

"We'll conjure him with your quilt and see what he has to say." Olivia waited. I said nothing, and she continued, "I'll pick you up at the station. Bring something that reminds you of Toby."

I passed through Leo's gate and felt warm again. It was winter, and the villa's gardens were washed out, but somehow they revived me.

Olivia I went to the studio, where she'd arranged a lunch of small sandwiches and salads.

"What did you bring?" she asked.

I pulled the Navajo marriage blanket from my bag. I also took out my old quilt, the one I'd started during my time in the West.

Olivia picked up a sandwich and went to a small chair in the far corner of the studio. "Now what?" she asked.

"I have no idea. I guess we wait." I unfurled the patches that had sprung from my hands last time I'd been in the studio. I threaded my needle and began to join the two quilts together.

"Do they tell the same story?"

I leaned in close to the quilt. "I don't know. The first part has never said a word."

Olivia finished her sandwich. "Well, if you made it, I'm sure it has a lot to say."

I laughed.

When I'd finished joining the two parts, I ran my fingers over the whole, wondering when Toby would appear. His actions, his desert magic, were visible, but Toby himself was absent.

Olivia finished her sandwich. "I think I'd better leave you alone." She touched the quilt on her way out the door.

I continued to look for Toby. But instead of hearing the magician, a new voice piped up. It came from the first part of my quilt, the part I'd begun in my early days out West. I located the patch, a tangerine bouclé taken from a Southern California hotel.

"He said he loved me, but I never really believed it. We were young. He was a magician. I was an assistant. I've read all the books. The magician falls for someone else. Well, that's not exactly how it went down." Eva paused. "At first no one noticed, you know," she scoffed. "Everyone was so distracted by how great his trick looked that no one in the audience imagined I was gone for real. You know the rest. And you could have stopped him from doing it again."

Before I had time to reflect on what Eva had said, a familiar voice piped up. "It was cool for a little while, being dead. When they heard about it back at my high school, everyone was talking about me. One girl even said that she saw me in some parking lot. Like I'd be hanging out in a parking lot! But then—" She snapped her gum again. "—then people sorta started to forget. Something else happened. Some local girl made it into a movie or whatever, and no one thought about me anymore. It totally sucked!"

When these two fell silent, I folded my hands and waited for my magician to speak. Just as my hand grasped a package of needles, I thought I heard his voice. It seemed to be coming from the Navajo marriage blanket—the scratchy wool a perfect vehicle for Toby's voice. I leaned in close, but the words were indistinct. I let the red-and-black wool rest between the scissors' blades, wondering if the woman who sold us the blanket had been wrong and that the only way to save my marriage was to destroy the blanket. I look a deep breath before letting my scissors race through the blanket, disrupting the geometric patterns, severing the cloud colors from the desert colors. It didn't take long to reduce the blanket to strips and squares. I wondered how these shapes would work their way into my patchwork. I kept cutting.

Finally, I reached for a needle and thread. I started sewing. The needle flew in and out of the fabric, creating a pathway of stitches that drew Toby and me together again in the dark desert. There he was, as he was meant to be, arriving at my table in the Old Stand Saloon. It was as if my patchwork had been waiting for his arrival. It seemed to shine and come to life. The glittery fabrics of Las Vegas sparkled, the desert reds hummed, even the oceans—Max's domain—vibrated.

"I'd been waiting for the two of you to come along." My needle trembled. My hand paused, allowing me to look at the patchwork maze. A black-and-white-checked fabric had appeared among the desert reds. It spoke with the voice of the waiter at the Old Stand Saloon. "I'd been waiting and I'd been hoping. Magic doesn't come to town twice in one week." When his voice faded, absorbed back into the fabric, my needle resumed its pace.

Soon the pieces of the marriage blanket were scattered among the desert squares. They stood astride the glittering, synthetic casinos and beneath the torpid swaths of sun. And from a square where the blanket intermingled with patches of white velour and red Vegas sateen, I heard a new voice. "They come and go, the couples. I don't really take no notice anymore. Maybe they in love. Maybe they drunk. Maybe she pregnant. Joo know? But they pay, they marry." The white velour from which the voice was coming gave a rattling cough. "But joos was different. Joos was meant to marry. Marry and then some. I say to myself, I've been waiting for a couple like this." Then the priest fell silent.

My needle had come to a rest. The patchwork continued to vibrate. I shook off my thimble. "So," I said to a scrap of the blanket, "I'm waiting." I tapped one of the Navajo scraps.

"I was waiting for you that day. And you made everything better."

"Until I couldn't."

"It's not important how we came together. We fell in love."

If you can conjure me, you can send me away, I almost told the quilt. But these were words meant for Toby.

When Toby fell silent, I turned to the Max shapes, hoping to be comforted by my brother's voice. I let my eyes run along the quilt, watching Max's story unfold. I saw his escape into the river. I saw our swim with the whale. And then I came to the patch that told of my fall through the ice—a patch I'd sewn during my last stint in the studio, capturing the muddy brown of the hill and the cherry red of Max's coat. This patch looked different now, fuzzy and un-raveled. Unlike the Max patches that led up to this one, my sewing seemed careless here and imprecise. I closed my eyes, trying to remember both the patch and the day it recalled. My recollection was just out of reach. I folded the quilt away and ran toward the villa. On the pathway, I collided with Olivia. Her cheeks were flushed with excitement.

"The rabbits," she said. "The ghost rabbits. They're back."

We arrived at the hutches, where Leo and the Christophs were staring at three rabbits snuffling about the enclosure.

"Just three?" I asked.

Leo folded his arms. "Erik always expected more. I expected less."

Now a rustling came from the woods behind the hutches.

"I indulged him. I always thought that this was some sort of joke." Leo looked at the three lost bunnies. "Maybe it's just a co-incidence."

I was about to share Toby's theory on coincidence, when the rustling grew louder. Then came a rolling wave of white, not from the sky but from deep in the pines. It poured through the trees and slipped over the carpet of needles.

"Rabbits," Leo said, dropping his arms to his sides.

Hundreds of rabbits were gliding over the ground like mercury. They came in waves. They slipped around tree stumps and hopped over roots.

"The rabbits," Leo said again.

Soon the hutches were teeming with the ghost rabbits.

"They're real," one of the Christophs said, pulling a woolen hat over his ears.

"Where do they come from? Where were they?"

Leo looked at me.

"I wonder if Toby found the rabbits," I said.

"Toby?" Olivia asked. "What does he have to do with the rabbits?"

In the low light, the rabbits' fur was ghostly white. Their outlines melted into one another.

"I think Toby's magic is confusing the past with present."

The forest was silent once more. The rabbits were snug in the hutches.

"How did they know where to come?" Olivia wondered, picking up a rabbit.

"They're lucky," I said. "Someone was waiting for them."

"Leo," she called, "come. They're soft, like pom-poms."

Leo wasn't listening. He was staring past the hutches and into the woods. "He knew. Erik knew they would come back. I wonder." I looked into the pen. The rabbits' pink eyes had taken on a piercing glow. Their shifting forms made me uneasy. Leo was still staring into the woods. "The rabbits came." He took a deep breath. "They came like a blizzard. But he's not. He shouldn't." Leo wound his fingers through the fence. "He left by choice, wandered off in the middle of a hiking trip. We are from a flat land. Erik should have known better to fool with mountains. The leader of the expedition simply said that when he turned around, Erik was gone. I'm not sure whether he wanted to leave for good or he simply got lost. All I know is that he's not coming back. But the rabbits, they never had any choice. They were sent away. Whatever magic claimed them doesn't last forever. There's some comfort in that." Leo watched three rabbits squeezing into the same hutch. "Somehow Erik knew."

I nodded. "Maybe there are no perfect tricks," I said, thinking how the cocoon of magic that trapped Eva on her mesa slowly began to dissolve.

"I wonder where they've been?" Leo said.

"I have an idea," I replied, wondering what words to use to describe the intermediate world of Toby and Theo's magic. "It's not a happy place. But one that can be escaped. Had Toby found the rabbits as a way of atoning for his mistakes, or was their return just a by-product of his explorations of the Dissolving World?

Leo put an arm around my shoulder. "Let's go back to the villa. You will have a bed to sleep in instead of the studio floor."

A fire was blazing in the main hall of the villa.

"Something happened to my quilt," I said to Olivia when we were alone. "Some of the images of my brother are fading. They're taking my recollection of Max with them." I bit my lip. "My memory is all I have left of my brother."

"Why is it happening?" Olivia sat forward in her chair.

"Toby's playing with the past. He doesn't think it will affect the present. But it does."

"He's making your brother vanish?"

I told her about the Dissolving World.

Olivia had only one question. "Where was the last place you saw your brother."

"In the ocean."

"So, tomorrow, that's the first place we'll look."

Sixteen

Olivia and I set off early the next morning into an escalating storm. We took the train through a countryside that was stretched as flat as a fitted sheet. It had been placed on the ground with impeccable care in a palette of greens, browns, and grays. Rows of perforated depressions that marked the path of the harvest ran perpendicular to the canal and bike path—a drab Mondrian print bordered by slate-color roads. Two-story farmhouses with red-brown roofs sprang from the dull land as if from the pages of a pop-up book. Each disruption of the flat landscape surprised me. But soon the appearance of the houses established a rhythm that fell into sync with the clatter of the train wheels—simple chords that marked time over its persistent drum roll.

Olivia and I rode in silence, letting the train cut through the advancing storm. Finally we arrived at the beach town and found a tram that would bring us to the sea. The tram rattled through half-deserted streets. The swelling storm gave the city a hollow sound. As we approached the beach, the air grew damper. Sand, borne by the wind, dirtied the tram windows and crusted our lips. The beach seemed to be coming to us—the sticky mix of salt and sand that I hadn't tasted in years.

The tram deposited us in front of a grand hotel, asleep in the off season. The pennants flying from its towers danced madly in the rough wind. The sea was hidden behind a wall of shuttered surf shops where towels, visors, Frisbees, and sunscreen hibernated until late spring. A promenade of more empty stores inside a dirty glass atrium led back to the beach. Iron grates were pulled across the arcades. The video games sat blindly in their cages. Seaside souvenirs smiled sourly inside the darkened stores. As we walked, our footsteps echoed like the march of giants.

"I'm not really comfortable around the ocean," I said, catching sight of the gray sea for the first time. "I haven't been near it since Max left."

Olivia took my hand. "It's going to be fine. This is the best place to show you that Toby can't control everything."

I looked through the salt-sprayed window of the atrium at the furious water and wondered if I dared to look for my brother, I could retrieve the memories that were slowly fading.

Olivia didn't let go of my hand as we left the atrium and headed down the boardwalk. "I'm sure your quilt is every bit as powerful as Toby's box," she said.

"It's just a quilt."

"It's better than magic. It's real."

"I always thought of my quilting as some sort of map or time line," I said, my voice trying to outdo the wind and crashing surf. "Toby ruined that."

"No. I'm sure you're wrong. We're going to find some new memory of your brother that will bring the old ones back."

Since the day Max swam off, I'd always turned away from the

water. But now, I knew I needed to face it. And maybe if I understood what remarkable force called him off, I would know how to find him before he swam further from my mind. I'm not sure how Olivia understood this. When I asked, she simply told me that she'd learned it from my description of my quilt.

To the far left of the horizon, a vertical funnel of storm clouds rose. It arched over the sea and the land until it disappeared into the city at our backs. As the black clouds started to move toward us, the wind kicked up the sand in stripes. Waves of sand crashed from the beach onto the boardwalk. I looked at the furious water. The ocean was devouring the beach—the waves curling across the shore in the same direction as the thrashing pennants flying from the hotel's domes. I couldn't imagine Max forsaking land for such a forbidding climate.

Across from us on the boardwalk a long, two-story covered pier ran straight over the sand, and then out over the sea, before forking into two cupolas. We started down it, but as we prepared to cross the border of sand and sea, I stopped. In the distance, a pair of kite surfers were being swept into the air by the wind. Once airborne, they twisted and flipped, before crashing back into the ocean. The sea nipped and growled at their feet. It tore and gnashed against the rocks and poles on the pier's underbelly.

"You see," Olivia said, leading me into the pier, "you'll be safe from the water."

I looked out to the point where the water melted into the sky. Like Bermuda, where the turquoise water was sewn to the turquoise sky, the North Sea was joined to the somber Dutch heavens. We arrived at the end of the pier and stepped out onto a ledge. At that moment, the thunder cracked, shaking the pier. I watched the kite surfers running for cover.

"Okay," Olivia said, "let's see what charmed your brother."

I tried to listen to the call of the water above the screaming

wind. I watched the waves merge and crash, duplicating and redu-
plicating into dozens of patterns. The color of the water changed
from dark to light as the waves approached the pier. I wondered
what it felt like to be wrapped in the arms of the stormy sea. I was
sure that Max knew how to submit to the water's power.

I gripped the handrail and forced myself to look deeper into
the water, searching for his slippery shadow. I took a deep breath
and let the wind tangle my hair. Soon I grew accustomed to the
arrhythmic chomp and swirl of the waves. And for the first time,
I could see the possibilities of the ocean. Like my quilt, it was a
breathing creature, evolving before my eyes.

Within the tumultuous waves, I now saw patterns of foam
and undertow. I was able to tease out a variety of shades from
what I thought was a uniform gray. I knew that each of these
shades would sing to Max the way my fabrics sang to me. I imagined him weaving his way between them, summoned by their
songs to explore deeper parts of the ocean.

I closed my eyes as the memories of Max came back, rushing like the return of the ghost rabbits. I leaned forward, letting
the spray brush over my face and the salt sting my eyes. Then I
felt Olivia take me by the waist and lead me back into the covered pier.

"You see," she said.

I nodded. We sat on a bench, and I took out my quilt. The
Max figures had all established themselves in their places, all except for the one that told the story of my tumbling through the
ice. This figure and the details of that day were gone for good.

"Let's go," Olivia said.

"No, I'm not ready. I want to get closer to the water."

We left the shelter of the pier and walked back to the beach.
We crossed the sand and came as close to the water as we could

without being struck by the pounding surf. I pulled Olivia to the ground and wrapped the quilt around our shoulders, protecting us from the flying sand and sea and wind. Olivia uncorked a bottle of wine, and while we drank, I listened for the first time to the songs Max loved.

"So what are you going to do?"

"About Toby?"

She nodded.

"The magicians were wrong when they told him he conjured me to his side." I watched the foamy tip of a wave crawl toward our toes. "I'm sure we were meant to meet that day, but it wasn't solely his doing. Toby needs to understand that not everything he touches is magic." I dropped my head. "I miss him, but even when we are together, I feel lonely. I'd rather be alone."

Olivia inched closer to me.

"Toby and Max think they are incapable of loving me, or anyone, as much they love something else. I watched for years as my brother slipped away until the day he left for good. I thought that there was nothing I could do to prevent it. I didn't try to pull him back. I won't make that mistake twice." We sipped our wine and watched the waves tangle with one another. "He's fading," I said. "Like the Max figures on my quilt faded. I need to bring him back or I'll lose him for good."

Olivia squeezed my hand. "I hope you understand that it isn't you they are escaping from."

From the corner of the street, I could make out a person in a puffy red coat standing in front of Piet's house. Even from a few feet away, I detected the scent of pot and wasted time that billowed from Amsterdam's black-lit coffee shops on a tide of trippy music.

"Can I help you?"

The red coat turned, and I thought I recognized Jimmy, Greta's boyfriend. "The magician's friend," he said.

"Wife," I corrected.

"Sure. Whatever." Jimmy's eyes were glazed and red. He looked at the ominous gray of the sky. "Does it always rain so much here?"

I nodded.

"I come from the desert. Never seen so much goddamned rain."

I fumbled for my keys. Jimmy was too impatient and rang the bell. When no one answered, he pounded on the door. I found my key and was about to fit it in the lock, when the door opened and Toby poked his head out. If he was surprised by Jimmy's presence, he didn't let it show. He looked past the teenager to me. "Are you making it a habit of staying away at night?"

"I'm not the only one," I said, pushing past him into the house.

Toby's eyes clouded. Before he could speak, Jimmy wedged himself between us.

"It took me forever to find you."

"I vanish easily."

They backed into the vestibule.

"Some guy in a magic shop told me there were a bunch of creepy old magicians living on this street. I've been ringing every bell."

"Creepy," Toby repeated.

Jimmy looked over his shoulder at the street and then peered down the hallway. "Perfect." He laughed. "This city and this rotten house are perfect for a couple of old-timers like yourselves. Couldn't really imagine you under the Vegas lights."

"You'd be surprised," Toby said.

"We're not as old-fashioned as you may think," I added.

"A magician and a—" Jimmy looked at me.

"A textile designer."

"Right out of the history books. Bet you don't even watch TV."

We shook our heads.

Then Jimmy looked down at his shoes. He pursed his lips and squinted. He pulled his puffy ski coat tighter. "Never cold like this back home."

"Can I get you anything? Something to eat or drink?" I suggested.

"Nah. I haven't found anything good to eat since I've been here."

"Maybe a coffee?" Toby offered as Jimmy looked up.

"A beer," Jimmy said finally. "I'll take a beer."

Toby and I looked at each other and shrugged. "Why not?" the magician said.

"Cool," Jimmy muttered, and took off his coat.

We sat at the kitchen table. "Only good thing in this city is that you can get fries everywhere."

"You can get fries a lot of places in America," I said.

"They're better here." Jimmy looked down at the table. "Like at that diner, the Route 66?"

I nodded as I remembered the place where we first met Greta.

"The fries there suck. The ketchup is really bad, too. They just pretend it's Heinz. But Greta always had to refill those Heinz bottles from some pump dispenser. Didn't fool anyone." He shrugged. "In Intersection, there isn't much choice."

Toby returned with three bottles of beer.

"Bottles," Jimmy said, "nice. At the bars here, the beers are so small."

"So it doesn't get warm while you're drinking," I explained.

"True," Jimmy said. "Greta'd probably be jealous if she knew I was sitting here with you. Or angry. Who knows." For a moment, no one spoke. "I miss her sometimes," Jimmy said finally. "I miss her a lot of the time. It's like, when she ran off to Las Vegas, I wasn't sure she'd come back exactly. But I never thought that I wouldn't see her again." He rubbed his eyes and looked at the table.

"I should have been more careful," the magician explained. "It was my fault."

Now Jimmy laughed. "That would make Greta so mad. She'd want all the credit."

Toby drained his glass.

"She was such a weird girl," Jimmy continued. "She talked about death like it was a person. It was like a popular girl Greta wanted to impress." Jimmy shook his head. "The weird thing is, she was fun. I mean, at least she had a thing. All the other girls at school—well, I don't know—they're pretty much the same." He paused. "I just don't understand what she was thinking."

"Some people just feel that they are meant to be elsewhere," I said.

"How do you hold on to someone like that?"

"You can't," I replied.

"That sucks."

"It does," Toby added.

"Can you find someone after she disappears?" He looked from me to Toby.

Toby shook his head.

"But you're a magician."

"That doesn't make any difference."

Jimmy drained his beer then pounded the bottle on the table with such force that the plates shook in the sideboard. "No," he said. "I don't believe it." His knuckles were white. "It's the only thing that does make a difference."

"Why?" Toby asked. His voice was calm.

Jimmy spoke slowly, trying to control a storm rising inside him. "When Greta left for Vegas, she said you were more than a magician. She said you could actually do stuff." Now he pounded the table again and half rose out of his seat. "So, do something."

"Please calm down," Toby said.

"It's just not okay," Jimmy said, standing and walking around to Toby. "Everyone says it is, but it's not. And you're not going to walk away a second time."

Toby stood and tried to lead Jimmy back to his seat, but the teenager didn't let him.

"Greta's dead, and you're on vacation," Jimmy said. "That just doesn't make sense."

"I'm not on vacation," Toby replied, struggling to speak calmly.

"It looks like it." Jimmy stumbled against a wall, then righted himself. "I'd like to blame Greta for what she did. But she's gone. So I'm gonna blame you. You killed my girlfriend."

Toby opened his mouth.

"And don't tell me it was her fault. It's your fault. You killed her."

"I'm sorry."

"Not good enough," Jimmy muttered, rubbing his goatee. "I'm leaving tomorrow. But not before you make it better." He jabbed a finger in Toby's direction.

"He can't," I said.

"Yeah?" Jimmy looked at Toby, who remained silent. "Then why doesn't he tell me himself?"

"What would you like me to do?" Toby asked.

Jimmy rubbed his goatee. "I don't know. You're the magician. So, something."

"Something," Toby repeated.

"Yeah, something," Jimmy said as water welled up in his glazed eyes. "Because I can't believe my girlfriend was dumb enough to step in front of a bullet during a magic trick. Death is not cool. I mean, I'd remember her forever if she hadn't died. She was my girlfriend—how was I gonna forget?" He looked from me to Toby, waiting for an explanation or an answer.

Jimmy sat down at the table once more. He slumped his shoulders and hung his head. "I used to like magic as a kid," he said, looking into his hands. "Shows came to Intersection, since it's on the way to Vegas. But now I think it's mean."

Toby crammed his hands in his pockets. He bit his lips, trying to remain calm.

"Why does someone want to pretend he's cutting one of my friends in half?"

"I don't know. It's a trick," Toby offered. "It's sensational."

"Why do you want to pretend to kill someone?" He sank deeper into his seat. "I guess you don't always pretend."

"Stop it," Toby whispered.

"Why?" Jimmy sat up straight. "Why?" he repeated, now on his feet. He approached Toby. "What is the point of being a magician if you can't make anything better?" Jimmy was inches from the magician's face. "You have to do something!" Jimmy yelled. "Greta said you could. And you will."

"I can't."

"I'm not leaving until you fix it."

"He can't," I said.

"Jimmy, please," Toby said.

"No," the teenager replied, throwing his hands up in front of his face, "don't talk to me. Don't." He coughed. "Don't do anything anymore. Not until you make it better." Then he began to cry. His sobs rattled the glasses and the coffee cups. I put a hand on Jimmy's shoulder. I felt him shake so hard, it seemed he would burst. Then I looked at Toby.

For the first time in many days, he looked solid and resolute. "All right," he said.

Jimmy looked up.

"I think there is something I can do."

"What?" Jimmy said, wiping his nose.

"I said, I think there is something I can do."

"You're kidding," Jimmy said.

Toby shook his head.

"So, Greta was right? You can do stuff for real?"

"I'm not sure what will happen," Toby said. "I can only try a few things."

I remained at the table while Toby showed Jimmy out. He returned with the same look of resolve.

"What are you going to do?" I asked.

I never got my answer. Theo appeared in the kitchen doorway, looking impatient and aggravated. "You will waste your talents on that boy."

Toby didn't reply.

"He'll find another girlfriend. They always do. Teenagers are fickle and often carried away by obsession."

"I don't consider easing his pain, or my own, a waste of my talents," Toby replied.

"You are keeping us waiting," Theo said, beckoning with his scarred fingers.

The magicians were sitting in the living room around the fireplace. In addition to Piet, Lucio, and Theo, the group contained several of the men I hadn't seen since our visit to the sanctum. Piet made a place on the couch for Toby. I hovered in the doorway.

"Now it is time for you to decide," Theo began, settling into an armchair farthest from the fire, "whether you are going to help us or not."

"Toby." Piet turned toward the magician. "I hope that I have done my best to show you a world of conjuring that can be yours."

"If I give this one up," Toby added.

"But why wouldn't you?" Theo asked. "What do you have here?"

"I have Mel."

"Perhaps you can convince Mel to go with you," Lucio said.

"No," I replied. "There will be no conjuring involving me."

"You see, no matter where you go, she is not planning to follow," Theo said.

"Stop talking about Mel," Toby replied.

Piet placed a hand over Toby's. "You love magic, but this time you live in does not respect your craft. There is no beauty or elegance to modern magic. Everything we created will still be in place when we return. The theater is set. The audiences are waiting."

"Then they will have to wait," Toby said, standing up. "I will not help you."

Theo's face darkened. "You are making a mistake."

"No, you made the mistake when you came to visit me in Vegas. Las Vegas has always been my dream. I might seem silly to you, but I want to be a magician of this moment. Or of the moment before everything went wrong."

"If you take us back, it will be to a time before that happened," Piet said.

"But I wouldn't have fixed anything."

"You will never fix anything," Theo said. "You will only pretend."

"Untrue." Toby stood up.

"If you will not help us, your time here is over," Theo replied.

"I have no reason to help you." Toby pushed past me into the hall.

Piet stood up, looked at me with his watering eyes.

"Did you really think I would go?" I asked the oldest magician.

"Before I met you, I had hoped."

I left the magicians in the living room. I knew where I'd find Toby. He had opened the door to the Dissolving World. I rushed to the box and pulled him back.

"Why are there only two choices?" I asked him.

"What do you mean?"

"Going back to Theo's heyday or returning to the night of Greta's death?" I drew Toby away from the box. "What about staying here?"

"What's the difference if we go back to that night and do it over?"

"Because we will always know it should have been otherwise," I said. I opened the door to the box and peeked inside. All I saw was four walls. I let the door close. "Toby, there are consequences to what you do in there. Things in the present are starting to change. The magicians don't care about this, because once they go into the past, the present, our present, won't concern them."

"What's the difference if a few objects from a past life pop up here?"

I thought about Eva, buffeted on a tide of Toby tricks, pulled from one moment to the next. I wondered where she was now. "Because it won't always be objects. Soon it will be people. You will hurt someone again."

The magician shook his head.

"You can't see past the possibility of succeeding in this one thing, in saving Greta's life. You need to consider the effect it will have on other people. Like me."

"How could saving Greta affect you?"

"After I fell through the ice, memories of my brother began to shift and change. Because you pulled me out, he was written out of that moment. When you save Greta, a whole different reality will open up. We cannot live in two worlds."

"If we go back, we will eventually get back to the present." Toby walked over and examined one of the illusions with menacing blades and saw teeth.

"What about all the things that have happened since we left Vegas? Do they matter? Should they cease to exist?"

"What has happened that's worth saving?" He ran his finger along the sharp edge of a circular blade.

I thought of Olivia and Leo. "I'd lose my friends."

"You can come back and find them again."

"They wouldn't know me. It wouldn't be the same." I backed away from the box and sat at the worktable. On the table was a yellowed playbill. It featured a picture of the Dissolving World with a painting of Theo's head crowned in smoke. Beneath the illusion was the inscription STEP INTO YOUR IMAGINATION WITH THE DISSOLVING WORLD: $1.

"You'd find a way to befriend them."

I shook my head. "As I said, I'd always know things were supposed to be otherwise."

Toby's eyes flashed. "Who are you to say how things are supposed to be?"

"Who are you?"

"I am trying to make things better, while you are content for everything to be the same."

"With magic," I said.

"Yes, with magic. But that is all I have."

I took a deep breath. "I have always loved you beyond your magic. I have loved you in spite of it."

Toby could not meet my gaze. He looked over my shoulder, through the dusty window where evening was coming too early, as usual. "In spite. As if it's a burden."

"That's not what I meant."

"You have always wanted me to sit on the sidelines of my art. You want me to play with it, but never use it."

I shook my head.

"It is as if I were to tell you to sew buttons instead of creating a quilt. You want me to become like Theo and the rest—sit by and watch as my magic dries up."

"Of course not. But the fact that I love you and not your art should tell you something."

"What's that?"

"That there is more to you than the skills that make that box work."

"Maybe."

"I need you to love me in this world." I stood up and grabbed Toby's wrists.

"I do love you. But it doesn't matter where. To me, one world's as good as the next. In my reality, things are forever shifting and interchangeable. I'm a magician, Mel. I never expect anything to be fixed. In fact, I demand the opposite."

"Tinkering with reality is different from changing it."

"Now that I've nearly found a way to undo the worst thing I've done, how can you expect me not to try?"

I blinked away my tears.

"Look around, Mel. Is this a place for my magic? Is this a place for us?"

I shook my head.

"If I don't repair what went wrong in Vegas, I'm going to spend the rest of my life hiding away, unable to perform. I'm going to become Theo—a bitter, frustrated magician with no magic." Toby paused. "We loved Las Vegas. It was strange, but we loved it."

"I remember."

"So, come with me."

"No. There will always be something else. Saving Greta is only the beginning."

We stared at each other, unable to find the words to close the gap between us.

"I love you, Mel. But I want everything to be better."

"Then you need to show it by staying here with me. Things can be better without them being exactly as they were before. There's nothing to fix. People aren't meant to be brought back to life."

Toby rubbed his hands together. "What if you had the chance to bring your brother back? Tell me you wouldn't."

"I did have the chance. I could have asked you. I could have asked to see him for a day, a moment, however long it lasts." I shook my head. "But I didn't. He chose to leave, the same way Greta chose to die."

"Her death was my fault."

"No, Toby. It wasn't."

The magician shook his head.

"Her death ended your run in Vegas. That is all."

"I need to try and save the girl."

"You are not saving her," I said. "You are only saving yourself. It's selfish."

"How can you say that?" Toby said.

"Because you are doing this to make yourself feel better at the expense of everything else. And if it works, you will stay and I won't be with you. You won't have the heart to come back. You will be blinded by your magic."

"I'll come back for you."

"No, Toby, you won't."

"This is my only chance," he said. "Tomorrow we will have to leave Piet's." He opened the door to the Dissolving World.

"Don't go in there."

"I do love you," Toby said.

"I won't follow you."

He stepped inside. And of course, I followed.

Seventeen

I open my eyes to an unnaturally gray sky. The looming clouds are stationary. Anyway, it's too warm to snow. Beneath my head is a heavy synthetic cushion.

Then I hear a familiar voice. "You getting up, or what?"

I look from the frozen clouds to the girl standing in front of me. It's Greta in her shredded peasant outfit. We're in the Winter Palace.

"Too much to drink?" the teenage waitress scoffs. "And it's so early."

"What happened?"

"She wants to know what happened? One minute you're, like, holding your drink. The next, you're taking my tray down with you." She narrows her eyes and peers at me. "Hope the carpet's all right."

"It's stain-resistant."

My forehead is tender from my fall. I can feel a small bump.

What was it that Eva said on top of that mesa? You can't bang your head against a dream, and if you scream, you wake up. Of course, this is no dream, and I wonder how to find Toby inside his trick.

"So, you gonna sit there all day?" Greta asks, not helping me to my feet. "You better not cause a scene over here. I need this job. I won't be fired because you can't handle a drink." She looks over her shoulder at someone approaching through the parting crowd. Sandra.

The Winter Palace manager appears in front of me, her face a mixture of pity and condescension. She's a cloud of perfume, champagne, and voile.

"Mel, get up." Sandra offers me her perfectly manicured hand. She's not wearing the dress I helped her pick out, but something brassier. "You can't be lying around. And in that outfit. This is VIP."

I'm on my feet. Despite the artificial cold of the Winter Palace, I'm having trouble breathing. "Quick," Sandra says in her stage whisper, "get into my office. Change into something suitable." She hands me her key card. In an instant, she's gone, leaving me with Greta.

Greta is about to walk away. "Greta."

She stops and give me a confused look. "Yeah?"

"There's going to be a magician, right?"

She shrugs. "You just passed out in public, and you're worried about a magician."

I make my way to Sandra's office, searching for Toby as I go. People are giving me strange looks. I guess, being dressed for a Dutch winter day, I don't exactly blend into a swanky Vegas crowd. Sandra's office is a tornado of discarded heels, dresses, and costume jewelry. I see the dress I helped her select from the mall at Caesar's discarded on the back of her chair. I rummage through the clothes. Most of the dresses are sateen, and their colors are strictly SoCal or Key West. If I had the time to listen, I'm sure they'd all be singing the chorus of a Jimmy Buffet song. I'm looking for fit rather than style, which leads me to a orange-coral knee-length number. It has spaghetti straps and tiny crystals along the bodice. I put it on and feel like I've wandered off from an Under the Sea prom night.

The opening party is flowing from the lobby into the Hermitage Salon. The shoulder-height vases bursting with hyacinths smell extraordinary. The motorized sledges whirl through the shopping promenade, carrying tipsy revelers bundled underneath the faux fur throws. Fireworks explode from the onion domes. A folk music trio in Cossack dress moves through the crowd. I look everywhere for Toby. Waitresses give me canapés. Another champagne flute winds up in my hand.

Sandra is at my side once more. She plucks the strap of my dress. "That's better. You look like one of us." She's riding high on a tide of champagne and adrenaline.

"Sandra, is Toby performing?"

"Toby?"

"The magician?"

"Oh, honey. Of course he's performing." She holds up her champagne glass and gestures around the room. "Why do you think all the ladies are here?"

I step back to avoid being doused with Sandra's drink.

"But believe me, you're gonna have to wait in line for his time, hon."

"I need to talk to him before the show."

Sandra gives me a look that lets me know I'm about to embarrass myself and her again. "Grab a drink and relax. I can't imagine a magician needs to be disturbed before his big Vegas debut." Now Sandra's voice becomes all business. "The carpets," she says, pressing the toe of her cream-colored shoe into the pile, "are they holding?"

"So far," I reply, my voice small and distant in my own ears.

The party continues. Everything is a little brighter and merrier than I remember. The champagne seems to pop with iridescent sparkles. Music pours from the speakers, inspiring the guests to tap their toes. Suddenly, a Russian juggling troupe bursts onto the floor and begins to toss their batons. The crowd parts, delighted by the flying sticks and balls, some of which are now on fire. Almost before the juggling is complete, guests shuffle toward the Hermitage Salon. I follow. Peering over the bare shoulder of a woman in a sultry cocktail dress, I see members of the St. Petersburg Orchestra playing as they arrive on the artificial ice in sledges.

The crowd's exuberance swells as an impromptu snowstorm gusts through the salon. I need to find Toby or Greta. I'm stuck, wedged in a sea of dresses, tuxedos, and cocktails as the tiny artificial flakes pour from the ceiling. The crowd looks up as snow covers everyone with a sparkly sheen.

I push my way through the crowd and begin to search for Toby. Instead, I find Greta sneaking a cigarette near the Red Square pub.

"Looks like you pulled yourself together," she says as I approach.

"I wouldn't smoke in that outfit," I reply.

"Yeah? And I wouldn't pass out at six P.M. Guess some people shouldn't drink."

I try to stay calm. "I didn't pass out."

"Whatever." She rolls her eyes.

"Listen, Greta . . ."

"I barely know you, so stop calling me that. Anyway, it's not Greta. It's Paula."

"Sure, Paula. The magician—," I begin.

She extinguishes her cigarette. "Yeah, sure, the magician. What do you care? You wanna get cut in half or something?"

"Me?"

Greta shrugs. "Lots of people volunteer for stuff like that."

I look down at her bodice, where I expect a bloodstain to blossom. "What about you?" I ask.

Greta laughs. "Yeah, right. His show bores me. I came to town 'cause I thought he'd do something cool. If I see another card trick, I'll puke."

"Good," I say, helping myself to a drink from the tray Greta abandoned.

"What do you care?"

I consider my glass. "Because magic is overrated."

Greta shakes her head. Teenagers always know better. "Nah. It's 'cause you want to volunteer yourself."

I finish the drink. "Not at all."

Greta smirks. "Right. We'll see if you get the chance."

Before I can respond, a fanfare bursts from the speakers, followed by an announcement proclaiming the arrival of the magician. I'm back at the gambling pits just in time to see Toby jump onto the blackjack table. He's not wearing the coat I'd sewn for him, but his black Western shirt. He reaches down and gives a hand up to his assistant, who alights next to him. It's hard to tell, but I'm pretty sure it's the girl Sandra recommended from the Rio.

It's the same show Toby put on months ago. This time around, he seems more self-confident, adding a little swagger and wink to his tricks. As usual, the women are thrilled. They find his silence alluring. They lean forward, hoping he will say something as he brings the frozen fountain to life. They look jealously at the assistant as she's levitated above their heads. A few catcalls disrupt the cocktail chatter.

I'm trying to keep an eye on Greta. She's standing a few feet in front of me, chewing gum and looking bored. Not doing her job with the tray of cocktails. Now Toby begins to introduce his final trick. The assistant holds up the card reading CATCH ME IF I FALL. She displays the gun for the audience. Then she asks for a volunteer. A dozen manicured hands shoot up. Mine joins them. And then something catches the corner of my eye: Eva. She gives me a look, her eyes telling me that we've been here before. And in this instant, Toby makes his choice.

Her. Greta. And again, that settles it. She allows Toby to help her onto the blackjack table. This time, he holds up her arm, and she pirouettes for the crowd. Then with a small curtsy, she takes her place behind Toby.

Toby ties the blindfold over his eyes. Greta looks out over the audience, proud and aloof. Then she holds her head up. She's the star. The showgirl aims the gun, and Toby braces himself. I know this part. I've seen it in my head, in my dreams, projected onto car windows, and in the place of television shows. The showgirl pulls the trigger. The magician recoils. The bullet is transformed into flower petals.

I step closer. The showgirl raises the gun for the second time. The crowd holds its breath. The shot rings through the gambling pits. The magician staggers slightly, but remains standing. Coins rain down onto the blackjack table. The spectators exhale and shift their feet.

Then I hear the woman next to me praise the showgirl for her daring. Her voice is liquor-loud and floats above the audience. She points and shakes her head in admiration. Greta scowls at her, then at the showgirl. This is her show. The showgirl lifts the gun. I see Greta stand up straighter, thrusting her shoulders back. The assistant is about to pull the trigger.

"No." My voice pierces the heavy silence. "Don't."

Without dropping the gun, the showgirl looks at me. Toby's nose and lips are motionless. I imagine that he is pleased. His illusion is complete. The danger seems even more real.

Behind me, I hear someone whisper, "There's always one who falls for it."

Greta shuffles her feet. Toby cocks his head to one side, noticing this adjustment. The showgirl's finger tenses around the trigger once more. And then, as I knew she would, Greta leaps. She's in front of the magician. She recoils, just as Toby reaches in front of her chest. The crowd gasps, then holds a collective breath. With one arm supporting Greta, Toby raises his free hand. Between his thumb and forefinger is a bullet. He holds it out to the crowd. A single drop of blood falls to the stage. I look at the bodice of Greta's peasant outfit, where a tiny bloodstain, no bigger than a penny, is quickly disappearing from view.

The magician lifts Greta to her feet and whips off his blindfold. His face is a mixture of shock and elation. Greta wants to take a bow, but Toby cuts her short, ushering her off the table as quickly as he can. She walks into the crowd as Toby fingers the bullet she'd wanted for herself.

The tide of relief that hits me as I watch Greta walk away from this show nearly wipes me off my feet. Maybe Toby was right—by saving Greta, we will save ourselves. I want to rush to him and congratulate him, but he is hidden behind a wall of women. They are circling him, holding their cocktails like weapons to fend off one another. I know the look on Toby's face. He's barely registering these women. His mind is wandering far above the Winter Palace, reliving the tragedy he's just prevented and the show he's just pulled off. I know he's thinking about what comes next, what pathway his magic will open for him. And for the first time in ages, I want to follow.

I push through the crowd.

"Toby," I say quietly. "You saved her."

His eyes narrow.

Sandra rolls her eyes and shares a knowing glance with everyone but me. "Oh, Mel, here, thinks that stunt wasn't planned."

Everyone laughs except Toby, who's still giving me an odd look, one that seems to say I've let on more that I should. "I'm sorry," I say, stepping away.

"Poor Mel," Sandra continues. "She was the one who tried to stop the trick in the middle. Thought she was saving a life!" She shakes her head. "Mel, honey, magic isn't real."

It's clear that Sandra wants to get rid of me. "Toby," she says, "I don't think you've met Mel, our fabric consultant. I'm sorry," she adds with a knowing look at her friends, "textile consultant."

Toby takes my hand. He blinks and shakes his head, trying to dislodge a memory. As if, somehow, I might have got stuck in a forgotten corner of his imagination. Then he gives me his showman's smile. "Pleased to meet you, Mel." Toby lets go of my hand and accepts another glass of champagne. As our hands fall away, the scenery we passed from Tonopah to Amsterdam rewinds and vanishes. Sandra's saying something to Toby. As they talk, the magician looks at me, but only for an instant. Then his attention is elsewhere. This is his reality. I am only a visitor.

I go back to the pits, watching the women fawn over Toby. He's enjoying the disaster he's turned into triumph. Now I know the answer to the question Eva asked me on top of the mesa. This is the loneliest I've ever been. I'd rather just be alone. But alone doesn't exists in Vegas. I'm lost inside Toby's trick with no idea of where I belong. And no idea of how to escape. I don't trust my surroundings, not even the fabrics I chose and refurbished. I look around at the once-familiar setting of this casino. Now I notice small adjustments. A fountain sits in a different corner. The garden has been planted with different flowers. The motorized sledges are frosted with fake snow. What else had changed in Toby's world? How many infinitesimal alterations and huge divergences has the magician created in order to save one teenager? Why can't I be by his side in the world where he succeeds?

I stand in the grand entrance of the Winter Palace, watching the sledges circle on their tracks, carrying tipsy partygoers who trail champagne in their wakes. Toby's name is everywhere. The partygoers are intoxicated by his performance—the heady thrill of the inexplicable adding to their substantial buzz.

I realize that I've been standing in one place for too long, neither drinking nor mingling. My immobility is drawing looks from the passersby. I'm ready to move, when I feel a sweaty palm wrap around my wrist.

"Mel Snow."

Swenson smells like a week's worth of nights out. "Jim Swenson."

He steps back and smiles, then sucks more whiskey from his glass. "I thought you'd know me." Swenson shakes his head. "You see, I don't know you. According to me, we've never met before. But I think you'd tell a different story."

I yank my wrist free from his meaty grip.

"Eva told me to keep an eye out for you. She had an idea you might be here. Whoever you are."

"Well, here I am."

"But you ain't supposed to be." Swenson cracks an ice cube. "Eva tells me you're another victim of Toby's magic."

I shake my head.

"Eva's not in the business of lying."

"If you've never met me, you won't understand who am I and what I'm doing here."

Swenson shrugs, making his leather blazer creak. He rattles the remaining ice in his glass. "Maybe so. All I know is that your magician's up to no good again. Probably gonna hurt you or someone else like he did Eva."

I shake my head.

"Well, there's an offer for you on the table here."

"I'm not interested."

"Me and Eva are heading up a new show. She's got a knack for fortune-telling. I'm always on the lookout for more color." He pats my shoulder. "You know."

"Absolutely not," I reply, stepping away.

Swenson sucks air through his teeth. "Once Toby crashes and burns—and don't worry, it'll happen. Over and over from what I've heard. Once he crashes, I'll be the next big thing."

"I doubt it," I say, and leave.

I exit the casino, walking against the tide of late arrivals. Fireworks are erupting from the onion domes over my head, and camera flashes are popping as more Vegas royalty makes its way down the red carpet. I hit the Strip, push past the tourists gawking at the spectacle of the Winter Palace's opening. In my time in Amsterdam, I'd forgotten the artificial vitality of Las Vegas, the nonstop flow of people, traffic, noise, and light. I'm easily and happily lost in this melee. The press of people in either direction erases the panicked loneliness summoned by Toby's imagination. I want to cocoon myself in the sound and energy of the Strip.

I walk until I come to one of the hard-partying casinos, where gambling takes second place to all-night drinking and dancing. I take the escalator through the music-themed lobby and find a bar called the Double Down Saloon, where patrons pay a premium for the Western dive-bar honky-tonk experience. It's the customers who provide the evening's entertainment, jumping on barrels and shaking it for the crowd in exchange for a free shot of whiskey or riding the mechanical bull with a cropped T-shirt as their reward.

In Sandra's dress, I look as if I've been left behind by a bridal party. But inside the Double Down, no one notices. Clearly, this is the sort of place a bridesmaid might come to drown her sorrows or seek comfort in the arms of someone other than the best man. Countrypolitan music is blasting from dozens of speakers, and tribes of women are hooting and hollering along, throwing imaginary lassos into the air. The crowd is a mix of Midwesterners out on hen night and hardcore cowgirls in up-to-there cutoffs, leather halters, and cowboy boots that look as if they might kill. College boys, taking in this controlled experiment in wilding women, lurk in the background, calculating their moment of approach.

A bullhorn goes off. Someone has just fallen off the mechanical bull. I'm about to order my drink when the bartender throws a shot of whiskey in front of me. Then she points overhead to a sign— HOOTENANNY HAPPY HALF HOUR 9–9:30 P.M. NO WHINING JUST WHISKEY. I throw back the shot in one gulp. Another appears. I'm about to pay, when a man in a business suit places a twenty on the bar. "Looks like you needed those. My treat." As I'm going to thank him, a new song comes on, and the crowd begins a line dance.

I don't know the moves, and my dress is a little tight in the thighs for this sort of dancing, so I work my way to an empty corner of the bar, where I find a table made from a reproduction wagon wheel surrounded by barrels turned into stools. I sit and lean my head against the wall, letting the rush from the whiskey subside. The stomping of the line dancers and the rhythmic music become my heartbeat. I watch the crowd step, slide, and spin. Will this world become my reality? Will I become carefree enough to join in? Or, like Eva, will I be buffeted from one place to the next, too removed or insecure to stay for long?

The line dancing ends. The siren calling someone to ride the mechanical bull wails. I am about to stand up, move on, get my bearings, and figure out what to do next. And then, the magician is standing in front of me. He's still in his Western shirt. A few streaks of stage makeup are visible along his jawbone.

"Toby." His name nearly gets caught in my throat.

He looks at my dress, then smiles. "Sandra's friend. Mia?"

"Mel. Mel Snow."

"Toby Warring." He smiles as he takes my hand. It's the smile he left behind in Nevada. "Mind if I sit?"

I shake my head and pat the barrel next to mine.

"The desert is no place for someone named Mel Snow."

"I've heard."

Suddenly two beers are in front of us. Toby catches my eye to see if I've noticed this trick. I pretend not to. I simply accept my drink as if the magician brought it with him from the bar.

"Is the desert a good place for magic?"

"That's quite a question," Toby says, swigging from his bottle. "Some places out here are, and some aren't. In the desert, you have to pay attention. Things have a way of going wrong."

"I know." I look down my bottleneck. "You're from back East," I say. "Mid-coast Atlantic?"

"How'd you know?" Toby's eyes sparkle. He moves his barrel a little closer to mine.

"Are you a magician?"

He nods.

"I bet you don't reveal your secrets."

"I don't have any." He replaces his bottle on the wagon wheel table. "Well, I have one. But I'm not telling. At least not yet."

His one secret—a magician who can actually do magic. I'm wondering how long it will take this time before he tells me.

"You're not from Vegas either," the magician says with one of his trademark conversational swerves.

I shake my head as we once again discover that we grew up along the banks of the same river back East.

"So you came to Las Vegas to work for a casino?" Toby asks.

You brought me here, I want to say. But in this world, I have no idea how I came to the Winter Palace. "I'm a textile consultant."

Now the magician stifles a laugh.

"You're looking at my dress?"

"What color is that?" he asks.

"I think the official name is Key West Coral."

"Some things should stay in Florida."

I looked down at the dress—its color, an awful match for my complexion. "I'm not so fond of sateen or crystal beading either."

"It kind of makes you look like a broken-hearted beauty queen," the magician says.

"When in Vegas," I say, quickly raising my bottle in front of my face.

Toby lifts his beer to meet mine. There is a clink of glass, and for a moment it seems as if time has stopped. The music is gone. The dancers frozen. And once again, everything telescopes to me and the magician. When I look up, the crystal beads on my dress have become irregular turquoise stones.

"I'm not going to ask."

Toby smiles. "As long as it makes you smile."

"So," I say, rolling my beer bottle between my palms, "shouldn't you be celebrating your Vegas debut back at the Winter Palace?" What fresh coincidence has caused us to collide this time in another improbable location? Did Toby once again conjure me to his side, or did I pull him to mine?

"The show is the satisfying part. The aftermath is a letdown."

"It didn't seem too disappointing," I reply, thinking of the women encircling the magician.

"In the end, the audience wants something I can't give them."

"They all want to know how it's done?"

Toby nods.

"But in your case, the explanation is impossible."

I ignore his surprise. I just smile and pat his knee. "In another lifetime, I spent a lot of time around magicians."

For a moment, Toby cannot speak. Instead he snaps his fingers, and two more beers appear. We raise them to each other. "To things better left unexplained," the magician suggests. And then Toby tells me about his childhood blocks that taught him about magic.

It doesn't bother me that I've heard this all before. Soon we are on our feet, dancing to revved-up hoedown music. Between songs, I ask, "Why did you come here tonight?"

Toby shrugs. "Why not?"

Next to us, a woman has climbed on top of a barrel. She's looped her shirt into an impromptu bra-top and is bending her knees, grinding her way down to her feet.

"You don't strike me as the cattle-call type."

"I'm not."

A new song starts. We're shouting now. "I wanted a moment alone," the magician says.

"This is a strange place to come to be alone."

He nods in time to the music and turns to face me. He puts his hands on my hips and pulls me in close. "And why did you come?"

I laugh. "Same reason." Falling in love with Toby is easy.

We dance, stomp, and tumble along with the music. The crowd throws our bodies together. It's a comfortable collision. And then we are in front of the mechanical bull. Toby catches my eye. I shake my head. "No way."

But he's insisting, and in an instant, I'm lifted over the wooden railing and waiting to be helped onto the bull.

I get in the saddle, and my dress rips. I grab the pommel and wait for the ride to start. A crowd gathers, hooting as the machine underneath me comes to life. Toby and I lock eyes. The machine revolves in small circles, then pitches forward slightly. I grip the pommel tighter. The magician doesn't blink as the bull accelerates. Soon it's spinning and dipping wildly. The crowd is whooping, their voices outdoing the music.

Then the Double Down Saloon gives way to a magic lantern show of our shared experiences. I see the Old Stand and the Laughing Jackalope Motel. I watch as the Rio and the other casinos we visited on our honeymoon spin past. I see the canyon and our picnic on the marriage blanket. I watch the *Desert Princess* chug into a corner of Lake Mead. I see the ranch house pop up between two mesas. Soon the illusion is shattered, interrupted by applause. The ride is slowing; then it stops. Two of the Double Down's employees leap into the ring and lift my arms in the air. The crowd is chanting, "Beat the bull!"

"Giddyup," the woman on my left yells, "we have a winner!"

"First person to beat the bull in months," the woman on my right says. She pulls a Double Down crop top over my head. "Five hundred dollars even," she adds when I've got my head through the neck hole. And she hands me five crisp bills. The crowd is chanting and cheering as I'm passed back to Toby. The magician takes me in his arms. "Who knew you were such a cowgirl," he says.

"What were you thinking when I was on the ride?" I ask.

"I was thinking whether you'd let me see you again."

A tall mustachioed man in a cowboy hat leans between us. He nods toward the bills I've got clenched in my hand. "Should be about enough right there."

"For what?" Toby asks.

"For a Vegas wedding. A girl can ride a bull like that's a girl worth holding on to."

I hesitate for a moment; then I shake my head. "I don't know about marriage, but I'm happy to see what comes next."

The night passes in a swirl of neon, fluorescent cocktails, and flashing lights as Toby and I wind our way down the Strip. Then, of course, there are the small touches of magic that make even the glitziest parts of Vegas shine a little brighter. In the presence of this Toby, it's easy to forget the gloomy magician I'd last seen in Piet's workroom. Finally, we arrive back at the Winter Palace. The opening party has evaporated into the general buzz of another Las Vegas night. At the entrance, Toby puts his hands on my shoulders. "I'm not good with people," he says.

I know, I want to tell him.

"But being around you comes naturally to me."

I close my eyes, waiting for his kiss. And when he kisses me, it does not, as usual, lift me up into the sky, make me float above the desert or wherever it is we are; it keeps me on the ground, as if this is precisely where I'm meant to be.

"I'll find you tomorrow," Toby says as I spin through the revolving door.

When I turn to wave, he is gone.

The artificial light of the endless Winter Palace day erases the intoxication of my night with Toby. I walk through the lobby, unsure of which employees to greet. I head for the front desk, where clerks dressed like Hussars guard the telephones and the reservations system. I find a female receptionist, give her my name, and tell her I've lost my key. She eyes my ruined dress—a frayed time line of my recent trip across the Strip. "Big suite for one gal," she says, passing me my card. "But I guess it'll be filled with high rollers now that we're opening."

I nod and thank her. I'm being shipped out.

On my way to the elevator, I pass the Red Square bar, where

Sandra and her friends are stretched out, ordering everything the harried waitress can bring them.

I walk away, hoping to make it upstairs unnoticed. The elevator glides up so quickly that it take a moment for my heart to catch up. The key card opens the Cherry Orchard Suite. Everything is as I would have left it. My clothes are folded. My books and magazines sit in orderly stacks next to the bed. My shoes are lined up under the window. The only thing missing is a sign of Toby. But of course, I expect that.

Without the magician, the suite is enormous. The king-sized bed envelops me. I press my ear to the bedspread, hoping to hear its stiff synthesized song, which used to comfort me during Toby's late-night shows at the Castaway. The bedspread is silent. So are the crisp cotton pillows. I stand up and explore the room. The fireproof curtains, with their cherry motif, no longer sound like caged woodwinds. The deep oboe notes of the plush pile carpet are barely audible.

I find my suitcase at the back of the closet. My quilt, the one made during my travels in the West, is neatly folded at the bottom. I open it on the bed. Of course, the gingham napkin from the Old Stand Saloon is absent. In its place are several fabrics I don't recognize as well as a couple from the Winter Palace. I trace my fingers over these, trying to imagine what part of my own history I've missed. Each fabric that I'd sewn onto this quilt had at one time sung or spoken to me, contributing its notes or story to my own. I lie down on top of the patches, imploring them to come to life. But there is no noise, only the blood-rush seashore in my own head. The fabrics are dead. I feel as if I might drown in their silence.

Without my fabrics, I don't know where to turn in the hours that stretch before me. My quilt is nothing more than a jumble of patches, a haphazard collection that runs in place. Looking at it, I understand why Eva cannot stay in any one place for long. My presence has been removed from what were once familiar surroundings. I feel myself written out of my own past. I have no idea how to catch up with this present.

Still lying on the quilt, I fumble for the telephone. I dial Leo's number. I need to hear a familiar voice, even if, in this world, we are strangers.

It's Olivia who answers, her voice warm with sleep. "Hello?"

"It's Mel," I say.

I'm met with silence at first. "Hello?"

"It's Mel. You don't remember me, do you?"

"Mmmm." I can imagine Olivia scrunching her eyes and wrinkling her nose, trying to tease my name out of her memory.

"Or maybe we haven't met." I suggest.

"Maybe not. That would make it hard to remember you."

I want to tell Olivia all the things I know about her. I want to do anything to keep her voice pressed into my ear. But then she says, "I think you have the wrong number."

"I probably do." The line goes dead, adding its silence to the fabrics'. I let the receiver tumble from my hand and dangle toward the floor. Soon I can hear the rhythmic buzz of the busy signal. I let it go on.

Eighteen

I'm lying in the middle of the king-sized bed, legs and arms spread wide. A castaway on a raft floating in the empty Cherry Orchard Suite. There's a knock at the door. I pull on one of the plush bathrobes with gold braided belts. I expect to see the magician. Instead I find one of the bellboys carrying the clothes I'd abandoned in Sandra's office.

Out on the Strip, the neon illusions of the Las Vegas night are gone. The harsh sun reveals the city's trickery, exposing the miniature skyline outside the New York, New York and the small Eiffel Tower in front of the Paris for cartoonish approximations. I weave between slow-moving tourists and pass the Mirage, where the volcano's lava roar is still sending more heat into the baking day. Finally I come to Fremont Street and enter the covered esplanade. As I knew it would be, Fremont is empty save for a few hard-nosed gamblers still at the tables since last night and those who set their alarms to catch their lucky dealers.

The Castaway is a swamp of cigarette smoke. The carpet is sticky with spilled drinks and trampled ash. I pass through the pits, listening to the hollow drop of coins. Men and a few women are hunched over at the tables, considering their cards. I arrive at the door to the small theater and push it open. Inside, I find a tangle of discarded furniture. Three-legged craps tables are turned on their sides. One-armed bandits stare blankly from the dusty dark. I look at the stage where the Ladies' Magician had performed. It's a jumble of fallen stage lights and discarded gels.

As I sit down, I hear someone approaching from the back of the theater. I hope for Toby, but it's Eva, gracefully negotiating the mess that separates us.

"You thought he would be here?" she asks.

"I wasn't thinking."

"Toby's shows at the Castaway exist in a time that cannot come again."

I nod while Eva lights a cigarette and takes the seat next to me. "So, you, too, were sent into one of Toby's tricks."

"How can you tell?"

"Because we've already met inside the magician's imagination. I've seen it all before."

"Seen what?"

"The show at the Winter Palace. The other outcome. And you were there."

"That wasn't his imagination. That was real."

Eva shakes her head, sending smoke from side to side. "Maybe for you. For me, it was just another intersection of his tricks."

I look around the theater. "All of this is an accident. Toby didn't mean for me to follow him."

"Follow him where?" Eva sounds uninterested.

"In Amsterdam, he discovered a trick called the Dissolving World. It can take him to any point in his memory.

"Toby never needed a trick to do that. He's done it before. Except it was me he sent there, not himself." Now Eva laughs with a sharp, cutting sound. "And after all this, he chooses to come back here." She shakes her head and squints into the dust. "I guess saving her life is more important to him than fixing mine."

"You're alive, aren't you?" I give her a cool look.

Eva exhales toward the ceiling.

We are silent for a moment. Then Eva kicks up her legs and places them on the seat in front of her. I watch dust settle on her patent leather heels. She smooths her stockings. "He came back here, but he doesn't know you. But you know him. Maybe your love is just stronger than his." There's a sharp edge to Eva's voice.

I shake my head. "He didn't know I was coming. He told me not to follow him." I looked down at my hands. "I guess he never imagined that I'd be part of this world when he stepped into it. He didn't create a place for me here. But we've met again."

"And it's all running so smoothly." Eva doesn't want a response. "Don't get too comfortable. You are always going to be an outsider. But you must have already figured that out. Your memories and Toby's can't line up. Your worlds will always be slightly different."

I don't reply. Despite last evening with Toby, I know Eva's right.

"The more time you spend here, the more edges will blur, corners will melt, and places will vanish. Because you are meant to be elsewhere, you will not be able to remain in one place for long. When Toby banished me to the mesa, the trick eventually broke. I was returned to reality. But I'd been gone for so long, reality and I no longer clicked. For your sake, I hope this trick ends sooner rather than later."

"What if I don't want that?"

Eva narrows her eyes into the dim light. "What happens

when something goes wrong for Toby this time? Will he rewind time, send himself somewhere else, forget about you again?"

"Toby didn't mean to forget me."

Now Eva places a hand on my leg and grips hard. "But he did. Even if it was an accident. Every accident is the manifestation of a secret intention. Toby banished me because he wanted to test the limits of his magic. And he knew that when he discovered what he could do, he'd leave me behind." She finishes her cigarette and tosses it onto the ground. I watch the ash burn down. "He's chosen magic over you."

I shake my head. "He loves me."

"Maybe," Eva says. "But he loves magic more."

"Last night was like starting over."

"Maybe." She doesn't buy it.

I look at her profile—her sharp coif and angular chin—and I remember a question I've been meaning to ask her. "Eva, where did you go that night on the mesa?"

"Somewhere else. Elsewhere."

I shake my head at this unusually imprecise response. "Tell me."

"I went to find Toby." Without looking at me, Eva says, "I was worried you wouldn't get through to him. And I was right. I told him, no matter what happens, he should never involve you in his magic." She puts a new cigarette to her lips, lights it, and exhales. "If he loves you. You should thank me."

"He listened to you."

"Until now."

"He didn't mean for me to follow him," I tell her again. "How do I make it stop?"

Eva shrugs. "Convince him. Convince him that things are better elsewhere." Then she shakes her head. "I don't think you have much chance." She's on her feet. I know better than to ask where she's going.

After a few months in Amsterdam, the heat of Las Vegas at lunchtime takes me by surprise. On the Fremont side, there are no air-conditioned walkways and skyways to take you between buildings—no trams or shuttles to save you from the sun. Only five minutes after leaving the covered esplanade, my sundress is drenched. I'm struggling back toward the heart of the Strip. I take a glance at the insistent sun and realize that I need a break.

The Stratosphere, the casino on the Strip closest to Fremont Street, has nothing more going for it than its looming space age tower—a haven for thrill seekers, romantics, and the occasional suicide. I had passed this casino many times on my way to watch Toby's show at the Castaway without ever being tempted to enter. Now, the promise of air-conditioning lures me into its lobby.

The interior of the Stratosphere resembles an airport terminal more than a glitzy venue to drop cash and press your luck. Maybe its allure increases as you ascend the tower, passing swimming pools and wedding chapels suspended high above the Strip. I buy a ticket for the observation deck and ride the elevator over a thousand feet in the air. The view does not thrill me. The tower is so much taller than the rest of Vegas that my eyes pass over the Strip, leading me to the suburban sprawl that runs toward the murky mountains in the distance. Looking down from the Stratosphere, Las Vegas is an array of drab concrete structures, skeletal buildings, and vast parking lots.

The crowd on the observation deck is divided into two groups—those intent on capturing this strange panorama on rolls of film, and nervous adventurers waiting in line to ride the world's highest roller coaster. The roller coaster is often closed due to high winds, but today the desert air is stagnant. It seems to suck the chatter out of my fellow tourists on the observation deck, muting their exclamations into silence. The only sound is the intermittent rush and roar of the roller coaster shooting over its rails.

As I peer out over the city and the desert beyond, I'm struck by the dizzying uniformity to the outskirts of Vegas—indistinguishable communities clustered so tightly, I cannot imagine how, if I were set down in one of them, I could find my way out. I begin to walk the circumference of the tower until I'm looking in the direction of Tonopah. I squint, teasing out the northwesterly road Toby and I first traveled together. I concentrate as hard as I can, trying to impose the memory of our meeting onto the world in which I'm currently standing. I conjure the image of the magician's beaten minivan, the desolate road where he found me, the splintered charm of the Old Stand Saloon. I run my fingers over the back of my hand where Toby first touched me.

As I'm looking over the desert, I feel the edge of my vision start to blur. The sharp diagonals of the highways ripple. The border of towns and mesas shake. I grip the handrail and prepare myself for the same heady swirl of plummeting through the Dissolving World. My knees buckle, and I'm ready to fall to the deck.

Then Toby catches me. "I'm guessing heights are not your thing."

It's a moment before I can speak. "If I didn't know better, I'd say it's quite a coincidence bumping into you here."

The magician leads me away from the railing. "Do you know better?"

"Because magicians don't believe in coincidence."

Toby gives me a strange look, then smiles. "You're right." He winds his fingers through mine. "I've been looking for you."

"And you had an inkling that I'd be hanging around the Stratosphere tower?"

The magician shakes his head. "I'm afraid psychic ability is far outside my powers. I followed you." He pauses, waiting for my displeasure. But all I do is smile. "Then I lost you somewhere in the depths of Fremont Street. I hung around the esplanade until you emerged."

"Why didn't you say anything?"

Toby bites his lip. "Nerves. I want everything to be perfect. Like last night."

I want to tell him that is impossible. But he has a look that suggests he's poised for disappointment. "I wanted to ask you to be my guest at a private show tomorrow. But I couldn't wait until then to see you."

"Did you consider leaving a note or using the phone?"

Toby shakes his head. "Too simple."

I am about to say yes, but manage to restrain myself. "Maybe."

"Maybe?"

I glance over the panorama. "If you let me take you somewhere first."

"Where?"

I'm not going to tell. We step into the elevator, and my stomach rises as we slide back down to earth.

I don't let the magician know how relieved I am to see his beat-up brown minivan, that he has not left it to rust at the edge of the desert. As I climb into the passenger's seat, Toby looks over at me. "Seems odd to see someone riding shotgun."

"I don't believe I can be the first." I crack the window. It's what I'm supposed to say.

"Magic doesn't leave much room for relationships. Especially my kind."

"Of magic or relationships?"

The magician laughs. "I was thinking magic. But that might change."

"You're going to change your magic?"

He shakes his head. "Maybe slightly."

"Why now?" I ask, as if I've known Toby forever.

"I'm tired of banishing things."

Toby puts the car into drive and slides from the parking lot onto the Strip. I direct him out of town, in the opposite direction from the suburban sprawl I'd seen from the Stratosphere.

"Magic is a lonely business. Can you imagine what it was like being a magician in high school?"

I fiddle with the door lock.

"Magic cut me off from my stepmother, my classmates. And then when I went to circus school, I discovered that my kind of magic cut me off from my peers." We come to the end of the Strip and roll past the famous Las Vegas sign. I crane my neck to see the Laughing Jackalope Motel shrink into the distance. "Loneliness is part of what we do. It's our job to make things disappear."

"But you are supposed to find them, too."

Toby nods. "I wish it were that simple." He presses on the accelerator, and with a familiar shudder, the van picks up speed. "It is also a magician's job to pretend a certain cruelty or danger on stage—to make people believe that we are cutting our assistants in half, shooting them, or impaling them on spikes."

"Fake danger."

"Usually." Toby exhales a slow and steady breath. "Last night, something changed. It wasn't supposed to happen that way, the volunteer jumping out in front of me."

"Greta?"

"You know her."

"Not really."

"I'd seen her around. I guess you could say she was a fan of mine. Came to a bunch of my small shows." The familiar static creeps into his voice. "She's supposed to stay put, stay behind me. Her presence is just a gimmick to highlight the trick's potential danger. Then she jumped." He shifts his grip on the steering wheel. "My magic is all about potential, the potential of anything to be anywhere at any given time. Mastering possibilities is what excites me. But this girl, she interfered. And instead of ruining my show, everything slid into place. It was as if I had been waiting for this moment. Sometimes my hands act unbidden, but this was different." He pauses. "Do you know what happened?"

I do. Sort of. But I want to hear it from Toby.

"Someone cried out in the audience." He turns to me and smiles. "You. And then I reached out and caught the bullet. Not caught it. Withdrew it." He draws out these last two words. "It was as if you were telling me to do so." Toby's voice changes, becoming confident. "I must sound ridiculous."

"No."

"Then I ran into you at that classy bar, and things sort of fell into place."

I know now that if I tell Toby that I cannot stay with him, I will break his heart. If I tell him I'm going to leave, will he follow?

"I'll never top last night's performance. And I can't shake the feeling that somehow you made it possible."

"I can't imagine how."

"Neither can I. But if you hadn't called out, maybe . . ." Toby's voice trails off as he imagines the scene I've replayed in my head hundreds of times. "So," the magician continues, his voice bright, "where are you taking us?"

Us. The word sounds fantastic, full of settled possibility. "I'm not telling."

We stop at a trading post by the small highway and pick up some food. Kachina dolls by local artists are arrayed on shoddy display cases. While the shopkeeper hunts for a bag for our groceries, Toby makes two of the dolls circle each other in a ceremonial dance. The dolls rattle the shelves as they settle back into place.

The shopkeeper looks up, his eyes flashing with disapproval.

"Too much?" Toby asks.

"Maybe you shouldn't mess with ceremonial objects."

The magician accepts the groceries with a smile that is not returned.

We continue down the dusty highway.

"Still no hint?" Toby asks as his fingers reach for mine over the shift.

I shake my head. I'm starting to worry that the blue ranch house will no longer be there. Or that someone has moved their life into our place. I'm worried most of all that imposing my memory of the ranch house onto this reality will make me seasick, as I was on the Stratosphere tower.

The van rattles over the uneven dirt, shaking as it hits ruts and rocks. The little blue house comes into sight. Again, I'm struck by its improbable color—a flash of cornflower—framed by two rusty mesas. I can tell that Toby is captivated by the house's improbable charm, just as he was the day we accidentally discovered it.

We try the front door. It's unlocked.

"What is this place?" Toby asks as we step into the strangely cool interior.

"Somewhere I'd once planned to live."

The house is empty, but not barren. Plates, cutlery, and glassware are stacked neatly in their cabinets. Dish towels hang from a rack along the wall. The immaculate silence reminds me of our visit to Toby's childhood home inside the Dissolving World—a sensation of otherworldly abandonment. The only difference since my last visit here is that the fabrics no longer sing to me.

"You changed your mind?"

"Something like that."

"Do you think you'll change it again?" Toby drums his fingers along the table.

I shake my head. "I love this place."

"So—"

"It's hard to come back."

Toby walks into the living room. The green floral couch and matching La-Z-Boy are still there. He sits on the couch and stares out the window at the two mesas. "It's like another world here, as if Las Vegas doesn't exist." The magician looks around the room. "Living here would make sense. You should reconsider." He nods and pats the space next to him on the couch—the same gesture he'd made on our first morning at the Laughing Jackalope Motel.

"I'd love to, but I can't. I don't stay in one place for long."

"Because you're a traveling textile consultant."

I smile at this simple explanation. "Something like that."

Toby loops one of his long arms around my shoulder and pulls my head onto his collarbone. "I feel so comfortable here. Like I've been here before." Then he swallows hard. "You're not seriously thinking of leaving town, are you?"

"I think I have to."

"But we've only just met."

"I've heard that love and magic don't mix."

Toby gives me a strange, thin smile. He shrugs. "I used to believe that. Until last night." He releases my shoulder and pulls away from me so he can look into my eyes. He takes my hands in his. "Ever since I discovered I could do magic, I've been searching for the perfect trick. My stepfather, Ernest, was an anatomist. I would hang about his office, staring into the jigsaw of blood and flesh and bone and wonder what form of magic could reassemble what he had meticulously taken apart." He squeezes my fingertips, causing small bubbles to rise into the air. "Unlike other magicians, my illusions are real. If a traditional conjurer pretends to cut a woman in half, he is pretending to put her back together. Of course, there is no pretending in my magic. This is why I don't cut assistants in half or shoot them from cannons." Toby presses my hands tighter. "Which is not to say I haven't been tempted. But last night, simply by accident, I performed the perfect trick. I didn't catch that bullet in time. I reversed it. I accidentally created and subverted actual danger onstage. I saved that girl's life. In my Vegas debut." Toby is beaming. "No magic trick will ever top that." He leans forward and kisses my cheek. "I'm never going to try. That trick will live in everyone's memory. A perfect moment never to be relived again."

"You wouldn't want to repeat or revisit it?"

Toby shakes his head. "It was the moment I'd been searching for since my childhood. A moment of purest magic. So, what I'm wondering is, now that this has happened, would you consider staying here in Vegas with me. I'm tired of banishing things. I'd like to do a less lonely form of conjuring."

I stand up quickly so Toby cannot see my tears. How can our happiness hinge on the outcome of a single magic trick? But in this reality and in the other, this is what Toby believes. He sounds so earnest and sure of himself. But magic will win eventually, carry him off, just as the water summoned Max.

I cross to the opposite side of the room. When something goes wrong this time around, I wonder what moment Toby will wish to return to. Will he come back to the day we met, or will he revisit to the scene of his perfect trick? I might be fooling myself, but I try to imagine that Toby will return to me, if only in a world of his magic.

"I'll think about it" is my answer.

If Toby is disappointed, he doesn't let it show.

As the afternoon slides into evening, I decide to forget that I am a stranger in this place conjured by Toby. I want to enjoy the ranch house and the mystical mesas. I never got the chance before. Our future is now telescoped to this single afternoon. I draw

Toby to his feet and lead him out into the desert behind the house. We walk through the sand, planning the future. We discuss the best place to install a picnic table and a cactus garden. We imagine our desert life, which seems to be unfolding quickly. Toby enchants me with details. He lures me into designing new curtains for the living room. We plan to rearrange the bedroom, so the view from the bed is of the sand, not the television. We decide to swap the smoked glass window in the bathroom for a clear pane.

Soon the sun is slipping between the mesas. Tentacles of black stretch out across the desert, creating pictographs in the sand. Toby sits at my side. We stare toward the mesas, at the place children believe is haunted by animal spirits. As I spread out the picnic, the pictographs begin to dance. They circle and weave; then they melt into the sand and emerge as new shapes. They steal toward our feet, curious explorers, then timidly vanish, only to reappear at a safe distance. As we eat, the pictographs rise from the sand, briefly forming into three-dimensional shapes. I recognize the spirits and creatures from the crafts sold at the side of the road. They last for only a moment, a beautiful two-step dance, before collapsing back into the desert.

When this dance is done, it is night. Toby stands up and draws a large circle in the sand with the toe of his shoe. I am at the center. He returns to my side and sits. As he does so, the circle bursts into low flames, protecting and illuminating us. We uncork another bottle of wine and drink in silence. The only sound is the low crackle of the flame and the scratch and snuffle of curious desert animals approaching the ring of fire.

Eventually the flames go out. I sense the magician readying for his next trick. I stop him. But I want something more. We return to the house and fluff the pillows on the bed. I pull back aside the drapes, so the desert stars shine into the window. We lie down side by side. I switch on the TV. The local news flickers to life. Toby and I link hands as the newscaster takes us on a tour of Vegas's minor happenings. We watch in silence, as if we had done this always.

The news fades away. Toby wraps his fingers over my shoulder and pulls me on top of him. The television is forgotten. He places his lips on mine, and I fully expect that his kiss will be magical, that I'll be carried away, lifted up to the stars or laid down on the distant mesas. But we stay in this room, on top of the buttercup bedspread. For the first time, I feel the full weight of the magician's body as we roll over the covers.

I am starting to fall asleep in the hollow of Toby's collarbone. I can feel the magician slide into his dreamtime conjuring, the semiconscious twitch of his fingers summoning long-forgotten objects. I lift my head. "Toby? Have you ever heard of a magic trick call the Dissolving World?"

He shakes his head. He's falling back asleep.

"I've heard that it's a perfect trick."

He's awake now, his eyes clear, his lips tense.

I rummage through my bag for the playbill I carried from Piet's.

Toby takes the paper from my hands. "Looks like any old box to me."

I snuggle back into his shoulder. "It can take you into any world you imagine, if only for a moment." I sit up in bed, wrap an arm around Toby, and pull his head onto my stomach. I comb my fingers through his tangled black hair, shaking out grains of sand. I tell him everything I know about Theo, Piet, and the Dissolving World. I finish my story. I feel Toby's jaw tense. Then I add, "I've heard that certain magicians can make this trick happen without the box itself. Who knows."

Toby exhales.

"That is magic I'd love to see." I close my eyes, willing my dreams to come. Toby stretches out next to me. I can tell that it will be a long while before he falls asleep.

Toby only half listens to me as we drive back to Vegas. His mind is lighting on mesas, running alongside the riverbank of his youth, flying over the roads that carried him out West. Every once in a while, he reaches over and pats my hand, reassuring me of his presence, if not his attention. He lets me off in front of the Winter Palace, barely finding time to kiss me and make a comment about preparing for his private show this evening. Then his eyes find mine, and he's with me once more.

"You're coming?"

I nod.

"Before it was only a maybe."

"I've changed my mind."

A gold-embossed envelope is waiting for me in the suite. It contains an invitation to A SOIREE OF MAYHEM AND MAGIC. At the bottom of the card is my name and the explanation GUEST OF THE MAGICIAN. I recognize the name of an established Hollywood actress and one of the fabled private venues in Las Vegas.

The private salons of Las Vegas are the refuge of tycoons, royals, sultans, and sheiks, where women come and go through hidden doorways and their customers vanish through underground tunnels. It was to one of these that Toby had summoned me.

I iron my only cocktail dress, a black silk sheath that had once purred like a sultry lounge singer. I twirl before the mirror. The dress looks bland. Toby unwittingly deprived it of its best feature. I'm dressed too early and pace around the suite. I finger the edge of the silent drapes and look over the expanse of desert that stretches away from the Strip toward the ranch house that will never be ours. I've spent my last night in the Cherry Orchard Suite. I've already thrown a few things into a suitcase that I'll probably leave behind. Anyway, I don't know where I'm headed, and I'm not sure I want to take anything with me.

I glance down at the Strip, now the setting for two conflicting tales of Toby and me, two divergent love stories heading in the same direction, but never reaching the same place. I will always know the magician better than he knows himself. Tricking myself into forgetting would be the only way to move forward. But there is nothing about my life with Toby I will ever willingly let go of. I let the drape fall, then close it altogether, blocking out all the landmarks of our various paths and our uncertain future. Then I sit, relaxing into my choice. I wonder how long I've known that this was the only possible ending.

If I could ask my brother one question it would be this: Did he wake up that morning in Bermuda and decide, *Today is the day I swim away?* Or did something in the water call him with a voice so sweet and insistent that he could no longer come up for air? I have a feeling he had known all along, ever since that day he survived the nighttime river. If I had my quilt, the complete quilt I'd left at Leo's, I would search it for a clue to the moment I knew that Toby and I had come to inhabit different worlds. This realization doesn't floor me or send me reeling to the chair with stomach-punch force. It creeps in, a slowly rising tide, on which I'm eventually going to float away. But, like my brother, I have a feeling that this ebb and flow will bring with it a melancholy freedom.

Sandra gives me a look as I pass through the lobby. I'm carrying the invitation in one hand.

"Where you off to, hon?"

"A party. A magic show."

Her eyes narrow. "Lots of magic this week."

"Guess Vegas is growing on me."

"Join me for a drink first." Sandra looks over my shoulder toward the Red Square bar, then at the envelope in my hand. I glance at my watch and shake my head.

"Suit yourself," she says, waltzing off to the bar solo.

I present myself to the concierge at the establishment mentioned on the invitation. I give him my name and am escorted through a maze of hallways to an unmarked and unremarkable door. The door opens to a small foyer piled high with silk cushions. A woman in Moroccan robes, refashioned to allow for an improbable amount of décolletage, takes my hand and leads me through another set of doors to a dimly lit room decorated in a grab bag of oriental and Middle Eastern styles. Chinese lanterns hang from a ceiling that's tented in *Arabian Nights* fabric, barely illuminating hookahs and Japanese tatami mats. Eight pointed Moroccan stars hang next to stencils of Hindu deities. Ostrich feathers fill ceramic vases while ornate shrines are set up to revere nothing in particular.

About thirty people are scattered through the room, reclining, drawing on hookahs, sipping green drinks. I recognize the Hollywood star, the hostess for the evening. She's in a silky red dress buttoned up to the throat. She's sprawled over cushions, extending her bare feet into a small crowd of admirers who silently consider their cocktails and suck on bubbling pipes.

Belly dancers, masseurs, tarot readers, and a hypnotist move around the room, whispering their offerings into the ears of the guests. It seem as if drugs and alcohol are not sufficient to charm the revelers' minds into submission. They require another type of out-of-body experience and need their futures to be laid out in vivid pictures. Behind a DJ booth, a man in a fez spins slow hypnotic grooves. After a couple of days back in Las Vegas, I realize how tired I am of these false enchantments.

I didn't see Toby enter. But he's at my side, wearing a black silk shirt with black embroidery.

He loops his arm through mine. "Would you indulge me before I make my rounds?"

"With what?" I let him kiss my cheek.

"A quick trick." Toby passes his hand over mine. I look down and see my green drink—absinthe and citrus—turn the color of the ranch house. He winks and is off.

I settle into a pile of cushions, not really caring that I have no one to speak to. I'm happy to watch Toby work, stretching out his elegant frame alongside revelers on Thai meditation pillows. I can't hear him, but I can imagine his voice as he asks if they would like to see his magic. I know the looks of surprise as cocktails are transformed into smoke, which then curls upward, taking the shape of Far East dragons.

Toby's routine is similar to the one he performed at the Castaway, but now it's tinged with Eastern mysticism. He transforms money into prayer papers, makes animal shapes appear inside the Chinese lanterns, causes the hookahs to billow multicolored plumes of smoke. Toby charms with updated classics, making an orange tree grow from an empty vase, plucking enamel carp from the air, transforming napkins into doves and then back again.

In this dark chamber, hidden away in the bowels of Vegas, it's easy to submit to the magician's charms. If we could lead our lives sealed in such boxes, staying with Toby, even in this world of his conjuring might be possible. But eventually the door will open and reality will leak in. Something will go wrong and the magician will resort to magic to repair the damage. I can't blame him, I think, as I watch him turn a woman's cuff bracelet into a iridescent lizard, before restoring it to a cuff.

Toby takes his time with the actress. He sits close to her and whispers in her ear. He holds one of her hands in his own, using the other to conjure an array of objects that might amuse her. She has an ostrich feather in her free hand and is using it to trace lazy circles in the air, keeping half an eye on the magic appearing next to her. Coins and tarot cards, birds of paradise, and hammered silver jewels arrive in her lap. Her drink turns to smoke, which then coils around her neck and solidifies into a silk wrap. Toby removes the wrap from the actress's shoulders and crumples it in his hands. He unfurls it, then he claps, folding the fabric together. As he does so, the silk vanishes, replaced by a tall green-and-orange flame, leaping upward from the magician's palm.

Toby's on his feet, making room for the hypnotist, who's been waiting to enchant one of the actress's companions. Soon the man leaps from the group, swirling and bobbing, sinks to floor, and, with a word from the hypnotist, is released from his spell.

I follow the magician to a corner of the room, where a four-paneled Moorish screen leans against the wall. He brings the screen into the center of the room and arranges it into a diamond shape with a small opening between the two end panels. He returns to the actress and her friends and extends an arm. The hostess allows herself to be lifted to her feet and led to the screen. Toby whispers something in her ear and escorts her into the space inside the panels. She vanishes from sight.

When she emerges, she swears she's been away for hours, transported to another world. Her friends line up for this new enchantment, each one emerging with a fantastic tale of a landscape far away. My heart leaps as another partygoer steps into this trick. Toby's success at the Winter Palace has clearly emboldened him, and he invites the entire crowd to be part of his magic.

Then it's my turn. Toby beckons to me, drawing me to his side. He passes an arm around my waist, and we stand in front of the screen.

"Wait." I step away from the magician.

"What is it?"

I take a deep breath, willing the words to come out. "I can't stay."

"The party isn't going to last forever."

"I can't stay in Vegas. My time here is up."

I see Toby's eyes cloud. "I don't understand."

"I don't expect you to." I look into my hands, searching for a way to explain.

"We've met before. But there's no way you'd remember." I pause. "It was at another time. One that seems never to have existed."

The magician's expression is blank. He's used to the inexplicable, so he lets me continue.

"I loved you there, too." I can't meet his eye, so I look into the opening between the panels. "We'd done so much together."

"So, why do you need to go?"

"I am inside one of your tricks. Like Eva, I've fallen victim to your magic. I want to leave before it happens again."

"Eva." The name catches in Toby's throat.

"You haven't seen her."

"Not since—"

"If you love me, maybe you'll follow me."

"Where?"

"I'm not sure. Maybe to Amsterdam, where we parted. Maybe back home to my parents." I shake my head. "I have a feeling you'll remain with your magic."

"I can take my magic anywhere." Toby's voice is overrun with its strange static.

"We can replay this scene hundreds of times in hundreds of different places, but I have a feeling you'll always choose magic in the end."

"I'm a magician. Am I supposed to choose anything else?"

I shake my head.

"So?"

I stand on my toes and press my lips against Toby's. His kiss is cold and distant. His lips are hard and trembling. I know that he's trying to navigate between anger and despair.

"I'll see you again," Toby says, and points to the other side of the screen.

I step into the opening of the screen. I turn to see Toby clasping his hands together, searching for some magic to bring this moment under his control. I shake my head and tell him that I'm sorry. He reaches out to me. But I step farther into the opening inside the four-paneled screen. I close my eyes and wait. I have no idea where he'll send me. I wonder if in a few moments I'll step back into the party and find my temporary place with the actress and her friends, or whether I'll wind up somewhere else entirely. Soon I feel the familiar static rush. I wonder where the magician is sending me. I wonder if I'll ever see him again.

Nineteen

Piet's house was boarded up. His magical memorabilia had been packed into boxes. I recognized the address on the labels as that of a famous magic museum in Nevada. The only illusion that remained was the Dissolving World, and I stepped out of it into the empty workroom. I had no idea how long I'd been gone.

All trace of Toby's and my passage in the house had been removed along with everything else. When I stepped into the screen in Las Vegas, I had been prepared never to see the magician again, but I wasn't ready to have all physical memory of him taken away. I'd hope to run my fingers over his black dress shirts and flip through his library of books on magic and anatomy. But most of all, I hadn't wanted to let go of the saltshakers and ashtrays he had palmed during our first days together. Like my quilt, I had always imagined that these souvenirs would help me retrace my steps to wherever I'd left Toby, even if only in my mind.

I left Piet's, and this time an usually clear Amsterdam evening was lost to tears. The streets sparkled with a wintry sheen. The canals glistened, reflecting the stars that rarely showed themselves above the city. Streamers of white lights in the shape of snowflakes framed the openings of the alleyways, foretelling the approaching holidays. Circus wagons selling freshly made doughnuts had popped up on busy intersections and alongside popular parks. The sound of Christmas music filled the air, accompanying me on my walk to the train station.

Olivia was waiting just inside the gate of Leo's villa. Before I could say anything, she threw her arms around my neck. "We've been so worried," she said. "No one's heard from you for weeks. We haven't been able to call the magicians."

I'd been gone for only a couple of days. But Toby's magic has a way of transforming time to suit itself.

"But you've come just in time."

"For what?" I asked. I was too tired to notice Olivia's outfit—a red-and-green velvet dress with synthetic pine needles at the collar and cuffs. I looked over her shoulder to the villa. It was lit up by hundreds of candles. A bonfire was burning on the lawn.

"It's Leo's saturnalia. The best party of the year."

"I'm not up for a party."

Olivia kissed my cheek, mulled wine on her breath. "Of course you are. It's the longest night of the year. So we stay up, beating back the darkness with candles and fire."

She linked her fingers through mine and began pulling me toward the festivities.

"It wouldn't be the same without you," she said, looking back over my shoulder.

"He's not coming." I drew a deep breath, filling my lungs with the scent of wood smoke, pine needles, and roasting meat. "Toby sent me to a place where we were strangers. I don't think he's coming back."

Olivia wiped away tears from my cheek with her palm. "I wouldn't count on that."

The villa and the lawn behind it were glowing like a sunset, each window shining with a shade of red, orange, or purple light. Streamers flew from the gables and Eastern European dance music filled the air. The evergreens had been strung with white lights, reaching from tree to tree until they disappeared into the depths of Leo's property. A trail of lanterns illuminated the path to the villa.

I followed Olivia to the lawn, which was lit with dozens of braziers. Several pits had been dug into the earth. These were filled with glowing coals for the skewers of meat. I looked down to the river where fairy lanterns were being launched downstream on tiny boats made from bark, their small flames bobbing and glittering in the dark water.

The yellow tent had been transformed into a dance floor. The shadows of the dancers dipped and wove in between the oriental flowers painted on the tent's exterior. The Christophs passed through the crowd, swinging censers filled with rosemary. One of them wore a crown of ivy and the other, holly. The rest of the revelers—satyrs, Roman courtiers, jesters, Elizabethan ladies, unfamiliar pagan deities—filled the tent. Olivia and I stepped inside. The Eastern European music stopped, and the dancers were clearing the floor, making way for a string quartet in Louis XIV costumes. Their faces were powdered as were their wigs.

"Finnish," the Belgian Christoph said, tapping me on the shoulder. "Apparently, back home, they even own a reindeer."

"Have you seen Leo?" Olivia asked the Christophs.

"The house," one of them replied. "More light."

"There will never be enough candles. Come, Leo will be so happy to see you," the other Christoph said.

Before heading toward the villa, Olivia and I helped ourselves to cups of warm, spiced wine. I could feel the alcohol bring a glow to my cheeks. She noticed and put her hands to my face. "That's better. Your face wasn't just pale. It was empty of color."

I finished my wine as we wove through the party and up the stone staircase that led to the terrace at the back of the villa. Boughs of holly, ivy, and other evergreens hung from each lintel and transom, as well as framing every window.

We found Leo in the kitchen stooped over a tray of candles floating in tiny finger bowls. He was dressed in a midnight blue velvet suit embroidered with the rings of Saturn. The gold embroidery was caught by the candlelight.

His face lit up when he saw me. "Aah," he exclaimed, "I knew you wouldn't be far behind."

"Behind what?" I let Leo embrace me.

He released me and held me by the shoulders at arm's length. "Behind your husband." Then Leo narrowed his eyes to mine. "You didn't know."

I shook my head.

I felt Toby before I saw him—an angular shadow in the back of the room. I turned. The magician stood in the doorway, framed by candlelight. He was smiling.

"Toby."

In an instant, he crossed the room and wrapped me in his arms. "You didn't think I would come," he whispered in my ear.

I pressed my head into his chest.

"Thank you for having me," Toby said to Leo.

"We haven't had magic here in years. But before anything we need more light. The party lasts until the last light—candle, fire, coal, whatever—burns out." He put a finger to his lips. "But be careful not to extinguish any yourselves. That is bad luck. It summons the dark too soon. Please?" He handed us each a lighter and pointed to a side table laden with pillar candles.

Toby waved his hand over the candles, lighting them all at once. Their flames rose upward in shades of green and blue, bringing the stars and planets embroidered on Leo's coat to life. Leo ran his fingers over his sleeve. "Saturn for my saturnalia," he said, then took us each by the arm. "Let us head into the night. But first, a toast." He pulled three small glasses off a nearby shelf and filled them with a thick brown liquid. "Sailor's drink. Wards off the dark, cold night."

We lifted the glasses.

"To everlasting life and everlasting bacchanalia." With these words, he vanished.

Toby and I stood alone in the kitchen.

"I didn't think you were coming. Ever," I said.

"I don't like being left behind."

"You saved her." I took Toby's hands in mine.

The magician nodded. "But only in that world."

"I know," I said. "But we were strangers. That was the price."

"We met again." A smiled played across Toby's lips. "You were pretty good on that bull."

I laughed. "And you were handy with the ladies."

"But there was only one lady I was interested in. And she left."

I nodded.

"I told you I'd see you on the other side of that screen. I had no idea how far away that was." Toby kissed away a tear. He re-filled our glasses from Leo's bottle.

"Do you remember now how things are supposed to be?"

"I'm not sure things are supposed to be one way or the other. But when you stepped into the screen and vanished, I knew I'd have to see you again." Toby linked his fingers through mine and squeezed tight. "I reached out to pull you back, but you'd already gone. And when my fingers missed yours, that's when I remembered." He knocked back his drink. "Not just that we'd met before, but everything. It made finding you easy." Now Toby looked into his glass. "I didn't wait long to follow you. The guests at the party in Las Vegas were starting to whisper. They'd seen you go into the screen and not come out. It was like Eva all over again. I felt dizzy. I was in two places at once. I had two overlapping memories of you and of Las Vegas."

I smiled, remembering my own seasickness as my Las Vegas experiences collided on top of the Stratosphere. "Now you know what it is like to be inside one of your own tricks."

"I had to escape."

"Into the screen?"

"I can't imagine what they are saying back at the party." Toby said. "The magician who made himself disappear."

I lifted my glass to my lips and wondered if it wasn't just me Toby was reaching out to in that screen, but also the ability to step into his imagination. I wondered how long it would be before he longed to go save Greta again. And with his customary conversational misdirection, Toby said, "Falling in love with you again was fun." He lifted me in his arms. "Shall we join the party?"

Before I could reply, he kissed me and carried me out into the crowd.

We found one of the Christophs in the middle of the lawn.

"You remember Toby."

Christoph's face lit up. "The magician. At last," he beamed, bowing slightly as he shook Toby's hand. "Would you like to be holly or ivy?" He extended his arms, one of which was ringed with holly crowns, the other with ivy.

"I have no idea," Toby replied.

"The two most important winter plants. I think you should be the Holly King." He held out the arm with the holly.

"Are you sure?" Toby asked.

"He's jolly and playful. A vegetation god. He's part of the seasonal cycle, and you're a magician. It's all about transformation."

The magician fingered the holly crown.

"And the ivy?" I asked.

"The cold gloom of winter. But evergreen nonetheless."

"I'll take ivy," Toby decided.

"You'll take the gloom of winter?" I asked.

Christoph wrapped an arm around my shoulder. "There are no bad choices. The ivy brings both good and bad luck. Although some say it represents mortality, the most common belief is that the ivy is eternal life and resurrection."

"Resurrection?" Toby said, reaching for one of the ivy crowns. "The ivy."

"I will, too," I said.

"It's the contradictions that appeal to you," Christoph said, kissing my cheek. "It also represents wine, ecstasy, and bacchanalia."

I returned his kiss.

"So when will the great show take place?" Christoph asked, turning to Toby.

"What is a bacchanal without magic?"

Toby looked around the tent.

With a synchronized stomp of their feet, the Finnish quartet began a waltz. A couple dressed as druids took to the floor.

"It looks like the last thing you need around here is magic," Toby said.

Christoph clapped his hands, and the wreaths tumbled down his forearms. "Magic is exactly what we need. Tonight there will never ever be enough. We need to keeps the lights burning as long as possible. And from what I recall, you are the man who can play with fire."

Toby smiled. "True."

"We are all at your command," Christoph said, bowing and stepping into the crowd.

The braziers roared and flickered. People were waving banners and dancing in circles. Toby and I accepted cups of hot wine from a man with elf ears and pointed shoes with bells. Another elf handed us skewers of meats on small plates.

"Beef spiced from Africa," the second elf explained. "You might as well eat frankincense and myrrh."

Toby laughed. "I'll stick to cardamom and cinnamon."

"Me, too," I agreed. We left the elf.

"After all, we are not the baby Jesus."

"That is what you sign up for with Leo. You get the true freaks, the fake freaks, and those who simply relish the hidden pleasures of the everyday."

"The elf," Toby said. "A little over the top."

I nodded.

The Finnish quartet was replaced by a motley band of a drummer, accordion player, flutist, and fiddler who were roaming the lawn playing gypsy music. Toby and I linked arms, and together with Leo we joined a group of dancers who had formed a circle on the grass. As we spun and twirled, Olivia appeared at our side and took Toby by the arm.

"Where are you going take us tonight?" she asked.

"I don't know what Mel has told you," Toby replied.

"Everything and really nothing," Olivia said.

Toby looked at me.

"She's exactly right," I said, reassuring him that I had kept most of his secrets.

Toby took two cups of the mulled wine from a passing tray,

handing them to us. Then he clapped his hands, and a third cup appeared in his palm.

Olivia stood on her tiptoes and kissed the magician before twirling away into the crowd.

The tempo of the music escalated. I could feel the lawn pulsing beneath my feet. Toby grabbed me and headed toward the heart of the party. I followed. He walked with his palms clasped together. When he opened them, a burst of fireworks shot upward. He spun his arms over his head, spinning streamers of silk from his fingers. I struggled to keep up as he proceeded down the lawn.

"A magician," someone said, falling into step behind us.

Toby waved his arms, and the streamers came together, taking the form of a Chinese dragon that flew upward, then disappeared into the sky.

More people began to follow. Toby quickened his pace.

He reached up into the air, palms opened wide. Two large multicolored balls descended into his hands. He tossed the balls up. When he caught them, they began to unravel into bright ribbons that trailed behind the magician and got tangled in his growing crowd. As they unwound, the ribbons changed to vines of ivy that flew from Toby's hands and wreathed his audience. The partygoers gasped and walked faster, hoping for more.

Toby was moving toward the river.

"More," someone from the crowd cried.

He didn't turn around. He simply reached back and began to withdraw more objects from the sky—golden candlesticks, a censer, a bough of rosemary and holly—passing each one to the crowd.

"Quick," he whispered to me under his breath.

The dance and jingle of the audience and their delighted cries were closing in behind us.

"Quick," he said. He tossed a handful of golden coins over his shoulder.

We were running now, outstripping our pursuers, who were caught up in drink, dance, and Toby's magic. "The real show will come later," he shouted to the throng. He reached into the air one last time and, in one of those pockets visible to him alone, found a large brass ring. He twirled it; then he tossed it high into the air. As it rose, it became a ring of fire that soared away into the longest night.

Now the magician wrapped his arm around my waist, and we continued our tumble forward until we'd almost reached the river with its fairy lights.

"What will you show them later?" I asked.

Toby shook his head and shrugged. "I don't know."

At the water, we turned left and walked in silence, letting the tumult of the saturnalia recede. Eventually we came upon a long wooden dock I had never seen before. It extended far out over the river. Toby leapt onto it, then offered me a hand. At the end of the dock, we sat dangling our feet over the river.

Even in the dark, I could tell he was smiling. The light of the party in back of us illuminated the sky. But as I pulled close to Toby, I felt a familiar tingle. I held up my hands. "Snow," I said. "It's going to snow."

"How can you tell?"

"I can feel it."

Toby raised an eyebrow.

"What? You can't?"

He shook his head.

"Can't you feel the air get heavier—the cold get heavier?"

"When is it going to snow?" he asked.

"Soon. Sometime tonight. Maybe even in the next hour."

"Shall we wait for it?"

"At least for a little while," I replied.

I leaned my head against the scratchy wool of Toby's collar and listened to its banjo twang. The sky had split into two levels. In the background, a drape of blue black had fallen. In front of this curtain, gray-tinged snow clouds had appeared. They flew so close to the river, I felt that if I climbed one of the trees on the riverbank, I might be able to reach out and comb them with my fingers.

Directly above our heads, the snow clouds were tied into a line like a chain of paper dolls. They looked like the skyline of a fairy-tale Arabian city. Domes and fortresses were clustered on one side. A lengthy barricade with an ornate watchtower sat in the foreground. Behind it was a steep hill dotted with small houses. A brief gust of wind shifted the pattern. Part of the fortress wall vanished, and more domes appeared.

"You're cold?" Toby asked.

"Yes. But I like it."

"Did you see Constantinople?"

"Babylon."

"Perhaps it was Moscow. The Kremlin."

"It was Mesopotamia."

"The Taj Mahal."

"No. Persia."

"Or maybe, it was the Taj."

"The casino in Atlantic City?"

"Or Disneyland. That magic castle or whatever it's called."

I laughed and turned back to the clouds. "Maybe it's Vegas," I said.

Toby smiled.

"Will you miss it?" I asked.

"Of course. But it's still there."

I nodded. Toby pulled me tighter. "And you've already gone back and done what you needed to do."

A long, thin breath escaped through Toby's lips. "I don't know."

"The problem with being a magician is that you seem to love things more in their absence." This was why Toby had come back—this and something else, I was only beginning to understand.

We turned back to the sky. For a while, my clouds took the form of ocean liners trundling through a lightless sea. Then they were massive suspension bridges. Then a lobster. Then a swimmer. Then a phoenix. I looked over at Toby and wondered what he was seeing—what form his clouds took.

"Do you think that you find the shapes in the clouds or that you shape the clouds with your mind?" I asked.

Toby shrugged.

I looked at the sky. I saw mesas rising from a desert—the same titanic tea tables Toby and I had driven past on our way to Intersection. And then on top of one of the mesas, a head emerged and looked around. From underneath the head, an adolescent body unfurled—the teenage waitress.

The cloud bank lowered until it was almost at the level of the river. The cloud-form Greta was standing, one hand on her hip, in front of the blue ranch house. I felt a strange tingle and looked down to see that my ring had changed to cloud gray. The waitress beckoned to us. Toby stood up. He pulled me up, too. The cloud-scape grew wider and more detailed. A highway stretched behind the house. There was Jim's Big West Donut. And at the end of the road, I could see the Las Vegas Strip.

As the clouds rolled past, I saw the road leading into Vegas. The famous WELCOME sign. I saw the Laughing Jackalope Motel. The panorama came to a halt in front of the Winter Palace. Fireworks the color of crystal were shooting out of the onion-domed turrets. I could just make out the distant sound of the St. Petersburg Orchestra tuning up inside. And suddenly I knew that the moment Toby and I set foot in this cloud-world, it would take shape, solidify into his perfect desert, his perfect Vegas. He would be back to the scene of his mistake.

He tugged at my hand. "We won't have to be strangers now."

I shook myself. I knew that once Toby discovered the possibility of gliding from one world of his imagining to the next, he would never rest. He would always be leaving me behind, returning less and less often, until one day, he would cease to appear.

"I belong here."

Toby didn't need to save Greta anymore; it was that he could. And this possibility and all the possibilities it led to were that undeniable calling that had been summoning him since the day his blocks had first opened his eyes to magic. It was only now that the voice had solidified and grown insistent. He would live between the worlds of his imagination, saving Greta in one, Eva in other. Testing the limits of his craft, rewinding time, and doing it again. I don't think he planned to stay in one place for long. Not even the Las Vegas stage could hold him. He would save his greatest magic for himself, skipping between places summoned by his fantasies and dreams.

Toby extended one leg. His foot hovered between the river and the clouds. He let go of my hand. He had not come back to me; he'd come to say good-bye. I looked back at the villa, at the warm light just barely visible through the tree. Then I sensed a movement at my side. I turned back and saw the clouds close around the back of Toby's wool coat. And without a word, the magician disappeared. Like Greta and Max, he didn't say good-bye.

I remained at the edge of the dock. The cloud cover lifted, rising to its accustomed height.

"Toby," I said quietly. But there was no response. I lay on my side. I closed my eyes, feeling the sting of tears. Before I left the dock, I took off my ring and dropped it into the river. Then I clenched my hand tight, and when I opened it, I was holding the key to the blue ranch house.

On the great lawn, an enormous bonfire was burning. The revelers had joined hands and were dancing around it, the flames highlighting their holly and ivy crowns. I worked my way into the circle, letting the dancers lead me around and around until my head spun. Eventually the ring of hands broke apart, scattering the dancers across the lawn. I found a seat underneath one of the great braziers. I leaned against it, turning my back to the party.

Cradling a cup of mulled wine, I listened to the escalating merrymaking. Soon a voice clamored to be heard above the crowd. "The magician," it called. "It's time for the magician."

Others joined in, clapping and calling for Toby.

The lawn was a tumult of cries for magic. People began darting to and fro, peering into the dark for my vanished husband.

I pulled in closer to the brazier's pole, wanting its heat to melt me. The cries for Toby grew louder, some now tinged with disappointment.

Then a shadow stretched across the brazier's orange glow. "He's gone, isn't he?" Leo asked, leaning down and kissing me on the head.

I nodded.

I sat on Leo's lawn until the last of the lights died out. As I felt the dark rise, I remembered the swell of the ocean after it had taken Max. And although the loss and the sadness were beyond expression, I knew that this time I would not wait for Toby. I would not look or listen for his footsteps. Unlike Toby, I would not attempt to undo what the magician chose for himself.

It has been three days since Toby left, and I've been wandering around Leo's villa between the winter-blooming plants and a soft

feather bed made up for me in the room next to Olivia's. Often
I go into the studio. My fingers guide me through Erik's fabrics,
choosing the ones that will tell of the rest of my adventures in
Holland and elsewhere. Their voices had returned the minute I
broke through the other side of Toby's trick, comforting me in
the magician's absence. I can make out Piet's and Olivia's voices.
Eventually, I'll come across Leo and maybe even Theo. Maybe
one day, I'll hear Toby again.

Despite the cold, I often walk along the river. I wear one of
Leo's coats and a wool scarf Olivia made for me. The water is
marbled brown and gray. I look at its surface, searching for the
first crystals of ice, and I remember that I promised myself I'd be
home by the time the Delaware froze. I always imagined that I'd
bring Toby with me, but now I'll make the trip alone.

One day, I take a thermos of coffee and sit on the dock where
I last saw Toby. I comb my fingers through the air, searching for
the portal of his escape. It's late afternoon, and an early darkness
is settling along the riverbank. Here the river is narrower, and despite the fading light, I can still make out the small road on the far
side. In all my time at Leo's, I have never seen a car or a bicycle on
this road. So I am surprised when the silence of the falling dark is
disturbed by the faint purr of an engine.

I look upstream and watch a car come into view. The engine
sounds tired and lugs slightly. When the car is directly opposite
the dock, it stops. Even in the failing light, I know it's a brown
minivan. No one gets out. The engine continues to idle. I lower
my feet over the river and trace the toe of one boot through the
cold water. There is no sound except for the rhythmic swish of
my shoe in the water and the irregular drone of the engine on the
other bank.

I wonder how cold the water will be if I decide to cross. And
if I cross, I wonder if the water will remain water at all, and on

what bank I will arrive. I close my eyes and remember how happy I was when I turned around on a deserted Nevada highway and saw the van for the first time. I remember the tingling in my fingers when I tried to brush them over Toby's as he put the van in gear. Even without magic, the desert landscape appeared to me to be enchanted.

I have to stop myself from calling his name. The Toby I want cannot be pulled into the world on my side of the river. Soon, the silhouette of the minivan fades into the night. The only way I'm assured of its presence is the rattle of the engine.

It's dark now. The river is indistinguishable from the bank. I can barely make out my boots above the water. As I sit there, trying to feel Toby's gaze cutting through the night, I realize that he cannot draw me to his side. And now I smile, confident that he never did so in the first place. I relax, as I let our first meeting replay in my head—a chance encounter in an improbable place. Then I hear the windfall of coins in the remote gas station, and I know that this, too, was not his doing.

I will sit there in the near-presence of my magician until the last moment, but I'm not going to cross over. I will remain in a world governed by chance and coincidence. I want to call out to Toby to tell him that I was right—he has learned to love me more in my absence. And this tells me how truly empty his conjured world is.

It takes me a few minutes to realize that the engine is no longer humming. The van has not driven away. It is simply gone. I stand up and walk back to Leo's.

The Delaware froze late this year. My mother tells me it was waiting for my return. Together we walk down to the riverbank and slide across the ice. We skid past the spot where Max allowed himself to be stolen by the water for the first time. The bright sun makes the thick ice sparkle. Underfoot, the river creaks and groans, settling into its winter skin.

We slide downstream, letting the ice skaters twirl past our uncoordinated stumbling. We stand in the middle of the river, clinging to each other for balance. We are almost underneath the rusted iron bridge when snow begins to fall. My mother looks up, startled by the absence of clouds. Skaters stop to stare at our private snowstorm. I wriggle out of one of my gloves and hold out my hand to catch the flakes. My back is to the bridge. I wonder if I turn around, will I see the tail end of a brown van disappearing up the road? But I don't want to look. I just want to close my eyes and imagine the magician and me zigzagging past one another. As the snowflakes hit my face, they turn to tears. But soon, these, too, melt away. Then I take my mother's hand and urge her onward, away from the improbable snow.

ACKNOWLEDGMENTS

Abundant thanks to my wonderful agent, Kim Witherspoon, and her assistant, Julie Schilder, whose perseverance on my behalf brought this book into being. Thanks to Hilary Rubin Teeman at St. Martin's Press, a remarkable editor and a superb reader who understood what I was trying to say. Love and gratitude to Susan Kamil, a spectacular mentor and better friend. Many, many thanks to Mary Kelley and Judyth van Amringe for their creative demonstrations of love and support. And most important, thanks to my parents, Philip and Elizabeth Pochoda, for their patience when they didn't understand where I was or what I was up to, and their untiring help when I was lost inside my own head and words.

1. There is an immediate attraction between Toby and Mel. What is it about their characters that draws them to each other? Why do they decide to get married after such a short acquaintance?

2. Toby is a capable of both strange and wonderful things. But there is an unknowable and perhaps darker element to his craft. Why is Mel so accepting of this?

3. How does Mel's childhood prepare her for her relationship with Toby?

4. This is primarily Mel's story and not Toby's. In what ways does she wield power over him? How is Mel capable of her own brand of magic?

5. What is it about Toby that draws women to him in Las Vegas? What draws Greta to him?

6. What is Mel's relationship to fabric? What is the function of her quilt? Do you believe that she can actually hear voices in the fabric?

7. Las Vegas is a city of heat and Amsterdam is a city of water and rain. How do these climates affect the lives of Toby and Mel?

8. The Dissolving World is powerful illusion. What does it represent for Toby? What does it represent for Mel? Does the possibility for their love exist inside this illusion?

9. Toby and Theo at one time each possessed extraordinary powers. How do their philosophies of magic differ?

10. Compare the fates of Max and Toby. What do you think happens to both of these characters?

11. After finishing the book, do you think it is a coincidence that Toby and Mel met at the Old Stand Saloon?

For more information, visit www.readinggroupgold.com.

A
Reading
Group
Guide

St. Martin's
Griffin